HOLIDAY HEARTS

JOSIE RIVIERA

INTRODUCTION

To keep up on newly released ebooks, paperbacks, Large Print Paperbacks, audiobooks, as well as exclusive sales, sign up for Josie's Newsletter today.

As a thank you, I'll send you a Free PDF … The Beauty Of …

Josie's Newsletter

Did you know that according to a Yale University study, people who read books live longer?

Holiday Hearts

5 STAR READER REVIEWS

Amazon Review by Aunt Sis

5.0 out of 5 stars

They were really a beautiful testament to Christmas, wherever you spend it. And as Christmas is live, the three loves in these books were wonderfully written!

Amazon Review by A. Kollasch

5.0 out of 5 stars

"I love Christmas stories! This set did not let me down!"

Amazon Review by Blackeagle (A Snowy White Christmas)

5.0 out of 5 stars

"If you love Christmas miracles I would highly recommend this book to you believe me you won't be disappointed. This novella is beautifully written with a heartwarming storyline."

Amazon Review by Amazon Customer

5.0 out of 5 stars (Candleglow and Mistletoe)

A wonderful Christmas story! There is much to like about this book. The characters are well defined and likable. The story makes you laugh and cry. The descriptions of all the places are so well done that you feel like you are there. I am anxious to read another of this author's books."

Amazon Review by glendaleone

5.0 out of 5 stars (A Portuguese Christmas)

"Oh how I LOVE Josie's writing!! !! !! I devoured this at one sitting because I just had to see what happened next!! I was immersed from the moment I started to read. Krystal and Adolfo were about as opposite as can be but ohhhh the chemistry. I loved the back and forth of their emotions, fighting themselves and each other! They were realistic and relatable! I don't want to give anything away so I will just say READ IT AND ENJOY !! !! !! It is a wonderful clean story meant to be enjoyed by all."

DEAR FRIENDS

A heartwarming story is the hallmark of a romantic holiday. Savor the magic with my three joyful, sweet, clean and wholesome contemporary romances.

This set includes the following books:

A Snowy White Christmas

Margaret Snow no longer believes in fairy tales, but she's determined her young daughter will experience a real, upstate New York Christmas, not LA's fake...everything. Giving up glitz and glamor to return to her hometown is easy, but facing her high school sweetheart, Fernando Brandt, is another story. Especially when the sparks flying between them illuminate the insecurities that could prevent her from accepting the true gift of Christmas—unconditional love.

Candleglow and Mistletoe

When Noelle Wentworth's bus crashes, one deep, rumbling voice calms her racing heart—then a handsome face kicks it back into allegro. But love is a concerto she never learned to play.

Noelle once saved Gabriel Waters from a high school bully. There's no recognition in her eyes, but there's something else that tugs at his heart—pain and distrust. Unexpected attraction burns warm and sweet, but their pasts could turn the promise of love to ashes.

A Portuguese Christmas

Injured during a Portuguese surfing competition, Krystal is determined to defy doctor's orders to make it home to Rhode Island by Christmas. First, though she has to get past handsome, arrogant Adolfo Silva.

Keeping Krystal safe is Adolfo's first priority, but this bold, courageous woman's wings won't be clipped. Somehow, he must convince her that spending Christmas with him isn't the end of her world. Because she's become the center of his.

Cozy up under a quilt with a cup of hot cocoa and lose yourself in this wonderful season of love.

These books and audiobooks are also available separately.

PRAISE AND AWARDS

USA TODAY bestselling author

A Snowy White

CHRISTMAS

a contemporary romance novella

USA TODAY BESTSELLING AUTHOR

JOSIE RIVIERA

This book is dedicated to all my wonderful readers who have supported me every inch of the way.

THANK YOU!

CHAPTER 1

*S*ometimes Margaret Snow's guilt would go away for a few minutes. But it always returned. Insistent. Dull. Intense.

She was a terrible mother. Check.

She'd never amount to anything. Check.

She only thought about herself. Check.

These negative thoughts chattered incessantly, tucked ever so slightly behind everyday activities. Like uncaged wild animals waiting to pounce at the first opportunity.

She glanced out her office window. Despite the wind and ice, city workers were adding cheery red bells and silver holiday trimmings to the streetlights. It didn't help. November in upstate New York promised gray skies, bitter sleet, and not an ounce of cheeriness until spring. Today was no exception.

What was the weather like in California? She checked the weather app on her phone. As expected, sunny skies in Los Angeles were predicted throughout the Thanksgiving holiday.

"Unbelievable," she whispered. "How could two places be so different?"

And why was she stuck in the lesser desirable of the two?

It was her own fault. She'd forgotten her lines during her last audition because she'd been preoccupied with her daughter's insistent cough that had lingered for weeks. But her agent, Sid, and the casting director hadn't been interested in excuses, and they just dismissed her as a wannabe actress who didn't take the acting profession seriously.

"Stick to modeling," they'd said.

She sighed. She'd been back in her depressing hometown only three weeks and already felt limp and exhausted.

But her daughter Amelie seemed content, and only Amelie mattered. Margaret grinned, remembering the impish smile Amelie would flash whenever she had rolled round and round on their favorite California beach. She'd emerge covered in sand, her small eyeglasses placed carefully on a nearby towel. Her incessant coughing spells would follow, but the physician assistant she saw assured Margaret this was normal in a frail child, and as long as Amelie didn't develop a fever, there was no need for concern.

"See? I'm fine, Mom," Amelie would say, giggling while demonstrating a perfect cartwheel in the sand. "Now let's go for peppermint ice cream."

Margaret's heart did a funny little turn. Amelie was so much like her father. A perfectionist and a planner. And that was why she'd ensured that Amelie would never know him.

Grumpy, her African grey parrot hanging upside down from the top of its cage, chirped an out-of-tune melody.

"Talk. Say something," she said, knowing he couldn't hear her.

He stared back and shook his head.

She sipped her cup of cold black coffee and shuffled through the stack of blank applications on her desk. The famous actress she'd hoped to become was now relegated to this, a talent agent looking for talent in a town that had none. So demeaning, but at least she was able to provide for her daughter. She sighed, louder this time, twisted the wadded-up handkerchief on her lap and dabbed at her eyes.

A familiar Christmas carol played faintly on the radio, an instrumental arrangement of "Jingle Bells." Shouldn't there be a law prohibiting the playing of Christmas music before Thanksgiving? She clicked it off and gazed absently at the cornucopia wreath tacked lopsided on her office door. Her office was a mess, with boxes piled in a far corner, but she'd only been in Owanda a few weeks and hadn't had time to unpack.

A loud knock brought her attention to the present. Lucy, Margaret's best friend since childhood, opened the door. "Are you busy? You are, right?" She blinked twice, the signal they'd devised years ago for impending disaster.

"Should I be?" Margaret stuffed the handkerchief into her skirt pocket and set the coffee cup on her desk. Formalities weren't observed in upstate New York. One simply rapped on the door and barged in because everyone was considered family. But the only family she'd known lived in a fairy tale. No mother had ever bounced her on her knees or sung lullabies at night. Her mother had been too busy hiding from her drunken, violent husband.

"One of your elves is here for his interview." Lucy actually said this with a straight face. Her blonde hair was styled into an angled bob, soft wisps cascading around her broad cheekbones. She never left the house unless she looked picture-perfect, even if she was only heading to the grocery store. Hollywood had changed her. It had changed them both.

"I tried to stop him, but he knows us too well." Lucy stepped closer and cupped her hands around Margaret's ear. "And take my word, he really knows *you*."

9

Sure he did. Margaret felt the scowl settle on her forehead. She'd been a swimsuit model, and men had excellent memories when it came to bikinis and the women who filled them. She'd never modeled topless—never. But skimpy? Well … yes, if it paid the bills and Amelie's tuition. And this elf could request her autograph with a gold pen and silver paper, but he'd be leaving her office empty-handed.

Lucy shook her head. "He was always so demanding."

He was always …

"Send him in," Margaret replied. She'd dealt with pushy fans before. He could take his autograph book and—

But he'd already barged into her office, all six feet of charm. He was, after all, from upstate New York. See above if you forgot.

With a wave as if she were leaving for a trip abroad, Lucy said, "I'm in my office if you need me." She retreated into the hallway and closed the door.

"My lovely princess," he was saying, "you're as beautiful as ever." He glanced at the parrot. "And I see some things never change. Your house always resembled a pet hotel."

She gaped, stunned by the deep voice and all-too-familiar endearment.

She caught her reflection in the mirror on the opposite wall. "Mirror, mirror, who's the fairest?" he'd always teased. She wasn't beautiful, but her cheekbones were high and her skin smooth and clear. The rest of her had been gangly arms and legs and too-dark eyebrows.

Was she sitting or standing? All the poise and modeling classes were forgotten in the space of a second. Fernando. Fernando. Fernando. It couldn't be, not after all these years. She drew in a breath and held it.

He brushed a hand through his dark hair, dampened from the icy weather. "I heard you were back in town."

She swallowed. How did a man look so put together in

this type of weather? Her voice returned and matched her shaking body. "You live in Owanda?"

"I thought I did, although you're making me question it." He looked around, a slight smile gracing his mouth. "Remember we lived two blocks from each other?"

Except she'd lived in the double-wide trailer at the edge of a trailer park and he'd lived in a cozy bungalow with white shingles and a red front door. She looked off for a moment, needing to focus on something else, anything else. Grumpy appeared to be sleeping.

"How could I ever forget?" she asked.

Fleeting hurt dimmed his gaze, but the smile remained. "You forgot quickly, actually." He took a step forward, seemed to think better of getting closer, and halted. "I've missed you." He glanced at the parrot. "Don't tell me, let me guess. He's blind."

"Deaf."

"Does he talk?"

"No, but sometimes he sings off-key." She looked pointedly toward the street. "Probably because he's speechless at the terrible weather."

Fernando laughed. "It's not so bad here. Summers are very pleasant."

It took everything in her to remain calm and silent. He was digging in for more conversation, offering small talk before he began his interrogation.

"I brought you a gift." He retrieved a small box, wrapped in gold foil paper with a silver bow, from beneath his wool coat and held it out to her. "Welcome home."

"Thank you, Fernando, but this isn't home." There. She was able to say his name aloud.

When they'd been together, he'd always surprised her with little wrapped gifts—her favorite drugstore perfume, technical books about nursing injured animals, a small leather journal for her notes. Inside the package he'd always write in his bold, neat script: "To my snow white princess, all my love."

"And I can't accept any gifts," she added.

"Of course, you can." His dark brown eyes gleamed with a certainty that she would, indeed, accept it. He carried his belief confidently on his muscular shoulders that life around him went according to his plans. He hadn't changed.

"No, I can't." She pushed back her chair so quickly, it clattered to the floor. Gracefulness had never been her forte and, yes, she'd been sitting. Fortunately, the falling chair gave her something to do—scramble and bend to retrieve it, taking longer than necessary because frustration and memories collided. When she stood, she held the chair upright in front of her like a lion tamer. She'd read a magazine article that a lion tamer used the chair in the ring to confuse the lion, not as a form of defense. All she needed was a whip in the other hand, but the same article had assured that the tamer's whip was only for show. So she stood face to face with Fernando, holding a useless chair and a non-existent whip that wouldn't have helped anyway. Tanned and attractive, he watched her with desire in his gaze. He resembled a sexy magazine ad for a man who desperately needed a shave and didn't care.

He moved her small Christmas tree to the corner of her desk, then placed his gift on the opposite corner. "Please. I bought this especially for you many years ago."

"What are you doing in my office?" Not waiting for a reply, she turned and placed the chair behind her. Swiveling back, she smoothed her lemon-colored skirt and focused on the framed photo hanging on the opposite wall. In the photo she was arm in arm with a famous male actor, and they both held a glass of champagne. Her silk dress was low cut, inappropriately tight, and beyond short. What had they been toasting? She couldn't remember. Her hazel eyes in the photo stared back, glassy with too much drink. Her gaze darted to Fernando. His smile had changed, now slow and insolent as if he'd read her mind and agreed she'd been too provocatively dressed for a twenty-year-old girl. The gleam in his eyes was gone, and he'd reverted to his default setting of disapproval, one of his favorite settings. She'd never met his expectations of the cloyingly cute, content upstate New York girl.

"I thought you lived in Los Angeles," he said. "That swimsuit photo shoot you were in for the sports magazine was the main topic of conversation in this town for several weeks. You and that minuscule yellow bikini made the cover."

"I do. I did. What did you say you're doing here?" She braced both hands on the edge of her desk. Her palms were sweating. What was the advice when confronted with an uncomfortable situation? Stay calm and imagine the other person naked. Yikes! That didn't work as images of his naked, muscular body flooded her senses. She inhaled so loudly, the sound filled the stark room. As she fingered the wadded handkerchief in her skirt pocket, her gold bracelets jingled with a busy clink, reflecting her agitation. Lazy afternoons in his bed when they'd ducked out of high school early were forever seared into her brain. Years of therapy obviously hadn't helped. One minute with him and she reverted to a flustered schoolgirl.

An impish grin moved across his face.

"I'd heard you'd moved out of the area and worked in Florida for some real estate company," she said.

"Don't believe everything you hear. I'm back and forth." His gaze lingered on the top buttons of her blouse. "I'd read in one of the tabloids you were considered for a leading role in a Hollywood adventure film."

She stiffened. "Don't believe everything you read."

Rejection was part of the acting business. Her agent had explained that the role had ultimately been given to a younger upcoming actress who'd worked in classical theater. "Things will pick up in January," he'd assured her.

Fernando shook his head. "An adventure film doesn't seem suitable for an actress with your talent. You probably would've been running around scantily clothed while the action took place all around you." His tone held kindness and understanding. "Besides, the role was for a blonde, and you wouldn't want to change your hair color again. You're stunning when you're a brunette."

"Thanks. I'll be sure to pass your opinion on to my agent." She resisted the urge to touch her hair and shuffled the applications on her desk instead.

"Are you in Owanda for a couple of days visiting friends?"

Please be here for a short while. Like one day. In the meantime, she calculated how long it would take to pack her and Amelie's suitcases and leave town. Two days, maybe three. And how would Amelie adjust to the news? Today was her first day at a reputable public school for the deaf and things were settling into a new normal. Margaret squeezed her eyes shut for a moment. She needed this job to buy back her trailer. She needed a big break in Hollywood so that Amelie could return to her private school. She needed to get out of this decrepit town if Fernando was here.

His gaze had taken permanent residence on the low neckline of her green blouse. "No friends you'd know." He loosened the wool scarf around his neck and turned to the window, a look of feigned surprise on his face. "So you're gracing us with your famed presence because you'd prefer to interview elves rather than star in million-dollar movies or appear on the covers of magazines? Are the paparazzi camped outside? I don't remember seeing any."

"They couldn't work on their suntans in upstate New York."

"Are you visiting anyone special for Thanksgiving? Your parents passed away a few years ago."

Probing, as usual. Leave. Please leave. Don't ask any more questions.

She swallowed. "Yes, both my parents are gone." Always, the sorrow she should've felt wasn't there.

Sadness blurred his striking features and tiny lines creased his forehead. His face showed his thoughts like a road map, although the road map looked more mature and a tad worn. Perhaps he'd aged as much in six years as she had.

"I'm sorry for your loss," he was saying. "They weren't perfect, but I believe they loved you very much."

"They didn't, but thanks." Her throat ached at the recollection of the childhood whippings she'd endured at the hands of her father while her mother sat silent.

"You're still a woman of few words," he said.

"Who's interviewing whom?"

"Just like old times. I talked and you responded in monosyllables. I never knew what you were thinking."

She shifted. "Why are you here again?"

He unbuttoned his long gray wool coat. The sable-black scarf hung loosely around his neck. "Don't you know why?"

"No, I don't, but if this is a game and I'm supposed to guess, then I'll change the subject to the weather because I'm not good at guessing." She glanced at the clock. Still time to make an escape from his certain interrogation. "How's this? I haven't experienced a white Christmas in a long time."

"I only returned a few months ago, but I imagine the winters are as harsh as ever," he said.

"So you live in Florida? The weather is warm and sunny there."

"I didn't say for certain, but I appreciate you trying to

check up on where I live." That seemed to please him, and a smile appeared. "You looked surprised when I walked in."

Surprised? Talk about understatements. An eye roll was in order, but he was watching too closely. She stood straighter. "You mean when you barged in. And yes, you were the last person I ever expected to see again."

"After high school graduation, there was nothing left for me, so I left the area," he said.

"You always said you liked this depressing, freezing town."

"Owanda is comfortable and familiar, but it wasn't the same without you."

Because you disappeared without a word. He didn't say it. He didn't have to. His road-map features showed anger, then hurt. Why couldn't he hide his emotions? All the men in Hollywood said one thing while meaning another. But they were actors and agents, and he was an open, honest canvas. Right and wrong. There was no gray area for him.

"You know I needed more than what Owanda offered," she said.

"Certainly more than I could ever offer."

The gentleness in his voice was unexpected, and the shock she'd felt when he entered was draining away to something else. He'd offered her caring and security. And love.

She suppressed a rush of sudden tears. "I've never been satisfied. I wanted more than a Saturday night at the local movie theater followed by a keg party."

"A woman as lovely as you wanted something better than a guy from a small town who spent his nights partying."

"You were popular. Hockey team, class president, you managed it all."

He smiled. "I was always true to you."

His smile was so genuine, she returned it. "I know you were."

They were allies for a moment. But if he suspected she was hiding anything, he'd board the truth train and never get off. She snapped her thoughts away from panic and inhaled a steadying breath. He'd never know. He'd never know.

He held up his hands, palms out, a gesture of understanding. "I'm not asking for an explanation for why you left. I've never analyzed people's motives nor judged them."

"You've always been the better person."

When you weren't drinking.

He dropped his hands. "So you decided to leave sunny Los Angeles to work for your former talent agency at the coldest time of the year and interview elves?"

"It's temporary. I'm between jobs and doing my agency a favor."

She was desperate.

"Plus," she continued, "this allows me an opportunity to spend the holidays in an authentic winter setting to research my next role as a snow princess in Alaska. Of course, the screenplay is only in the planning stages." She glanced at him, hoping he actually believed her story. He seemed relaxed, his expression suggesting interest. Perhaps she was a better actress than her agent thought.

He nodded. "The weather doesn't get any more wintry than upstate New York."

"For this current project, my agency has asked me to audition men four feet ten inches or shorter for jobs at the mall as Santa's helpers." She glanced at the neatly wrapped package on her desk. "If you're trying to bribe me with a gift to get a job …" She gazed up at his tall, lean frame and gave a rueful laugh. "Sorry. You don't fit the role requirements."

His gaze locked with hers, a wry smile on his lips. "Actually, I'm here to represent my twin brother, Michael. If you recall, he's a dwarf."

She nodded slowly. "Of course. I'm sorry, I'd forgotten about him."

Years ago, she'd enjoyed weekly Sunday dinners at Fernando's home. Michael had worn a hearing aid because the bones in his ears were so small, but the Brandts' good-natured teasing and shouting made up for any hearing impediment. She'd learned sign language because of Michael. Ironic, as signing was one of the main forms of communication she used with Amelie. The remembrance of mouthwatering sausages, green vegetables, and sauerkraut simmering on the Brandt kitchen stove teased her nostrils. His mother was Spanish—hence Fernando's Spanish name—but had cooked German food to please her husband.

Margaret had sworn off German food after leaving Owanda because it brought back too many memories. His family had been so demonstrative, so caring, so unlike her own. Her mother had never cooked a hot meal. In fact, she'd never cooked any meal. And Margaret had had only two conversations with her father in her entire life. Both times he'd been sober. Two times, in eighteen years.

Fernando's mother had always sent Margaret home with leftovers in case there wasn't any food in her house. There never was.

She cleared her throat. "I didn't advertise for dwarfs."

"You advertised for elves, but dwarf is a politically correct term. Michael can be Sneezy today because he's coughing and having chest pain. However, I took him to our family physician, and he's fine." Fernando smiled. He had those crinkly laugh lines around his eyes she remembered so well. "Now you only need to find six more dwarfs. What were their names again?"

She held up a hand. "Thanks, I know the names of the seven dwarfs. And I'm looking for elves, not dwarfs marching off to a mine every morning."

"The dwarfs were searching for diamonds. Some were kept and some were discarded, but all diamonds are rare and precious." He gave her a long, appreciative look and then glanced at the applications on her desk. "The economy didn't recover here as well as it did in other parts of the country. Most people in our town will take any job available."

Our town. Owanda was his town but it certainly wasn't her town. She was a California girl now.

She offered him an application and pen. "I need to leave soon, so you can mail it back to the agency. The address is at the top."

"This won't take long." He grabbed the pen and pulled a chair up to the opposite side of her desk. He shrugged off his coat and scarf, slung both behind the chair, and sat. His absorption in the application gave her time to retuck her blouse into her skirt and quickly feel that all the buttons were securely fastened. She lifted her chin and offered an in-control smile just in case he looked up, hoping she gave the appearance of a self-confident movie star. If only she could wipe away the sweat gathering beneath her fringe of bangs without looking insecure.

She glanced at the clock. Two fifteen. Amelie was dismissed from school at three o'clock.

He pushed the application toward her, along with the business card he recovered from the pocket of his well-tailored gray suit. "I'll give you one of my cards."

"Thanks." She stuffed the card into the top drawer of her desk without looking at it, along with his gift.

He quirked a dark brow but said nothing.

She perused his neat handwriting on the application, instantly recognizable even after all these years. Her mother had forwarded his unopened letters to California. He'd written her love letters pleading with her to return. He'd admitted he had an addictive personality and vowed to give up drinking.

She never answered him. At eighteen years old and pregnant, the bright lights of Hollywood were a beacon for a wealthy new life she could achieve on her own merit. She was an independent woman who relied on no man.

She studied the application. "Your brother still lives at your old address?"

Fernando loosened his navy tie. "Yes."

"With your parents?"

"Sadly, my father passed away several years ago. Michael lives with my mother, although he had his own apartment for several years. Lately he's prone to seizures, and I insisted he no longer live alone. He's also recovering from a major operation."

"I'm sorry. I hope he's up to working."

Fernando's gaze drilled into hers with a silent plea. "Work is the best therapy for his recuperation, and it will take his mind off his ailments. Nothing like being an elf in the world of make-believe to forget all your cares."

A beat passed.

"Without dreams, life would be boring and empty," she said.

"Keep your head in the clouds if you want to, but your feet should be firmly on the ground." A deep smile emphasized his dimple. He hadn't outgrown the light sprinkling of freckles on his nose and cheeks. He'd been the best-looking guy in the senior class, rugged and lean, his T-shirt worn untucked. He'd offered her love, but now something else simmered beneath the surface, a resolve edged with tenacity.

He studied her face. "This is the point where you're supposed to press me for details about my life."

She offered him an indifferent shrug. He returned the

shrug. A shrug contest. Who could act the most disinterested?

"All right, if you're not interested in me, let's talk about Michael." He leaned back in the chair and crossed his arms. "Do you have any information regarding the job? That is, if you decide to hire him."

She grinned. "There's a shortage of elves in Owanda, so he's got the job. The local mall is setting up a Christmas display in its center court and needs several elves to assist Santa while the children wait in line to see him." She scanned the application. "You listed Michael's phone number and e-mail, so I'll contact him directly. The job will begin the day after Thanksgiving and end Christmas Eve. I hope he's prepared to work nights and weekends, because Christmas isn't all fun and games."

"Of course it is." His dark eyes were filled with warmth again. "I love Christmas."

Snowball fights in the Brandts' backyard. Multi-colored lights and silvery tinsel decorating the Christmas tree, the scent of fresh pine in their living room. The savory aromas of almond crescents and cinnamon stars wafting from the warm kitchen.

Her own childhood house with no Christmas tree, broken lights permanently strung along their front porch, and a drunken, drug-addicted father permanently strung out on the living room couch.

She chewed her bottom lip, a habit from childhood. Her voice softened. "Christmas isn't joyful for many people."

"You and I used to laugh together, sometimes over the silliest jokes. You loved holidays, especially Christmas."

"I'm an aspiring actress. Maybe I was pretending."

He shook his head. "I know you well. Very well. You weren't acting."

She waved a hand dismissively. He was watching her too closely. "Christmas is for children."

"Christmas is for everyone." His voice had a slight catch, but perhaps she imagined it. "Nothing is more precious than seeing a child's face on Christmas morning and the assurance everything's right in the world."

His words almost finished her. Tears sprang to her eyes. There wasn't room in the air for shiny expensive gifts and high expectations. The clock on the wall ticked the minutes, hours, days. Only forty days until Christmas. She'd never be able to stay in Owanda if he were here. She straightened her shoulders and met his probing stare, reminding herself she was not the destitute, dependent girl she'd once been.

CHAPTER 2

*F*ernando was the one to break the stare. He glanced at his gold watch for the second time in five minutes. It must be fake, she thought. He could never afford anything so expensive.

"I'm late for a meeting, but can we get together while you're here?" he asked. "I'm certain my mother would want to see you for a chat. And our favorite pizzeria, Antonio's, is still in business. We can enjoy a pizza and grab a slice of ricotta cheesecake for dessert."

And there he went, planning her life right down to dessert.

She kept her expression nondescript. "I can't commit because of my schedule. I'm sure you understand."

The perfect vague excuse people used to get out of things they didn't want to do. People always prioritized what was important to them and what wasn't. In truth, she wasn't about to chat with his mother in her intimate kitchen about a Christmas sugar cookie recipe or how California weather differed from New York's. Not when there was a matter of far greater importance his mother knew nothing about.

"Of course," he said. "You're a successful model with a full agenda. You've gotten exactly what you've always wanted."

"There's nothing wrong with being financially independent."

He pointed to the photograph on the opposite wall. "Even if it means giving up your integrity? That's not the woman I knew." With a nod, he stood, pulled on his coat and scarf and strode to the office door.

Only he wasn't striding, he was limping and holding his side.

"Are you hurt?" she asked.

He turned. "Just a sprain. I was working on my car yesterday."

"You always said you weren't mechanical and didn't know the difference between a steering shaft and a steering wheel."

"People change." He looked at his watch again. Three times since he'd entered her office. And his cell phone kept buzzing. "Good-bye, Margaret. I hope your Christmas display is a success."

That was it? He wasn't going to press to see her again?

She gazed at him, this darkly attractive man who was looking more amused than disinterested, and stepped around her desk. "Fernando, wait."

She didn't want him to leave. She didn't want him to stay. A tenderness for him, a rush of longing, made her want to explain, if only she could. *I'm not rich any more. Your beautiful daughter looks like you. She has your eyes, your smile, and your kind heart.*

But she'd never tell him because he'd never allow them to leave if he knew the truth. So instead she said, "I'd enjoy seeing your mother again."

She mentally shrugged, telling herself he'd hound her until she consented anyway. Besides, she loved his mother's sugar cookies, as well as pizza and ricotta cheesecake from Antonio's.

"I invited you to spend a relaxing evening with me. It's not a jail sentence." He ran a finger along her chin. "So you can smile."

She obliged, hesitantly. "Sounds perfect. And I'm looking forward to seeing your brother again."

Something sad crossed Fernando's face, but was quickly replaced by his usual optimistic grin. His finger glided to her cheek. So light, so exquisite. So like him to roll kindness and encouragement into a caress.

"Michael faced some challenges this past year. He was on dialysis, but they found a kidney donor, and he's much better. This job will be good because he needs to know that he matters and is a useful working adult."

"Of course he matters. Michael was such a contented, carefree child."

"He's still mildly autistic."

"He was all the more loving because of his autism. I remember when I was at your house, he was obsessed with driving a cherry-red toy train across your mother's dining room table. She'd scold him, but everyone knew she didn't mind."

The laughter and joking had been nonstop at the Brandts'. Her eyes welled. Amelie had a loving family she'd never meet.

She reached to wipe a tear away, but Fernando was faster. He tipped up her chin. "These are happy memories."

She attempted a laugh. "I never used to cry, but now I get weepy all the time."

He grabbed her hand and held it. "Michael's red train sits safely on a shelf in his bedroom, although he doesn't play with toy trains anymore." One corner of his mouth twitched, and he looked suspiciously like he was laughing at her.

She'd been made fun of enough in her life. She shrugged off his hands.

He backed away. "You're a self-sufficient woman now. Forgive me for forgetting." The cell phone in his coat pocket buzzed again. He ignored it.

"I cried when I was younger," he said softly.

This was unexpected. She forced a quiet, disbelieving laugh.

"You called me a baby once," he said.

She shifted. She remembered but couldn't recall why she'd been so angry and had lashed out at him. "I'm sorry. I'll blame it on being young and ignorant. I now know there's nothing wrong with a man showing his emotions. It's a sign of strength, not weakness."

"I never cry anymore," he said. "I quickly learned crying doesn't change anything."

She wanted to run her hand reassuringly along the dark bristles on his strong, determined chin, but her arms felt too heavy, and she couldn't lift them. And the room was too hot. Maybe she was getting a fever. She needed some fresh air and glanced toward the window. No yellow ball of California sunshine shone back, only gray, gloomy skies. A worker bundled in a hooded, military-green parka was sweeping the sleet from the sidewalk.

The clock chimed two thirty.

"Perhaps," he said, "that's the reason why you decided not to date me." He grabbed the door handle and opened the door a crack. He hunched over but quickly straightened.

Margaret figured Lucy had her ear pressed to the door and was eavesdropping on the entire conversation and was surprised her friend didn't fall into the room.

"Don't assume you know everything about me," she said.

He stepped back toward her. She breathed in his familiar scent of the outdoors and cold air. No expensive men's cologne for him. "But I do know everything about you." His tone had changed, warmer now, sensual.

No, no. Not this. She moved away. "We never agreed about anything."

"We agreed about one thing," he said. "And beneath your stardom and expensive clothes, you're still the same passionate woman. Somewhere along the way you've lost sight of what's important. I understand."

"I have a therapist in Los Angeles. I don't need your advice."

He grabbed her shoulders and pulled her closer. His dark brown eyes reminded her of melted chocolate. "You'll find everything you're looking for right here."

She wasn't prepared for the tenderness in his voice. "Who am I, Dorothy from *The Wizard of Oz*?" She jerked away. "I'm not wearing ruby slippers and don't need a lecture. There's nothing in this depressing town for me."

He brushed his fingers along her cheek. "You used to enjoy when I held you. You said it was comforting." His glance slid to her lips.

She inhaled sharply. "Not every situation can be arranged by you because—"

"Of course it can." His arms locked around her, and his lips came down on hers in a long, demanding kiss. "So enchanting."

She leaned against him as he deepened the kiss. He'd been so good to her and they fit so well together. Her perfect match. Her soul mate. Her protector.

"My stunning princess," he whispered. "You're as beautiful as Snow White."

She twined her arms around his neck. She shouldn't. She did. She'd always loved when he'd called her Snow White because of her shiny ebony hair, chin length and parted in the middle and her contrasting pale skin. A thousand lifetimes ago. But life changes—one last time in his bed, an unplanned pregnancy, a resolve to pursue her dreams.

She drew a great gulp of air and dropped her hands. "I have to leave."

"So do I." Melted chocolate cooled, and he moved back a step. "When can I see you again?"

Never. Had she said the word aloud?

CHAPTER 3

She must have, considering how quickly his gaze turned cold.

She turned to the closet in the corner of her office, pulled on a royal-blue coat lined with a fleece collar, and tied a checkered scarf around her neck.

"Am I being dismissed?" he asked.

She slung her black leather tote over her shoulder. "You're not the only person with commitments."

Lucy chose that perfect moment to appear in the doorway. "Margaret, don't forget your three o'clock appointment."

"You're ever efficient, Lucy," he said. "Always hovering over Margaret like the older sister she never had."

"So glad to see you, Fernando." Lucy narrowed her eyes. Her bubble-gum pink lipstick had faded. "What are you doing here? I was told you'd left town years ago."

He turned up the collar of his coat, genuine puzzlement on his face. "And why would you have inquired about my whereabouts?"

"Lucy was looking up people from our high school yearbook

29

in case anyone wanted to get together for a Christmas reunion," Margaret smoothly interjected. She certainly was honing her acting skills today. Her next audition was bound to be a success.

"Are you living in Owanda or just visiting?" Lucy asked him.

"That seems to be the question of the day, and I assure you I'm not peddling apples." He smiled. "Should I be flattered by your interest?"

"Absolutely not," Lucy responded with exaggerated gaiety.

He stepped nearer to Margaret. "I'm unsure of my holiday plans, but apparently that makes two of us."

And our child makes three. Margaret gasped aloud. Now where had that thought come from? The silence stretched, as the seconds ticked by.

Fernando turned to her. "See you soon. You'll love Antonio's. The pizzeria hasn't changed." His fingertips slid lightly along the edge of her hairline, and he pressed a quick kiss to her forehead. "This holiday is turning into more of a celebration than I ever dreamed."

She swallowed. And more of a disaster than she'd ever imagined.

* * *

"WHAT ARE YOU DOING?" Lucy demanded as soon as Fernando's footsteps had retreated down the hallway and the front door slammed.

Margaret pointed at Lucy. "You're the one who let him barge into my office."

Lucy put her hands on her hips and stood straight to her full height of five feet. "And you're the one who agreed to see him again!"

"You know he'd never leave me alone until I consented. One night, a brief dinner, and he'll be satisfied."

"When it comes to you, he's insatiable. I saw the way he still looks at you."

Margaret shook her head. "Not anymore. We're all grown up."

"He loved you enough once to want to marry you. How will we ever hide Amelie from him?"

"We've done a good job these past five years."

"Yes, when we were separated by three thousand miles. But here in the same town, it's impossible. You should've told him years ago." She shook her head and sighed deeply. "I knew we never should've returned."

"We didn't have a choice. I'm paying bills and plan to buy back my old trailer."

"Why? We need the money for more important things like rent and food."

"I was fortunate that my former agency set up this winter-wonderland gig for me just when California was so uncertain. They've taken care of all the expenses at the mall and the office and I'll still make money. When I learned about the foreclosure a couple of months ago, I knew I needed to return for a few weeks."

"That rusty old thing has probably disintegrated. What are you trying to prove?"

That she no longer was the needy, poverty-stricken girl who lived at the end of Spruce Street. But she didn't say her belief aloud.

"Fernando doesn't suspect a thing," Margaret assured Lucy. "Besides, he doesn't know our home address. Amelie will attend school while we work in the office during the day, and we'll be gone in six weeks."

"He found your office."

"Coincidence. He didn't know I was working with this agency again."

Lucy shook her head. "He always had a bloodhound sense when it came to you."

"But he missed the most important part, his daughter." Margaret fished in her tote for her car keys. "Did my LA agent call? There's another casting for a drama starring some very famous actors."

"Nope."

Margaret pushed aside the thought of not booking any more jobs in Hollywood. People had short memories, and one blockbuster film was a matter of one successful audition.

"I'll see you tonight at the apartment after I pick up Amelie from school and stop at the grocery store. I want to try a new recipe for stuffed peppers."

"You're becoming domesticated?"

"I'm changing my life for the better, remember?"

As long as it wasn't German food, she could manage anything.

He'd hoped his gift would bring her gladness, a reminder of happier times, but she hadn't bothered to open it.

CHAPTER 5

*A*s usual she was running late. Margaret steered her small white Volvo around the narrow country roads and forced away the thought of Fernando's unexpected appearance. She'd wanted to launch into a tirade about his perpetual planning before he'd smothered her words with a kiss. His hands had caressed her back while pulling her close to him. They fit together intimately-- they always had-- and she knew he'd guard her with his life. He'd gazed at her with unbearable tenderness. Seeing him again, she realized how much she'd missed him, his indulgent smile and silent strength.

She chewed her bottom lip. What was wrong with wanting to feel needed and loved? She glanced out the side window at the cloudy skies and endless precipitation. Nothing, for the average woman living in Owanda. But not for her. If she ever married she'd be a full partner. She wasn't looking for a lord and master who believed he could make all the decisions because he controlled the paycheck.

She gripped the steering wheel and kept her gaze on the road. The sleet had stopped, and she pulled the car up to the curb at precisely three o'clock, just as the school bell rang. She got out and soon spotted her daughter racing toward her from the building.

"Mom! I love school! And I didn't cough once!" Amelie's voice was a loud monotone as she ran to the car. Her small form was dwarfed by her new berry-red parka and the sparkly polka-dot book bag on her shoulders She carefully carried a tiny white kitten. "Look what my teacher said we could have. It's a boy and he only has one eye."

Margaret stared at the kitten. "So cute, but we can't keep him. We're only here until the end of December and don't have room for anymore rescue animals in our small apartment."

Her daughter's mouth quivered, and she plopped a kiss on the kitten's forehead. "We had lots of strays in California, and you said a kitten is almost as good as a daddy."

Margaret shook her head. Opening the car door, she pushed some office supplies off the front seat onto the floor and placed the kitten on the seat. "This isn't California and I never remember saying that."

"All the other kids in my class have a daddy, but mine can't live with us, right?"

Amelie brought up the most sensitive subject when least expected.

Margaret blinked back threatening tears and braced her hands against the car door for support. "No, he can't. He's … busy."

"Will he come back someday?"

"Remember how much I love you. Daddy not living with us isn't your fault. There're all kinds of families, and our family is you and I and Lucy."

"And our new kitten." Amelie jutted out her small, determined chin. "I know Daddy will come back some day."

Leave it to a child to display unguarded optimism.

Margaret regarded her daughter with heartbreaking admiration. She had such resilience. She tucked Amelie in the backseat and pulled matching berry-red insulated mittens on her small hands, then buckled the seat belt. She placed the book bag on the floor.

"Let me speak with your teacher," she both signed and spoke. Amelie was hard of hearing and wore a hearing aid. Margaret always made eye contact with her daughter, as Amelie relied on visual cues and gestures as well as lip-reading and signing.

Mrs. Henderson, the kindergarten teacher, waddled over. Her crop of wiry-gray hair was pulled back in a messy bun. Her beige wool coat was buttoned securely around her large body.

"The first day went well?" Margaret spoke aloud while signing so Amelie was included in the conversation.

"Very well." Mrs. Henderson glanced at the front seat. "Can you take the kitten home? I found him on my front step this morning, and your daughter told the class you took in strays in California. My mother lives with me and is allergic to cats, or I'd keep him. With only one eye, this kitten has a slim chance of being adopted if I take him to a shelter."

"Please, Mommy?" Amelie offered her most persuasive smile. And the kitten was already curled up and sleeping in the front seat.

"We already have Grumpy," Margaret argued.

"Grumpy needs a friend," Amelie signed.

"A parrot doesn't necessarily want a kitten for a friend."

"Grumpy is safe in his parrot cage. Please, please, Mommy?"

Margaret sighed. "All right, but I can't commit for a long period of time."

"Yay! I knew you'd say yes!" Amelie signed, and then

cent lights glaring from the ceiling and making his head pound. "Your daughter distracted me."

"Perfectly fine. We're through for today. I've talked enough about business and am ready to head home." Scott slid back his chair. "Once the auction is finalized and the sale price agreed upon, the only distraction you'll need to concern yourself with is where to spend all your money. But if I know my daughter, it'll be an easy task."

Fernando offered a half-hearted laugh. "I appreciate your assistance in financing this real estate deal. An outlet mall requires a lot of capital."

Scott's forehead creased, or tried to. "Those trailers should've been torn down years ago. My investors and I are doing this decrepit town a favor. It's been stuck in a time warp. Think of all the new jobs we're creating."

He stood, and Fernando did as well, striding over to Scott and extending his hand. He forced a smile as the men shook hands. "Thank you for your generosity," Fernando said.

"I believe in winners. You're diligent and skilled in this business, and your instinct is good for sound investments. As soon as you move permanently to Florida, there are several other properties we can develop together. I guarantee your real estate business will double within the next year."

Beneath the tan and trimness, Scott appeared much older close up, Fernando noticed.

"Thank you, sir."

"My daughter's a lovely girl. She's all I have, and I'd give her the world."

Fernando gave a brisk nod. That statement was as loaded as it got.

Scott offered a genuine smile in her direction. "I'll wait for you in the foyer, Diana."

"I'll only be another minute, Dad."

Fernando figured she'd likely be much longer, but she was

used to people waiting for her. The two of them watched as Scott exited.

"Dinner at my place tonight?" Diana asked. She followed Fernando back to the table as he arranged the paperwork into one bundle. She didn't have a head for business, only pleasure, and he knew where the conversation was headed. An exquisite meal, a bottle of wine, and then he'd spend the night. Under her attractive demeanor, she was ruthless when it came to getting what she wanted. He'd witnessed her negotiation skills in action when she'd purchased her current home near the Atlantic Ocean. She had wanted all the expensive paintings the owner had collected through the years, and she'd gotten them. The owner hadn't stood a chance.

"Angelina, my housemaid from Florida, is broiling sirloin steak with roasted potatoes and chocolate pie for dessert. In the morning, Dad and I will be returning to Florida, so it'll be the last time I see you for a few weeks."

He placed a hand over where his kidney had been removed. "I can't. I'm more tired than I anticipated."

"You never should've donated one of your kidneys. Just because Michael's your brother doesn't mean you owe him anything."

"It was a privilege, not an obligation."

"He could've waited on the list for a donor."

He held up a hand. "I'll not argue anymore about this."

"But are you all right? You've lost weight since the operation."

"I'm here, aren't I? And yes, I'm fine."

But he was the opposite of fine. He lifted a dismissive shoulder, reached for his water glass, and took a sip. He placed the glass back on its coaster and wiped at the water spots on the table with the folded napkin. "I'll meet you at the airport in the morning to see you off."

She didn't look happy but went into satisfied mode. Lowering her voice, she asked, "Are you taking the pills my doctor prescribed? I didn't tell him they were for you. They're magical, aren't they? Let me know when you need a refill."

He nodded, patting the pill bottle in his shirt pocket. "I needed a few to get me through a rough time. I didn't heal as fast as I thought."

"You work too hard and never take any time off." She touched his hand, close to his abdomen. It was an intimate gesture. Her hands were smooth because she'd never done a day of manual labor. Who flew in their housemaid from Florida, anyway?

"When you relocate permanently to Miami, you can relax and spend your days sailing with Dad and me."

"I can't leave my mother to look after my brother by herself, as her eyes are starting to fail and she doesn't drive anymore. Besides, Michael's condition could worsen at any time."

"He rented his own apartment until you demanded he move back with your mother."

"He wasn't well and couldn't be alone."

She shrugged. "Your family will understand your life is in Florida with me. They can manage on their own and we'll hire in-home care. You can commute between Miami and Owanda."

"I won't fly. I tried it once and vowed never again. Must be the air pressure."

She laughed. "A flight from Florida to New York State takes less than three hours. Sit in first class, enjoy a couple of drinks, and you'll be fine."

"I'll take an overnight train," he said. "Besides, I like this town and don't want to leave it permanently. It's home."

"Then you'll have two homes. But this holiday you

promised to spend Christmas in Florida and stay through New Year's."

"Of course." He glanced at his watch. He didn't belong here.

She was his fiancée. She was supposed to act interested and loving. So was he.

Her crystal-blue gaze searched his. "Tell me that's what you want. We'll take trips to Europe after we're married."

"Of course." Same response, with an even more incredulous tone, as in "How can you possibly think otherwise so please stop asking."

She sighed an exaggerated sigh. "Sorry your brother can't withstand long trips. It's better if he stays here with your mother."

She didn't look at all sorry, and he knew she'd never had compassion for sick people. Sometimes he had the feeling she only put up with his family to please him.

He squeezed her hand. "I'll take an early morning train to Florida on Christmas day."

"Good. We'll celebrate Christmas night on Dad's sailboat." She smoothed her hand across his shirt sleeve. The two-carat diamond in her engagement ring flashed in those damn fluorescent lights. He'd spent a fortune on it after her father had contributed a substantial amount of money to his real estate venture in Florida. The shopping center and apartment complex had proven a success.

He gazed at her platinum-blonde hair, her tiny turned-up nose. She was a lovely woman, and she cared about him. Sure, he was her rebound fiancé after her former lover had left her at the altar. At least, that was the story she'd told, although it had changed several times. Still, they respected each other. She was exactly who he deserved, persistent and aggressive. Besides, no one married for love anymore.

He assumed she'd drop her hand, but she gripped tighter. "What do you want for Christmas, darling?"

The room fell silent.

He brushed a polite kiss on her cheek. "Nothing special."

She jerked her hand from his sleeve. He blamed his non-answer on his fuzzy brain, although he knew what she wanted him to say. He just didn't say it.

CHAPTER 7

$\mathcal{I}$f ever a person wanted to be humiliated, standing in the middle of the local mall dressed as an elf on Black Friday was the perfect place to do it. Margaret's insides cringed. She'd vowed never to be put in a position of feeling awkward and uncomfortable again, but the ever-present need for money forced her to do embarrassing things.

"Santa, you must wear your beard at all times." She applied eyelash glue to Gus Stefano's chin. He was the local plumber and part-time Santa. She waited several seconds for the glue to become tacky, then pressed the white beard onto his chin until it stuck firm.

He took a long pull from his mug. "This beard itches and the glue doesn't hold properly."

She wiped her sticky fingers on her red velvet pants. Wisps of white beard stuck to her thighs. "If the beard falls off in one of the children's hands, you'll never work as Santa in this town again."

"No kid should be pulling on my beard," Gus said. "If they do, I'll threaten that Santa won't bring them any toys."

"You won't do any such thing. Laugh like a jolly fellow

and say 'ho, ho, ho.'" She tightened the shiny black belt around her emerald-green elf's jacket. One of the seven elves she'd hired had called in sick, so she'd stepped in. Technically the men weren't elves, they were merely short in stature. Michael was the only dwarf.

She glanced at the large mall clock as it chimed nine o'clock. The elves were all late on their first day of work.

Amelie and Lucy were at the apartment baking Christmas cookies, although Lucy would never actually eat a cookie because she was always counting calories. They'd spent several evenings perusing recipes and had decided on three favorites: a peanut butter with a chocolate kiss in the center, a round cookie made almost exclusively of butter, and home-made chocolate fudge. When Margaret returned home, the kitchen would be warm with the aromas of sugar and chocolate.

Gus took another sip from his mug. "I'm sixty-four years old and had one heart attack. I should be retired and sitting on a beach in the Caribbean."

"Rumor has it you love this job and would never give it up."

"Rumor has it wrong. These days I tire easily."

"For a guy named Santa, you complain quite a bit. As soon as the mall doors open, you'll be surrounded by children." She stared directly at his mug. "And that better be coffee in there."

"You're bossy for such a pretty elf." He stared at her pointy green shoes. "If people learn a famous swimsuit model is here, you'll be surrounded by a mob clamoring for autographs."

She laughed. "The public is fickle and fans want a new fresh face. I'm yesterday's news."

Gus set his gaze on the mall entrance doors, their glass dusted with snow. A line of shoppers snaked around the building. "Who takes their kids out the morning after Thanksgiving, anyway? My grandkids are at home in their pajamas watching TV and playing games." His blue eyes twinkled. He looked so much like Santa. Despite his gruffness, he had one of the kindest hearts of anyone in the world.

"I'd prefer to stay home in my pajamas too," she said.

That's what made Gus a good Santa. He couldn't come to grips with the commercialism surrounding Christmas, and neither could she. She'd much rather fill her apartment with abandoned stray animals than a roomful of designer dresses.

"Yep," he said. "Every dedicated shopper in America is eager to buy, buy, buy. Some have waited outside the mall all night to be first to snag the best deals."

She tilted her head and eyed his red velvet suit. "How many years have you played Santa?"

He was comfortably leaning back in his chair, his large stomach bulging, and one of the shiny brass buttons on his Santa suit was ready to pop. He set down the mug and adjusted his wire-rim glasses. "Over thirty years."

"Then go take your rightful place on Santa's throne." She led him to a peppermint-striped candy-cane throne in the middle of the holiday display. Two gingerbread houses flanked the throne. Several artificial Christmas trees completed the scene, each decorated with oversized gold and peacock-blue bulbs. A sign above the throne said "Wish." Gus bumped his head on the sign as he took his seat.

"That sign should be mounted higher. Or should I say I *wish* the sign were mounted higher?" He rubbed his head and sighed loudly. "Fortunately, this throne gives me the perfect vantage point to admire your shapely little derriere while you prance around in that elf suit."

"Derriere? Is that a new word in your Santa Claus vocabulary?"

"Perhaps later we can ..."

She shook her head. "Never happen."

"Aren't you interested in older men? I'm divorced and single."

"I've sworn off all men, young, old, and in-between. They're way too much trouble. What's more, I could never date Santa Claus."

"Little Margaret." He smiled good-naturedly. "I'm glad you returned for the holidays. I still remember you as a tall, skinny girl who played hop scotch on the sidewalk."

Her trailer had been dark and narrow. She'd stayed outside as often as she could, despite the typically bad weather. An old tool shed had housed several of her rescue animals.

"What were you running from when you left?" he asked.

She gave an incredulous laugh. "You really don't know? How about my terrible life?"

"I heard Fernando was devastated and searched everywhere for you."

She couldn't answer. She hadn't known.

"And what were you running toward?" he asked.

Much harder question. She stood quiet before she answered. "In truth, sometimes I don't know anymore."

Success she'd earned on her own, a shot at fame, a taste of wealth. Had any of it mattered? She'd moved to LA to make a better life for her daughter. But the money had slid from her fingers as she'd attempted to keep up with the mounting bills for health insurance, tuition, and medical treatment for Amelie.

"You were always such a kind child, especially to animals," Gus said.

"I'm not in Owanda on a kindness mission. I need the money to pay my bills."

"I came from nothing too, you know. People like us think money equals peace of mind, but it doesn't."

Her memory drew the cold, empty walls of her childhood bedroom, and a muscle tightened in her throat. "I'm planning to purchase my old trailer because it's in foreclosure. I'll tear it down and put up a real house, a white bungalow with a red front door."

"Don't forget the white picket fence." He nodded. "Sounds like you're changing your life into a make-believe board game. You can't fix everything in your past by tearing it down and replacing it with a fancier substitute."

She chewed her lower lip but kept her back straight. "Watch me."

She'd been pathetic and poor, but she had succeeded. Some of it was luck, yes, a simple roll of the dice that she had been born attractive. But hard work and ambition had made all the difference. She wouldn't accept failure. And she'd never be poor again.

She picked up his mug to discard the contents and sniffed a suspicious whiff of blackberry brandy.

She frowned. "You told me ..."

"Ho, ho, ho." He patted his large stomach with white gloved hands.

A bell on the garland-decorated clock chimed nine fifteen, and a stampede of shoppers raced through the mall doors and into the brightly lit stores. Several had small children in tow, and they lined up so their children would be the first to sit on Santa's lap.

"Has Santa been drinking?" a flushed woman shouted for everyone in Santa's Wonderland to hear. She juggled a chubby-cheeked toddler in one arm and an older child in the other.

"He drinks only coffee," Margaret lied. She briefly wondered if Gus had hidden the brandy bottle amidst the burlap-wrapped Christmas trees and if she could sneak a swig.

At nine thirty, five short men and one dwarf strode through the mall and stopped when they reached the edge of the Christmas display.

Michael dabbed his irritated red nose and sneezed. "We're here!" He was thinner and paler than she remembered and sported a short dark beard.

She hugged him. "It's good to see you. I hope you're feeling better."

A familiar deep voice came from behind Michael. "I don't remember receiving that same warm, fuzzy greeting from you. Instead, you demanded to know what I was doing in Owanda."

She stiffened and ignored Fernando. "Thanks for showing up to be Santa's helpers," she said aloud to the elves. "Unfortunately, you're all late."

"You told us to report at nine thirty." Buster, the shyest of the men, stroked his long gray beard and kept his head down.

She propped her hands on her hips. "I said to arrive before the mall opened."

"It's six elves against your word," Fernando said. "Admit you're wrong."

She swung around to him. "Who are you, the elf lawyer?"

He gestured toward the camera at the foot of Santa's throne. He was such a good-looking man, resembling a lean hockey player on the cover of a sports magazine. "I can stay a few hours if you need someone to take pictures. I'm your Prince Helpful offering free labor."

She paused and then nodded. Amelie and Lucy weren't due to meet her at the mall until early evening. "All right. Thanks." She smiled.

"I took a photography class in college." He pulled his cell phone out of his coat pocket and snapped a photo of her.

"Well, then you're more than qualified," came her sarcastic reply. She pointed to the heavy camera. "After you take a photo of each child, I'll ask the parents if they'd like to purchase it for five dollars."

"What do I get in return?"

"Nothing, because you volunteered. I'm already over budget for this project."

He grinned. "Want to take a selfie with me?"

"No." She raised a hand to shield her face. "I'm the wrong subject and not sitting on Santa's lap."

"A man can dream, can't he?" He examined the photo on his phone and grinned before tucking it into his pocket. Then he shrugged off his coat and grabbed the heavy camera. "I'll use an action setting and begin snapping pictures as soon as each child approaches Santa. Some of the best photos occur when the subject isn't posing for the camera because that's when you can see the real emotion on a person's face."

"Thank you, Robert Capa," she said, referring to the world-renowned Hungarian World War II photographer.

An older child holding an oversized rainbow-colored lollipop jumped out of Santa's lap. "I said I want two trucks, not one! That's my wish!"

Gus looked at Margaret and lifted both hands as if to say "It wasn't my fault if he's greedy" as the mother raced after her child.

Margaret sighed. "You missed that shot, Fernando."

He snapped another photo of her. "But I found a much more intriguing subject."

* * *

THREE HOURS LATER FERNANDO SAID, "I'm expected at a meeting in town. Sorry, because we make a great team."

"Prince Persuasive is leaving his damsel in dire need?" She picked up a lemon-lime slushy drink left on the floor and discarded it in a nearby wastebasket. "Are you meeting your stockbroker?"

He threw an amused look. "Not today. Call me if there's any problem with Michael."

"Can't Michael drive?" she asked.

Fernando shook his head. "He has his license, but I've never encouraged it. Besides, he can't afford a car."

Michael was in line facing them with several children. His face was flushed as he held out a deck of cards facedown. "Pick a card, any card. I'll show you the card you chose."

"How?" one of the children asked. "You're gonna peek."

Michael winked. "It's an illusion."

"Where did he learn magic tricks?" Margaret asked Fernando.

"He's spent many days in the hospital this past year. I introduced him to a magician in New York City, and he's been perfecting magic tricks ever since. Magic takes skill and technique."

She folded her arms together. "It's not real. It's what you want people to believe while you're diverting their attention elsewhere."

He turned that probing gaze on her again. "People have used diversion in their lives to avoid important topics, especially when they're trying to hide something."

Her breath caught. Surely he didn't know about Amelie. She looked up at him.

A good-natured smirk was planted on his face. No suspicion there. "You have my business card with my phone number?"

"I left it at the agency office." In truth, she hadn't bothered to look at it.

He reached into his saddle-brown leather wallet and handed her another one. His cell phone buzzed. As usual, he ignored it. "I'll pick Michael up in a couple of hours. I'll be at my office if you need me."

He had an office? It certainly added credibility to his incessantly ringing cell phone. With a quick wave to the group, he strode past several boutique stores, pushed open the mall doors, and exited.

She walked to the line of squirming children and impatient parents. "Santa will be with you shortly so show him your best behavior."

"Or we won't get any toys for Christmas," one of the children intoned.

"Something like that." She continued to the group of elves who were straightening the metal poles that held the line in place. "Do you want to arrange half-hour lunch breaks among yourselves?"

Michael smiled up at her. "We can stagger the breaks so there're always several elves available in case it gets busier."

Buster glanced in Michael's direction. "He should go first. He's turning white."

She turned. Dear heavens, Michael was swaying on his feet as he limped toward her. Her hands stopped their straightening. "Michael! What's the matter?"

"I'm a little tired." He dropped the deck of cards and held his side. Someone else had done that recently. Someone else had limped and held his side.

Her breath caught in her throat. Fernando, the day he'd left her office. He'd said it was a sprain because he'd been working on his car.

Michael stumbled toward her. "My brother should take me home."

She caught his shoulders. "He left a short while ago. Don't you remember? You waved to him."

Michael picked at invisible lint on his elf suit and

smacked his lips. His gaze had turned wild. So strange to see his eyes bulge. "Where did he go?"

"He went to his office." Although what could be so pressing in any office the Friday after Thanksgiving was beyond her.

Michael twitched in her arms. "I need him." He wrenched from her grasp and dashed through the line of children, knocking over several metal poles.

"I'm dreaming of a white Christmas ..." piped through the mall's speakers amidst the screams of several toddlers. She fumbled for her cell phone. Hadn't Fernando handed her his business card? Her hands shook as she dialed 911 and ran toward Michael. His limbs convulsed, and he collapsed on the floor, taking one of the large Christmas trees into the aisle with him. The silver bulbs shattered. Blood spurted from a gash near his temple. She pressed the cell phone close to her ear and knelt beside Michael. "Answer, someone please answer," she whispered.

Michael gave a puzzled look. "Who are you?"

She tried to wipe the fear off her face. "I'm Margaret. You've known me since you were little."

Gus knelt beside her. "You'll be all right, Michael." He appeared so calm while her heart was pinging a loud beat in her chest.

Gus pulled off his white gloves and Santa Claus hat and propped them beneath Michael's head as a pillow. Then he loosened the top buttons of Michael's green tunic and nudged him onto his side.

"He's having a seizure," he whispered to Margaret. "But don't worry, he's okay. Take a deep breath."

Her heart flip-flopped as her throat constricted. A blank dial tone buzzed in her ear.

She gripped the sleeves of Gus's Santa suit. "My 911 call

didn't go through." She shook her head. "I can't even dial three simple numbers correctly."

"We can't be good at everything." Gus met her gaze. "This seizure shouldn't last more than a couple of minutes. No need to call an ambulance because I'm trained as a paramedic."

Michael's eyes rolled up, his eyelashes fluttered. He was shaking.

"Should we put something in his mouth in case he bites his tongue?"

"Doesn't help. In fact, it might harm him, and we don't want him to break any teeth." Gus surveyed the gawking crowd. "Get rid of these parents and their kids. That'll give you something to do. You're as white as Michael."

She stood on wobbly legs and walked over to the elves. They stared up at her with wide eyes. "Buster, please escort the children and parents away from this area," she said. "Then put up a sign saying we're closed for the remainder of the day."

A security officer strode over to Margaret. He planted himself in front of her, his massive arms crossed over his chest. "Is there a medical problem here?"

"Santa can explain." She pointed to Gus and then walked away to offer candy canes to the children and parents. "I'm sorry but we need to close unexpectedly. Please come back tomorrow." She walked back to Gus and the officer. Michael was standing now, leaning against Gus.

"Yep, everything's okay, officer," Gus was saying. He blinked and patted the officer on the back. "I didn't recognize you at first, Jacob. How are you?"

The officer tilted his head back and rested his hands on his hips. His black short-sleeved polo shirt emblazoned with the word *Security* was too tight for his broad chest. "I got a job at the mall while the police department works on my reinstatement. You may have read about a drug bust in the newspapers, but I wasn't at fault, just doing my job to get these derelicts off the street." He lifted his shoulders in a semblance of an explanation.

Jacob patted Michael on the shoulder. "And you, little man, shouldn't be working so recently after your operation." He narrowed his gaze on Margaret. "Why did you hire Michael when he's still not well?"

She stepped back. "I was told he'd recuperated and the job would be good for him." She fished in her pocket for Fernando's business card and plugged his number into her cell phone.

"Michael had kidney failure," Jacob said. "Four months ago he received a new kidney from Fernando. You probably know all about it."

She inhaled sharply because in the space of a few seconds, everything came together. The limping, the side holding, the hunching over. The lying by omission. Damn him. How dare he keep this secret from her? She fumed as she dialed his office number. His gold-embossed business card read, "Fernando Brandt, real estate broker, commercial and residential."

A woman answered. "Brandt Realty."

"Fernando Brandt, please."

"Who should I say is calling?"

"Margaret Snow."

"He's in a meeting."

This man had more meetings than the president. "Tell him it's urgent."

His voice came on the line a few seconds later. "Margaret? What's the matter?"

"Michael's suffered a seizure but he's coherent."

"When? Why didn't you call me sooner?"

"It happened so fast. Fortunately Santa's a paramedic."

"I'm on my way." He hung up the phone so quickly, she stared at it for a full ten seconds, outraged, before heading back to the elves. Fernando was beyond arrogant if he believed he could pick and choose what he told her to suit his purposes.

Michael was now sitting on Santa's chair. Jacob, Gus, and the elves surrounded him. "Fernando shouldn't have left on my first day of work." He gazed at her with sweet, soulful eyes, so much like Fernando's and Amelie's that her heart squeezed. She bent to pick up the deck of cards scattered on the floor and handed them to him.

"He's coming very soon."

Jacob stared openly at her. "Hey, you're Margaret Snow. Don't you belong in a magazine wearing a bikini?"

"I'm sorry, do I know you?" She gazed up in the air as if she were checking for the answer on the ceiling. In reality, she was searching for an escape from another lecherous fan.

He slicked back his streaked blond hair. "We were in English class together, sophomore year. I always thought you were the prettiest girl in high school. Wow! Wait till I tell the guys Margaret Snow is in town." He openly perused her, no shyness there. "Great polka-dot bikini you were wearing on the cover of that magazine. Remember the song, 'She wore an itsy bitsy teeny weeny ...'? The guys used to tease Fernando with that song when we'd see him. He let a gorgeous gal sneak off right out from under him."

"One of Bobby Darin's greatest hits."

Her ears burned, and she avoided his gaze. Her agent had urged her to pose for the shoot in the tiniest bikini she'd ever seen, saying it was a stepping stone for her career. She'd dieted and exercised furiously for two weeks beforehand, avoided carbohydrates like the plague, and at times imagined she'd turned into a salad topped with a can of tuna fish. (Packed in water, of course.) When her weight hadn't plunged as much as the swimwear company wanted, she'd taken laxatives. The laxatives had worked to help her shed the last five pounds, but her health had paid for it for months afterward. Lucy had dieted along with her, although Lucy's weight had never returned to normal. She remained stick thin.

"Let's get together," Jacob said. "I've always wanted to try acting. Can you get me an audition with one of your big-time agents?"

"Sorry, I'm very busy." Her theme song for deterring men.

One of the elves caught her gaze. "Do we get paid for today?"

"Yes, of course."

Really? she asked herself. How? With no more money being generated by photos, she'd be forced to borrow from the little savings she had to cover payroll. And that money was reserved for the foreclosure.

"I'll take care of all the wages," Fernando said.

She spun around. "How do you appear out of thin air?"

Smiling, he put his hands in his pocket, pulled out his checkbook, and signed the top check. He tore it out and extended it to her. "I opened the mall door and walked in. You were preoccupied with mall security."

She struggled to keep her anger in check and locked her hands behind her. "Thank you but I can't accept your money."

He grabbed her hands and placed the check in one of them. The smile disappeared. "I insist. I realize you're a wealthy woman, but give the elves a raise if you don't know what to do with all your money."

He didn't wait for her response and started toward Michael. She tucked the check in her pocket and followed him. She'd tear it up later.

Fernando placed his hand on Michael's shoulder. "I heard you were the center of attention today."

Michael sipped from the insulated cup of coffee he was holding. "I was more tired than I thought. Gus helped because he's a paramedic."

"Thank you." Fernando extended a hand to Gus, and the men shook. "I'll take my brother home now." He turned to Margaret. "Why didn't you call me sooner? I gave you my cell number twice."

"I misplaced your business card."

He let out an exasperated breath. "Does my family mean so little to you?"

She forced herself to meet his gaze. "I'm sorry. I panic in an emergency, and there's a lot on my mind."

"How could I possibly forget how busy you are?" It wasn't a question laced with understanding.

"And how can I possibly forget how manipulative you are?"

"What's that supposed to mean?"

She pushed out a breath in frustrated impatience. "Why didn't you tell me you donated one of your kidneys to Michael?"

He slipped his hand around her forearm and held tightly as she tried to pull away. "We discussed more important topics in your office because we hadn't seen each other in over five years. I expect you to be more understanding."

She wrenched from his grasp. "You expect the world to turn as you planned."

Jacob strode over and laser-tagged his gaze on Margaret. "I'm off work tomorrow. How about dinner at Antonio's?"

A muscle tightened in Fernando's jaw. "Sorry, she's already committed for that restaurant."

"Don't speak for me," she said.

Jacob raised a bleached brow. "I didn't realize you two were still an item."

"We're not," she and Fernando said at the same time. If she weren't so angry, she might've laughed.

Fernando turned and draped an arm around Michael's shoulders. "My car is parked by the entrance. Can you walk a little way?"

"Margaret, let's plan on the Royal Palace for egg rolls," Jacob was saying. "We can check out the Gentleman's Paradise Club afterward."

As she watched Fernando and Michael walk slowly toward the mall exit, she opened her mouth to tell Jacob she'd never be sharing egg rolls with him at the Royal Palace or any other palace, but then she saw Lucy and Amelie enter the mall. They walked directly toward Fernando and Michael, and the four all stopped and greeted one another.

Margaret swallowed and resisted the urge to dash toward them and pull them apart. Time ticked by. Fernando smiled at Amelie, bent down, and began signing. Their hands moved rapidly. Amelie's head tilted up, and Michael joined in the conversation. Lucy walked away, apparently lured by a designer purse sale.

Margaret's breath caught. Surely Lucy wasn't leaving them alone.

Fernando laughed aloud, mussed Amelie's hair and straightened. From across the mall, his probing gaze locked with Margaret's. He nodded.

Her heart stopped, just for a moment. Then it started beating again.

CHAPTER 8

*M*argaret was aware of Lucy's gaze boring into her back. She whirled and blinked twice, their secret signal. "What's going on?"

Lucy didn't blink back. She gestured toward the small crowd. Amelie scampered off to sit on Santa's throne. "I was going to ask you the same question."

"You go first," Margaret said.

"We finished baking cookies earlier than we anticipated, and I inhaled at least two thousand calories just by sniffing the air. Doc is sleeping contentedly by the fireplace, and Grumpy is probably perched upside down in his cage. Oh, wait." Lucy put a hand to her forehead. "We have Doc and Grumpy, but we don't have a fireplace."

Margaret took hold of Lucy's shoulders. "Isn't there a more important issue to discuss?"

"Amelie and I met Fernando and Michael."

"So I noticed. And you strolled away while Fernando chatted with Amelie. How could you?"

"Amelie was safe. She was with her father, and he was funny and engaging."

"And now you're giving him secret father tests?"

"He's one of the best-looking men I've ever seen, even by Hollywood standards."

"And that makes him father material? How did you introduce Amelie?"

Lucy shrugged. "He must've assumed she was with me, and he was preoccupied with Michael. Remember when he was madly in love with you?" She hesitated, then added quietly, "Some women wait a lifetime for love and devotion."

"The last man I'd ever want is one who controls every aspect of my life. And your precious Fernando has his own secret. I discovered he donated one of his kidneys to his brother, something he purposely hid from me."

"He was always the type of guy who'd do anything for anyone. Remember how compassionate he was to the people in the homeless shelter? He did a lot of volunteering, serving meals and transporting them to and from the hospital."

Firmly, Margaret shook her head. "Whose side are you on?"

"You don't feel obligated to tell the truth about Amelie, yet you're judging him for donating his kidney?"

Margaret gritted her teeth. "What is it about this town that turns everyone into a psychologist?"

Gus shuffled over with Amelie. "This little girl belong to someone?"

"She's with us." Margaret grabbed her daughter's hand.

His smile was kind and thoughtful. "Well, she's coughing really hard. Better watch that."

Margaret bent to Amelie. "You haven't coughed since we left California."

"Just a cough, Mommy. It'll go away," Amelie signed.

"I assume it's you three ladies living alone while you're here," Gus said. "And kids need a male role model in their lives. If you ever need me, I'll come around. I'm experienced and have grandkids, plus I can build an excellent fort out of Popsicle sticks and cardboard boxes. And"—he winked—"I'm Santa Claus."

"Thanks. I'll keep your offer in mind," Margaret said.

Lucy produced a pair of buttery-yellow leather gloves and fanned them at her cheeks. "The kitchen was blistering while we were baking, and I was getting hot flashes."

"Me too, Mommy!" Amelie waved her face with red mittens.

"I bet ice cream will make everything better, cutie." Holding Amelie's hand, Margaret veered toward Owanda's Creamery, the local ice cream parlor.

"Ice cream is almost as good as a kitten and a daddy, right, Mommy?" Amelie asked.

"Right," Margaret assured her.

Lucy shook her head and followed, pushing open the swinging glazed doors of the creamery. She staked a claim at a small yellow table and three chairs near the entrance. "So, no more photos with Santa today?" She pulled up a chair and drummed her fingers on the wrought iron table. What she really meant was, "How are we supposed to pay the mounting bills?"

"We'll open again tomorrow." Margaret studied the chalkboard menu hanging on an adjacent wall. Thirty ice cream flavors were listed, including twists, sorbets, and custards. "I'll miss Michael. He won't be returning because he's obviously not fully recuperated from his operation."

She turned to Amelie and signed. "Two scoops of peppermint ice cream?"

Amelie nodded. "With chocolate sprinkles."

"And a small caramel cone for me. What about you?" Margaret glanced at Lucy.

"Nothing, thanks." Lucy toyed idly with her gloves. Margaret knew she was too weight conscious to be interested in ice cream, especially after stuffing herself with Thanksgiving turkey yesterday and sniffing Christmas cookies today. Lucy eyed a fashionable women's store across the way. "Won't you meet Michael again when you see Fernando?"

"Fernando's decided I'm insensitive, so I doubt I'll hear from him again." She swallowed. For some reason, her heart hurt when she said that.

"Why not, Mommy?" Amelie signed with one hand while tugging on Margaret's velvet pants with the other. "Everyone likes you because you're nice."

She gave a bitter chuckle. Because nothing she'd ever done had met Fernando's high standards, and she wasn't a nice person. She was weak and money-minded and unlovable. She'd tried being a good daughter, but her parents hadn't cared about her. Her childhood friends except for Lucy were non-existent. She'd always been an unpopular, awkward loner who never fit anywhere.

"Sometimes I'm not a nice person," she murmured.

She'd said too much. Lucy's reproving glare confirmed it.

She'd left Fernando because she wouldn't be restricted to a small town. Although, she admitted with a pang of regret, he was everything a man should be. Decisive, intelligent, and caring. Her heart sank when she thought of telling him the truth about his daughter. Would he ever forgive her, ever understand? He'd seemed so cheerful when he was taking photographs of the children on Santa's lap, engaged and interested in each child.

A woman who'd stood in line with her little girl smiled and waved good-naturedly. Margaret smiled and waved back. Small town living was certainly friendlier than California.

Jacob sauntered to the ice cream parlor's entrance and strode inside. "This is my lucky day. I'm seeing two beautiful women and this cute little girl again in one afternoon." He stared at Amelie and then Margaret. "Who's she with?"

Lucy leaned forward. "Both of us."

"How old is she?"

"Five."

"What's her name?"

Lucy paused and shot a glance at Margaret. "Her name is Amelie."

"Pretty." Apparently satisfied, he set his full white-teethed beam on Lucy. "Do you remember me?"

"Of course." Lucy tilted her head as the reflection of the overhead Tiffany lamp doubled the platinum in her blonde hair. She wore black false eyelashes. Fortunately, she didn't bat them. "You poked me with your pen during algebra class when we were in high school."

He leaned nearer. "Because you copied all my answers."

She actually giggled, aloud, with no embarrassment. "You never studied a day in your life. You sat behind my desk and copied all the answers from me."

"Will you join me for dinner? I always thought you were the prettiest girl in our high school."

Margaret raised her brows. That line sounded familiar.

Lucy grabbed her cell phone from her suede, blazing-pink purse. "I'm free any time and you can text me."

He added his number to her phone contacts. His enormous satisfied grin resembled the Cheshire Cat's.

Margaret sighed. Jacob had asked her to accompany him to a gentlemen's club. Was that the reputation Hollywood had branded on her? After endless auditions, casting calls, and trying to memorize lines, she was known only for a skimpy bikini on a magazine cover.

She glanced at Amelie. She'd taken off her glasses, and her bright shining gaze was focused lovingly on Margaret. She offered her daughter a small smile and cleared the sadness from her throat. If only she didn't need to make so much money to be self-reliant. If only her need to prove herself by being a critically acclaimed actress could be calmed. If only Fernando would forgive her, because she did care about him and his family. And Lucy was right. He'd be a wonderful father.

She pulled in a deep breath. *Pluck that thought out of your mind. Your career would end right here in this worn-out town.*

She stood and weaved through a clump of teenagers with pierced eyebrows to the front counter. She switched her order from a small caramel ice cream to a large peppermint sundae. Then she added whipped cream, hot fudge, and a maraschino cherry. After all, it was the Christmas season. Time for good cheer and celebration.

Jacob stepped in line behind her and tapped her on the shoulder. "She's your daughter, isn't she?"

She whirled. "I'm sorry. What did you say?"

"Amelie. She's your daughter."

"Unless an unemployed cop in New York State has different rules from the ones in California, Amelie is none of your business."

"And I decided I know who the father is."

Deny. Escape. Any Christmas spirit she'd felt was quickly turning to panic. She held firm and erected a cool, inscrutable mask over her features. "No one's interested in your outrageous opinions and decisions."

A merry holiday song played through the ice cream parlor's loudspeaker, but still she heard Jacob's soft voice as she whirled around. "I won't tell. Get me that audition so I can vacate this crummy town and move to Hollywood."

CHAPTER 9

*S*now and hard-driving sleet were the order of the day. Fernando must have forgiven her for any imagined thoughtlessness toward his family because he'd called her office and arranged a date two weeks after Michael's seizure. The visit to see his family was postponed until Michael was feeling better. However, dinner at Antonio's was still on. So here she was amidst the scents of tomato sauce, Parmesan cheese, and freshly ground black pepper. She inhaled deeply with appreciation. She'd been eating California salads far too long.

Fernando stood waiting near the entrance of the tiny pizzeria and escorted her to their table. His gaze and smile were all approval. "You're looking lovely."

"Thank you for politely lying because we both know I'm a wet, bedraggled mess." She raised a hand to her face and shook off the sleet that had settled on her red tartan scarf. Her coal-black eyeliner was probably streaming halfway down her cheeks, and a bad hair day was an understatement.

His light brown hair was damp from the sleet, and he pushed a wavy tendril back from his forehead. He wore snug denim jeans and a navy pea coat, and she grinned at him appreciatively. The good-looking teenage boy had become one of the most striking men she'd even seen. For a moment she was caught in the spell of his persuasive brown eyes.

"You're looking well," she said.

"I feel much better, and the pain has lessened. The doctors told me that it would take several months to fully recover, but I tend to be impatient." A faint smile touched his lips. He leaned toward her, his mouth moving closer to hers. "I would've picked you up at your house."

She looked away. "I live out of town in a very nice rental apartment."

No, it wasn't nice. It was freezing, with cold air seeping through the cracks in the walls. Plus, the roof leaked. She shuddered just thinking about the place. That was the problem with lies. Sometimes, most times, they made her very, very tired.

She'd hoped her LA agent would have returned her call regarding prospective auditions, but her cell phone had sat silent for days. Many of the fashion magazines were scheduling January shoots in the Bahamas for their summer issues. It was not encouraging that her agent hadn't answered her call and hadn't called her back.

Lucy was spending a cozy night at their apartment with Amelie and Doc, the rapidly growing kitten. For a kitten with one eye, Doc was surprisingly mobile. Gus was stopping over to play Go Fish with Amelie.

Tomorrow, Lucy was seeing Jacob again. She'd gone out with him three times, always meeting him in Owanda. She'd become adept at lying, too, and had told Margaret she continued to sidestep his inquiries about Amelie's parents. But how long before Margaret confided in Lucy regarding Jacob's threat?

Fernando tucked Margaret's hand possessively in his and

swept her to a corner table. A small fire crackled in the fireplace. He helped her off with her coat, then shrugged off his own and draped both over their chairs. She hung her purse over the back of her chair and examined the reindeer salt and pepper shakers in the middle of the table.

"This pizzeria hasn't changed. Plastic reindeer are a charming addition," she said.

He laughed. "Much different from your fancy California restaurants. They probably use real fir trees as centerpieces."

She set the reindeer on the table and perched her chin on her hands. "Those restaurants are too health conscious, and I can only eat so much tofu. I used to love Antonio's eggplant."

"I already placed your order. Eggplant parmesan and a side of angel hair spaghetti for you and a double order of the same for me. And we can share a cheese and spinach pizza." He smiled. "I assume you're hungry after working at the mall all day."

This was the part when she was supposed to thank him for remembering the food she loved and being considerate, but instead she bristled and said nothing. He was well-meaning but she had a more accurate description: controlling.

The owner, Antonio, greeted them and filled their water glasses. His white mustache, weathered face, and kind dark eyes made him easily recognizable. "I heard we had a famous swimsuit model in our midst. My little Margaret, still as lovely as ever."

Fernando nodded. "She's perfect."

She shook her head. "I disagree, but thank you." No matter how many times she was complimented, she still saw herself as the awkward, too-thin girl who lived at the end of Spruce Street.

She accepted Antonio's warm hug. He smelled of mozzarella and fresh basil.

"How long are you in town?" he asked.

"I've tried for an answer, but she's mastered the art of evasiveness," Fernando said. "I'm hoping she'll grace my mother's home with a holiday visit."

She squeezed her hands on her lap. Memories of his house at Christmas time came back in a rush. Silver tinsel hanging on pine branches, the scent of butter cookies sandwiched with raspberry jam. Handel's *Messiah*, the grandest of all choruses, sounding from the CD player. And if she entered that house, her heart would break for the family and endless love Amelie had lost. Instead, Amelie had a mother who'd put her Hollywood career above spending time with her daughter. Ironic. She'd wanted to be independent and create a perfect life for her daughter, but she couldn't spend quality time with her because she was too busy working.

And she was still doing it, waiting for her agent's call.

Get your priorities in order.

She sat straighter and willed the chatterbox in her head to stay silent. No recriminations. One big movie role and she'd retire because her money problems would be over.

Antonio took a step back. "Seeing you two together is like old times."

"And old times are the best times." Fernando's gaze met hers, warm with admiration. "Although she's always been out of my league."

Caught off balance by his compliment, she touched the corners of her eyes to catch the tears. He'd been the hockey star, while she was the excluded, dirt-poor outsider. She wanted to say something but knew her voice would break. This town, this man, this eggplant, threatened to defeat her. Her memories had been safely stowed to be brought out at a later time when she determined. But her therapist had been wrong. The memories sprang from their compartment whenever she was within two feet of Fernando.

"Can I get you a bottle of wine, a celebration for two high school sweethearts reunited?" Antonio asked.

She covered her empty wineglass. "None for me, thanks."

Fernando lifted a brow. "Your Hollywood reputation precedes you. Aren't you a party girl?"

She shook her head. "I learned that alcohol isn't my friend. Have you ever heard other friends say they were having problems, and then they started drinking and all their problems disappeared?"

Fernando laughed. "None for me either."

Antonio smiled and walked away.

Fernando reached for her hand across the table, his thumb lightly caressing her fingertips. "You're a good influence."

"My decision isn't necessarily your decision. I know what's right for me."

He smiled at her as if she were extraordinary and precious. He squeezed her hand, his grasp warm and familiar. "And I respect you for that."

She sighed with pleasure. Many of her girlfriends in high school had wanted him at their side to enjoy his popularity and the male strength radiating from him. Yet, he'd wanted only her. He brought her hands to his lips and brushed a light kiss on her palm. A smile of contentment touched her lips. And he still wanted only her.

At the table behind her, a young couple shouted at each other. Their toddler had been playing peek-a-boo with Fernando.

"See that little boy?" he asked. "He's the reason I never want children."

She pulled her hands from his grasp, turned and caught a glimpse of a child with the face of a cherub. She whirled back and placed her professional actress expression on her face. "I'm surprised. I thought you loved children."

"Other people's children."

She picked up her water glass and took a long drink. For a couple of beats her heart felt crushed in a vice. So, she'd been right in never allowing him to know his daughter. She set down her glass and nodded slowly as if she were pondering his words. "Children are a lot of responsibility."

"Do you know why I don't want children?" he asked.

No, no, no. She tried an interested half smile. "Why?"

His face grew serious. "My brother suffers from sickle cell syndrome. It's a hereditary gene and we're twins. Seeing my brother struggle ... Well, I couldn't bring children into the world knowing they might need to fight to survive as he has had to. His life has been a series of hospitals and sickness, and it's been difficult watching him suffer and knowing there isn't anything I can do." Fernando thumbed at the corners of his eyes and looked down.

"Were you tested for the gene?" she asked.

"Yes. And I have the sickle cell trait, which is different from sickle cell syndrome. I don't suffer from any symptoms, and it's not a disease. Just no mountain climbing or scuba diving for me because of the change in oxygen levels." He laughed but didn't sound amused. "However, if my wife had sickle cell syndrome, our children would have a 50 percent chance of having either the trait or the syndrome."

"And if she didn't?"

"Still 50 percent. Besides Michael's dwarfism, the syndrome has resulted in fevers, chest pain, and coughing. But enough about illness. We're here to celebrate our reunion."

She chewed her bottom lip as her mind raced back to the day when Amelie was born. The hospital had checked for sickle cell syndrome, hadn't they? It was a routine test administered to all newborns.

Breathe. Stay calm. She stared into the cheerful flames of

the fireplace and inhaled the scent of wood smoke. Amelie had been born with a hearing impairment, but she deserved every second of life. Margaret couldn't imagine even one day without her precious daughter.

She glanced uncertainly at Fernando.

He gazed back with a look of deep pride, and her heart gave a peculiar little lurch. "I'm proud of all you've accomplished in California. You're extremely smart and courageous and selfless."

She swallowed. He was crediting her with his own honorable traits. He was noble and thoughtful and kind. She placed a hand atop his, and he smiled. There was no mistaking the look on his handsome face. Without a doubt, he still cared.

Behind her, the toddler's chubby fingers pulled on her coat. She spun around as he stood on his chair. Her hands flew out to grab him before he tipped over, but his young mother was faster, elbowing Margaret out of the way while scolding him.

Margaret turned back to Fernando and folded her clammy hands together. "Whew. Close call." She choked out the words. "You name the emergency, large or small, and I panic."

"You reacted quickly. I didn't see that coming and I was facing him," he said.

Because in your effort to control everything, you don't see what's in front of you.

Her eyes clouded. She'd been two months pregnant and had already gained ten pounds when she'd left Owanda. At eighteen years old, her breasts had been heavy, and none of her jeans fit around her waist. She'd been sick every morning before school. Nonetheless, he hadn't noticed. He was one of the most astute people she'd ever known, but he hadn't noticed. And if he had, he would've taken charge and provided for them. She knew him; she knew that. Or maybe she didn't. Her mother had waited for her drunken husband to provide for them, and he never had. Instead, she should've taken matters into her own hands and gotten a job. Even now her mother's hopeless, wistful face haunted Margaret's dreams.

Through the pizzeria's foggy window, a thin sheet of icy snow cast a blurry view on the outside world. The winters were endless here, the cold persistent.

"Who was the little girl with Lucy at the mall?" he asked. "Something about her looked so familiar. Is she Lucy's daughter? She was charming and couldn't wait to tell me about Doc, her new rescue kitten. Lucy said the girl's name was Amelie."

Margaret clutched the base of her water glass as a stab of panic went through her. Lucy had told him Amelie's name? Margaret made a mental note to throttle Lucy when she got home. "I hope you and Amelie had a nice chat," she managed to say.

"You always found at least one stray animal to nurse back to health when you lived on Spruce Street."

The teenage waiter interrupted by placing a large pizza rack in the center of the table, then deposited a piping hot cheese and spinach pizza on the rack. His upper lip was pierced. Face piercings, Margaret thought. It must be a prerequisite for teenagers in this town.

"I remembered you liked spinach pizza as much as I do." Fernando handed her the first slice. "You look beautiful when you eat."

"That's three."

"Three what?"

"Three compliments in an hour." She smiled at him around a bite of pizza. The sauce was exquisite, the perfect blend of spices and comfort.

Her cell phone buzzed.

"Excuse me. I'm expecting a call from my agent." She opened her purse and retrieved a text message from Lucy.

Come home. Amelie has a fever and she's coughing.

When did it start? she texted back.

A few minutes ago, Lucy responded.

Sickle cell syndrome. No, it couldn't be. Margaret's head began pounding. She shoved her plate aside and bolted to her feet. "Something's happened ... at work." She pressed her lips together, knowing her whispered explanation sounded painfully quiet.

She could feel the restaurant patrons watching her. She wouldn't scream. She wouldn't cry.

He vaulted from his chair, and his dark brows flicked up with a measured look. "You're leaving?" He threw some bills on the table. His voice sounded far away.

Her hands shook as she texted. *I'm on my way. Call paramedics.* She grabbed her coat and dashed around tables. She couldn't stop running. Alarm swelled in her throat, and she dragged air into her lungs. This couldn't be happening.

Her phone buzzed. The text message from Lucy read, *I already did.*

CHAPTER 10

*F*ernando's fingers grazed her elbow as he took long strides through the restaurant to keep up with her. "Where are you parked?"

At the pizzeria's entrance, he saw the sleet had turned to snow, which flew across the ground and shone silver in the moonlight. Margaret pulled away from him. Her face was flushed and she was breathless. "My car is parked at my office."

"Is that where you're going? To your office?"

Tears sparkled in her eyes. "Lucy texted me. I'm driving back to my apartment."

"Why?"

She twisted her tartan scarf until her knuckles turned white. "Amelie is sick."

His attention was diverted by another text message on her phone. She typed a quick reply and turned away from him. Her pace quickened as snowfall swirled in the street lights. Her footsteps muffled by the snow, her black leather boots left small imprints in the blank white sidewalk.

A traditional red kettle was stationed at the next corner, a shivering volunteer ringing his bell, and Fernando threw some spare bills into the kettle. Then, for the second time, he caught up with her. He studied her stricken features and slid his hand beneath her arm. "I'm parked around the corner. I'll take you home."

She shook her head. "My car is only a few blocks from here."

He tightened his grip and steered her toward his car. "I'm closer."

"No." She jerked away and rushed headlong into the street. Several cars swerved, their horns beeping a loud warning.

Cold air pressed against his skin as he raced across the street. "You're in no condition to drive on these icy roads!" His thoughts circled, searching for some sense to her urgency. "What happened?"

"Amelie needs me!" Without a backward glance, she continued running. Heavy black clouds blocked any light from the moon and stars. The red lining of her coat flashed as she ran, and her ebony waves blew wildly around her face. With lengthy, brisk strides, he closed the distance between them, grasped her shoulders, and turned her to face him.

"That's enough. You're coming with me. I'm sure Lucy has everything under control." He deliberately spoke in a level and authoritative tone.

She threw him a murderous look and jerked back. "Believe me, she doesn't!"

Why was she acting like a raving lunatic?

He grabbed her arm and whirled her around to face him. "I insist I take you home." He was surprised when she stopped arguing, but didn't hesitate to guide her around the block to his car. Reaching for the handle, he opened the passenger door. "Don't panic. I'm certain Lucy is an excellent mother."

Margaret closed her eyes and blew out a breath. "Yes, I'm sure she will be. Someday."

A tendril of doubt settled in his stomach. The cold had taken on a bitter edge, and he shivered. "Amelie isn't Lucy's child?"

Margaret shook her head.

"Is Amelie a stray child you adopted in California?"

Her eyes snapped open. "You're joking, right? You're comparing Amelie to a rescue animal?"

She was certainly protective toward the little girl. Perhaps she and Lucy had raised Amelie from birth. He waited, but then sighed when no explanation was forthcoming. "The faster you get in, the faster we get there."

She flicked a glance toward the sidewalk, as if again considering taking her own car.

"I'll get you home safely and quickly, and Amelie will be all right. I promise." He tipped her face up to his and lightly stroked her shiny black hair. Deep inside, the familiar surge of protectiveness rose. He'd happily strangle anyone who tried to hurt her. That is, if she allowed it, because she'd grown from a shy, uncertain teenager to an independent woman with a mind of her own.

Her eyes were shadowed with alarm. She nodded woodenly. With a resigned slump, she slid in and buckled her seat belt.

He ducked into the driver's seat. "Where's your apartment?"

She expelled a long sigh. Her gaze was riveted to the road. "Old Towne Road. You've lived here all your life, so I'm sure you know where that is. Just drive fast."

CHAPTER 11

*S*he lived farther out of town than he'd imagined. The only apartments he knew on Old Towne Road were in an old, run-down building. What would Margaret be doing living there?

He glanced at her. She kept her eyes on her phone, but no other text messages came through.

"Bad reception on these country roads," he said. His side hurt again, and he could have used a pain pill, although the pain had subsided, becoming less and less each day. He'd discarded the bottle of little yellow pills when Diana left for Florida, though. He couldn't concentrate with the pills fogging up his brain, and he had found himself becoming more and more dependent on them. Addictions, he'd vowed to himself years ago, would never take hold of his life again.

Margaret sat ramrod straight and sobbed softly. Tears glittered in her beautiful hazel eyes and dampened her long dark eyelashes. She looked vulnerable and desolate. "Drive faster. Please," she said.

He held his breath and pressed the accelerator. Trees and

branches heavy with snow whizzed by. The road was dark and snow covered, but in spots ice lurked under the snow, and a couple of times his car slipped across the patches of ice. His cell phone tinged with a text, most likely from Diana. She'd been back in Florida three weeks and had contacted him every day. He glanced down, trying to remember where he'd placed his phone.

Too late, he looked up to a car's headlights shining at him. He swerved. Margaret screamed a warning and clutched the dashboard. He'd drifted several inches into the other lane and narrowly missed the black SUV traveling in the opposite direction. A blast from the driver's horn forced Fernando to overcompensate, but he safely negotiated the car back into his own lane.

He glanced at her pale face. "I'm slowing down. This ice and snow are hazardous."

"If you'd kept your eyes on the road, that wouldn't have happened. A skilled driver would never—"

"I'm doing the best I can. I know this area and we're a couple of minutes away from your apartment."

"Then speed up."

He frowned, pushed harder on the gas pedal, and skidded to a stop in front of her apartment. As he'd suspected, the brick building was low and dingy. Blue and red emergency vehicle lights shimmered in the snow, and several vehicles were parked haphazardly in the driveway.

"Thanks for the ride. Drop me off here and you can leave." Margaret flew from the car and slammed the door behind her.

"The hell I will," Fernando muttered. He parked at the edge of the driveway, closed the distance between them, and firmly placed his arm on her shoulders.

She flashed him a defiant glare. For a moment he thought

she was going to physically push him off the small stoop before they entered the foyer.

A squawking parrot hanging upside in his cage, several people talking and laughing, and the television, set to a piercing level, greeted them. Amelie sat curled up on the living room couch with her legs tucked beneath her. Gus sat beside her holding a deck of cards.

It's a Wonderful Life was playing on the television. Fernando glanced over, recognizing the part where George walks back to the bridge where he was going to jump. He pleads to Clarence for his life, and Pottersville once again becomes Bedford Falls.

Margaret rushed to Amelie's side, hugged her, and knelt beside her on the worn carpet. She felt the girl's forehead. "You don't seem warm, thank goodness." Briefly, Margaret closed her eyes and the worried expression on her face relaxed. "Are you coughing?"

Gus placed a card face up on the couch. "Yep. She coughed a couple of times, and I told Lucy not to alarm you. Fevers in kids are common and come and go. To stop Lucy's fretting, I called my paramedic friends to check on Amelie. They're in your kitchen grabbing a short dinner break."

"Go fish!" Amelie placed her card triumphantly on top of Gus's, grinned at Margaret, and signed, "It's just a little cough."

Arms folded, Fernando leaned against the door frame. The African grey eyed him from his cage. A basket of Granny Smith apples and plump oranges sat beneath the cage amidst a pile of animal magazines and a laundry basket full of clothes. Margaret had never been interested in housekeeping, perpetually losing track of time when absorbed with her animals.

Amelie waved and signed, "Hi Fernando. Are you taking

me ice skating like you promised? I'm planning to wear my red parka so I won't get cold."

Margaret jumped to her feet and glared at him. "When was this arranged? Amelie can't go ice skating with you. Absolutely not."

"Why? I'm a former hockey player and I can skate fairly well."

Lucy emerged from the kitchen with Doc snuggled against her chest. "Sorry, Margaret, false alarm. I tried to call you after I texted, but there was no signal." She glanced at Fernando. "What are you doing here?"

"Is that the only question you can ever ask me? You gave Margaret quite a scare."

Jacob emerged from the kitchen carrying a plate piled high with pizza.

Margaret stared at him, looking like she'd been hit across the face. She gave Lucy a long, meaningful look and then blinked twice. "I thought he didn't know where we lived."

Lucy lifted her chin. "He missed me."

Jacob shrugged, his jaw tightening. "I'm here a lot. Lucy's a grown woman and can do whatever she pleases. She knows several agents in Hollywood, so I don't need you, but let's be honest, you didn't plan on helping me anyway." He looked at Amelie, and then at Fernando. "Cute kid, isn't she? Such pretty dark eyes."

"She's adorable," Fernando said.

Margaret's gaze narrowed at Jacob. "Amelie is not part of this conversation."

Jacob's cold gray eyes appraised her before he focused on Fernando again. "Amelie can sign because of her hearing impairment, similar to your brother's. Kind of like a common bond."

Fernando looked intently at Amelie. She shook her wavy

light brown hair away from her face, then took off her glasses and rubbed her eyes. Looking at him again, those dark brown eyes gleamed impishly. "Fernando, do you like our new kitten, the one I told you about?" she signed.

He nodded as a shiver of realization skipped through him. "How old is she?"

Margaret looked as if she'd been punched in the stomach, but she answered him. "She'll be six years old soon." Her shoulders stiffened. "Thanks again for driving me. I'll walk you out and get my car in the morning."

His feet were firmly planted on the floor. He stared from Amelie to Margaret. Memories flooded across his mind, the unexplained questions he'd shrugged off. Because he was young. Because he was so certain of their future together, he'd grown complacent. The weight gain he'd never mentioned for fear he'd hurt her feelings. Her sickness every morning before school, which he'd attributed to her staying up late with her rescue animals. Her abrupt departure after graduation. For years he'd been devastated, too blinded by hurt and anger to analyze what was clearly apparent in hindsight.

But not anymore. His heart hammered violently. How could he be so blind?

They locked eyes. Her gaze was steady, though her eyes revealed her exhaustion.

Blood roared through his veins, forcing his heart to pound in his ears. He knew. God help him, he knew. He glanced at Amelie, giggling on the couch, absorbed in her card game with Gus.

"You need to leave," Margaret said. "You're blocking the paramedic truck." She stepped past him and opened the front door.

He clamped down on her hand and dragged her out with

him, slamming the door behind them. The frozen night waited, and a tremor rippled through him.

"Is it true—what I'm thinking?" he asked.

She swallowed hard. The color drained from her face. She blew out a long breath and met his gaze. "Yes."

One word. The silence suffocated him. A sudden gust of freezing wind made him shiver. Pointedly, he dropped her hand and looked away. "Why didn't you tell me?"

She twisted her fingers together. "I wanted to. You know I loved you. It wasn't that."

She'd never answered his letters. Now she finally was telling him she loved him, now that he was seeing her for who she really was—a woman who'd do anything for fame and fortune, even if it meant denying him and his daughter.

"You wanted to, but what, it slipped your mind?"

"I was afraid you'd come for us." She avoided his gaze. "I wanted other things."

He gave a bitter laugh and stared down at her beautiful, anguished face. She'd betrayed his love, his trust, and left him cold. His perfect princess. "We had our life all planned."

She chewed her bottom lip and shook her head. "Your plans."

"It could've been the three of us. I knew you had a hard life, and I wanted to give you something better. I wanted to keep you safe."

Her fists clenched at her sides. "Your idea of saving me was living here in this horrible town and keeping me on your leash."

"I never restricted you."

"You didn't need to because everything was already decided—where we were going to live, what we were going to do. I didn't want a life of being married to a high school hockey coach while I stayed home and baked cookies."

"So you kept my daughter from me. Why? For your glamorous career? What's more important, a child raised in a loving family or your precious money?"

A quiet fury boiled inside him. He'd lost all those years— Amelie's baby steps, the first time she smiled, her first words. So many questions, so much he wanted to know. When had her deafness become apparent?

"We're leaving as soon as this mall job is finished," she said. "I've made a home for Amelie and me in California."

"I'll fight for custody."

Tears sprang to her eyes as she drew a ragged breath. "Try it. You'll never win because you'll never find us."

The front door creaked open, and Amelie skipped onto the stoop clutching her red parka around her. "Mommy, don't yell at him. Jacob just told me that Fernando's my daddy." She extended her arms to him, signing and talking all the while. "I told Mommy you'd come back. Why didn't you tell me? Did you want to make it a surprise?"

"I wanted to make it the best surprise, sweetheart." He picked up her delicate, slim body, smelling of strawberry soap and innocence, and cuddled her close.

She clasped her hands around his neck. Her chocolate-brown eyes sparkled. "Mommy said you couldn't live with us, but now you can," she said in her loud monotone.

He kissed her baby-faced cheeks. "I would've come sooner …"

"You were busy, Daddy. That's okay."

He sniffled and turned from Margaret with his daughter in his arms because he didn't want Margaret to see him vulnerable. Amelie wiped at his cheeks as his tears flowed. He set the girl down and stared at her charming face, the slight gathering of freckles across the bridge of her nose, her tiny glasses fogging in the cold.

She tugged on his hand. "I've been hiding this under my

bed. I didn't want Mommy to see because she gets quiet if I talk about my daddy." She reached into her jacket pocket and held up a crayon picture of a man and woman holding a child's hand. They stood on the edge of a sandy beach gazing at the ocean waves. A parrot was perched on the man's shoulder, and the woman held a cat. A dog with three legs stood beside her.

He swallowed and cleared his throat. "It's beautiful," he signed.

Margaret sank to the edge of the stoop and shook her head. "Amelie. You're such a precious and precocious child." She stared up at the dark winter sky. "Why wasn't I paying attention to what my daughter was saying?"

Fernando didn't answer. He stared at Margaret's profile and saw her bottomless kindness and her misguided and reckless logic. She'd been young and headstrong and imprudent when she'd fled, but she was all he'd ever wanted in a woman. If only she'd desired him as much as he'd desired her. If only she'd allowed him the opportunity to prove that he'd give her everything she deserved.

"You've done a wonderful job raising her," he said.

"Lucy helps." A wry smile grazed Margaret's lips. "Believe me, Amelie's a handful."

He extended a hand to her. A beat went by before she accepted and stood. Mere inches separated them but he didn't pull her closer. "We can work this out together."

Her gaze was proud, her spine straight. "Perhaps."

"For Amelie's sake," he said, "anything's possible."

Amelie had been catching snowflakes on her tongue. "Daddy, listen! Tomorrow we can ice skate and then stop for peppermint ice cream with chocolate sprinkles in the mall." Her hands signed rapidly. "Mommy will be helping Santa, but we can say hi." She tugged on the hem of his coat. "Bend down, Daddy. I have a secret to tell you."

He bent so their faces almost touched. "What is it, sweetheart?"

"That's not the real Santa in the mall," she whispered loudly in his ear. "It's Gus pretending to be Santa. I know because his beard is fake and falls off. And I heard Mommy tell Lucy that Gus drinks too much blackberry brandy, and I can smell it on his breath when he pretends to be Santa."

CHAPTER 12

"*D*addy and Mommy, watch me!" Amelie wobbled precariously on tiny white skates and stuck out one leg. Margaret laughed from the bleachers and clapped vigorously. "Be careful," she signed. Fortunately, she'd managed to find an ice skating rink in California and had taken Amelie skating a couple of times.

Fernando, on his own skates a few feet away, added his applause. "Perfect skating today, sweetheart," he signed. "The rink is closing, so let's clear the ice. We can come back tomorrow." He grabbed her hand, and they skated over to Margaret.

Margaret opened her arms and wrapped her daughter in a big hug. "This is your third time ice skating, and you're becoming a wonderful skater! I'm so proud of you."

He deposited Amelie on a bench, removed her ice skates and then handed her several dollar bills. She laced up her furry, hot-pink boots and scampered to the rink's snack bar for hot chocolate and a pretzel.

Ice skates decorated with evergreens and pine cones were

displayed on the rink's bulletin board, reflecting the holiday spirit. *The Twelve Days of Christmas* sounded over the loudspeaker. The air smelled of leather, hockey skates, and stinging cold.

"Our little girl is always hungry," Fernando said, laughing. "Wintry air and vigorous exercise perks up an appetite."

Margaret tipped her head toward him. "Just like her father."

He smiled shamelessly and led her to a corner of the snack bar. She eyed the booth and blinked. "Why are we sitting back here?"

He put his hands in his pockets and shrugged boyishly. "We used to sit in this booth after my hockey practice."

"I well remember."

He glanced at the concession stand. "We can see Amelie perfectly from our booth."

She slid into it, and he settled beside her, the hard muscles of his leg touching hers.

"Our daughter's a natural on the ice," he said.

"Just like her father," Margaret repeated.

"She could be a graceful figure skater, or she could play ice hockey when she gets older. We'll make every opportunity available to her."

Margaret raised her eyebrows. "It's only been two weeks. We're taking this slow, remember?"

Sadness touched his gaze. "I'm thrilled she's in my life, and there's so much I want to give her."

"You're forgetting about my career in California," Margaret said, although exactly what that career entailed she wasn't sure anymore.

With a grim but encouraging smile, he said, "You're an ambitious, successful, woman, and I won't prevent you from pursuing your goals. Nor would I want you to hinder my career."

"Good. We're in agreement."

"And I forgive you."

She flinched. "Forgive me for what?"

He shook his head. "I've pondered and prayed. What's done is done, and I want us to move forward, not backward." He gave her a long, assessing look filled with respect. "Your Christmas display brought you to this town. For whatever reason, be it spiritual or all the stars aligning, I'm forever grateful."

"It was financial." She held her chin defiantly high. "I came to Owanda so I could pay my bills and buy what I needed to buy."

He directed his gaze toward the miniature pine tree near the rink's entrance. The Christmas tree sat in a galvanized metal bucket, adorned with gold painted acorns. The branches hung heavy with whimsical miniature ice skates. So simple and perfect.

His expression softened. "How do you spend Christmas in California?"

"I tried to create an old-fashioned Christmas despite the seventy-five-degree weather. Several years ago, Lucy insisted we purchase a pre-lit upside-down Christmas tree, and I've used it every December. Lately, she's usually absent with whoever her current boyfriend happens to be, so Amelie and I attend Christmas Eve service at a local mission church."

"Sounds lovely," he said.

It was also lonely, but she wouldn't tell him that part.

"Christmas morning is spent baking sweet rolls and opening gifts, and in the afternoon we visit the local animal shelter," she said.

"No doubt looking for an animal with deformities you can rescue and take home."

She nodded. "Like Grumpy, our African grey. He's part of

the family, as Doc is now. Amelie knew I'd never be able to return that kitten after I took him home."

"I love animals almost as much as you do," he said.

She grinned. "Almost?"

"Animals create chaos."

"And they offer unconditional love and companionship."

"If rescue animals are your passion, then I support you." He kept her gaze. "Christmas Eve is a week away, and I'm hoping you and Amelie will spend it with me." His invitation was made softly, unbearable tenderness laced with guarded hope. "Lucy mentioned going to Las Vegas with Jacob for Christmas, and I don't want my two special girls to be alone. Michael doesn't have a large appetite, and I can't eat all my mother's turkey and chestnut stuffing by myself."

She smiled. "We both know you probably could eat all the turkey and a plateful of Christmas cookies besides. Lucy and I would love to have your metabolism."

She touched a light hand to his sleeve, and he moved closer, apparently pleased and surprised at her involuntary touch. She could almost sniff the sauerkraut and apples braised in white wine wafting from the Brandts' kitchen on Christmas Eve. When she was young, Christmas in her mobile home had smelled of cheap beer and musty odors. Her parents never seemed to realize it was Christmas.

"I'll let you know," she said.

His sigh was quiet, as if he were reconciled to the fact she might refuse. "Amelie would love my mother's cinnamon star cookies, and I kept my copy of *The Night before Christmas*."

She swallowed the aching lump in her throat at the remembrance of him reading the book aloud, along with good-natured pantomime and laughter. "You're the most persistent man I've ever met."

"Although the book's a tad worn, it's our Christmas tradition to read it in its entirety."

"The book is only thirty-two pages long," she said wryly.

He tilted his head and laughed. "Is that a 'yes'?"

His laughter was infectious. She grinned. "Yes, and thank you. Amelie and I will love a real family Christmas celebration, and I enjoy seeing your mother and brother. They're such fun to be around."

The silence in the ice arena was comfortable, punctuated by the laughter of children and parents filing in for hockey practice. Comfort and contentment, emotions she hadn't felt in a long time.

"Did you know your smile warms this entire rink?" He took her hands in his and kissed her forehead and eyes, then brushed an affectionate trail to her lips. Their breaths mingled.

She darted a glance toward the entrance. "Not here."

His arms wrapped around her, and warmth flooded her veins. "We used to sit in this corner and kiss after hockey practice."

The look in his eyes was all male, and her pulse thumped a steady beat. "You were all sweaty."

He laughed, his lips close to hers. "I always searched the stands for you. I would've been crushed if you ever missed a practice or a game. Our team would've lost."

"And I was always cheering when you scored the winning goal."

His mouth pressed against hers with hurried urgency. She kissed him back, glorying in his need and the dizzying passion she'd always felt in his arms. He'd always chased away the aching sadness and isolation plaguing her.

A group of young boys with ice skates over their shoulders hooted as they passed. She pulled away, disoriented, incensed at herself and Fernando. They were at the public ice skating rink, kissing with the passion and abandon of two starry-eyed teenagers.

He gazed down at her with exquisite tenderness. "I can't believe we have a daughter."

"It wasn't right, what I did," she whispered. "It was selfish and self-centered to keep her from you. I'm so sorry."

"Thank you for apologizing. It means a lot." He stroked her hair. "You have the strength and resilience of a thousand men, and you're the most compassionate woman I've ever known. You'd never intentionally hurt anyone." He rested his chin against her forehead and whispered, "You know I've always loved you."

His gentleness prompted unexpected tears, and she ducked her head against his jacket. After all she'd done, he forgave her and he loved her.

"I kept telling Lucy I wanted to call you, but there was always another audition, another—"

"Shh. I understand. You don't need to explain further." His finger touched her lips. His gaze smoldered with admiration. The unique connection they'd felt since high school, that they were best friends and could confide everything to each other with no fear of being judged, surged between them. He bent his head to kiss her again, and she met him in the middle, finding confirmation of his forgiveness in one more kiss.

With a loud squeal of delight, Amelie, with a ring of whipped cream around her mouth, ran over to their booth, prompting a return to reason.

Margaret attempted to draw away, but Fernando draped his arm protectively around her shoulders. "On Christmas Eve, we'll attend services at the church, then have dinner at seven o'clock."

"Perfect." She couldn't help but note his expression of joy. Despite all the happiness she'd taken from him, she thought, with heartbreaking contrition, that he was looking toward the future.

* * *

LATER THAT NIGHT after Amelie was tucked in bed with Doc, Margaret pulled on a silk nightshirt and slipped into her bed. Shadows crept across the worn carpet as the moon passed behind a silvery cloud. Wide awake, she stared at the cracks in the ceiling. The apartment was quiet except for the ticking of her illuminated alarm clock. Lucy was spending the night at Jacob's place, wherever that was. Neither was forthcoming about where he lived, and Margaret's conversations with Lucy had become stilted.

Amelie, though, was thrilled about her new-found daddy. Already she had blossomed under Fernando's watchful eyes, and her pale pallor had been replaced with a healthy glow. He'd proven in a short while he was indeed a wonderful father, and his mother had welcomed Margaret and Amelie with tears of delight. No recriminations, no turning away with aversion and loathing. She'd understood Margaret's sincere explanations and treated her like a daughter, just as she always had. Michael had demonstrated his magic tricks and chuckled when Amelie called him Uncle Michael. He'd also complained to Margaret that Fernando was preventing him from renting his own apartment.

"It's for your own good," Fernando had said. "Suppose you have another seizure and you're alone? I want to keep you safe."

Typical Fernando, Margaret had thought, always practical, always trying to protect everyone.

She sighed and tucked her hands behind her head. Wasn't this where they belonged—in her hometown, where she and her daughter could be loved? She enjoyed Fernando's company and valued his friendship. He made her laugh. He was trustworthy and neat and honest to a fault, and he supported her love of animals. Perhaps, she considered with a smile, they'd continue growing their family and be blessed with another child. Amelie didn't carry the sickle cell trait or syndrome, and neither did Margaret. They'd both been tested, and Fernando had responded to her news with a strangled cry of relief.

She rolled to her stomach and buried her head in her pillow. New York City was a few hours from Owanda by train. She'd check with her agent, and perhaps there were jobs on the East Coast better suited to her modeling career. If she had another child, there were categories for lifestyle models that she could age into while they raised a family. She smiled and imagined Fernando's delight when she told him, knowing in her heart he'd support her decision to continue modeling. She had reconciled herself to the fact she'd never be a movie star. So they'd never be wealthy, but she'd be able to keep her financial independence and work.

She gave up trying to sleep. Propping up the pillows, she watched the sleet clinking against her bedroom window, the snow outside white and frozen.

How did Fernando earn a living? He'd offered a vague explanation that his real estate office was on the other end of town, and he had a business in Florida. Judging by his expensive clothes and car, he must be selling a lot of homes.

Her smile deepened. He loved her. She'd seen it in his eyes, in his smile, and she loved him. And this time when he discussed marriage, she'd actively participate in the planning. Amelie would be the flower girl, strewing delicate red rose petals, and Pachelbel's Canon in D would swell from the church organ as Margaret walked down the aisle. With a sense of peace, she rested her head against the pillows and welcomed slumber, although her mind was busy and the ideas ran together. She was adding a scalloped hemline to the flared sleeveless wedding gown, as well as a crimson chiffon bow at the waist, when she slid beneath the covers and fell asleep.

This time, nothing would stop her fairy tale wedding to the man who had once been her prince.

CHAPTER 13

"*I*'ve never attended a foreclosure auction." Lucy tightened the faux leopard fur belt around her waist and adjusted her periwinkle satin blouse to show more cleavage. "Am I overdressed?"

"Not if you plan on attending a mid-morning cocktail party," Margaret replied. She'd worn a proper cream silk blouse over a white camisole, a tan pencil skirt, and beige heels. On a whim, she'd added a jaunty red headband to offset her black wavy hair and add a festive air to her outfit.

"Jacob's taking me out to dinner. Does that count?" Lucy asked, her voice rising.

Jacob was a subject Margaret avoided. She'd come to an understanding with Lucy. As long as he wasn't mentioned, they wouldn't argue.

When Margaret didn't answer, Lucy rolled her eyes. "You shouldn't blame him for what happened. I'm the one who told him he could come to our apartment. I am, after all, a grown woman who can make her own decisions. Besides, Fernando forgave you, and you should forgive also."

"I understand. You're in love." *Again.* But Margaret didn't say that aloud.

She gazed at the ornate real estate office, a restored bank lobby. Marble floors and gleaming wood paneling were offset with tasteful crown molding.

Lucy's gaze followed Margaret's. "Real estate and property must be better than I imagined because someone's getting rich in this town. Who owns this building?"

Margaret shrugged. "I don't know much about real estate, but it's obvious some big company put a lot of thought into this restoration. I heard they're building apartments in this complex also."

Lucy adjusted the flashing poinsettia brooch on her collar.

Margaret covered her mouth with her hand to suppress a giggle. "Should you still be flashing?"

"Oops! The battery has a mind of its own." Lucy yanked at the chain, and the poinsettia returned to its red shiny state. "I hope none of these important people saw me flashing."

Margaret laughed aloud. "With any luck, they won't be interested in my dilapidated mobile home." She inspected a sign in the lobby listing the foreclosure properties, then nodded toward the glass elevator across the hall. "The auction is on the fourth floor." She opened her handbag and fingered the certified check for five thousand dollars. Her fingers were cold and clammy, and a premonition of disaster followed her. So much money—and the last of her savings. All those weeks of nonstop work at the mall, calming frustrated parents and crying toddlers, hadn't brought in as much money as she'd anticipated. Gus hadn't been able to work for several days because he'd developed a heart arrhythmia and she couldn't find a replacement Santa. The week before Christmas was one of the busiest times, and she'd been forced to shut down the Christmas display.

"Perhaps I should drop this entire auction idea and save money for more important things," she murmured.

"Now you're having second thoughts? All you've talked about for two months is buying back your trailer."

"I'm inexperienced in real estate. I've never attended a live auction."

"Don't take offense, but you're interested in something no one else wants. They'll probably give it to you."

She couldn't help but grin because Lucy was always brutally honest.

"Maybe it'll only sell for one thousand dollars and I'll have four thousand dollars left over."

Another call to her agent had gone unanswered, although she'd left a message requesting him to send her head shots and résumé to an affiliate agency in New York City. He at least had returned her call, just that morning, when she'd been in the shower. He'd left a voice mail regarding a feature film. He said it was urgent and to call him immediately, but everything in Hollywood was urgent. She would call him after the auction.

She smiled. Yes, things were definitely looking up, and Amelie would have a wonderful Christmas. With the money she hoped to save on the auction, she'd buy Amelie the doll-house, complete with furniture, tiny dishes and family pets, that she'd been eyeing in the mall.

As they stepped into the elevator, Lucy asked where Fernando had been lately.

"He had a lot of business to catch up on." Although when she'd pressed him for details, he'd been elusive. She had hoped they'd spend some time alone so she could tell him of her plans to settle in Owanda permanently, but she hadn't had the opportunity. He had called every night to talk with her and Amelie, but she wanted to tell him her decision in person. Now with Christmas Eve only a couple of days away, she'd surprise him then.

"When are you flying back to California?" Lucy asked.

Margaret shrugged, suppressing a secret smile. "I'm not sure."

"Jacob and I are flying to Las Vegas on Christmas Eve, then to California for New Year's. We'll rent an apartment once we get settled, so I won't be moving back in with you and Amelie."

Margaret nodded, and they rode the elevator in silence. When the door opened on the fourth floor, Fernando stood directly in front of them carrying a black leather briefcase. She heard his sharp intake of breath as he stepped back.

"Margaret?" He stared at her with a blank expression. She'd never seen him like this. His face was usually a road map showing every emotion.

Her eyes widened, and she sucked in a breath. She must've stepped from the elevator because the doors closed behind her with a ping. She felt her face flush. "Fernando?"

"What are *you* doing here?" Lucy blurted.

He gave a pained look and gripped his briefcase. "Just once, can you greet me with a simple hello?"

"What *are* you doing here?" Margaret asked.

His muscles bunched, causing his superbly tailored gray suit to crease at the shoulders. "There's a foreclosure property ... I'm interested in. What about you?" He spun to walk with them. He didn't brush a light kiss on her forehead as he usually did, nor did he touch her arm to guide her.

"My mobile home is in foreclosure and I'm buying it back," she said.

His dark brows set together in a frown. "Why would you want to do that?"

"Because it's mine."

"Not anymore. The bank owns it."

Lucy flashed an encouraging smile at Margaret. "Well, if Fernando's advising you, then you don't need me. I'll wait in the lobby and call Jacob, or maybe I'll get a tattoo on my left thigh." She waved a hand dismissively and clicked on her poinsettia pin. "Just kidding." She swiveled on her calfskin-leather stilettos and clicked down the hallway.

Margaret double-checked the room number, and Fernando followed her into a large area set up with armless chairs. She picked up a list of the auctions from a table at the entrance, then seated herself in the front row. He slid into the chair beside her and set his briefcase on his lap.

"You don't want your old trailer. It's a sad remembrance of those lonely years, and it's been empty so long it'll need numerous repairs," he said.

His flat dismissal of what she wanted and didn't want sounded a little too authoritarian. Her chin came up. "How would you know about the condition?"

"I'm in real estate, and trailers depreciate."

Her fingers tightened around the list. "I'm not buying it to make money." She swallowed. "It means a lot to me."

"You'll need to tear it down."

"That's exactly what I intend to do. I'm putting a house on the land."

Briefly, he closed his eyes. "Margaret." He touched her hand, the first time he'd touched her. "There's something you should know. I'm also bidding on the property."

She dropped the list onto the floor and was silent. When she bent to retrieve it, she could feel her whole body stiffen. "Why?" Her tone sounded pinched, like she couldn't get enough air in her lungs, or like a glass of cold water had been pitched at her face. That feeling of disaster hung in the air.

She took a deep breath and retrieved the list. Perhaps he was planning to gift it to her and Amelie as a Christmas surprise.

She looked at the list and saw that the starting bid for the trailer was one thousand dollars and thankfully affordable. However, the adjacent mobile home park, added to her listing, brought the price up to one hundred thousand dollars.

One hundred thousand dollars.

She pointed to the list. "Is there a mistake?"

"No, your trailer and the park are being sold as one parcel."

She raised her brows. "Why? My trailer was never in the mobile home park."

"Because I—"

He jerked around as a breathtakingly beautiful woman in a flowing variegated silk dress sashayed in, commanding the attention of the entire room. Heads swiveled as the woman headed straight for him.

"Surprise, darling." She pressed a kiss on his cheek while rubbing her hand on his forearm. "I love dove-gray suits on you."

His hands tensed into fists on top of his briefcase. "Diana, what are you doing here?"

She patted her shiny blonde hair, elegantly coifed and sprayed into place. "Dad and I flew up from Miami. He's talking with one of the bankers for additional financing. I wanted to be here to support you." Her hand stopped stroking his arm as her crystal-blue gaze raked Margaret with complete distaste.

Margaret drew back. "I don't believe we were introduced," she said to nobody in particular.

Diana seated herself on Fernando's left and then leaned around him. "You're the little pauper who ran off to California to enjoy her fifteen minutes of fame flaunting her body in a swimsuit. Fernando told me all about you."

Margaret flinched and swallowed. "I'm sorry, but I don't know who you are."

Diana ran an intimate hand along his. "Hasn't he mentioned me? He's my father's real estate partner and I'm his fiancée."

The silence of an abandoned cemetery settled over the large room. Margaret stared down at the foreclosure list in her hands, trying to focus on it, but her eyes were swimming with tears. All the while he'd accepted her apologies, kissing her, holding her, nodding sympathetically, he'd been engaged to another woman.

She pushed back her chair and threw the list on the floor. She wouldn't be able to bid because her throat was closing.

He grabbed her hand. For a moment, she curled her fingers around his for support. Then she remembered and pulled from his grasp.

"I didn't know you were interested in your trailer or I never would've listed the parcels together," he said.

"You arranged this?" she whispered.

Diana heard her and laughed. "You should thank him. Perhaps you can give him your portion for what a rusty trailer's worth—five dollars."

He swung around. "Enough, Diana. That trailer was Margaret's childhood home." He turned to Margaret. "Please. I'll do what I can to fix this."

She shook her head, a frantic, insistent *no* as the auctioneer took the podium and outlined the auction rules. She tried to stand, but Fernando grabbed her hand firmly. Tears of righteous anger sprang to her eyes as she looked around, trying to spot a way out. Several people in the room were parents from the mall, and they smiled and waved, obviously recognizing her as the former swimsuit model who'd been in the elf costume.

Somehow, she held her chin high, waved back, and faced front again. She was the aspiring actress, she told herself.

The bid for the parcel started at one hundred thousand

dollars, and the price kept rising, thousands of dollars for a trailer park the developers planned to tear down. Or rather, Fernando and his real estate company. Mutely, she calculated the minutes until the auction was over and she could crawl away, far from him and his precious Diana. Far from the frozen town of Owanda. Far from elves and dwarfs. She stared at the floor as Fernando seized the winning bid, over half a million dollars. But she was done. It was over. And she couldn't bear to stay in the room another minute. She crumpled the list, tossed it in her purse, and pushed back her armless chair.

Fernando grabbed her hand again and he spoke quietly. "I'll talk with the auctioneer. Don't leave."

She shook off his hand and stood. "Lucy's waiting, and then I'm picking up Amelie after school."

"I'll call you tonight."

"Don't bother." She choked out the words. "Congratulations. You won."

Carefully, she composed her features to a cool disinterest. Her shoulders straight, she grabbed her purse and kept her gaze fixed ahead as she marched from the room. She rode the elevator alone to the first floor and Lucy, surprise, surprise, wasn't there.

Margaret walked slowly to her car. Sleet assaulted her cheeks along with the tears, and she slipped several times on the icy sidewalk. The disappointment inside her ached, a constant reminder of how elusive happiness was.

She started her car and stared at the frozen windshield. Must it always sleet? Where was the snow in this infernal town? Not the wet slushy snow or the icy snow they'd had so far, but those fluffy white flakes that were supposed to coincide with the Christmas season?

As a child, she had loved to wake up and gaze out her bedroom window at the piles of feathery snow that had fallen during the night. Sledding on crisp, cold mornings meant afternoon lunches of toasted cheese sandwiches and tomato soup, followed by cups of hot chocolate topped with frothy whipped cream.

Ha! She brushed her bangs aside, tore off the red headband, and flung it to the backseat. None of those events had occurred in the Snow household. Her imagination was conjuring remembrances of a childhood she'd only read about in books.

She swiped at her eyes and chewed her trembling lip.

All this heartache. She never should've come back, and she'd go mad if she stayed in town another day. She'd book a direct flight for her and Amelie back to California on Christmas Day; airfares would probably be cheaper because of the holiday. If they left early morning, they'd arrive by noon because of the three-hour time difference.

They'd spend Christmas like they always had, attending a quiet church service and then serving at a rescue kennel. Perhaps they'd adopt an animal with half an ear, or half a tail, a cat or a dog no one else wanted. And they'd take the animal home and save it from being put down.

"Because their spirits aren't broken," one of the workers at a shelter had once said.

And Amelie would have an enjoyable Christmas, minus the snow, of course, because snow didn't fall in California.

Margaret sniffled and caught one of her tears with her tongue. She kept her gaze glued to the windshield, but the wipers kept freezing up. She had to keep stopping to clean the windshield because the wipers were so thin, they were worthless.

CHAPTER 14

"*I*'m headed to the kitchen for some fudge. I read somewhere there are no calories in Christmas sweets." Lucy stopped at the entrance to Margaret's bedroom and plopped one hand on her hip. "You're supposed to laugh and correct me. It's a joke."

"I smiled. Does that count?"

Lucy sighed and shook her head. "Fernando called again. He's taking Amelie to a Christmas play after they have dinner. He said he's grating some type of egg noodle batter and Amelie is helping him. Shouldn't you talk with him before you leave?"

"It's spaetzle. His mother used to make it all the time." Margaret placed her suitcase on the bed and opened it. "He's seeing his daughter and will be with her until we leave for California."

"But he wants to see you too, and I'm tired of relaying messages back and forth between you two."

"There's nothing further to say." Her shoulders hunched forward. Surely the knot wanting to take up permanent residence in her stomach would dissolve. "No one can blame him for moving on after all these years, but I'm not discussing Diana with him."

It was too painful. She'd imagined a happy ending after their make-out session in the ice arena. He'd imagined one also, but with another woman.

She choked on her own fury, done with foolish dreams and crushing hopes. She'd wept each night since the auction with nothing to show for it but bloodshot eyes and a dejected spirit.

"Do whatever you want, you always do." Lucy's voice was clipped as she continued to the kitchen. "But I think you're throwing away a good life with him."

Margaret's cell phone rang. She picked it up while folding her favorite cotton blouse and placing it in her suitcase. "Hello?"

"Margaret? It's Sid, your agent. Why haven't you returned my call?"

Good question. She shook her head. "I'm sorry. There's a lot going on here."

An impatient huff rang through the line. "You know the feature film you auditioned for?"

The audition she'd botched. "Yes?"

"The casting director has slated you for one of the minor characters. Lots of bathing suit stuff, but your looks are what you're known for."

She tightened her grip on the phone. Her heart leaped. "You mean I got a role after all? Are there a lot of lines?"

"That's the good part. You have to walk beneath a waterfall and say how good the water feels on your skin, or something like that. Because it's a major motion picture, your salary will be in the high six figures."

She squeezed her eyes shut. A huge amount of money would ensure she'd have the funds to provide for Amelie's education and health needs for a long time. But the good part, he'd said. What was the bad part?

"Then you can move to New York City like you mentioned in your voice mail," Sid went on. She thought she caught something in his voice, a faltering, but he never faltered.

"I've had a change of heart and am moving back to California as planned," she explained.

Sid didn't respond to that. "There's one more thing," he said, and then hesitated. "When you walk beneath the waterfall ... you'll be topless. It's a view of your back, so not full frontal exposure. I'm assuming you're good with that because nowadays, it's expected."

Silence. A slow, sick feeling added to the knot in her stomach. This was life in the Hollywood lane, the fast road to success. "You know how I feel about nudity, Sid. Let me think about it."

"You can't keep these guys waiting, and this role is a great opportunity. There's a thousand actresses in line behind you."

"I realize that and thank you. I'll call you the day after Christmas."

She clicked off her cell and studied her suitcase. It was too small for the sweaters she'd bought in Owanda. She'd donate them to a women's shelter in the morning.

Grumpy squawked from its cage in the living room. Walking out there, she grabbed an orange from the basket on the floor and fed him several small pieces. He stared at her with pale gray eyes.

Lucy was slouched on the living room couch, a plateful of homemade chocolate fudge perched in her lap. Her gaze was glued to the television and a cartoon version of *A Christmas Carol.* Doc was curled up beside her. Lucy had already moved all of her clothes and personal items from the apartment, but a designer suitcase stood in the foyer.

"I couldn't help but overhear," she said around a mouthful of chocolate. "That was Sid on the phone."

"Yes, he offered me a part in the feature film I auditioned for."

That news prompted Lucy to sit up, which caused a landslide of fudge to the carpet. "Congratulations! Jacob will be thrilled because you'll get to know some powerful people."

"I'll be sure to put in a good word for him," Margaret said.

Lucy picked up the fudge and popped another piece in her mouth. "The one-second rule," she explained. Chewing thoughtfully, she added, "Jacob and I leave tomorrow, Christmas Eve. It doesn't matter if we'll be traveling on a holiday as long as we're together."

"And Amelie and I leave on Christmas morning."

Lucy hesitated. "I hate the thought of you being alone on Christmas Eve."

Margaret shook her head. "It's like any other day, and Fernando's family will keep Amelie entertained. I'll finish packing, then head to the office. I've hardly spent any time there since the mall job started, and I need to clean out my desk." She sighed and looked around. "I never had time to get a small Christmas tree, and I denied Amelie Christmas memories."

Lucy laughed. "You set up the forlorn tree at the office, and Amelie is enjoying a wonderful holiday. Your Christmas display at the mall was festive, she went ice skating, and she's spending time with her father. The Brandts always knew how to celebrate Christmas with lots of merriment and festivity."

Margaret swallowed. To change the subject, she asked, "How's Gus?"

"He was admitted to the hospital because of the arrhythmia, and the doctors had to insert a pacemaker. But everything's well now."

Margaret sighed. "I'll call him before we leave. He's been so good to Amelie."

A car horn beeped, and Lucy jumped from the couch. "Jacob's a great guy, but he can't keep track of time. He's an hour late, as usual." She gave Margaret a quick peck on the cheek and grabbed her coat and boots while cramming the last piece of fudge in her purse. "Merry Christmas! See you in California!"

Margaret turned off the television, instantly regretting the silence.

She sat on the couch to snuggle Doc, but the kitten permitted her one stroke before arching to be put down. "You'll be flying as carry-on baggage, so you better behave."

Animals were so much better than humans. They never broke your heart, never talked back. They simply wanted to love and be loved. If only humans could give love as freely.

Grumpy swung upside down in his cage and stared at her.

"We're going back to California," she said to the parrot. "You'll be flying as checked baggage."

No answer. She walked to his cage and began peeling an orange. She offered him a slice.

"If only you weren't deaf and could talk to me," she said.

The bird stopping swinging. "Change of heart," the parrot said.

She dropped the orange to the floor. "All this time, you could talk and were listening to us? We would've adopted you from the rescue shelter, no matter if you were deaf or not." She reached her hand into the cage and patted his head. "You were too cute to ignore."

Grumpy stood on his perch and wiped his beak. "Merry Christmas, spaetzle."

CHAPTER 15

*A*s Fernando strode toward the hospital entrance, he glanced at his watch, mentally planning every detail as Christmas Eve neared. First, he'd stop by his real estate office and finalize the mobile park sale. Then he'd head home to Amelie and his family to assist with last-minute Christmas Eve preparations. He tightened his grip on his briefcase, relieved he'd gotten one more gift for Amelie before the mall closed for the holiday. The air was brisk and cold, the smell of snow in the air, perfect for Christmas.

He pushed open the door to the hospital, mildly surprised to see Gus sitting in a wheelchair, a plump, beardless man with a twinkle in his sharp blue eyes.

"Ho, ho, ho," Gus said in his jovial Santa imitation. "I heard you were leaving for Florida. Don't take offense, but you look like you haven't slept in days."

Fernando scraped a hand over his jaw. He'd spent two sleepless nights staring at the ceiling in the dark, thinking about Margaret. She had smiled with such happiness as she'd admitted that she and Amelie would love a real family Christmas celebration with him.

"What are you doing at the hospital on Christmas Eve day?" Gus asked.

Fernando slid onto a bench near the older man. "I picked up my brother's doctor's report. He's recuperated nicely since the operation, and thankfully there's no more dialysis for him. His blood tests confirmed that the transplanted kidney is functioning properly. He'll take medication to prevent transplant rejection, but he's able to lead a normal life. And in turn, we're blessed to have him in our lives." Fernando cleared his throat, reminding himself not to take anything or anyone for granted. "Are you being discharged?"

"Yep. Waiting for my daughter to pick me up because our car is in the parking lot. The doctor was concerned about my heart and inserted a pacemaker. I'd like to think I can slide down the chimney with a sack of toys." Gus sighed. "But I'm feeling more tired than usual these days."

"Perhaps it's time you retired," Fernando said.

In the hospital archway, an animated display of old man winter, complete with snowflakes, began flashing and playing a cheerful Christmas tune.

"I'm supposed to quit drinking brandy and every other beverage I enjoy to avoid any heart complications, and the doctor wants me to sit around all day and do nothing," Gus said.

"Will you take his advice?"

"Maybe, as long as I can still play cards with someone." Gus shrugged, reached in his pocket, and tossed Fernando a crushed white beard. "Your brother can play Santa Claus next year."

Gus's hand had developed a small tremor. Illness was a funny thing because it made you appreciate life. How easy it was to become unappreciative of the things that really mattered. Fernando's mind flashed to his brother, and he knew that Michael would agree to the Santa role. He loved children and would probably add a magic trick or two. He placed the beard in his briefcase. "I'll mention it," he said.

"Margaret called me this morning. She and Amelie are flying to California tomorrow. Hardly any snow has fallen since they arrived." Gus glanced at the icy slush outside, apparently to prove his point.

Fernando stared at the revolving hospital door, not wanting to face the bitter defeat of losing her a second time. "Yes, Lucy told me. Amelie's creating a gingerbread house with my mother and brother this afternoon, and I'll take her back to their apartment early Christmas morning."

He didn't know how long he could bear that sort of living arrangement, with his daughter and Margaret three thousand miles away from him. What was she thinking by refusing to speak with him? She wouldn't give him an opportunity to explain. Didn't she understand he'd waited years before beginning a new life, settling for a wealthy woman who was happy to fund his work pursuits? *Settling*. What an interesting description of his relationship with Diana, but money had blinded him. Perhaps he'd wanted to prove to Margaret that he could be as successful as she had become.

"Can you imagine?" Gus asked. "Our little Margaret's been offered a role in a major motion picture. She'll be appearing on the big screen in all the movie theaters across the country."

Fernando's cell phone buzzed. He glanced at it; Diana's phone number was displayed on the screen. They had argued after the auction, and she'd left in a huff for Miami, leaving him an ultimatum that he better immediately follow her. He hadn't. He stared again at the revolving hospital door. Some of the people entering and leaving appeared to be patients; others were probably visiting family and friends. Young people walked quickly while older people shuffled along, some with canes.

"I'm planning an equitable arrangement and won't fight for custody." He scowled while he spoke, his expression contrary to his words. In reality, Margaret had responded to his phone calls with silence, as if they were opponents rather than former best friends, lovers, and parents to a beautiful five-year-old girl.

"So you'll be flying to California from time to time?"

"I don't fly. I'll take the train or bus," Fernando admitted.

"I was certain you two were meant for each other, but I must've been wrong. Diana, from what I've heard, is more your type."

Fernando fixed his gaze on a pole-mounted display of spiral snowflakes near the hospital entrance. "Diana's goals aren't complicated and she leaves the business decisions to me."

"And Margaret would fight you all the way."

Fernando chuckled. "Yes, she probably would."

"It's a shame, letting a woman with her kindness and bravery slip through your fingers a second time. She's got such a big heart." Gus nodded slightly. "But I understand Diana's father's wealth is enticing to an enterprising man like you."

This time, Fernando met Gus's gaze head-on. "I don't need her father's money."

Gus stayed quiet for so long that Fernando continued to stare at him.

"Once you tear down the mobile home park and Margaret's old trailer, how will you fund an outlet mall that'll cost millions of dollars?" Gus finally asked.

Fernando shook his head. "I've shelved the idea for an outlet mall. Instead, I'm turning the area into a park with a man-made pond for fishing in the summer and ice skating during the winter months, something the entire community can enjoy at no cost. And I'm developing some other plans also."

"Margaret wanted to build a new home on her old property. She mentioned a white bungalow with a red front door." Gus performed a brilliant interpretation of a man who'd just said something he shouldn't by putting a hand over his lips.

"Sounds like you're describing my childhood home." Fernando's heart did a quick flutter. Could she have been yearning for his house all these years?

"Margaret said you're leaving early Christmas morning for Miami," Gus went on. "She's spending this afternoon at her office cleaning out her desk."

Fernando tightened his grip on his briefcase. "Good to know." All this cheerful information about Margaret was wearing thin on his taut nerves. And where was Gus's daughter? It didn't take that long to retrieve a parked car.

"What has Margaret told you about the Hollywood film?" Gus asked.

"We haven't spoken, remember?" he said impatiently.

"They want her to wear a bathing suit for the role. Or rather, half a bathing suit."

Fernando rose to his feet. "Is that what she said?" His gaze narrowed as he frowned. It might be Christmas, the time of harmony and good cheer, but he was in the mood for a confrontation. She damn well wouldn't be appearing topless in any film.

Gus's mouth was wreathed in a wide grin as Fernando turned on his heel without saying good-bye and strode away with long, purposeful strides.

"Merry Christmas!" Gus called. "There's snow in the forecast. Drive slow."

* * *

AS HE DROVE to Margaret's office, Fernando phoned his mother to tell her he'd be later than planned. "Start preparing the turkey without me," he said. "And tell Amelie I'll be back soon."

He kept seeing the image of Margaret in that tiny iridescent yellow bikini plastered on the cover of a sports magazine a couple of years ago. Hadn't he stood by as other men gazed lustfully at her enticing body, all the while making lewd comments? That had been a difficult and trying time in his life, and he had decided once and for all that she didn't want him. And then he'd heard she had returned. He'd gone to her office to tell her about the auction, at the last minute taking the gift he'd bought her years before. He'd kept it in his bureau all these years. Upon seeing her, he quickly realized he still loved her with an urgency he couldn't explain. But if he was honest with himself, he'd known that all along.

He sighed inwardly. If she hadn't left him without a word after graduation, if her hair wasn't the perfect shade of ebony, if she wasn't so proud and determined, he'd never have gotten engaged to Diana in the first place.

He stopped the car and punched in Diana's number, doing what he should've done months ago.

CHAPTER 16

*E*very few minutes Margaret pulled her white Volvo over to the side of the road, got out and scraped the snow off the windshield. Her cold car engine idled loudly. The warning of an impending snowstorm—which seemed to have arrived already— blasted from the radio, and she hoped to be finished packing things from her office by dusk. One could usually count on a snowy Christmas in Owanda, which brought with it, she realized with surprise, not a sense of frustration but of tranquility.

She'd never excelled at parallel parking but found a space near her office. The streets were noticeably quiet, the stillness broken only by ice crackling beneath her boots as she walked. Nonetheless, she could feel an air of anticipation for the special holiday. She sniffed appreciatively the scent of wood fireplaces and wondered how she and Amelie could ever leave the town that was her home.

She fumbled with her office entry keys and then flicked on the lights in the cold hallway as she entered. The worn waiting room chairs sat empty. Glossy magazines featuring movie stars and their secret lives were displayed neatly on the coffee table. She picked up one of the magazines. People believed movie stars were blessed with physical attractiveness and a charisma that hurled them into stardom. She'd learned it was also hard work and required difficult decisions. In a society valuing wealth and fame, she'd succeeded. All she'd had to give in return was her integrity.

She placed the magazine back on the table. One more set of keys and she entered her office. She loosened her coat, wet from the snow, and slung it over a chair. Then she wandered aimlessly around the stark, quiet room.

She pulled a chair up to the window and watched snowflakes falling thickly on the streetlights. Cheery red bells and silver holiday trimmings were being covered by a feathery white blanket. A true winter wonderland icing everything in its path.

Now, with no one around, she could congratulate herself on all she'd achieved and grieve for what she'd subsequently lost. Fleeting success, brief wealth, an opportunity to pursue her greatest dream—a film career.

Check. Check. Check.

She brushed tears from her cheeks. But, oh, what she'd sacrificed. She'd defied Fernando, shamed him, lied to him, while believing that, somehow, he'd always wait for her. A bleak pain grew in her throat because she'd lost a man who'd truly loved her. In return for his trust and affection, she'd caused him to be an object of ridicule in his beloved hometown and kept his daughter from him. She wanted to replay Diana's intimate voice while she'd touched his arm possessively at the auction, the insults she'd hurled at Margaret, and her stunning beauty.

Instead, Margaret remembered the way Fernando had held her protectively in his arms at the public ice skating rink, how he'd teased her about her deaf parrot the first day in her office, or when he'd whispered in a voice tender with emotion, "I can't believe we have a daughter."

She stared out the window at the never-ending snow, the pearly-gray clouds covering the sky. If she didn't hurry, she'd be stranded in her office on Christmas Eve. Quickly, she walked to her desk and knelt on the floor. A pile of boxes sat beside her, which she loaded with pens, pencils, and blank applications. Fortunately, she'd never unpacked several boxes that still stood in a haphazard pile against the wall.

She opened the top drawer of her desk and hesitated. His beautifully wrapped gift sat unopened. She took it out and turned it around with her fingers. At the bottom was a small card. With a choked sigh she read his bold handwritten script aloud: "To my snow white princess, all my love."

She drew a long tortured breath and slowly expelled it. Although she hadn't spent any time at her office, she should've opened the gift when he'd first offered it to her.

Hesitating, she stood and set the gift on her desk. Too late now. She'd take it back to California and open it there, a token gift for herself on Christmas Day.

Somehow, she had to accept his impending marriage to another woman, a sophisticated woman who made Margaret feel unrefined and gauche. She leaned against her desk and briefly closed her eyes. How could she live in California and raise their daughter without him?

She straightened away from her desk. What was she doing? She'd declared to anyone who asked that she made her own decisions and therefore controlled her own destiny. She would create a new life in Owanda, and Amelie could continue to see her father and his family. Sure, it would be difficult knowing he was with Diana, but he'd never be so unkind as to flaunt their happiness and break her heart. Besides, her heart was already broken.

She reached for her cell phone. This time she would truly

be the woman she wanted to be, a woman her daughter could be proud to call *Mommy*.

Your agent will never speak to you again if you make this call, a little voice in her mind rebuked. You're giving up everything you worked so hard for. Hollywood is an unforgiving town and won't forget.

Quickly she dialed Sid's number before she changed her mind.

Her call immediately went to voice mail. "The answer is no, Sid," was all she said. She pressed the end button on the phone. Somehow she knew that Hollywood would roll on without her. In the space of a brief phone call, she'd lost her Hollywood identity so she could establish a new one by creating a permanent home for her and her daughter.

The front office door slammed and footsteps strode purposefully through the hallway. Her office door flew open as he barged in, a familiar, handsome man from upstate New York in a well-tailored navy suit. He said nothing, just wheeled a suitcase into the middle of the room with one hand. In the other he held out a package wrapped in gold foil paper and tied with silver ribbon. His chocolate-brown eyes stared into hers.

You know I've always loved you, he'd whispered to her in the ice arena.

"I have a gift," he said aloud.

The room tilted, and she lurched from her chair. She nodded and swallowed, hoping to control her trembling voice. "You offered me a gift wrapped exactly like that six weeks ago." She pointed to the neatly wrapped package on her desk. "So now I have two."

He placed it beside its identical twin on her desk. "This one isn't for you."

She drew back to admire both gifts, then stared down at her hands.

To do something, anything, not to meet his probing gaze, she turned her gaze to the small Christmas tree on the corner of her desk. A sad reminder of how little she'd put into holiday decorating, its spindly branches were bare.

"Poor forlorn little thing," she whispered.

He leaned closer. His nearness was disconcerting, a hairsbreadth away. "Anything I can do to help the situation?"

"Do you know anyone who can decorate a Christmas tree?"

He grinned boyishly and took a step nearer. "I load up a tree with lots of tinsel because that disguises any imperfections. Small, twinkling colored lights and a star at the top works wonders."

She smiled. "Twinkling lights? You sound like a television commercial."

"Your mind always seems to gravitate toward Hollywood."

In a small voice she said, "Not anymore."

He came around her desk, pulling his suitcase, and gazed silently at her.

She dug her nails into her palms. "Are you leaving for Florida this evening instead of tomorrow so you came here to say good-bye?" she asked. "If so, where's Amelie?"

"Our daughter's building a gingerbread house with my mother. And no, I'm not leaving for Florida, I'm flying to California." There was a curiously quiet gravity in his voice. "With you."

She blinked, brushing her bangs from her eyes, and then she stared at him.

"I don't understand. Amelie and I are staying in Owanda."

He dropped the handle of the suitcase to the floor. "You mean I won't have to fly to California and live there?"

"Not unless you're planning on becoming an actor."

His eyes held a sheen of tears. "That settles it then."

"Settles what?"

"Where we're going to live in order to be together." He closed the space between them and pulled her to him, wrapping his arms around her. "I've missed you so much."

He smothered her joyous murmur with his kiss. "Not as much as I've missed you," she was finally able to say.

His breathing was ragged when he lifted his head. "Will you marry me?"

"As long as you're not marrying anyone else." She tilted her head back and looked up into his earnest gaze.

"No one but you, my princess." With a brief nod, he added, "Diana wasn't in the best of humor when I called off our engagement, but she'll find another man before the New Year rings in." He pressed her head against his chest. "What about your movie role?"

"I'm not an actress, I'm a mother."

"And soon to be my wife," he added.

This was where she belonged. The exquisite feeling of his strong lean body fitting against hers and his hands massaging her back made her shudder, fearing that if they ever broke contact, her life would be shrouded under a vast emptiness she couldn't bear.

He tangled his hands through her hair. "Have I ever mentioned you remind me of Snow White?"

"About a thousand times. It's embarrassing to be named for a fairy-tale woman who was tricked into eating a poison apple by a witch."

"But first she lived with dwarfs who took care of her."

She gazed straight into his deep chocolate gaze. "I can't imagine living with seven men when one will do perfectly."

"I love you," he whispered solemnly. "I've always loved you."

She choked back tears of joy. "And I've always loved you."

He sat on her chair and settled her onto his lap. He

clasped her tighter as she laid a hand on his unshaven jaw. "Merry Christmas, darling," she said.

His eyes took on a devilish gleam. "It's not often we're alone, between deaf parrots and one-eyed kittens and our daughter." He took her lips in one long kiss and then eyed the pile of boxes on the floor. Slowly he unbuttoned the top button of her cardigan sweater and gathered her body close to his. "I have a plan. If I placed those boxes straight across on the floor as a bed ..."

* * *

TWO PAIRS of footsteps ran through the hallway.

"Mommy! Daddy! Look what I got!" Amelie's loud voice echoed through the room as she placed a tiny calico kitten with no tail on the desk between the two gifts wrapped in gold paper. She signed eagerly, "Uncle Michael said you'd be here because Daddy called him. We stopped at the animal shelter first."

Margaret leaped up from the pile of boxes and quickly buttoned her sweater. She crossed the room to hug her daughter, then looked at Fernando who had quickly stood as well. "You arranged this? You knew they were coming?"

He glanced at his watch and then glared at his brother striding quickly into the office. "You're a half hour early."

Michael tapped his hearing aid fitted unobtrusively behind his left ear. "Sorry, I didn't hear you."

"Michael, you're driving?" Margaret asked.

He nodded. "I bought a car, and I'll move into my new apartment at the end of the month. I got a good job with a prestigious real estate office located at the other end of town."

Margaret stared at the kitten attempting to scramble off

her desk. "Amelie, we can't possibly take on another rescue animal," she signed.

"Yes, we can, Mommy."

Fernando and Michael nodded simultaneously.

Margaret searched her mind for an explanation. With a helpless glance around the room, she asked and signed, "Can someone please tell me what everyone seems to know except me?"

Michael answered. "My twin brother isn't building an outlet mall on the mobile home property. He's building a public park for everyone to enjoy, and I'm in charge of the development."

"And, Mommy, where your house used to be, Daddy is building a brand new animal rescue shelter. It's a secret and a surprise."

Fernando strode to Margaret and Amelie and put his arms around them both. "It's a no-kill shelter." He spoke slowly and directly to Amelie so that she could lip-read. "We'll offer free spaying and neutering, as well as training people to provide good homes for these animals. But only on one condition."

Laughter and giggles from Michael and Amelie greeted his announcement. Margaret turned to face him. "We can only keep five animals at a time in our home?"

"Even better."

Margaret attempted to hide her smile. "And what is that condition?"

"That you'll work by my side as an equal partner."

"Got it all planned?"

He shrugged. "Call it a character flaw." He reached for the two gifts on her desk, handing one to her and the other to Amelie. "Will you please do me the honor of finally opening this?"

She laughed. "Only if Amelie opens hers too."

"You go first, Mommy," Amelie said.

"They're similar. You can open them together," Fernando prompted.

Amelie unwrapped her gift quickly and held up a tiny diamond necklace with a fine gold chain. "Daddy, I love it! Put it on me."

He fastened the necklace around her neck and she twirled in a proud circle.

He laughed. "Mommy's next," he said.

Margaret slowly unwrapped the gift, placing the gold foil on her desk. She snapped the lid up on a small box in the shape of an apple, exposing a small, exquisite single diamond. She stared at him. The laughter was gone, and his look had changed to solemn hopefulness. He seemed unsure, almost hesitant. "Do you like it?"

She gazed at him a long moment. "I love it."

"I bought this diamond for you a long time ago, after our graduation. It's small. I know it's small. I can get a bigger one if you want."

She shook her head, laughing through tears of happiness. "It's perfect."

"You can make it into a necklace, or a ring."

She held the diamond up to the light to admire it. "I prefer a ring."

He pulled her and Amelie closer to his chest. "I love you both so much."

"When's the wedding?" Michael asked. "I'll be the best man."

"Tomorrow," Fernando said.

Margaret shook her head. "Impossible. We'll need at least six weeks to plan the wedding. Besides, no church will marry us on Christmas Day."

"My church will. It's all planned," he said with a smile. "Assuming we're not snowed in."

Margaret twined her arms around him. "You mean you can't control the weather?"

He grinned. "Unfortunately, even I have limitations."

She narrowed her eyes. "Weren't you planning on flying to California with me? Did you have a wedding planned on both coasts?"

He offered an impish grin. "Lucy is on standby. The wedding would've been quickly arranged, and she even offered to skip Las Vegas and fly directly to California. Owanda was my first choice, though."

"I'll be the flower girl," Amelie signed. "A Christmas wedding, Mommy! We can have it outside in the snow, and Daddy can rent a sleigh, and then we can get a horse." She picked up the kitten. "Won't it be fun?"

Fernando wiped his eyes and held his daughter closer. "Amelie, I love you, sweetheart." He kissed her, then Margaret.

Amelie giggled and signed, "And we all lived happily ever after!"

The End

* * *

A NOTE FROM JOSIE

Dear Reader,

Thank you for reading *A SNOWY WHITE CHRISTMAS!* I hope you enjoyed my sweet romance. Please help other people find this book and post an online review.

I love going home for the holidays, and especially enjoy second chance romances. Margaret and Fernando were a joy to write.

Happy Reading!

Josie Riviera

This book is available in ebook, Audiobook, paperback, Hardcover, and large print paperback.

Spotify Play List Here.

RECIPE FOR PEANUTTY CHOCO SURPRISES COOKIE

A favorite combination- chocolate and peanut butter!
Yields approximately 8 dozen cookies

Ingredients:

2 cups Peanut Butter (any brand- smooth or crunchy, and may use reduced fat, if desired.)

2 sticks butter (leave out of refrigerator at least 1-2 hours beforehand)

2 cups packed brown sugar

4 eggs

4 cups flour

2 tsp. baking powder

2 teaspoons cinnamon
1 bag candy kisses, wrappers removed

Cream peanut butter, butter, and sugar. Beat in eggs. Combine flour, baking powder, and cinnamon. Add gradually to peanut butter mixture until well blended. Stir by hand.

Chill dough at least 60 minutes for easier handling.

For each cookie, roll 1 teaspoon of dough into small ball and place on ungreased cookie sheet. Press in candy kiss. Bake for 10-12 minutes in 350 degree oven. After cooling, sift confectioners sugar on top, if desired.

Enjoy!

USA TODAY BESTSELLING AUTHOR

JOSIE RIVIERA

Candleglow AND Mistletoe

A rising pianist and a
pro stuntman winding down
his career find love amid
the glow of Christmas candles

* * *

Candleglow and Mistletoe

Copyright © 2016

Josie Riviera

CHAPTER 1

*N*oelle Wentworth never liked long bus journeys, especially when the bus was being driven by a preoccupied driver who kept glancing down at his cell phone. She shifted in the worn bus seat and fished through her purse for dry soda crackers to calm her motion sickness. Then she pushed down the impulse to march to the front of the bus and suggest that the bus driver slow his speed and concentrate on the snowy, frozen road ahead.

She glanced out the window. The traffic lights in Fisher's Crossing, the last small town before Snowing Rock, North Carolina, would force the driver to slow.

Noelle leaned back in her seat and blew out an exhausted breath. She'd been traveling since morning and longed to unpack, enjoy a long, hot shower, then practice piano for her upcoming concert.

She glanced at Anjali, the sleeping, five-year-old girl she'd met a few hours earlier. She'd started talking to Noelle, and Noelle had invited the little girl to sit in the empty bus seat beside her. Noelle smiled at Anjali's mother, Mrs. Fernandez, seated across the aisle.

The woman nodded back, her gaze tired, her hair graying at the temples. She zipped her long, red puffer jacket up to her chin and closed her eyes.

Noelle tucked her curly blonde hair beneath her hat, envisioning the picturesque town of Snowing Rock ahead. The town had been listed as one of America's top ten 'Christmas Towns' because of its quaint charm. She hoped nothing had changed in the fifteen years since she'd last visited. Although this wasn't a visit, she corrected herself. She'd agreed to temporarily manage her Aunt Joy's candle shop while her aunt convalesced from a hip injury.

Noelle's orderly private life would be disrupted for a few weeks while she helped out her aunt, but Noelle had agreed, purely out of duty. Although she was busy preparing for her concert, there was no other family, and her aunt needed someone she could trust.

Noelle knew that feeling all too well. She'd lost her parents a year ago and missed their support and guidance, especially after her bad marriage, made even worse by her illness. Along the way, Noelle had learned a hard lesson. She was leery of trusting anyone.

Absently, Noelle ran her fingers across her lap in silent piano arpeggios. Her upcoming concert was only a few weeks away. She fidgeted, pushing away the worst-case scenarios rushing through her mind. Suppose she ran off the stage again? Suppose the audience hadn't forgotten what had happened last time? She'd be performing in the magnificent Forum Theater in Saint Augustine, calling attention to herself, leaving herself open to criticism.

She inhaled deeply, then exhaled. No worries. As the months had gone by and she'd agonized over each excruciating detail of her previous, embarrassing performance, she'd rationalized that the experience had made her stronger.

She'd oversee Aunt Joy's candle shop during the day, and

practice on her aunt's piano in the evening. Besides, a quiet, restful break from hectic Saint Augustine was exactly what Noelle needed.

When she returned to the stage, she'd be well rested and well-practiced, proving to Colin Rudovich, her ex, that she was once again a professional concert pianist who captivated her audiences. This time in Saint Augustine, there'd be no memory lapses. This time, a disturbing doctor's report wouldn't interfere with her concentration. Fortunately, the cyst on her ovary had been removed and the biopsy had found the cyst wasn't cancerous.

Coils of smoke drifted from the chimneys of gable-roofed bungalows as the bus idled at a stoplight in Fisher's Crossing. The light changed from red to green, and the bus picked up speed, whizzing by snow-covered, jagged rocks.

The whine of cold winter air seeped through the bus's window. Noelle gratefully breathed in the fresh air and closed her eyes, hearing the beginning bars of her Chopin concert piece.

"Miss Noelle, want me to sing 'Rockin' Around the Christmas Tree'?" Anjali tugged on Noelle's sleeve. "My Daddy taught me all the words."

Noelle opened her eyes to Anjali's almond gaze.

"Sure, that's a fun Christmas song." Noelle glanced at her watch, then back at Anjali. "Aren't you tired? You've only slept a half hour since we got on eight hours ago."

Anjali's dark-complexioned face fell into a frown. "My Mommy said I don't need much sleep."

Noelle smirked. "I agree with her."

From across the aisle, Mrs. Fernandez laughed aloud. "My husband dotes on her. She sings all the time and he's encouraged her to join Snowing Rock's kindergarten choir next year."

Noelle felt that familiar, lonely ache in her gut. She swallowed her desolation and summoned a cheerful smile. "I remember hearing the choir when I attended Snowing Rock High. And I loved the sound of the children's voices blended together."

"Do you know how the song starts, Miss Noelle? You can sing with me." Anjali snapped her small fingers and began singing, "'Rockin' Around the Christmas Tree ...'"

Sleet tinkled against the window pane and Noelle glanced outside just as the bus flew by the last street sign in Fisher's Crossing.

She stood. "I'll be back, Anjali. The driver should reduce his speed. He may not know these mountain roads, but I remember them."

"Miss Noelle," the little girl asked, "What comes after 'At the Christmas party hop?'"

"'Mistletoe hung where you can see,'" Noelle sang softly.

The girl pushed up her small glasses. "'Every couple tries to—'"

"The truck on the other side is swerving into our lane!" a man in the front of the bus shouted. "It'll plow right into us!"

A pair of oncoming headlights reflected the road's icy glare. A sharp blast of the rig's horn followed. The bus driver threw down his cell phone and jerked the steering wheel hard to the right. The brakes shrieked, the wheels skidded.

Anjali pressed her fists to her ears and wailed.

"Anjali!" Mrs. Fernandez shouted from across the aisle.

Noelle's head jerked toward the window. She instinctively held up her arm to prevent Anjali from pitching forward.

The bus swerved, veered off the road, and screeched to a stop.

Darkness. Smells of gasoline. Muffled crying.

No, this couldn't be happening. With her heart racing, Noelle surveyed the darkened bus. Thankfully, none of the passengers appeared hurt. The bus was upright, although passengers crowded the aisle, tightening near the doors, pushing and shoving as they exited.

Noelle shot a glance across the aisle. Mrs. Fernandez's seat was empty.

"We need an ambulance!" the bus driver shouted into his cell phone.

Tears coursed down Anjali's dark cheeks. "Miss Noelle, where's Mommy?"

"We'll find her." Noelle slung her purse over her shoulder and squeezed Anjali's small hand reassuringly. They both jumped at the sounds of crunching metal as the bus sank deeper into the snow near the edge of an embankment. Several passengers screamed.

Stay calm, Noelle told herself. Stay calm. She brushed at a wetness on her forehead and noted blood on her fingertips. Now where had that come from? Perhaps she'd hit her head when the bus had swerved.

Through the clamor, she and Anjali pressed through the crowd and exited the bus. Fortunately, Noelle had picked up some winter clothing online before her trip. Their boots crackled on the icy snow as they made their way to the other passengers standing at the edge of an embankment. Several pointed to a gully, their conversations quiet and anxious.

Noelle peered past the edge and her chest tightened. The broken body of Anjali's mother in her familiar, red, long, puffer jacket, lay sprawled at an odd angle.

Noelle held in a gasp. Mentally, she chastised herself. Why hadn't she warned the bus driver sooner, insisting he slow his speed?

"Miss, do you need any help?" A deep male voice sounded through the crowd.

Noelle swung around.

A tall man, easily over six feet and sporting the beginnings of a dark beard, approached her. "Are you two all right?" he asked.

"Yes, yes I think so," Noelle said.

He was lean and extremely fit, wearing an olive green parka and gray wool hat. "I'm parked there." He pointed to a black Land Rover on the side of the road. "I was driving behind the bus and my heart hit my throat when the driver took that last curve so fast." He stepped forward and touched his gloved hand to Noelle's forehead. "You're bleeding."

Self-conscious, she stepped back and tugged her hat lower over her forehead. "I must've hit my head on the window next to my seat."

The man's dark brows drew together. He drew a white cotton handkerchief from his parka and gently wiped her forehead. "Hold this on the cut to stop the bleeding," he said.

"Thanks. I'm okay, really." Taking judicious note of Anjali's quivering jaw and tear-stained face, Noelle dabbed at her forehead with his handkerchief, then handed it back to him.

"This is Anjali, and she's more important than my cut forehead." Noelle dropped her voice to a whisper and signaled toward the gully. "Anjali's mother ..."

"My Mommy fell down that big hill and she's hurt really bad!" Anjali's thin face pinched with tears. Her teeth were chattering and she shoved her tiny hands into her coat pockets.

The man knelt beside her. "I'll bring your Mommy back safely." He secured Anjali's pink beanie securely over her ears and offered a comforting smile.

"Promise?" Anjali sniffed.

"Yes. I'm a man of my word. You stay here with this woman, all right?" He came to his feet and nodded to Noelle.

Before Noelle could reply, he'd climbed over a guardrail and inched down the steep, icy embankment. He pulled his cell phone from his parka, lighting a path with his phone's flashlight.

Noelle stamped her frozen feet. Winter weather had smothered the mountain and had left a chilling, dark calmness. Trees groaned under the weight of the snow. She smoothed Anjali's wet hair from her cheeks and zipped the purple parka up to Anjali's chin.

A growing crowd gathered, cheering the man on. He'd reached Mrs. Fernandez, grabbed a branch, and fixed a splint beneath her leg.

An ambulance flashed to the scene and braked to a halt. Two paramedics leapt from the vehicle, shouted inquiries, then raced down the embankment carrying a stretcher. With the help from the bearded man, they shifted Mrs. Fernandez onto the stretcher and hoisted her up the embankment.

Noelle stopped one of the paramedics as he hurried past. "This little girl is Anjali and she's the injured woman's daughter."

"The woman's leg might be broken, her pulse is weak, and she's shivering. We're transporting her by ambulance to Snowing Rock Hospital," the paramedic replied without stopping.

"No! No!" Anjali screamed. "Ambulances scare me!"

"Ambulances scare me, too," Noelle admitted. "However, we need to get you to the hospital to be with your Mom."

"Sorry, we don't take kids," the paramedic said over his shoulder. "And only one person can ride in the cab."

The engine of the ambulance started, the flashing red lights triggered.

"Mommy, don't leave me!" Anjali broke free from Noelle and darted toward the ambulance.

The man in the olive-green parka caught Anjali as she dashed by. He bent to her height and gently grasped her forearms. "Mommy isn't leaving you. The doctors will make her better." He spoke with quiet, relaxed confidence. "I'll carry you to my SUV, and we'll follow the ambulance. Your friend will stay with you once we get to the hospital. All right?" He glanced at Noelle.

Noelle swallowed, her mouth dry. "I ... I haven't stepped into a hospital since—"

The man raised a dark brow, then bent to Anjali. "Do any of your aunts and uncles live in Snowing Rock?"

"My Aunt Nancy and Uncle Joe Fernandez live next door to us," Anjali said.

"Good. We'll call your aunt and uncle when we reach the hospital."

"No! I don't wanna go to the hospital. I'll wait for Aunt Nancy and Uncle Joe to come get me here."

The man looked toward the road, shining like polished ice beneath a round November moon. "The hospital is a better place to meet your aunt and uncle. Then everyone will be safe."

Anjali crossed her arms. "No!"

He wiped the snow icicles dripping from her nose with his handkerchief and took hold of her hands. "Why aren't you wearing gloves on such a wintry night?"

She pulled from his grasp and scratched her red, raw hands. "My Mommy forgot to pack them and she was really sad about it."

"I'm sad, too, because your hands are so cold. Take my gloves. That'll make Mommy happy and you can show her the gloves at the hospital." He removed his thick leather gloves, guided her small fingers into them, and grinned. "Do you want my parka next?"

"No! Your parka's too big for me. So are your gloves!" Anjali giggled and flapped her fingers. "I'll go to the hospital if you carry me and Miss Noelle can come, too."

"Miss Noelle?" He stiffened for a moment, flicked a

glance in Noelle's direction, and smiled. He had strong, handsome features and hazel eyes.

Something about the admiration in his smile, the hint of gold specks in his hazel eyes, stirred her memory.

He cleared his throat and brought Anjali to his broad chest. "It's all right to be scared."

With Anjali in his arms, he called to one of the paramedics climbing into the back of the ambulance. "We'll follow you, Stan."

"These roads are hazardous. Maintain a safe speed, Mr. Waters," the paramedic said.

"I drive slow when I'm not working." The man regarded the snow-studded tires on his Land Rover. "I've traveled these roads many times and I'm prepared for every emergency."

As they made their way to his vehicle, Noelle said, "Thanks for reacting so quickly and so bravely."

He shrugged. "I do this for a living."

"You drive fast or you save people?"

He paused, studying her with open interest. "I act brave."

She blinked and studied him in return. His features were tanned and he probably spent a great deal of time outdoors, whereas she hardly ventured farther than her front porch. Still, something about him tugged at a long-ago memory.

She rubbed her lips and shook her head. Impossible, considering their apparently different lifestyles.

He held out his hand. "I'm Gabe. Gabe Waters, by the way."

"I'm Noelle Wentworth."

He clasped her hand and smiled warmly.

She glanced around. "Do we know each other? Your name sounds familiar."

He dropped his hand and rubbed his bristled chin. "Are you staying in Snowing Rock?"

He hadn't answered her question.

"I'm managing my Aunt Joy's candle shop for a few weeks," Noelle said. "I'll be living in her cottage while she convalesces from a hip injury in the town's rehab center."

"I love Snowing Rock. The town's beautiful, especially at Christmas."

"Have you lived in Snowing Rock a while?" she asked.

"I was in California for a few years, although I moved back to Snowing Rock because I always felt the town was my true home."

"The cool temperatures will be a welcome change from Saint Augustine," Noelle remarked. And she'd have plenty of time to perfect her performance pieces.

Gabe's gaze swung sharply. Lights flashing, the ambulance was speeding up the icy mountain road towards Snowing Rock. "We need to follow them," he said.

A battering gust of wind hastened their steps as they hurried to his Land Rover. Promptly, he buckled Anjali into the child seat in the back.

"You have children?" Noelle asked.

Inwardly, she chided herself for asking a stranger such a personal question. Judging by his rugged appearance, he was probably a mountain man, married with a dozen kids.

"No children," he replied. "My cousin, Holly, flies here often from Virginia and she's the proud single parent of a four-year-old son, Devin."

Gabe grabbed an army surplus wool blanket from the trunk and wrapped the blanket around Anjali's legs. Despite the icy conditions, he strode with ease to the passenger side and opened the door for Noelle.

"Sorry, I only have one blanket," he said.

Noelle sank into the luxurious leather seat of his Land Rover and fastened her seat belt. "I thought you were prepared for every emergency?"

His eyes twinkled with a hint of mischief as he closed her passenger door. "I'm only one person and assumed I only needed one blanket."

He slipped into the driver seat and started the Land Rover, adjusting the heater to full blast.

"Better?" His smile was directed at Noelle, that comforting smile he'd used earlier with Anjali.

Noelle snuggled into the seat. "Perfect."

She glanced at his profile. His nose was straight, his jaw authoritative, yet his body language was gentle.

He eased his SUV onto the road, coasted through a hairpin curve, eased up on the gas when the vehicle slipped, then sped up slightly before reaching the steep incline.

A few minutes later, his Land Rover idled quietly at the entrance to Snowing Rock Hospital before he switched off the engine. He skirted from the vehicle and unfastened a sleeping Anjali from the child seat.

"Will you be all right from here?" he asked, coming around to the passenger side to open the door for Noelle.

She took his hand and stepped from the SUV. "It might be better if you brought Anjali—"

"I may be needed at the accident scene. Is your luggage on the bus?"

"Yes." Noelle nodded. "And my piano music's in a separate suitcase stowed beneath."

"I'll retrieve your luggage and tell the bus company to contact you." He lifted Anjali, preparing to place the child in Noelle's arms.

Noelle shifted and kept her arms at her sides. She shook her head. "Sorry, but—"

"But what? Didn't you say your aunt's recuperating in a rehab center?" he asked.

Noelle's body quivered from the cold. Her gaze darted to the daunting hospital, the brightly lit ambulance entrance sign. "A rehab center is different from a hospital."

He cuddled the sleeping child to his chest. "You acted very competently at the accident scene, Noelle. I'm sure you can sit in a hospital waiting room."

The hospital doors slid open as a wheelchair squeaked past. Smells of bleach along with stainless steel assaulted her nostrils, the same hospital odors she remembered from the night of her parents' deaths. Through the hospital window, Noelle saw two sweating and shivering women as they sat side by side and stared at her through the glass.

Noelle licked her lips and lowered her tone to a whisper. "I'm sorry. I can't go in."

Anjali snapped her eyes open. "Miss Noelle! I want to see Mommy!"

"I'll take you to see Mommy," Gabe said quickly. Noelle couldn't determine by his expression whether he was furious or disappointed with her.

She swallowed. She was putting her own selfish fears before the numerous accident victims who needed this man's help. Still, she couldn't control the panic welling inside her. She wasn't a nurse, she told herself. She wasn't capable of handling medical emergencies, or talking with doctors, or sniffing hospital antiseptic ...

She kissed Anjali's cheek. "I'll call the hospital to check on your Mommy as soon as I arrive at my aunt's cottage. I know you're in capable hands with Mr. Waters."

"Gabe," he reminded her.

"Yes, well, I'll be leaving, then, Gabe." Noelle rubbed the back of her neck. "My Aunt Joy lives at 10 Oak Street, and I remember her cottage wasn't far from the hospital."

"Oak Street is two blocks in that direction," Gabe pointed to a side street. "If you want to wait until Anjali's aunt and uncle arrive, I can drive you."

"No ... No, the walk will do me good after sitting on the bus all those hours." Noelle granted him a self-assured smile she didn't feel.

"Plug in my cell phone number in case you need anything while you're here."

"I'm sure I won't ... need anything. Thanks, anyway," she said.

"All right." He pivoted and strode through the hospital doors carrying Anjali in his arms.

A short walk afterward, Noelle reached her aunt's single-story cottage, where she gratefully thawed out her frozen limbs. She called her aunt to inform her that she'd safely arrived, brewed a hot cup of tea, and gratefully immersed herself in memorized piano pieces on her aunt's old, upright piano. She was determined to return to Saint Augustine and perform a triumphant concert.

Nothing, she decided as she played, could stand in the way of being well-prepared and conquering her paralyzing memory lapse once and for all.

Not even a freezing cold town, an out of tune piano, and a bus accident.

CHAPTER 2

*J*n the space of a few seconds, all the memories of
fifteen years ago had collided with the present
when Gabe's gaze had connected with Noelle's shining,
emerald eyes.

Noelle Wentworth. The cool, unattainable beauty who'd
briefly attended Snowing Rock High. She was his high
school crush and girl of his dreams, the brave young woman
who'd lived in an affluent world he could only fantasize
about. She'd been surrounded by classical music and nights
at the opera. He'd been surrounded by poverty and sickness.

Nonetheless, in his senior year of high school, she'd
impressed him with her courage. He remembered the inci-
dent well, he thought with a grim smile. He was small, sickly
with diabetes, and was constantly bullied. One of the biggest
high school bullies had pushed Gabe into a locker, and Gabe
had responded, ready to fight, arms upraised and fists
clenched, although his heart had beaten madly in his chest.

Noelle had marched up and pried Gabe and the bully
apart. With her jade-green eyes flashing, she'd scolded them
both in a tone of frustrated impatience.

She hadn't known that her bravery had saved Gabe from a terrible beating, although he'd held his own in a fight with that same bully several months later. More importantly, Noelle had spurred Gabe to confront and manage his worst enemy, diabetes. Her intervention had provided the impetus for him to get strong.

An intercom paged a doctor, bringing Gabe's reflections back to the stuffy hospital waiting room. He shifted in line at the reception desk and jostled the dark-haired little girl in his arms.

Anjali snapped up her head and looked around. "Are my aunt and uncle here yet?"

"They'll come soon," he reassured, his memories drifting back to his remembrances of Noelle.

To his knowledge, Noelle hadn't flicked a glance in his direction after she'd broken up that fight. And why would she? He'd been the frail, skinny senior whereas she'd been the gorgeous, prim and proper freshman.

Gabe stepped to the hospital reception desk, aware of the clatter of computer keyboards combined with the smell of burned coffee.

"May I help you?" the receptionist asked.

"I'm checking on Mrs. Fernandez, who was brought here earlier in an ambulance," he said. "This little girl is her daughter, Anjali. We need to notify Anjali's aunt and uncle."

The receptionist poised her fingers over the keyboard. "Last name Fernandez?"

"Aunt Nancy and Uncle Joe," Anjali whispered loudly in Gabe's ear.

The receptionist searched the computer and tapped a phone number, speaking briefly on the phone. She laid the receiver on the cradle and said, "They're on their way. The hospital personnel will deal with insurance when they arrive."

"Thanks," Gabe said.

The receptionist offered a playful grin. "You're the stuntman from 'Force of Thunder One'! I recognized you immediately, Mr. Waters. How long are you in town?"

"Indefinitely," he replied.

"Your newest movie, 'Force of Thunder Two', is being released on Thanksgiving Day. I have an extra ticket if you'd like to come with me."

"I never watch my films," he said.

Because he was simply the man on the screen, pretending to be someone else.

"I've heard you're a perfectionist." She handed him a pen and pointed to a sign-in sheet. "You're as handsome as any of those movie stars."

"Thanks." He grabbed the pen and her hand glanced over his. She smiled and twirled a strand of her hair.

He wrote his name on the sheet and handed her back the pen. "Let's get this little girl taken care of," he said.

In long, strides, he obligingly took a seat in the waiting room with Anjali in his arms.

* * *

ANJALI'S AUNT and uncle arrived at the hospital soon afterward, the proper insurance information was filled out, and Anjali was playing checkers with her cousins when Gabe departed.

Mrs. Fernandez had explained to Gabe and her family that when the bus had stopped so suddenly, she'd been jostled forward and had raced off in panic. She'd searched for Anjali in the darkness, unexpectedly slipped, and fallen down the snowy embankment.

After brief conversations with the nurses, Gabe learned that Mrs. Fernandez had been diagnosed with a displaced fracture. Her fracture would be splinted for at least a day to allow the swelling to subside, then casted.

"I'm impressed by what a brave girl you were tonight," Gabe complimented Anjali before he left. "I'll check on you and your Mommy in the morning. How about a high five to the side before I leave?"

Anjali giggled and slapped his hand hard.

With a quick wave to Anjali's aunt and uncle, Gabe returned to his vehicle.

He shifted his Land Rover to a lower gear and braked carefully as he made his way down the snowy mountain. He skidded a couple times on black ice and let up on the gas, carefully rotating his steering wheel back toward the road. Soon, he eased the Land Rover to a stop near two police cars.

He got out and strode to an officer photographing a roped off area. "Need any help?" he asked.

"The right shoulder metal beam stopped the bus from rolling down the embankment." The officer's wheezy breath puffed out warm steam in the cold air. "Some passengers suffered minor cuts and bruises, a few broken bones. The accident could've been much worse."

"I offered up a prayer for all the passengers. You know prayer helps," Gabe said.

"Do I?" The officer dismissed Gabe, then yielded toward the road. "Incoming traffic to Snowing Rock has been rerouted. You can either drive around the mountain and use the back roads to head back to town, or wait for the plow. They're scheduled to clear a path shortly."

"I'll wait." Gabe tramped through the snow to his Land Rover, feeling a slight dizziness. His heartbeat came rapid in his chest, a sure sign that he needed to eat and his blood sugar was dropping. He settled into his vehicle and opened the glove compartment. As he'd done hundreds of times since he'd been diagnosed with Type I diabetes, he pricked his finger and put a drop of blood on a test strip, then checked the results on a blood sugar meter that he kept in the inner pocket of his parka.

He peered at the near-blizzard conditions, the police ordering motorists to turn around because the unplowed, steep mountain road made traveling too dangerous.

Gabe rubbed his hands over his face and grabbed a granola bar from his pocket.

He couldn't afford to have his blood sugar drop too low again. Last time it had almost killed him.

CHAPTER 3

*E*ven from rehab, Noelle thought, Aunt Joy was a take-charge person, insisting her candle shop open promptly at nine o'clock every morning.

Conversely, Noelle had never been an early riser, especially the day after a traumatic bus accident that left her weak and slightly dazed. Her head hurt and a small bump had appeared on her forehead where Gabe had pressed his handkerchief to stop the bleeding.

Earlier that morning, Noelle had been pleased to find her two suitcases deposited at her aunt's front door. After downing two cups of coffee followed by a warm shower, Noelle had changed into a fisherman knit sweater and black skinny jeans. She carried her black leather flats in her tote bag and secured her curly blonde hair with two ivory hair combs.

She couldn't resist a quick scale warm-up, which promptly developed into a run-through of the entire Chopin two-piano arrangement.

Following a hasty C Minor finale chord, Noelle hurried out to walk three blocks to the candle shop. The gravel-gray skies were silent, the town bleached in a dazzling white snow.

Noelle reached the entrance to 'Scents of Joy' fifteen minutes later, pausing to admire the elegant fresh wreath topped by a long red velvet bow hanging on the shop's arched entrance door. She stepped inside and the aroma of beeswax, a subtle honey scent, greeted her nostrils.

"Hi!" A young woman waved from the opposite corner of the shop. "I'm Caroline Crockery." Caroline's short, red hair was highlighted by thin purple braids, her bangs cut awkwardly over her forehead. Clad in ripped blue jeans and a long-sleeved denim blouse, she topped her outfit with a white, ruffled apron and tied the long ribbons around her waist.

Caroline leaned forward on a wooden stool and regarded Noelle. "Yup, you have curly blonde hair and green eyes, so judging by your aunt's description, you're Noelle. Thanks for bringing our first official winter snowfall, Miss Saint Augustine."

Noelle responded with a smile, her gaze sliding meaningfully to the wall clock. "I apologize. I'm late for my first day of work."

"No worries. I'm glad you're here because this shop has been crazy busy."

"Do you know of a good piano tuner?" Noelle asked.

"That's an odd question. Oh right, you're a musician." Caroline put a hand to her mouth, her round face furrowed in thought. "Sorry. I don't play a musical instrument. Alan plays guitar, though. I can ask him."

"Who's Alan?" Noelle asked, walking to the back room to hang her coat and change from boots to flat shoes.

"He works at the pizzeria in town. He's a friend I met recently."

Noelle stepped back into the brightly lit shop. "I'll check for piano tuners on the internet tonight."

"The internet, as in the world-wide web?" Caroline amplified. "Good luck. Both the internet and lights go out a lot in this town because of the wintry weather."

Noelle shot a cautious glance at the customers beginning to file in. Here goes, she thought. She'd never had retail experience. She hurried to the cash register while Caroline measured a mason jar, then cut a length of wick two inches longer than the jar.

"My aunt told me you're the most dedicated part-time worker she's ever employed," Noelle said.

Caroline's brown eyes gleamed, reflecting her jolly smile. "A candle shop is my favorite place. It's so warm and cozy and the scents are wonderful, especially during the holiday season. Who doesn't love making candles?"

"Me, for one," Noelle raised her hand in reply while she surveyed the shelves overflowing with a vast array of candles in a variety of sizes and shades. "I've never made candles. Is it difficult?"

"Very easy," Caroline assured.

"When I visited this shop many years ago, it was much smaller and more sparsely stocked," Noelle said.

"Your aunt expanded her business last year using her retirement savings."

"She never mentioned anything to me." Noelle made a mental note to ask her aunt if she needed money. Noelle didn't have much to give because her concert engagements had been close to none for the past year, but any money she had she'd gladly share.

"Your aunt's a seventy-year-old entrepreneur," Caroline said. "She rented the adjoining shop's space so she could offer candle-making classes."

"Sounds like I have a lot to learn." Noelle retrieved a

white, ruffled apron from behind the counter and tied the apron at the waist. "What should I do first?" she asked.

Caroline swept out her hand. "Hah! Where should I start?"

* * *

BY NOON, the shop was crowded with customers, and Noelle's hair had fallen from the ivory clips, hanging in unruly waves around her shoulders. She hadn't had a moment to tend to her hair, nor think, nor breathe. All the shop's details, including the appropriate music softly playing in the background, had been decided beforehand in meticulous notes left by Aunt Joy. The CD, featuring dulcimer and acoustic guitar playing an instrumental arrangement, had gone around for the fifth time.

Noelle apologized to a middle-aged woman standing at the cash register because Noelle had made her umpteenth mistake ringing up the customer's credit card. Inwardly, she rebuked herself. Perhaps her ex had been right. Perhaps she was inept at everything she touched. Perhaps the customers would begin judging her as harshly as the music critics had.

Caroline came to the register to correct Noelle's mistake, working briskly and efficiently. "That's Lucia Crandall," Caroline whispered, as an attractive woman, dressed in an elegantly tailored camel wool coat and brown suede leather boots, paraded into the shop. "Lucia owns Misty Mountain Candles, the other candle shop in town. Although her shop's doing extraordinarily well, she checks up on us once in a while—probably assessing her competition to remind herself she's still in the lead." Caroline shook her head. "We don't have her unlimited advertising dollars, although when I attend NYU next year and earn my degree in market research, I plan to marry a rich banker and offer my expertise to your aunt." Caroline added, "Lucia's rich husband died last year."

"I'm sorry for her loss," Noelle said.

Caroline snorted. "You're probably sorrier than Lucia was."

"I'm surprised this small town can sustain two candle shops. When I lived here fifteen years ago—"

"Snowing Rock has become a trendy vacation hideaway for wealthy people from all over the world," Caroline interrupted. "Some have bought permanent residences here."

As Lucia waltzed to the cash register, Caroline beamed a bright, artificial smile. "Looking for anything special today, Lucia?"

"Nothing in particular." Lucia glanced at her stunning reflection in one of the shop's hanging mirrors and arranged her shining black hair to show off a stylish pixie cut. "You're Joy's niece?" Lucia asked Noelle.

"Yes, and it's good to meet you, Lucia," Noelle replied.

"Will you be kicking off your shoes and prancing around the shop barefoot like your slightly insane aunt?"

"I'll leave my shoes on, thanks, although I may only wear socks," Noelle recovered admirably.

"I assume you've had retail experience?" Lucia asked.

"None," Noelle said.

"Know anything about making candles?"

"Not a thing."

Lucia smirked. "This will be my most successful holiday season in years." She opened the lid of one of the candles on a nearby shelf, one of 'Scents of Joy's' handmade candy-cane candles. "The wick's too small for this candle's diameter, Caroline," Lucia pointed out. "You poured the wax too high. When the wax begins to change shape, stop pouring."

Caroline saluted Lucia. "Thanks for the tip."

"Did I mention I'm opening a second shop in New York

City? My late husband's business originated there and I'm considering a store front on Fifth Avenue."

"Do keep us posted," Caroline replied. "We'll be waiting with bated breath."

Lucia made her way down the shop's aisles, examining price stickers on the bottom of each candle jar. "Joy and I enjoy a friendly rivalry," she said to one of the customers.

"Yeah, right," Caroline whispered to Noelle. "Friendly rivalry my—"

Noelle grinned. She glanced at her watch, counting the minutes until she could break for lunch. If she hurried to Aunt Joy's cottage and skipped lunch altogether, she could practice the difficult octaves in the Brahms sonata.

Just you wait, Colin, she thought, envisioning the smug face of her ex. I realize you're trying to exploit me again, although I'm ready this time because I've learned not to trust you. In fact, I don't trust anyone. She smiled just thinking about his heated features, his jaw dropping as they performed the crowd-pleasing opening measures of the Chopin duo-piano arrangement.

"When are the shop's candle-making classes?" one of the customers asked. Her question brought Noelle's musings back to the cash register.

Noelle lifted her shoulders and directed a quizzical brow toward Caroline.

"Every Saturday evening from now until Christmas," Caroline said. "Our candle-making class is free, although customers can purchase the supplies here on the first night of class. And we'll be serving hot chocolate and homemade sugar cookies."

Noelle twisted to Caroline. "Who's making homemade sugar cookies?"

"You are. I'll bring the hot chocolate. Your aunt said she was leaving her sugar cookie recipe in the cottage."

"I've never baked a cookie in my life."

"Just follow the recipe."

The woman who'd inquired about the candle-making classes inclined her head toward Noelle. "Your aunt must be so grateful that you were able to help her out. She's bragged about your accomplishments for years." The woman reached across the counter and patted Noelle's arm. "From what she's told us, you're a concert pianist. Can you play background music for our ladies' luncheon at Snowing Rock country club in December? That piano hasn't been played in years."

Noelle blinked. Once, she'd performed in large concert halls and commanded astronomical fees. That is, before her last dismal performance, because offers no longer flooded her email inbox. Perhaps, though, it had been partly her fault. She'd chosen to hide away in her apartment and had closed all her social media accounts after the performance, rendering herself virtually unreachable.

"I'm sorry I can't commit to any engagements," Noelle replied. "All my free time in Snowing Rock will be devoted to practicing. When I return to Saint Augustine, I'll share the concert stage at the Forum Theater with Colin Rudovich."

One of the customers at the register pressed her hands to her chest. "Mr. Rudovich is one of the finest pianists in the world! I've bought all his recordings!"

Noelle sighed heavily, said nothing, and finished counting the woman's change.

"I've heard praise regarding Noelle Wentworth's performances, also," a familiar, deep male voice rang through the shop.

Noelle snapped her head up. The shop grew quiet as Gabe Waters entered. He removed his sunglasses, placed them in his pocket, and pushed back his wavy chestnut hair. He'd shaved. She hadn't expected to see him again, but here he stood, looking tall, dark, and well ... extraordinarily handsome. He wore black fitted jeans and the same olive green parka. His hazel eyes mesmerized her, and her feet decided to root themselves to the floor.

"Gabe?" Noelle asked. He was so masculine, with his broad shoulders and powerful build, and he seemed out of place in a candle shop wafting with feminine aromas of lavender and beeswax.

"I think so." He exaggerated a look around, then met her gaze. An unhurried smile worked its way across his features. "Did you get your luggage?"

"Yes, the bus company delivered my suitcases this morning." She paused, feeling her cheeks warm with embarrassment because of her panicked reaction at the hospital. "Sorry about last night ... I had so much on my mind."

She'd acted like a coward and had run off with no plausible explanation. For the past year, she'd fought hard to overcome her fears and insecurities, although she'd failed miserably at the hospital.

He held up a hand. "Perfectly understandable after the trauma of the bus accident. I could've driven you to your aunt's cottage if you'd been able to wait."

"You were needed in two places at once, the hospital and the accident scene," Noelle said. "You didn't need a third obligation when my aunt's cottage was within walking distance."

"You're not an obligation, Noelle."

"I called the hospital and a nurse told me that Mrs. Fernandez will be monitored a few more days," Noelle said. "How's Anjali?"

"She seemed fine when I left. She's staying with her aunt and uncle until her father gets back. He's been working out of town. Fortunately, kids are resilient."

"I plan on visiting both of—" Noelle began.

"I assume you'll wait until Mrs. Fernandez gets home to visit them," Gabe finished. They both smiled.

Lucia Crandall made a beeline for Gabe, wrapping her fingers around the slight, wispy side layers of her hair. "When did you arrive back in town, Gabe? You usually call me."

"I arrived a couple days ago," he replied.

Lucia playfully touched his sleeve. "Dinner at my place tonight?" she asked, her lilting voice loud enough for the entire shop to overhear.

He kept his gaze on Noelle. "I'll text you, Lucia."

"I'll be waiting," Lucia's hand lingered on his sleeve while she eyed Noelle with disdain. "I couldn't help overhearing, and the invitation to play for our ladies' luncheon at the country club next month still stands. I'm on the board and background piano music would be delightful."

Before Noelle could respond, Lucia strutted to the door, pausing at the shop's front window where Caroline arranged several cranberry glass votives on a silver tray, affixing pine cones and holly berries to the glass.

"One of your candles is smoking, Caroline. Your distributor used too much fragrance oil," Lucia said. She swiveled, gave a smart wave in Gabe's direction, and exited the shop.

Noelle sighed. "Everyone's a candle expert except me."

An enigmatic smile tugged at the corner of his lips. "And me."

She met his gaze. "May I help you find anything?"

His gaze warmed. "I'm shopping for my cousin, Holly. Remember I told you about her last night? Our dads were brothers. She's getting married on December twenty-second and I'm the only groomsman."

"And her little boy, Devin, is the reason you keep a car seat in your Land Rover."

"And Devin is the ring-bearer."

Aware of how quiet the shop had suddenly become, Noelle glanced around. Every customer seemed preoccupied with candles and pricing, although Noelle had the feeling they were listening intently to every word of her conversation with Gabe.

"Holly wants to have both her wedding and reception at my place. I converted one of the old barns on my property into a large hall." Gabe grinned ruefully. "That is, if she doesn't change her mind, because she's canceled the wedding once already."

"Doesn't she want to get married?"

"She's the restless type. She's finishing a Master's Degree in Interior Design at Virginia Tech. She knows I'm a planner, and she's asked me to arrange the candle details."

"Candle details?" Noelle repeated.

He nodded. "She wants an evening candlelight ceremony and she's insisting on one particular scent from your shop." Gabe pulled a piece of paper from his wallet. "Candleglow and Mistletoe."

"Your cousin has excellent taste because Candleglow and Mistletoe is our signature holiday fragrance." Caroline held up a deep-green candle and waved Noelle and Gabe over to the display. "There's notes of sandalwood and vetiver in the aroma."

"I'm not sure what vetiver is, although I detect a hint of cedar and fir trees. The scent is woodsy and a little sweet." Noelle laughed and held up the jar. "At least that's what the description says." She handed the candle to Gabe.

He sniffed and shrugged. "My house is in the woods, and my cousin wanted a Christmassy wedding, so this candle fits the bill."

Noelle laughed and walked to the cash register. "You're certainly easy to please."

He grinned, the dimple on his chin prominent. "Whatever

makes my cousin happy. I'm overprotective of her, but she's marrying a great guy. His name is John and they're crazy about each other. He's responsible and stable and he'll be a good father to Devin."

A few minutes later, Gabe took his place at the back of the cash register line, his arms laden with a dozen Candleglow and Mistletoe candle jars. When he stepped to the register, he placed the candles on the counter and handed Noelle his credit card. "I'm setting up six long tables for the reception and will put two or three candles on each, so I'll need a half dozen more. I'll pay for all of them now. Some of them I may put aside as extra gifts for Holly."

Caroline called from the display window. "Candleglow and Mistletoe is in short supply because we keep selling out, but we should be able to get more in. Let me check." She disappeared into the back room.

Noelle bit her lip and attempted to appear confident. "Would you like these candles gift-wrapped?" she asked crisply. She was all thumbs when it came to wrapping gifts.

"Yes, please."

Fortunately, the transaction went smoothly. Uttering silent appreciation to the heavens above, Noelle handed Gabe back his credit card and thanked him for his purchases.

She glanced at the clock. Twelve fifteen. At this rate, she'd never break for lunch and practice octaves. She whirled, measuring and cutting festive gold paper, wrapping each candle separately. She tied on bright satin-red bows, stepped back, and smiled approvingly. Not bad for a beginner, she decided.

"Very nice, Noelle. Thank you," Gabe said with a grin. "Now I'd like to take you to lunch."

Adamantly, she shook her head. "Thanks, but I'm too busy."

"There are details about my cousin's wedding I can't

begin to comprehend and I'd appreciate a competent, beautiful woman's advice," he said.

Her smile faded. "You picked out the candles."

"Even I know there's more to a wedding than candles."

Yes, Noelle thought. There was commitment in good times and in bad.

And trust, feeling certain that she could rely on her husband, assured that he would be there for her. She sighed. All of that had been lacking in her marriage to Colin Rudovich.

Sadly, the word 'love' hadn't come to mind because, in hindsight, her relationship with her ex had been one-sided. She'd been impressed with his drive to succeed. He'd married her solely to further his career. After a time, she was just a pretty, crowd-pleasing accessory. The media had loved seeing the husband and wife duo perform together on the concert stage.

With a weak nod, Noelle said, "My dreadful marriage to a flamboyant, domineering concert pianist ended in divorce. You'll have to look elsewhere for wedding advice."

"Therein lies the problem," Gabe countered. "My dreadful marriage to a narcissistic, British film star ended in divorce. So. besides attending the same high school, we share something else in common. Our divorces."

CHAPTER 4

$\mathcal{B}$efore Noelle could ask what Gabe had meant by his high school comment, Caroline emerged from the back room.

"Bad news and good news, Mr. Waters," Caroline said. "The bad news is that Candleglow and Mistletoe candles are almost out of stock. The good news is I've been able to order more and the candles should arrive before Christmas."

"Thanks, Caroline." Gabe bestowed a charming smile. "If you don't anticipate the shop being busy for the next hour, I'd like to take your boss to lunch. I'll pick up the candles later."

Caroline waved toward the door. "Yup, not a problem. The shop quiets around this time and I'll take my lunch when Noelle get back. If business slows this afternoon, I'll teach her how to make candles."

Noelle gulped back horrified laughter. "Do I really need to learn?"

Making candles seemed too difficult, involving wicks and hot wax and proper temperatures.

Caroline blithely flung Noelle's question aside. "Yes, if

you want to teach our first class on Saturday night, Miss Saint Augustine."

A few beats later, Noelle pulled on her high boots and cream-colored jacket. Whirling a scarf around her neck, she tucked her hair beneath her knitted cap. "I can't be long for lunch because I want to practice Brahms," Noelle said, as Gabe guided her to the shop's doorway.

The charming smile lingering on his features vanished. "I won't take up much of your time. There's a sub place a few doors down and the service is quick." He pointed toward a building at the end of the street. "Do you want me to call ahead and place a rush order?"

He watched her closely, without a hint of animosity in his gaze.

She glanced uncertainly at him. "I'm sorry I was rude. There's no need to hurry."

The corners of his lips turned up, apparently mollified by her abrupt change of attitude. "You arrived in Snowing Rock last evening by a bus that crashed. Understandably, you're overwhelmed and preoccupied," he said.

A fierce blast of cold wind caused Noelle to lose her breath as she stepped onto the frozen sidewalk beside him. Her hair blew off her forehead.

Gabe gently touched her temple. "That bang made quite a bump."

She shrugged off his hand, pausing to regard her reflection in the candle shop's front window, adjusting her side-swept bangs to cover the bump. Then gliding past him, she slipped on the ice.

His hand shot out and captured her elbow. "Winter in Snowing Rock is a lot different from Saint Augustine. Fortunately, I'm here to save you from bus accidents and slick sidewalks." His white teeth flashed a leisurely, wide smile.

While they walked, Gabe kept a firm grip on her elbow.

Noelle stopped to marvel at the streetlights decorated with holly and ivy. Bright purple bows glittered like sparkling icicles from each of the storefronts. She sniffed the fragrant, sweet smell of roasted chestnuts when they passed a street vendor. People stood in line, walking away with brown paper bags brimming with warm chestnuts.

"The town feels so Christmassy, although it's only early November," she noted.

"Snowing Rock is considered Christmas Town, remember?"

She tried to capture the memory nagging at her. "Have you and I met before?"

"If we did meet, I couldn't bear to imagine that I was so forgettable," he said softly.

She bit her bottom lip. "Before my parents and I moved to New York City, I attended Snowing Rock High for one year, when I was a freshman."

"And I was a senior and looked different fifteen years ago."

She nodded politely while pushing the notion that they'd ever met from her mind. She hadn't had time to date when she'd been in high school. All her free hours had been devoted to piano practice. That's why she needed to get back to Saint Augustine and perform, to prove to herself that all those practice hours hadn't been in vain.

Gabe brushed a snowflake from her face and reclaimed her elbow. He nodded toward the end of the street. "There's Hal's Subs. You can see the sign from here."

A few minutes later, he opened the door for her, guiding her inside the bustling restaurant, tipping his head to people as they passed. He stopped a teenage waiter and placed an extra order, giving an address Noelle didn't recognize. Then he accepted her coat, removed his parka, and hung their coats on a coat rack near their booth.

Noelle checked the time on her cell phone. If their order came quickly, she'd still have time to reach her aunt's cottage and practice Brahms.

"Coffee?" Gabe slid into the booth seat across from her and stretched his long legs beneath the table. He wore a v-neck navy blue sweater that emphasized his muscular build. He grabbed two menus and glasses of water from a passing waiter and handed a menu to her. "I recommend the whole-wheat turkey sub topped with grilled vegetables because it's the best in town."

Noelle perused the menu. "Thanks, but coffee and a chef salad is perfect." She regarded him, surprised he was sweating despite the cold weather. "You look pale," she remarked.

He shrugged. "I worked out this morning and probably pushed myself too far."

Preoccupied, she nodded and glanced at the time on her cell phone, calculating how long the waiter would take to revisit their table so they could place their orders. She curled her hands together beneath the table and darted Gabe a glance. He was smiling at her. She, on the other hand, was being bad-mannered to a man who'd been very kind. Didn't she at least owe him her attention during a short lunch?

The teenage waiter headed over, paper and pen in hand. After they'd finished ordering, Gabe leaned forward and asked, "How do you like working in your aunt's candle business?"

Noelle composed her features, unwilling to admit how under-qualified she felt.

"It's not the antiquated shop I remember from fifteen years ago," she said. "And Caroline mentioned that my aunt plans to continue the expanding, selling homemade beeswax candles online, and perhaps internationally."

Gabe grinned at her over the glass's rim. "Your aunt must be tech-savvy."

"She isn't, and neither am I." Noelle waved her hand dismissively at herself, then perched her chin on her hands. "What do you do for a living? I'm guessing you might be a lumberjack?"

"Why would you think that?"

She shrugged. "You seem so outdoorsy. I visualize you living in a cabin in the woods."

He smiled. "I'm a stuntman for feature films."

She blinked. He'd spoken so nonchalantly. The resultant beat of silence was punctuated by the hum of people's conversations and the juke box playing 'I'll Be Home For Christmas' sung by Bing Crosby.

Noelle laughed nervously. "You're a stuntman for famous actors who don't want to perform their own stunts?"

"Something like that."

"Isn't that a dangerous gig?"

He laughed softly. "The industry calls them gags, not gigs. Many stunt people are free-lance and in order to keep their jobs, they don't publicize their injuries."

"Have you ever been injured?"

"I'm known for driving fast race cars."

He was hedging, she thought. "Race cars that crash?" she pressed.

Gabe focused on the teenage waiter preparing their food behind the counter instead of meeting her gaze. "I've leapt out of a burning car or two."

"Were you ever hurt?"

Gabe was unnaturally quiet for a moment.

She clasped her hands together in her lap and regarded him. "I'm sorry. I'm asking too many questions."

"I don't mind." He met her searching gaze. "And yes ... I was hurt once. The race car I drove overturned and set fire.

It was a treacherous, high-risk stunt and the accident occurred for two reasons. Partly because I lost control, and partly because a shortcut had been taken regarding safety precautions."

"Were you okay?"

He grinned. "I'm here, aren't I? And 'Force Of Thunder' was a box office hit."

"I've never seen the film," Noelle admitted. "Although I can't imagine ..."

He brushed his knuckles across her hand. "No one was seriously hurt. Afterward, the director was delighted because the shot was spectacular."

"The director should've been more concerned with safety issues than a box office hit."

"I agree."

Judging by his curt response, Noelle assumed the subject of safety and uncaring directors wasn't a topic Gabe was eager to pursue, so she grappled for a lighter subject.

"So, you work with famous movie stars?" she asked brightly.

"You name one of the multi-million-dollar action movies in the last five years, and I've probably been featured in a car chase or two."

The teenage waiter brought their sandwich, salad, and coffee. Noelle said grace and Gabe joined in. Then she placed her napkin on her lap and sipped her coffee.

"You should eat," Gabe said. "You had a long, distressing night and busy morning."

She picked up her fork and eyed the sumptuous array of lettuce, cold cuts, and sliced avocado before taking a bite.

Gabe concentrated on his sandwich. When he was finished, he said, "Tell me about the illustrious musical career you're known for when you're not running a candle shop."

She set down her fork. "As I mentioned, I'm performing

in Saint Augustine on December fifteenth, so I'll only be in Snowing Rock a few weeks."

She tried to dispel the thoughts chattering through her mind—that no matter what she did or how hard she tried, the audiences would never forget her poor performance. After one memory lapse, she'd assumed her fans would rally around her. However, she'd learned she couldn't trust a fickle audience, making her fearful of counting on anyone.

Gabe's expression softened. "All that piano practice when you were a teenager paid off. I remember listening to you from the weight room at Snowing Rock High."

All she'd done in high school was practice chord balancing and scale technique. She'd never had a normal adolescence, never dated, never attended proms like the other girls.

Noelle's reflections were interrupted by the teenage waiter pouring her more coffee. She extended a 'thank you' and studied Gabe's rugged, chiseled face.

"I don't remember you, although you obviously remember me," she said.

"Your piano music from that practice room motivated me to bench press four hundred pounds. I decided if you could practice that hard, then I could work out in the gym even harder."

"What did you do when I played slow, dreamy, piano pieces like Debussy?" she joked.

His smiled widened. He reached across the table and claimed her hands in his. "I'd slow my pace to match yours and do five squat thrusts instead of ten."

Throughout the remainder of lunch, she sat straight and alert as Gabe shared his most dangerous stunts and exploits with her. He answered her questions promptly while she relished the food, enjoying the bustling, upbeat atmosphere of the sub shop. He was witty and charming. He made her laugh out loud, his light-hearted banter contagious.

When the waiter waded into their conversation and placed a check on the table, Noelle realized that she and Gabe were somehow still holding hands.

She pulled from his grasp. "I need to get back to my aunt's cottage and practice before I return to the shop." She stood and pulled her wallet from her purse.

Gabe stilled her hand. "Please. I insist on paying."

"No." She shook her head, immediately mistrusting his motives. She didn't want to owe him anything. "I'll pay for myself."

He looked genuinely annoyed. "I invited you, remember? And we never got to discuss my cousin's wedding. You can reciprocate next time."

"I'm sure all the details of the wedding have been planned perfectly." She handed him the money for her portion of the bill. "Sorry, but there'll be no next time. I'm returning to Saint Augustine in a month and between the candle shop and practicing, I'm too busy."

* * *

As HE ESCORTED Noelle to her aunt's cottage, Gabe shielded her from the wind by walking backwards in front of her. He shared hilarious tidbits about well-known movie stars, continuing to wave off the perilous aspects of his job.

When they reached the doorstep of her aunt's cottage, he told her that he'd be spending the remainder of the afternoon at an outreach center he'd recently opened for wayward teens.

"Would you like to see the center sometime?" he asked. "We're putting together a Christmas musical to give teens something to do and keep them off the streets. We could use your musical expertise."

"Perhaps."

"Good answer." He chuckled. "I'll call you at the shop, all right? In the meantime, take care of that bump." He waited for her to step into the foyer, then changed direction and strode down the street.

Inside her aunt's cottage, Noelle waited for the kettle to boil, folded her aunt's red crocheted blanket neatly on the flowered couch, then eyed the fireplace. How festive the wooden mantel would look decorated with fresh poinsettia plants, embellished with deep green Candleglow and Mistletoe candles flanking each corner.

Noelle leaned back on the couch, a surprising heaviness in her chest at the thought of leaving the cozy cottage, nestled in the pine trees, for her air-conditioned Saint Augustine high-rise.

What if she spent Christmas in Snowing Rock after her performance? She and Aunt Joy could hang two red burlap stockings on the mantel and decorate a pine-scented Christmas tree with multi-colored, twinkling lights.

Noelle hadn't celebrated Christmas since her parents had passed, because she hadn't had the heart for festivities. And Colin, her ex, hadn't been interested in Christmas, declaring the entire holiday commercialized and a waste of time.

She set her teacup on an end table, went to the piano, and adjusted the squeaky piano stool. She tilted her head back and closed her eyes, visualizing the music before she played. Her hands struck a deep, resonant, bass octave, the last passage of the Brahms.

Her right foot pushed the damper pedal and something inside the piano snapped with a sharp cracking noise. The damper pedal stuck, the most important pedal on the piano, and every note of the bass chord she'd struck with gusto rang on and on.

She groaned aloud. The vertical rod must've fallen out.

On her phone, she searched the internet and found a listing for a piano tuner and technician in Fisher's Crossing. She called the tuner and left an urgent message.

Assuring herself she still had five minutes before reporting to the candle shop, she stretched out on her back and peered inside the piano.

She identified the problem and attempted to insert the pin back into the lever hole. The pin failed to cooperate, and she bumped her head as she slid out from beneath the piano.

Now what? Noelle closed her eyes for a moment, then stood and straightened.

Simple. As soon as she arrived at the cottage this evening, she'd try again. Because if the damper pedal couldn't be fixed, the piano was useless, and she couldn't practice.

She sank onto the couch and gulped an unsteady breath.

Her heartbeat raced at the thought of another failed performance on stage. If that happened, would her concert career truly be over?

CHAPTER 5

*A*fter Caroline checked out early the following day to see Alan at the pizzeria, Noelle planned to close the candle shop by six. Whenever she'd had a moment, she'd gone over in her mind the steps to fixing the piano's damper pedal. Perhaps she needed more light when she was beneath the piano. Perhaps she needed to consult an instruction manual. Perhaps she should try calling another piano technician.

She shook her head repeatedly. She'd only been in Snowing Rock a short while and she'd already lost valuable practice time.

Through endless false smiles, six o'clock sped to seven, and Noelle rang up the last customer of the evening. She congratulated herself on how adept she'd become at running the cash register in only one day. And the ledgers had tallied up perfectly.

In the darkness of a cold November night, Noelle walked the few blocks to the town's senior rehab center. Humming the opening Chopin melody softly to herself, she stopped at her aunt's room on the first floor, knocked once, and stepped inside.

"Noelle?" Aunt Joy sat in a wheelchair by the window and craned her head. She opened her arms and Noelle rushed into them. Her aunt's shoulders shook with weeping. "My dear niece, you look beautiful. You're so slim, so tall," Aunt Joy dabbed her eyes with a hot-pink fringed handkerchief she clutched tightly in her hands.

Noelle planted a kiss on her aunt's wrinkled cheek. Aunt Joy was the only family she had left, now that Noelle's parents had passed.

Noelle stepped back. "And you haven't changed a bit in fifteen years."

Aunt Joy wore a red, white, and blue tie-dyed tee shirt and no make-up except for bright blue eye shadow, which highlighted the pale blue of her eyes. Her long gray hair flowed over her shoulders and heavy green bohemian earrings dangled from her pierced ears.

Fresh tears stung Noelle's eyes. She'd missed her independent Aunt Joy, a woman who spoke her own mind. Surprisingly, she was beginning to feel very much at home here in this picturesque, quirky mountain town.

Coyly, her aunt slanted a straw fedora hat on her head. "Do you enjoy working at 'Scents of Joy'?"

"You'll be pleased to know that your shop was very busy." Noelle evaded the question. "As long as Caroline doesn't quit, everything will continue to operate smoothly."

"You're a capable young woman and I know I can rely on you as well, dear." Aunt Joy offered a convincing smile. "Although, I'll miss Caroline when she attends NYU next year. She's been offered a full scholarship."

Noelle met her aunt's smile. "She plans to study marketing and marry a successful banker."

"Sounds like Caroline, planning her life in ambitious detail."

Noelle pulled off her cream-colored jacket. "Anyway, how are you feeling?" she asked.

"The doctor said I should be able to return to the shop by the first week of December. I've done enough physical therapy and rehab to last a lifetime and I'm ready to leave." Aunt Joy scraped a hand through her hair. "Do we need to order more inventory?"

"Probably by the weekend," Noelle replied. "Certainly Candleglow and Mistletoe candles are big sellers."

"I stocked more than a half dozen boxes of candles."

Noelle threw open the heavy draperies and gazed out at a flint-gray sky. "Those candles were sold. A customer named Gabe Waters came into the shop and bought them all."

Aunt Joy gave a bark of laughter and Noelle pivoted.

"Gabe Waters came into my shop? He's one of our most famous residents and he's the highest paid stuntman in Hollywood, although lately most of his film work has been shot in Wilmington."

Aunt Joy's face glowed with chirpy interest, which Noelle attributed to her aunt's avid fascination with show business. When her aunt was younger, she'd been featured as an extra in a movie and had talked about the experience for years.

"He was at the bus accident the other night and acted quickly to save a woman who'd fallen down an embankment, and—"

Her aunt stopped Noelle with a sharp smile. "He recently opened an outreach center for disadvantaged youths near the edge of town where he lived when he was a teenager. Gabe's younger cousin hung out with a bad crowd—drugs, alcohol, you name it. That cousin, I believe her name was Holly, was a heap of trouble. Both cousins had neglectful, drug-addicted parents. They were left alone quite often."

Noelle considered the information. "Holly's getting married in Snowing Rock in December. At least, Gabe hopes she is," Noelle clarified. "I helped him select candles for the wedding. Well, mostly Caroline helped. Then he took me to lunch."

Aunt Joy swung her wheelchair round to face Noelle. "He renovated a house in Snowing Rock and is now living there because he dislikes big-city living. Here, he's treated like one of the locals."

"He said he remembered me from high school," Noelle said.

Her aunt sat straighter in her wheelchair, her gaze observant and alert. "He was constantly picked on by bullies because he was a weak, sickly kid. Years ago, I remember someone saying he had a mad crush on you after you stopped a fight between him and—"

"A fight." Noelle hesitated, the remembrances coming back in a rush. When she'd been a freshman, she'd seen two older guys shouting at each other outside a classroom. The bigger guy was pushing and shoving Gabe, jabbing at Gabe's chest with his fingers. Gabe didn't back down, but he didn't throw his fists at the bully, either.

She drew a breath, the words tumbling out. "After I shouted at the guys to stop fighting, Gabe would never meet my gaze in the hallway again."

"He was a senior and probably embarrassed because a freshman girl had protected him in front of his classmates."

Surprise mingled with Noelle's protest. "I hardly protected him. From what I heard, before the end of the school year he'd fought that same bully and won."

"Remember the high school Christmas dance?" Aunt Joy asked.

"Yes." Noelle's recollections circled. "My parents had bought me a red sequined dress. I felt uncomfortable—I didn't know where to stand, where to put my hands. I didn't relate well to my peers because my parents didn't stay in one place long enough. They were always searching for a better piano professor for my lessons and subsequently, I never developed true friendships." Noelle shook her head. "I left the dance early. There was a mistletoe in the doorway and I looked around to be sure no one was watching before I dashed under it and out the nearest exit."

"I was a chaperone and you looked stunning that night. Gabe couldn't take his eyes off you."

Noelle paused, calling to mind the small, thin teen, now a strong, rugged man. "Gabe looks like an actor."

Aunt Joy's eyes gleamed shrewdly. "And most attractive, especially on a big movie screen."

Noelle smiled, envisioning his rough, attractive features.

'I couldn't bear to imagine that I was so forgettable,' he'd said softly.

Her smile wavered. If she had more than a few weeks in Snowing Rock, she might enjoy spending time with him. He was funny and endearing and interesting.

Noelle kissed her aunt on the cheek as she prepared to leave. Her conscience nagged because she was already two days behind in her practice regimen. "Also, Aunt Joy, the damper pedal snapped on your piano. I called a piano technician in Fisher's Crossing."

Aunt Joy sank back in her wheelchair. "No technician will venture up the mountain until the snow subsides, and another storm is predicted within the next couple of days. Have a bite to eat tonight, and rest. Your practice can wait."

Determination fluttered in Noelle's chest. "I'll rest after December fifteenth. My performance must be extraordinary or I'll never be accepted in the concert world again. After what happened last year I'm surprised that Colin forgave—"

"Knowing your ex, he's gaining in some way, probably

through increased ticket sales," her aunt interrupted flatly. "And I won't forget how he treated you when you weren't feeling well."

"I had assumed my bloating and nausea were related to exhaustion and stress," Noelle said. "And Colin was either practicing or performing. You know how driven he was, especially after his mother died. Then his father's expectations rose even higher." Noelle shook her head. "I'm sorry I waited so long to see a doctor, because he said my fertility might be decreased. I don't want children yet, but someday ... and if I can't ..."

Noelle paused, remembering the empathy Gabe had shown toward Anjali. Her ex, on the other hand, couldn't tolerate children. They were too noisy and jumpy, he'd declared.

Aunt Joy patted Noelle's hand. "If you slow down, someday you'll have children. If not children of your own, then you can adopt." Her smile was gentle, her tone kind-hearted. "Don't let ambition cause you to lose sight of what's really important."

Noelle gazed directly into her aunt's perceptive eyes. "All my parents wanted was for me to succeed. I wasn't there for them when they died, and they were always there for me. I failed them."

"What could you have done differently? You were in a different state when the car crash happened and you arrived at the hospital shortly afterward. Confront your supposed failure, view it as a learning experience, and keep moving forward." Aunt Joy's hand stayed resting on Noelle's. "You're mistaking your parents' ambitions with your own. You'll succeed by not overdoing things."

After quick farewells, Noelle departed for her aunt's cottage. She didn't take time to rest, nor eat, as her aunt had suggested. Instead, Noelle lay on her back, shining her phone's flashlight at the small lever beneath the piano.

She cursed the piano, something she'd never done before, because the lever didn't fit no matter how hard she tried.

And if she couldn't practice, she'd fail. And if she failed a second time, how could she ever show her face on the concert stage again?

CHAPTER 6

On Friday evening, Noelle was able to leave the shop by six o'clock. That hadn't been easy, because closing meant restocking, dusting and mopping, and balancing the shop's tills.

With a relieved sigh, she pulled on her red, wooly gloves and cream-colored jacket, covered her ears with her red wool hat, then trooped four blocks to the Fernandez's two-story house. Snowing Rock reminded her of a make-believe, wintry hamlet, the icy-blue snow reflecting the glow from polished brass street lamps.

She stepped to the entrance of the Fernandez household and rang the front doorbell.

Anjali opened the door and threw her arms around Noelle's waist. "Hi, Miss Noelle! Come on in!" Her child-like enthusiasm was infectious.

"I'm so glad to see you again!" Noelle laughed.

"Mommy's home from the hospital!" Anjali grabbed Noelle's hand and towed her to the living room.

Mrs. Fernandez sat on the couch with a plaster cast on one leg, a pair of crutches set beside the couch.

Noelle hugged Mrs. Fernandez, then handed her a jasmine candle with a red velvet bow.

Mrs. Fernandez opened the candle jar and sniffed. "Thank you. Jasmine is my favorite fragrance. So delicate."

"And Jasmine is supposed to be a good scent for sleeping," Noelle pointed out.

"Who can sleep in this busy house?" Mrs. Fernandez gestured around the living room, littered with an array of plush stuffed animals, a dollhouse, and a ballerina puppet.

A woman strongly resembling Mrs. Fernandez stepped from the kitchen into the room. She had graying hair at the temples, her hair pulled back in a severe bun, accentuating her round cheeks and double chin. She flashed a smile.

"This is Nancy, my sister. She lives next door," Mrs. Fernandez said. "She's assisting me with my Christmas baking orders. I can't get around easily and the doctor said I'll wear this cast another six weeks. Apparently, it takes a while to heal from a broken leg."

Anjali did a cartwheel across the room. "Our house always smells delicious because Mommy and Aunt Nancy bake cookies for everyone in Snowing Rock!"

"Not everyone, Anjali," Aunt Nancy corrected, before swiveling back to the kitchen.

"What's your specialty?" Noelle asked Mrs. Fernandez. "Cakes or cookies?"

Mrs. Fernandez glanced sideways toward the kitchen. "Our plain butter Christmas cookies are very popular. We use powdered sugar, butter, flour, and vanilla."

For a moment, Noelle speculated about asking Mrs. Fernandez if she could offer any tips on baking sugar cookies. That is, until she spotted the upright piano half-hidden behind a pile of blankets in the far corner of the room.

Noelle revolved in a deliberate circle. "You own a piano?"

"Yes. I mentioned on the bus that Anjali's very musical."

For a few minutes, Mrs. Fernandez kept up a one-sided conversation about Snowing Rock's kindergarten choir while Noelle eyed the piano.

"We adopted Anjali from India when she was a baby," Mrs. Fernandez was saying. "My husband wants her to take piano lessons when she gets older."

"Piano lessons will give Anjali the solid foundation she needs to understand music and play other instruments." Noelle edged closer toward the piano. With a spurt of inspiration, she inquired, "May I play your piano? I'm staying at my Aunt Joy's cottage and the pedal on her piano is broken."

Mrs. Fernandez relaxed against the sofa. "Ours is an old player piano. There should be a music roll in the spool box. Pull the lever bar, open the compartment doors, and start pumping the pedals. 'A Holly, Jolly Christmas' is on the spool."

"I don't need to pump the pedals. I'm a professional pianist and I'm preparing for a concert in Saint Augustine next month." Noelle moved the blankets to the side, sat on the bench, and played several octaves.

Nancy appeared at the kitchen doorway with a soapy dish in her hand. "You're a professional piano player? Can you play 'We Need A Little Christmas'? I enjoy hearing music when I'm washing dishes."

Noelle's forehead knit into a frown. Apparently, a serious Chopin etude wasn't the top choice on anyone's play list.

Anjali dashed to the piano. "I can play! Wanna hear, Miss Noelle?" Anjali found the E key and pressed three times. "Jin gle bells, jin gle bells. Isn't that good?"

"Excellent!" Noelle clapped her hands in approval while Anjali gave a triumphant hoot.

"If you need a piano to practice, you're welcome to come over on Sunday afternoons," Mrs. Fernandez said.

"Thanks," Noelle accepted, abandoning the idea of practicing during this visit.

She stood and admired the huge floral arrangement set on the shelf beside the piano, a 'Be Happy' mug bursting with yellow roses.

"The bouquet was delivered yesterday," Mrs. Fernandez remarked. "It's from Mr. Gabe Waters, the famous stuntman. Anjali said he was the first person to come to my aid at the bus accident."

Noelle flicked her gaze upward. Somehow, the conversation had shifted from piano practice to Gabe.

"Yes, he acted swiftly and bravely," Noelle agreed.

"The doctor said that Mr. Waters saved me from developing hypothermia."

Noelle sniffed the sweet fragrance of the roses, and read the hand-written card attached. 'I wanted to brighten your home and your spirits. Wishing you a speedy recovery. Gabe.'

In fairness, he was generous and considerate. And he hadn't hesitated in risking his life to rescue Mrs. Fernandez.

"He also sent dinner last night from the sub shop on Main Street," Mrs. Fernandez finished.

Anjali twirled around the living room and landed on the floor beside her mother. "I love subs! How did Mr. Gabe know my favorite sub was wheat bread with banana peppers and turkey? He's a super-hero and can read minds!"

"Anjali, Mr. Waters called me to find out your favorite sub ahead of time," Mrs. Fernandez clarified.

Anjali rubbed her eyes. "Do superheroes always win, Miss Noelle?"

"Always," Noelle said emphatically.

The little girl tilted her head. "Then Mommy's right and Mr. Gabe's not a super-hero. Wanna hear how I know?"

"Absolutely!" Noelle lowered her gaze and hid her laugh.

Anjali's almond eyes gleamed. "Mr. Gabe played checkers

with me in the hospital and he couldn't beat me. Not once, although he said he really, really tried." Anjali embellished her deduction with another twirl.

Noelle smiled. She had to admit that Gabe was pretty great, even if he wasn't a superhero.

CHAPTER 7

$\mathcal{N}$oelle rushed into the candle shop at nine on Saturday morning wielding a tray of homemade butter cookies. Admittedly, some of the cookies were doughy because she hadn't waited for the oven to pre-heat, although she'd been able to salvage two dozen. The rest of the cookies had been burned beyond recognition because she'd forgotten about them as she'd tried to fix the piano's damper pedal.

She'd been unsuccessful, and silent piano practice wasn't going well.

A shriek of cold wind helped blow the candle shop's door open. She shook her tingling fingertips and changed into flat, red shoes to offset her black leggings. Then she pulled off her light gray wool scarf, winter wool hat, and smoothed her red tunic sweater to her wrists.

Her body shivered while she thawed out and admired the glow of lit candles placed around the shop, sifting scents of eucalyptus, cranberry, and Fraser pine through the air.

"Good morning, Miss Saint Augustine," Caroline greeted Noelle with her usual happy grin. She stood behind the cash register and flipped a turquoise skinny braid behind her ear. "Those cookies look good."

"Thanks." Noelle stepped to the back room, hung her coat, and placed the sugar cookies on the counter. "Last night, I ate a dozen that burned and I'm still on a sugar rush. If I keep eating at this rate, I won't be able to fit into my black formal gown for my piano performance."

"You're tall and trim and will look dazzling in a long black gown. Besides, calories don't count if the cookies are burned." Caroline laughed, then grew serious. "We've received an order for ten vanilla scented beeswax votive candles this morning from Mr. Waters."

"I thought he wanted Candleglow and Mistletoe candles for his cousin's wedding?"

"Apparently, he wants beeswax candles, too."

"Do we have any in stock?" Noelle asked.

"A few. I placed an order this morning for the additional candles, and they should arrive well before the wedding."

An hour later, Noelle realized that the time had passed in a blur. Polar-white snow battering against the shop's front window hadn't deterred the enthusiastic candle shoppers.

"I wish our candle-making class started earlier tonight, don't you, Noelle?" Caroline prompted when the endless stream of customers had slowed.

Noelle would've rather wished for her aunt's piano to have a working damper pedal, although she didn't want to confide that wish to Caroline and deflate Caroline's enthusiasm.

"I've never made a candle before, remember?" Noelle softened her response with a kindly smile.

"You'll love it! And I'm available as long as you need me tonight because Alan is working at the pizzeria until midnight."

"Your relationship with Alan seems to be getting serious.

With your math skills, I thought you wanted to open a successful office and marry a New York banker?"

Caroline shrugged. "Alan's a nice guy and treats me like a princess." She beamed a welcoming smile to two customers entering the shop. "Welcome to 'Scents of Joy'!"

In spite of Caroline's endless exuberance, Noelle rubbed her forehead. It didn't take a genius to realize that Saturday was going to be a very long day.

* * *

NOELLE CLOSED the candle shop at six, placing a sign in the window to remind customers the candle-making class began at seven. Outside, battering gusts blew the street lights back and forth, and people held their coats close against them as they battled the onslaught of the wind.

Noelle had an hour to cash out and clean before organizing the supplies for the candle-making class. She made her way to the shop's tiny bathroom and wrung out several paper towels, pressing them against her forehead as a cold pack to refresh herself. She washed her face in the small sideways sink, then applied a dab of rose blush and red lip gloss.

She was tired and hungry. Surely her waistline would forgive her if she ate one tiny, doughy, butter cookie? She was still debating when she wandered to the front of the shop and peered out the window. The snow was falling hard and heavy, and occasionally a screech of wind rose up, then died down.

At six forty-five, a line of customers had formed. Winter had filled the streets and a pale moon hung high in the sky. It had stopped snowing and the clouds had moved on.

Caroline draped two long tables with plastic tablecloths and covered the tables with newspaper. Small mason jars, glass measuring cups, scissors, roughly chopped beeswax, and wicks sat in the center of each table. On a side counter, she'd plugged in a dozen crock pots in a row of extension cords. Several old washcloths were placed alongside for clean-up.

"There are supplies for at least a dozen people." Caroline lit several beeswax candles and placed them on the table, then veered to Noelle. "Can you get the butter cookies and make hot chocolate? I'm using a mix, so stir in boiling water."

"Sure." With a plan to eat at least three cookies, Noelle walked down the hallway to the storage room, stopping in mid-step when a large boom rattled the building. All the lights in the candle shop went out simultaneously and the hallway went black. She gripped a corner of the wall and looked around.

"Hey! You okay?" Caroline hurried toward Noelle carrying a stubby, lit candle. "A transformer must've blown because of the weight of the snow. Let's test all the fuses in the breaker panel and switch on the generator. I let the customers inside and invited them to find a seat."

After checking all the switches, they started the generator. The light in the shop would be low, but efficient. When they returned to the front, a half dozen women were seated at one table. From the corner of her eye, Noelle noted that a handsome man was seated at the second table.

"Hi, Noelle." Gabe stood and shrugged off his olive green parka.

His hazel eyes gleamed, his wavy chestnut hair wet with snow. He looked super attractive in dark, slim jeans and a cream-colored wool sweater hugging his sculpted shoulders.

"Gabe?" she asked blankly. "What are you doing at a candle class?"

"I've been at my outreach center since dawn. I was driving by the candle shop on my way home and saw the lights go out. I thought you might need some help." His gaze drifted appreciatively over her clingy, red tunic sweater. His admiring appraisal made her pulse quicken and she attributed her reaction to relief, knowing his capable presence could fix any problem if another should arise.

She extended her hands. "Thanks for stopping by. Caroline and I were able to figure out the generator."

He held her hands in his. "I called the power company and the estimated repair time is four hours." He glanced good-naturedly at the candles arranged on the tables. "You're definitely in the right business for this town."

"Snowing Rock might be good business for candles, although it's not so good for pianists who need to practice." Noelle surveyed the darkened shop and cash register and an appealing idea occurred. Without electricity, she wouldn't be able to ring up any supplies, therefore, she couldn't offer the candle-making class. Elation hummed through her veins. She could head back to her aunt's cottage to practice.

She dropped her hands from his. "Because of the power outage, we'll need to reschedule the class for next Saturday evening," she announced, amidst groans of dismay from the ladies. "Please help yourself to the cookies I baked before you leave. Have a safe drive—"

"Nonsense. You're all welcome to stay!" Caroline interrupted, oozing with enthusiasm. "There's candle power and enough electricity so the crock pots will melt the beeswax."

The ladies seated at the opposite table applauded their approval.

"And I'll pay for all the supplies." Gabe tipped his head toward the cash register, then back to Noelle. He winked. "You can add the cost to my wedding bill."

Noelle opened her mouth to sputter an objection and he lightly placed his finger on her lips. "As we say in the acting business, the show must go on. To repay my kindness, all I want is a cookie in return."

Pivoting on her heel, Noelle grabbed some cookies and napkins, tramped back to her seat, and handed him two cookies.

"Thanks." His lips twitched. "Have you ever made a candle, by the way?"

"Never. Have you?"

"No, but I'm willing to learn and I'm certain you're an excellent teacher."

One look at his joking grin and Noelle half-sighed. "I'm a pianist. I'm not qualified to teach this class."

"I am, though, Miss Saint Augustine." Tying a fresh white apron around her thick waist, Caroline called for attention. "In the center of the table are small-mouthed mason jars and #4 cotton square braided wicks." Caroline held up a mason jar. "Joy and I found that a fifty/fifty blend of palm oil mixed with beeswax will produce beautiful candles."

"Why palm oil?" Noelle asked.

"Because palm oil is softer, with a low melt point." Caroline grabbed some beeswax, measured twelve ounces in a glass measuring cup, then encouraged the class to do the same. "The crock pots are set on low and will allow the beeswax to melt slowly."

Noelle smiled. The brilliant math senior with the ever-changing hair color and merry demeanor spoke passionately about candle making and, consequently, made the topic interesting.

"While we're waiting, we'll waltz back to the table to measure and cut our wicks." Caroline held a fistful of wicks in her hand and danced back to the table. "Then we'll dip the wicks into the melted wax."

Gabe rested his arm on the back of Noelle's seat, his hand brushing against her shoulder.

"May I suggest the longer wick to your right?" He

stretched his legs beneath the table, his hard muscles pressing intimately against hers.

She took a bite of the second butter cookie he hadn't touched and leaned back, feeling content. "After one class you think you know more about making candles than I do, I presume?"

He chuckled. Reaching around her for the wick, his hand touched hers, his gaze drifting to her face. "I'd say we're equals."

He really was the most provoking man she'd ever met, she mused with a grin. "And I'd say that I'm the boss," she said.

They were so close, his face stopped within an inch of hers, his warm breath glancing over her cheeks as he tipped her chin up to meet his hazel eyes. "Whatever you say, boss."

An hour later, Noelle stood to admire her and Gabe's candles. He'd touched and brushed against her so much during the lesson, she almost didn't care that she'd missed precious piano practice time.

Her gaze met his. They'd poured in palm oil when the beeswax was completely melted and stirred each other's wax with a skewer.

"Caroline's instructions were to pour only one half inch of wax in the jar. However, I'll hold your wick in place if you'll hold mine," he said. "You'll notice that my wick is standing up on its own."

Noelle gulped back an exasperated laugh at his sensual insinuation. "So we're both officially candle makers." She poured the remaining hot wax into his jar, then hers, leaving a space at the top in order for the wax to harden.

He nodded toward a row of lit beeswax candles set in the

middle of the table and grinned roguishly. "You're beautiful by candlelight, Noelle. Red suits you."

"Always the charmer, Gabe." She felt herself flush, caught in the spell of his persuasive gaze. She offered a bright smile, submitting to his attraction, admitting to herself that she truly enjoyed being with him.

She looked around, taking in the empty shop. She and Gabe had been so absorbed with each other that she hadn't realized a couple of hours had sped by and all the customers had left.

His white teeth flashed an indulgent, slow smile. "I learned a new skill tonight."

Her gaze fell to the lively flickers of burning candles, the scents of honey warming the air. "Yes, it was fun."

Lightly, he pushed her hair back and touched her forehead. "Your bruise is gone."

"Bruise?" With awkward hands, she tried to restore order to her hair. "I'd forgotten about it."

He slipped his arm around her and pushed a wayward curl from her face. "Caroline said my candle is a bright, sunny yellow. How about yours?"

Noelle laughed aloud, realizing that since she'd sat beside him this evening, she hadn't fretted about her upcoming performance or her practice schedule.

"Caroline said that my candle hardened back to its original beeswax shade, which is the color it should be," she admonished him with a laugh.

His eyes were warm, a deep golden, the color of beeswax honey.

His gaze darkened. Unhurriedly, he bent his head and she knew he was going to kiss her.

She didn't resist, gazing up at the attractive man who offered her gentleness and affection. His lips came down to caress hers in a tender, unhurried kiss. His arms wrapped around her, pulling her closer. She closed her eyes and touched a hand to his sculpted chest.

Caroline cleared her throat. "Well, you two," she interrupted, bringing Noelle plummeting back to the reality of the candle shop.

Noelle stepped away from Gabe, feeling her ears heat, most likely to a bright red. Caroline had strolled over just in time to observe their quickly broken kiss.

Attached to her cell phone, Caroline continued, "Alan's getting out of the pizzeria early and treating me to a late-night date."

"Go have fun, Caroline," Noelle said. "I'll clean the shop. You deserve extra pay for all you do."

"You're not getting paid, either," Caroline reminded. "Your aunt said you're refusing the weekly salary she offered you."

Gabe's gaze shifted to the crock pots, discarded wicks, and strewn scissors. "And I won't let you to clean this shop by yourself, Noelle."

"I don't need any help." Noelle hesitated and took a long breath. Yes she did, if she wanted to retreat to her aunt's cottage and practice all thirty-six major and minor scales before midnight.

A fierce blast of wintry wind blew into the shop as a college-aged man strode in. His hair stood straight up in a military buzz cut and several piercings gleamed from his ears. His protruding nose was a deep, dark red, resembling the color of merlot wine.

Caroline tossed a glance toward him and her lips parted. "Hi Alan. This is Noelle and Mr. Gabe Waters."

"Hi everyone," Alan nodded. "And hi, hot stuff." Alan blew Caroline an air kiss while holding up a pizza box and bottle of water. "Anyone like pizza?"

"Thanks, I'm famished," Noelle said. Mentally, a part of

her tried to calculate how long it would take to eat a few pizza slices so that she could get back to her aunt's cottage and practice.

She stole a glance at Gabe's expectant, smiling expression, his handsome face. The other part of her acknowledged that she wanted to share a few extra minutes with him.

"The candle wax is easier to clean once it's hardened, and the newspaper should've caught most of the spills," Caroline was explaining to Gabe. "If you wash the crock pots, remember not to pour any of the water down the drain. I've clogged the drain a couple of times because there's always some melted wax left at the bottom of the pot."

After quick goodbyes to Caroline and Alan, Gabe grabbed an armload of paper towels and headed for the storage room. "I'll take these supplies and check on the generator, Noelle. Then we'll eat, all right?"

Noelle gathered wicks and empty jars. She eyed the empty cookie tray, feeling shaky and exhausted. She quickened her pace past the crock pots on the shelf and caught her foot on an extension cord. She tripped, bracing her right arm on the shelf to stop her fall while the wicks and empty jars clattered to the floor. The crock pot overturned, and a blinding pain seared through her as hot, melted wax poured across the back of her right hand.

She gasped aloud and stared at her burning hand. How could she practice piano? How would she perform at her concert? She froze, the air bursting in and out of her lungs.

"Noelle!" Gabe appeared in an instant. "What happened?"

Hastily, she wiped the tears coursing down her cheeks. "I tripped on the crock pot cords. I was rushing. I should've been paying closer attention."

"Don't be so hard on yourself. Those cords aren't usually there and were easy to miss." He examined her hand, steered her to the bathroom, and ran the cold water. "Looks like a first-degree burn, although it's too early to determine yet. Leave your hand beneath the water. I'll get my Land Rover and take you to the hospital."

Noelle complied, gasping at the stinging spray of cold water cutting into her hand as a knifelike burn. She tried to pull her hand away. "Please, Gabe. No hospitals."

"All right, I'll take you to your aunt's cottage." His expression changed from worry to acquiescence. Carefully, he rolled up the sleeves of her tunic. "You don't want your sleeves getting wet and changing to icicles."

"We can't leave Aunt Joy's shop such a mess." Nervously, Noelle fingered the hem of her tunic with her left hand. "The shop isn't cleaned and my aunt's very fussy—"

"I'll clean the shop later." Gabe stroked the hair from Noelle's forehead in a slow, soothing motion. His gesture made her tears flow harder, and he withdrew a clean white handkerchief from his pocket and wiped her cheeks.

"Keep your hand beneath the cold water while I get my Land Rover, all right?" He shrugged on his parka and grabbed the pizza box and water on his way out.

A few minutes later, he strode through the shop's entry and stamped the snow from his black work boots. He shut off the bathroom faucet, extinguished the beeswax candles, and helped her put on her boots, hat and coat.

Bleakly, she stared out the candle shop's front window, feeling imprisoned by a winter-white specter of glaring snow and naked trees. She dried her eyes once more with his proffered cotton handkerchief, thankful that her last gush of tears had eased. Ruefully, she shook her head. "Please, I can manage, Gabe."

"You don't have to be brave for me, Noelle," he said quietly.

She searched his face, seeing kindness and compassion etched on his strong features. "I'm too much of a bother."

He kept one arm around her and led her to the shop's entrance. "You'll never be a bother to me, all right?"

Briefly, she closed her eyes to will away the burning pain as she watched his tall frame trudge through the snow to open the passenger door, then hurry back to assist her.

He needed a shave. He'd admitted he'd been at his outreach center since dawn.

Yet he was concerned and endearing, never complaining nor asking anything in return. She didn't need to prove anything to him.

She handed him the keys to the candle shop and he assisted her into his Land Rover.

With a quiet exhale, she sank back into the comfortable leather seat and closed her eyes. Perhaps just this once, she'd rely on someone else, trust someone else. Just this once.

CHAPTER 8

Gabe watched Noelle's tight expression as he drove the short distance to her aunt's cottage. The streets were tomblike, dark and silent, the power still out. He parked in front of 10 Oak Street, slid out of the driver seat and used his cell phone's flashlight to guide Noelle inside.

The cottage was a single-storied house, cozy and old-fashioned. A snow shovel sat by the front door, and a woodsy fir tree scent lingered in the hallway as they entered the living room. Two Candleglow and Mistletoe candles, along with old, twisted matches, sat on the coffee table. Logs and kindling were neatly stacked beside the ceramic, wood-burning fireplace.

He flicked on the light switch for when the electricity would be restored, then helped Noelle take off her jacket and boots. He steered her to the flowered couch, setting a red crocheted blanket to one side. He placed the pizza on a nearby table and lit the candles.

The cheery warmth flooded the room.

Noting Noelle's slumped posture, he said calmly, "Let me see your hand again."

She held out her hand. "How bad? Tell me the truth."

"The burn site is swollen and red," he said. "Is it painful?"

"It stings." She frowned, then ventured guardedly. "Why?"

"Because the blister hasn't swelled nor opened." Carefully, he pressed on the burn and she winced. "The blisters whitened and that's a good sign. So far, the burn looks first-degree. Still, it can get worse and change to second-degree without warning."

"How long before it changes? Then what?"

"If the burn becomes red and shiny and swells more, we'll decide what to do next."

Her gaze flitted around the room. She fidgeted with the sleeves of her tunic sweater. "What if I can't practice? If I miss a day, my technique will suffer. I'll be in the limelight in Saint Augustine, and my performance must be perfect, without a mistake."

Gabe started for the kitchen. "Don't worry about practicing now. Sit back and I'll get a bowl of cold water."

"Should you add ice?" Her voice choked with tears. "I thought I'd read—"

As compassionately as he could, Gabe answered, "Ice causes frostbite and might damage your skin. Cold water will pull the heat away." He rummaged through the wooden cabinets in the tidy kitchen, surprisingly modern considering the rustic, stone exterior of the cottage.

He opened the stainless-steel refrigerator, relieved to find orange juice, because he felt a drop in his sugar levels imminent. He quickly checked his levels, found them low, then poured himself a glass of orange juice. Fortunately, they'd be eating pizza within fifteen minutes.

He tried to take good care of himself, managing his

diabetes by watching his diet and staying physically fit, although sometimes he got sidetracked.

While he filled a bowl on the counter with cold water, he blew out a breath. He was sidetracked all right, by power outages and candle-making classes and a beautiful, distressed blonde.

He returned to the living room to find that very same blonde curled up on the couch, blowing on her hand. Her hair fell in wisps around her heart-shaped face and she lifted her long, graceful fingers to push a strand behind her ear. Despite her lackluster movements, she presented such an entrancing image by candlelight that he forced himself to shove back the urge to pull her onto his lap and comfort her. Instead, he shifted and set the bowl of cold water on the coffee table.

"Put your hand in the water," he said. "And blowing on the burn doesn't help. In fact, it can lead to infection. Any chance your aunt keeps antibiotic cream and gauze and Ibuprofen in her medicine cabinet?"

"Probably, knowing how meticulous Aunt Joy is," Noelle replied.

He was already striding out of the room. He came back with some Ibuprofen tablets, glasses and two turquoise ceramic plates from the kitchen, along with antibiotic cream and gauze.

"I'll serve pizza first and then you can take Ibuprofen to head off the pain." He studied Noelle's complexion, devoid of color, and frowned. "When was the last time you ate?"

She half-smiled. "Do burned cookies from last night count?"

"No. Eat a slice of pizza, then take the Ibuprofen."

Her gaze narrowed briefly. "Can I remove my hand from the cold water?"

"Yes." He went to the bathroom sink and washed his

hands, returned to the living room with a hand towel, and dried her wound. Then, he applied antibiotic cream, gauze, and a bandage.

"The power and heat should be back on soon," he said. "In the meantime, I'll light a fire in the fireplace."

Using the dry wood and kindling and old twisted matches, a cozy fire soon spat at them.

A few minutes later, some color had touched her face, and her cheeks had pinkened.

"I like cold pizza," she said.

"I do, too." He poured water into their glasses and raised his glass. "A toast to cold pizza and warm fireplaces." He added a conspiratorial wink.

"And candlelight."

"And Candleglow and Mistletoe candles," he said.

She gave a thumbs-up with her left hand, then picked up her glass. She broke into a smile and they clinked glasses.

He gazed appreciatively over her slim form. Her attractiveness and feminine allure had prompted many high school guys to stop and stare, doing things, trying to impress her. She'd brushed them all off.

He sat beside her on the couch and patted his arm, signaling for her to lean against him. "You must be exhausted. I'll stay awhile and monitor your burn."

She stared fixedly at the bluish-orange flames of the fire and didn't answer.

He swept his arm around her. "All right?"

She nodded and leaned closer. "I've wanted to light a fire in the fireplace all week, but I'm so weighed down by all the responsibilities of running the shop. I don't have a moment to think and when I get back to the cottage at night it's so late and I'm tired and ..." She swallowed.

"Sometimes, life doesn't go the way we planned," he said softly.

She tipped her head up. "And you weren't always a stuntman."

He offered a non-committal nod. He'd needed to over-come his diabetes and build up his physique in order to fight all the bullies who'd picked on him. He'd been a skinny guy from the poorest section of town who'd learned to become self-reliant in order to survive.

Gabe dropped his arm from her shoulders, leaned forward on the couch, and fingered the rim of his water glass. "Life took me in a different direction," he said.

She examined the bandage and furrowed her brow. "I should be grateful the burn is on the back of my right hand. I'm left-handed. At least I can still eat."

He set down his glass and turned to her, gently running his forefinger across her high cheekbone. He'd always admired her dedication and perseverance. She was every-thing he'd remembered, fresh, vivacious, and astonishingly fearless despite her fragile outward appearance.

"You inspired me to succeed, did you know that?" he asked.

She waved a flippant hand at herself and leaned back. "Me? Hardly. Your success is your own and you should claim it. I've heard that you're the highest paid stuntman in the business and in great demand."

"And you've made a celebrated name for yourself in the music world." He observed the piano in the corner of the living room. "So this is the piano you're practicing on for your performance?"

Her lovely mouth downturned. "Yes, except the piano doesn't work. The damper pedal broke and I don't know how to repair it, so I'm practicing silently without touching the keys. Although when I visited Mrs. Fernandez the other day, I discovered she owns an upright player piano." Noelle licked her lips, her posture stiffened. "She said I can practice at her house on Sunday afternoons. In the meantime, I'll read more about Chopin's style. That type of knowledge helps me connect with the composer."

"Sounds like an agreeable solution," Gabe surmised.

"I should be resigned to scrambling for a piano because I've never actually had one since living in an apartment. In Saint Augustine, Colin and I practiced at the university because we both taught music theory classes there part-time. Pianos and apartment high-rises don't go together. The neighbors would complain about the noise."

"I'm still getting over the fact that a concert pianist doesn't own a piano." Gabe brushed his fingers along her neck, up to her temple.

Noelle shivered and gave a small smile. "I inherited a beautiful baby grand piano in an ebony, glossy finish from my parents. They'd engraved my initials, N.W., inside the fallboard, and I kept all my old sheet music inside the matching bench. They settled in a suburb outside New York City after I moved to Saint Augustine. And then, they died unexpectedly in a car accident. My terrible performance occurred one month later." She rubbed her legs with her uninjured hand, and tears spilled from her sea-green eyes. "I avoided everyone afterward. I've just gone back to playing a few months ago."

Gabe offered her shoulders a comforting squeeze and murmured in her ear. "Why was your performance a disaster, Noelle?"

As if an interval of several minutes hadn't ticked by, she replied, "I wasn't concentrating and, consequently, suffered a memory lapse. I panicked and dashed off the stage. Colin was furious because we were performing a duo-piano concert and he couldn't finish the piece without me, and his father was watching. Colin's father is his worst critic." Noelle sighed and shrugged. "Anyway, Colin recovered brilliantly and performed a showy Liszt piano solo as a finale. He served me with divorce papers the following day and told me I was inept and didn't deserve happiness after what I'd done."

"For dashing off the stage?"

"Our marital problems had begun long before that particular performance. He was brought up by a nanny after his mother died, and his father only paid attention to Colin when Colin played flawlessly. Consequently, Colin was more interested in his performances than in me."

"You were always poised and professional."

"Not always. I cried so hard afterward because he was my husband and wasn't supposed to let me down. I had faith he would be there for me. When I confronted him, he said I was insecure and a coward."

She stared at the long shadows the fire in the fireplace had created across the woven wool rug. The fiery glow had gilded her blonde hair to shiny gold. She looked incredibly attractive in that soft red sweater, like a living flame, pure and vibrant.

"When I knew you in high school ..." he said.

She shook her head. "That teenage girl you knew was young and naive and didn't realize the hard road ahead of her. When you met me, I was a freshman. I was too cocky, too sure of myself. I soon discovered that music critics are merciless."

He pulled her closer. "And so was your ex," he said.

"Sometimes I don't believe I deserve a second chance after how poorly I performed."

"You deserve the world," Gabe said.

Something inside his chest squeezed. Despite the way she'd explained her poor performance by blaming herself, the aftermath had left her hurt and susceptible. She'd admitted her lack of trust in people. Yet, this brave, beautiful woman had summoned up the courage to return to the concert stage, the spotlight of her humiliation.

The tender affection Gabe felt for her multiplied. For the first time, he realized how devastated she must've felt after all her years of hard work and endless preparation. Her ex, as well as the critics, had been thoughtless and mean-spirited. And Gabe would've happily tossed the lot of them into the street and left them there.

Outwardly calm, Gabe said nothing. He lifted his glass and drained the water that was left. As she'd once protected him, he decided, he'd protect her from anyone who'd try to hurt her.

Noelle pulled from his arms and straightened. "Colin's given me an opportunity to redeem myself on December fifteenth at the Forum Theater."

Impatiently, Gabe fiddled with the sleeves of his wool sweater. "Somehow, I think Colin will benefit in some way."

"I've had reservations, too, although my need to prove myself outweighs my fear of exploitation. It's a professional gig and I'll be paid." She blew out a breath. "My performance will be a success, and then Christmas will be special again."

Gabe took her cold fingers in his. "Christmas isn't dependent on a piano performance. Christmas is about being surrounded by special friends and loved ones."

And cold pizza and glowing candles and a spirited, gutsy woman, he thought.

Her head bowed. "I haven't enjoyed a happy Christmas in a while. This town ... I'd forgotten how wonderful the holiday festivities were, the snow, the joyful decorations, although it's not even Thanksgiving yet."

"How's Christmas in Saint Augustine?" he asked.

She drew a long breath, then blew it out. "Lonely."

He considered her for a long, silent minute. Not this Christmas, he vowed.

"My parents talked about taking me to the O'Donnell farm for a sleigh ride, then cutting down a Christmas tree, although we never did. They were the scholarly type and weren't interested in outdoor activities. From the advertisements, I always admired the property."

Slowly, Gabe nodded. "I know that farm well."

Her green-eyed gaze widened. "Is the farm still open after all these years?"

"The farm opens Thanksgiving evening," he replied dryly.

"Do you know the owner?"

"Intimately."

He'd surprise her, Gabe decided with an inward smile. He'd bought the farm five years ago when he'd decided to make Snowing Rock his permanent residence. He, too, had admired the farm before it had fallen into disrepair. He'd purchased and renovated the house, barns, and rambling ten acres. His thriftiness during his lean years had paid off.

He couldn't help imagining the two of them running the farm together.

* * *

AN HOUR WENT BY, the fire had waned to silvery ashes, and Noelle slept soundly against his arm. Gently, he roused her. "I'll be leaving soon and will change your bandage. Is there anything else you need?"

With her eyes still closed, she mumbled, "No."

He placed several comfortable throw pillows beneath her head, covered her with the crocheted blanket, and placed a tender kiss on her forehead. She looked fragile and vulnerable, and he wanted to kiss away the remaining tension from her face.

This holiday season would be magical for her.

"Do you want to go on a sleigh ride with me?" he whispered.

"I won't have time." Her eyes remained closed. "I have to spend every minute ..."

"Practicing," he finished.

Carefully, he unwound the gauze to check the wound one more time.

Scarcely believing what he saw, his heart dropped.

CHAPTER 9

*N*oelle, wake up."

Shaken by a sense of prickling alarm because of the tenseness in Gabe's voice, Noelle's eyes snapped open. She stared down at the stinging, unbandaged wound on her hand with horror.

She half-rose from the couch. "The burn changed to second-degree? How?"

Gabe's hand tightened on her fingers. "The burn's blistering, however, it's less than three inches, so won't require medical attention."

Slightly, she rocked back and forth. "How long will a second-degree burn take to heal?"

"First-degree burns usually heal in three to six days. Second-degree will take days longer." He cupped her chin in his hands and forced her to meet his gaze. "Either way, I promise you'll be all right."

She felt her cheeks warm. Her panic was unreasonable when he spoke so encouragingly. The burn would heal. Despite her doubts, Gabe had known what to do. He seemed capable of handling any emergency.

"I'll get a fresh bandage." He stepped to the bathroom to wash his hands and returned, applying antibiotic ointment and rewrapping her burn in clean gauze and a bandage. Then he carried their empty plates and pizza box to the kitchen.

Suddenly, the lights flashed on with a hum, and Noelle blinked at the unexpected glare of the overhead living room light.

"Hurray, the power's restored!" Gabe called from the kitchen. "I'll reset the microwave and oven clocks."

In the overhead light, Noelle noticed hard slivers of candle wax, as well as spilled pizza sauce, clinging to her tunic and leggings.

"I should change," she said, half to herself. She stretched out her legs and blew out the candles.

Gabe peered through the kitchen doorway. "Go ahead. I'm almost finished here."

She padded to the bedroom. Slowly and with effort, she slipped out of her clothes and pulled on a slightly frayed pink cashmere lounge suit. The lounge suit was warm and soft, an investment piece from years earlier when she could justify the expense.

She studied her bandaged hand. How was she expected to perform in a piano concert successfully when she couldn't even change her clothes with ease? With a heavy sigh, she headed back toward the living room.

"For a damsel in distress, you look lovely." Gabe's voice checked her in mid-step. He still stood in the middle of the kitchen with a dish towel over his shoulder, the sleeves of his sweater rolled up to expose sculpted arms and a tattoo on his right forearm.

"I like a man who does the dishes." She came closer, reading the words on his tattoo. "'Running away from your problems is a race you'll never win.'"

"Words to live by," he said. "And I was drawn to the snowy mountain background."

She smiled resignedly. "I've always wanted a tattoo with meaningful words, although I was never brave enough to get one. Besides, my ex wouldn't allow it. He controlled my career, what I wore on stage, how low I should bow after a finale, and how many seconds I should wait before coming back onstage after a standing ovation."

"Your ex was a brainless idiot, and you're the most courageous woman I've ever known. You're being proactive by accepting his invitation and proving your resourcefulness." Gabe's admiring gaze slid the length of her body and a faint smile touched his lips. Slowly, he set the dish towel next to the sink and strode to her.

"Will you allow me one parting kiss to remember an adventurous evening?" he asked.

She drew a ragged breath and he brought her to his chest, kissing her long and lingering on the lips. She slid her fingers beneath the wavy hair at his nape, her heart beating in slow, unsteady lurches. An eternity later, he lifted his lips from hers and framed her face in his hands. "Let's exchange cell phone numbers and then I'll leave. You must be exhausted."

She nodded and quickly retrieved her cell phone. He typed in her number and sent her a text. 'You are unbelievably beautiful.'

"Are you trying to make me blush?"

"I'm stating the obvious truth. Now get some sleep." He pressed a kiss on her forehead and shrugged into his parka. In a tone that brooked no disagreement, he added, "If you need anything tonight, call me, all right?"

"I will."

Soon afterward, Noelle went to bed. She heard Gabe shoveling the outside walk, and she smiled. That was just like him, thinking of everyone and everything except himself.

She lay on her back and lifted her bandaged hand, staring at the bandage in the darkness, confident the burn would heal as quickly as Gabe predicted.

She buried herself beneath the blankets, trying to understand the rush of emotions he aroused in her. She didn't have time for a romantic relationship, she reminded herself, because she was resolved to practice diligently, then return to Saint Augustine and perform brilliantly. Nothing would change that.

Yet, all her thoughts drifted back to Gabe.

Because he was proving to be trustworthy and honorable. Because she enjoyed his company. Because when he was near, she felt protected and safe.

Through the lace bedroom curtains, she watched the polar-white snow falling softly to the ground. The frosty November moon was high overhead peeking through the clouds, and shiny icicles had formed on the window casing. Snowing Rock had remained the enchanting Christmas town she'd remembered from her youth.

Perhaps when her concert was over, she could return and finally put down roots, making this charming town her home. Her aunt would need more help as Christmas neared. Plus, Gabe lived here.

His humor was witty, his manner compelling. For the first time in several years, she was looking forward to Christmas. Despite her leeriness of attachments, it was alarming how easily she could picture herself making a life in Snowing Rock.

She sank deeper under the covers, planning every detail of the holiday.

First, a sleigh ride at the O'Donnell farm. She envisioned a majestic, spotted draft horse pulling a sleigh while she admired a breathtaking snowscape. She'd snuggle beneath a plaid wool blanket and inhale crisp mountain air. She'd be cozying up to Gabe, his body warm next to hers, the sound of sleigh bells and their laughter ringing in the air. The day would be picture perfect.

Noelle rolled to her side, reluctant to surrender those heart-warming thoughts as she fell into a groggy sleep.

One more thought made her eyes snap open. She stared at the empty shadows.

She was wary about allowing anyone to get too close. The wall she'd put up after her parents' deaths and her disastrous concert was one of self-preservation, tidily protecting herself from becoming too vulnerable.

Should she let down her guard, take a risk, and truly trust Gabe?

CHAPTER 10

$\mathcal{N}$oelle blinked at the bright, wintry sun streaming through the bedroom window and rubbed her eyes. Her cell phone rang insistently on the night table beside the bed.

She picked up the phone, noting Gabe's name on the caller ID. "Hello?"

"Good morning, gorgeous. I'm cleaning your aunt's shop, then shoveling her walkway. How are you feeling?" he asked.

She glanced at the clock on the night table and gasped at the time, past ten o'clock. Although she wasn't a morning person, she'd never slept this late.

She studied her bandaged hand with frustration, the previous night's memories flashing through her mind. "I feel tired and the burn stings," she confessed.

"Can you be ready in about two hours? I'll bring a late breakfast, change your bandages, then we'll go to the Fernandez's house. If you're up to practicing, I can discuss my cousin's wedding cake details with Mrs. Fernandez."

Noelle envisioned the bustling Fernandez household, wondering how she'd ever be able to concentrate on refining her piano pieces, especially using one hand, and with Gabe in the room.

"I'll entertain Anjali," he continued, as if reading Noelle's thoughts. "All right?"

She nodded into the phone, ended the call, then quickly called Aunt Joy and explained the events of the previous evening. Noelle ended with the reassurance that she was receiving excellent care from Gabe and that her burn should heal within a couple weeks.

Two hours later, the doorbell rang.

"Come in, the door's unlocked," Noelle greeted Gabe as he strode through the doorway. Dressed in his olive green parka and snug-fitting dark jeans, he looked so vital, so good-looking that she favored him with a gaze of appreciation that spanned the length of his athletic body.

Carrying a fast food take-out bag, his gaze drifted from her bandaged hand to her lips. "Does the burn sting?" he asked.

"A little."

"This'll make it better." His mouth descended on hers for a brief kiss.

He kept one arm around her and they walked into the kitchen. He set a corn tortilla filled with cheesy scrambled eggs on the table, along with steaming coffee. "High calorie, high protein diet from the nearest drive-thru restaurant will help you heal quickly. And a cup of coffee so you won't be tired."

She muffled a giggle and sipped her coffee while she stared at him, happily anticipating the upcoming Thanksgiving and sleigh ride they'd enjoy together.

After they'd eaten, he washed his hands with soap and water and unwrapped her old bandage. The wound hadn't gotten worse, and she watched, silently, allowing relief to sink in. He washed his hands a second time, wrapped her hand securely in dry gauze, and taped on a fresh bandage.

The sharp coldness of winter air bit into Noelle's cheeks as she and Gabe headed for his Land Rover. Within minutes, they approached the entrance to the Fernandez home and tapped on the door.

Anjali flung open the door. "Mommy! It's Mr. Gabe and Miss Noelle!"

"Come in!" Mrs. Fernandez, using crutches, crossed the living room and stared at Noelle's bandage. "Mr. Waters told me about your hand when he called this morning. I'm so sorry."

"I needed more practice with my left hand, anyway." Noelle shifted her gaze to the piano. "May I?" She stepped to the piano bench and sat, taking a quick look toward Mrs. Fernandez who bobbed her consent.

Anjali bound to the piano. "Miss Noelle, I can play piano, too, remember?" Anjali sat on the bench beside Noelle, found the E key, and began singing, "Jin gle bells, jin gle bells," while playing three consecutive notes.

Gabe came to stand behind Anjali. "Miss Noelle is preparing for an important concert, so let's go into the kitchen and give her some quiet time to practice, all right?"

Anjali continued to press the E key. "Mr. Gabe, do you know what note this is?"

His leaned over Noelle and Anjali. "I'm tone-deaf."

"That's okay. So is my Daddy, but everyone knows where Middle C is. Just find two black keys in the middle, and Middle C is the white key to the left," Anjali said.

Noelle pointed to Middle C, and Gabe reached around her and pressed the key three times. He sang, then gave a throaty laugh. "Thanks for giving me my first piano lesson."

"Any time," Noelle replied. "My rates are very competitive."

Anjali started playing again. "E is two notes up from Middle C. The piano is an alphabet." Anjali pressed three white keys in a row. "C, D, E."

"Thanks, Anjali. Let's go into the kitchen so that Miss Noelle can practice in private." Gabe scooped the little girl in his arms and carried her to the kitchen. "Can you help me pick out a flavor for a wedding cake that I've coerced your Mommy into baking for my cousin's wedding? Do you like chocolate or vanilla?" He turned, winked at Noelle, and mouthed, 'Have fun.'

Noelle practiced awkwardly at first, the pieces not making musical sense without the right hand melody. Her speed and accuracy suffered, and a slight heaviness weighed in her stomach with each wrong left hand note. Slowly, she tacked on new measures, drilling her left hand to play louder, then softer. Her senses heightened as she threw herself into the music, enjoying the intense, lush chords.

An hour and a half later, she was breathless. She stood and stretched, catlike. Her limbs felt lighter. Her practice session had gone well, the rapid arpeggios in her left hand never sounding better. Although she missed playing with two hands, she felt back on track, certain her right hand would heal quickly.

She wandered toward the kitchen, drawn by the enticing aromas of cinnamon and vanilla.

"All that music coming from one hand." Gabe made direct eye contact with Noelle and applauded. "You're amazing!"

"Bravo!" Mrs. Fernandez joined in the applause, along with Anjali. "I'd love to attend your concert, although I'll be too busy baking Christmas cookies."

Gabe grinned. "I'd love to attend, and I'm available because I'm not baking any Christmas cookies. I order them from Mrs. Fernandez," he said quickly.

Noelle tilted back her head, thinking she'd savor their

encouraging responses to reflect on later. The day had gone much better than she'd anticipated, and although the burn stung, she'd pushed through the pain. Once the bandage came off, she'd double up her practice and be well-prepared for a triumphant comeback. She might be asked to book concerts all over the United States, perhaps even Europe.

This group of wonderful friends emboldened her with self-assurance, convinced her she'd made the right decision to accept Colin's offer to perform on the concert stage with him.

Her smile wavered when she surveyed the gay atmosphere of the Fernandez kitchen. Gabe and Anjali were carefully mixing cake batter, then measuring powdered sugar into a large stainless steel bowl. All the while, he answered Anjali's endless questions with relaxed nurturing and endless patience. Noelle could hardly tear her gaze from him. He was all male, yet he carried off complete absorption and enthusiasm in the art of cake baking.

Stepping into the kitchen, she paused, feeling a puzzling shyness. She was beginning to care for him more and more, and there was no point in denying her feelings.

"Miss Noelle, wanna try the vanilla butter cake Mommy's baking for Mr. Gabe's wedding? Mommy said we're taste-testing." Anjali toyed with a plateful of cake. "Butter is delicious!"

Gabe sliced a piece of cake, hot and crumbling from the oven. He offered the cake and a fork to Noelle. She accepted, appreciating every bite of the warm sweetness.

"I recommend a caramel butter cream filling if you choose the vanilla butter cake for the wedding," Mrs. Fernandez said.

"What kind of icing?" Gabe quizzed.

"Torched meringue."

Gabe regarded Noelle over a forkful of cake. "Try the

pink champagne cake," he said. "Mrs. Fernandez recommended a rum filling and whipped cream frosting."

He watched Noelle closely as she enjoyed a bite of each. "Which do you prefer?"

Noelle tipped her head toward the pink cake and laid down her fork. "It's not my wedding, although I'm partial to anything pink, including pink champagne."

* * *

AFTERWARD GABE INSISTED on treating Noelle to dinner at Snowing Rock country club.

"I'm not dressed properly," Noelle protested, although he assured her she looked stunning.

After hanging their outerwear in the front reception room of the country club, he escorted her to a table near a huge marble fireplace. Noelle glanced down at her black wool slacks, crisp white poplin shirt, and long, gray pleated cardigan. The thick gold carpeting, the sweeping expanse of glass looking out onto a snowy golf course prompted her to realize that she looked anything but stunning in the affluent surroundings.

Gabe, on the other hand, looked extraordinarily fine in navy wool pants and a pin-striped shirt, emphasizing his athletic shoulders. His tweedy gray wool scarf was slung loosely around his neck. His grin was so boyishly appealing when she'd agreed to accompany him to dinner, she couldn't help but smile.

He recommended thyme chicken with roasted potatoes and Mediterranean vegetables. "A specialty of the house," he declared.

An hour later, after finishing more food than she normally ate in a week, she leaned back in her heavy wooden chair and sighed. "As always, you've done too much for me."

"Are you depriving me of the joy I feel when I've made such a special woman happy?"

She grinned. His teasing question, along with his kindling hazel gaze, warmed her.

He reached for her left hand across the table. "I've waited fifteen years for this moment. I've wanted to take you to dinner at the country club ever since I was eighteen, dreaming I could someday afford this place." He hesitated. "Ever since the day you soundly scolded me and that bully at school. I remember your green eyes flashed like dueling swords when you shouted for us to stop fighting."

She laughed. "Apparently my flashing eyes didn't deter you from fighting that bully, anyway."

Gabe shrugged. "He left me no choice. He wanted to sell drugs to my cousin, Holly. Regardless of my attempts, Holly went through a hard time anyway, but she's furthered her education, she's industrious and adaptable, and I'm very proud of her."

"She sounds like a woman who's gone through a lot and persevered," Noelle said.

"Will you attend her wedding? I'd like you to meet her."

Noelle heard the guarded, hopeful note in Gabe's voice.

"We both know I'll be gone by then." Even as she spoke she debated. Although she was determined to return to Saint Augustine and perform, she wasn't as excited as she had been.

"You'll miss Mrs. Fernandez's delectable wedding cake," he said.

Noelle pushed the leftover roasted potatoes and eggplant around on her dinner plate. "Honestly, I'd love to attend, although to journey back to Snowing Rock from Saint Augustine ..." She sighed. "I suffer from motion sickness and it's a long bus ride."

"Then I'll arrange your flight from Saint Augustine to

Fisher's Crossing." He caught her gaze. "Agree and tell me the matter's settled."

She smiled. "Okay. The matter's settled."

He went around the table, assisted her to her feet, and escorted her down the wall-papered hallway.

"And you can spend Christmas with me," he continued. "My cousin and her new husband will be honeymooning in the Bahamas and they're taking Devin along."

"I can't, really," Noelle protested. "Christmas is a special day and I'll want to spend the day with my aunt."

"You can both spend it with me." A roguish smile spread across Gabe's features. "You wouldn't want me to be alone on Christmas Day? What would I do with myself? I'll have no candles to make, no weddings to plan, no stunts to—"

She laughed. "Perhaps," she relented.

"And who's going to eat all that wedding cake?" He grinned mischievously and Noelle dissolved into a fit of laughter.

"You will! My waistline has probably doubled since I arrived."

Christmas in Snowing Rock with Gabe, she mused, wiping tears of mirth from her cheeks. A white, wonderful Christmas.

"Gabe Waters!" a lilting woman's voice came from the front reception room. "You've made yourself scarce since you've been back in town. You've only visited my place once."

Noelle swiveled to spot the ever-elegant Lucia Crandall strutting over. Lucia's hair was flawlessly arranged in her stylish pixie cut. She wore a tailored green silk suit, hugging her curvaceous, petite figure to perfection.

Gabe greeted Lucia, then turned to Noelle. "I'll get our coats."

Lucia's gaze traveled from Gabe to Noelle and her eyes narrowed. "I didn't expect to see you dining in a place like this." She swept out her arms, then studied Noelle's bandaged hand.

Noelle glimpsed herself in one of the ornate mirrors hanging on the country club's walls. She looked too pale, she decided, and her hair was unruly and uncombed. She shook back her blonde curls, feeling plain and unsophisticated beside the chic and well-groomed Lucia. Realizing that Lucia was regarding Noelle's bandaged hand expectantly, Noelle explained, "I burned my hand on candle wax after the candle class last night."

"Aren't you performing in a concert next month?" Lucia asked smoothly. "I know from experience that wax burns take weeks to heal, and you'll be left with a scar."

Gabe returned and assisted Noelle with her coat. "Ready to leave?" he asked.

Lucia placed a possessive hand on Gabe's wrist. "We're spending Thanksgiving together, remember?"

"As long as I'm back in town," he replied.

"No movie director will film over Thanksgiving weekend, so I'll be expecting you." Lucia swiveled to Noelle. "Don't forget the ladies club would enjoy background piano music for our Christmas luncheon." Lucia adjusted her fox fur coat around her shoulders. "We won't be able to pay you, though. Our club is in the red and I assume a famous pianist like you doesn't need the money, right?"

CHAPTER 11

*N*either Gabe nor Noelle broke the charged silence on the drive to her aunt's stone cottage. Tiny snowflakes melted against the Land Rover's heated windshield, and purple clouds drifted slowly across a darkening sky.

Gabe pulled into the driveway and shut off the engine.

He glanced at Noelle's tight profile and sighed. For the first time since the bus accident, he didn't know how to begin their conversation.

She sat with her hands clasped together on her lap, staring straight ahead.

After a lengthy silence, she said, "You promised the burn would begin to heal within three days."

"I didn't promise, Noelle. I said a first-degree burn would heal in three to six days, and a second-degree burn would take two weeks. I'm not a doctor and—"

"And don't be a liar, either," she snapped.

He gazed at her reddened face. How could she charge him with lying? Didn't she know him at all? He'd built a successful career based on truthfulness and good character.

His tone deepened. "I spoke from my experience on movie sets. There have been horrific fires, and guys have been badly hurt. I know how long it took for them to heal."

"Lucia is a professional candle maker." Noelle's voice rose. "Lucia knows from experience."

"And I don't?" Heat flushed through his body, reliving the stunt he'd performed the day of the stunt accident, how he'd almost blacked out, the people who could've gotten hurt because he'd neglected to care for his diabetes properly.

"And when were you planning to tell me you'd be gone until Thanksgiving?" she asked.

Despite her infuriated tone, he couldn't help smiling to himself. She obviously cared for him or she wouldn't be so upset he was leaving.

"I got a call from Christopher Swidering, my agent, this morning, and I can't refuse the stunt because I'm under contract until the end of the year," he said. "I planned to tell you when we got back to the cottage. The director wants to film an action shot because the weather forecast in Wilmington calls for heavy rain, which is the weather they need for the shoot. Handling the logistics of a movie scene like this is mind-boggling, and there's little margin for error, and everyone has to be present. Can you change your bandages yourself?"

Her laughter had an edge. "I'm not an idiot, Gabe."

"I'll phone you when I arrive in Wilmington, all right? It's a short flight."

She reached for the passenger door handle. "I'll be busy at the candle shop or practicing piano. If I don't pick up, leave a message. Oh, and enjoy Thanksgiving dinner with Lucia."

He shot around the SUV and captured Noelle's arm as she stepped onto the driveway. He studied her high chin and flushed face for a beat, then explained evenly, "Months ago, I promised Lucia I'd take her to the country club for

Thanksgiving because her husband had recently passed, and she didn't want to be alone for a holiday. She's an old friend."

Noelle stared at him with those flashing green eyes. "I couldn't care less about your relationship with Lucia."

"You've been glaring at me ever since we left the country club!"

She broke eye contact. "Of course your career comes first and my bandaged hand isn't a priority."

"I'll take Lucia to the club for Thanksgiving, then come to your place afterward." He rubbed his knuckles lightly across Noelle's smooth cheekbone and softened his voice. "Remember that sleigh ride I promised you?"

She bit her lip. "Of course I remember."

"We'll go on Thanksgiving night." He ran a hand through his hair. "In the meantime, say a prayer for me, all right? I'll be stunt driving a race car on two wheels while accelerating. It's up to me to keep the car under control at a very high speed."

"Yes, I'll pray." She pulled at a wayward curl on her forehead. "Gabe, will you be safe?"

"No worries. I'm a pro, remember?"

"Yes, but still ..."

His conscience nagged at the way he'd navigated around her question. He'd offered factual information, although he'd skimmed over his response. Stunt driving almost always involved an element of danger.

His forefinger traced her trembling lips. "I like knowing you're a tad worried about me."

She fidgeted with her jacket. The creamy skin beneath her eyes was darkened by shadows.

"I'm very worried," she said.

"I also like knowing you're a tad jealous."

Her eyes widened. "I'm not the least bit jealous."

He swallowed a smile. "In any case, a send-off kiss will take away the sting of our disagreement. Agreed?"

She sighed, then nodded. His hands shifted to her back, molding her to his hard form. His lips touched hers, tentatively at first, growing bolder.

Drawing a long breath, she locked her arms around his neck.

Her tender kisses and light touch nearly swept away his self-control. And they were in her aunt's driveway, the blast of a harsh winter wind piercing through the fabric of their clothes! Although it was almost dusk, the neighbors were probably all watching.

His chest tightened. Damn the neighbors. Damn the contract.

As the kiss deepened, he considered canceling the gag in Wilmington altogether. The director could scramble and find someone else.

Although Gabe knew he wouldn't cancel, for he was a man whom people could count on.

An eternity later, he lifted his mouth from Noelle's, wanting to feel her sweet lips pressed against his one more time. Only she could take away his parents' neglect, his need to prove himself and overcome his disease, his resultant risky profession.

Wood-burning fireplaces and the smoky smell of seasoned saplings scented the air. Nightfall had crept in, the purple clouds had darkened, the tiny snowflakes had changed to a mist of silvery ice. Noelle quivered, and he kept his arm around her while he walked her to the cottage.

They settled together for a few moments on the living room couch. After he changed her bandages, he checked his watch.

"It's getting late," he said. "My flight leaves early for Wilmington."

She didn't meet his eyes. "I know."

"I'll miss you. You'll answer your phone when I call?"

She slanted a slight smile. "Unless I'm too busy practicing."

"Then I'll keep calling until you pick up the phone." He brushed a soft kiss on her upturned forehead, his mind racing with all the things he needed to pack for his upcoming trip as he strode out the door.

When he reached his Land Rover, he couldn't bring himself to start the engine and head out. Instead, he sat in the driver's seat, steepled his hands on the steering wheel, and gazed at the rustic stone cottage.

He didn't want to leave Noelle. She was in Snowing Rock for only a short time. He'd waited years for the chance to see her again because he knew he'd fallen in love with her, although he hadn't admitted that fact to himself until now.

Love. He shook his head in frustration. Hadn't he learned from an ill-starred marriage that love was an impractical, idealistic concept? How could he ever be truly loved and accepted when his own parents hadn't cared about him?

He scrubbed a hand over his face and sighed heavily. Besides, his occupation was too hazardous ... his disease too complicated.

The last few days he and Noelle had spent together, he'd sensed she was becoming more attracted to him. In several instances, she'd sought his reassurances and embraces of her own accord.

Just thinking of Colin, her contemptuous ex, infuriated Gabe. How could Colin dare to dictate what she should wear, how low she should bow ...

Irritably, Gabe started the engine. He'd become preoccupied with an indescribably exquisite young woman who'd stolen his heart in a high school hallway.

He rubbed his whiskered chin. He needed a shave. Since

Noelle had arrived in Snowing Rock, he'd neglected his work-outs. He decided to hit his home gym and string together a double routine and longer set before retiring for the evening, being sure to check his blood sugar levels beforehand. He hoped he wouldn't regret his decision in the morning. A stuntman couldn't perform a back flip over a speeding car with a limp.

CHAPTER 12

*A*s Aunt Joy had predicted, the Wednesday before Thanksgiving was a quiet day at the candle shop with few customers. Noelle used the extra time to prepare for the shop's Black Friday sale, replenishing the shelves with tapered Christmas candles. Caroline had taken the day off to spend with Alan, promising to open the shop early on Friday morning.

An hour passed before Noelle greeted the first customer of the day, a red-haired woman with pin curls in her hair.

"Welcome to 'Scents of Joy'!" Noelle greeted with a wave. She was trying her best to be cheery, although she wasn't feeling it with Gabe gone.

The young woman acknowledged the greeting and raced through the shop, muttering and shaking her head as she picked up two cranberry scented votive candles. "I'm visiting my parents for Thanksgiving Day. Can you recommend an appropriate gift I can take?"

"Certainly." Noelle led the red-haired woman to a cornucopia featuring Wasabi Pear tapered candles and the woman quickly agreed with Noelle's recommendation. Noelle ran the woman's credit card transaction with no problem, then gift-wrapped the centerpiece.

"The pear scent is fresh and bright and the ideal candle to light after a heavy Thanksgiving dinner," Noelle explained.

After the customer departed, the remainder of the day dragged with few customers.

Before Noelle closed the shop at six o'clock, she unpacked tea light candles from a distributor. She frowned at some of the wicks because they were broken off and needed to be returned because the flame would never burn big or hot enough.

When she had finished and had tallied up the receipts, she glanced at her cell phone, anticipating her nightly conversation with Gabe. Although she hadn't seen him in two weeks, he'd phoned every evening. They'd talked for hours, about their work, about their pasts, about their high school and college years. He'd begun every conversation by asking for a detailed account of her burn wound and how it was healing.

But he wasn't in Snowing Rock, and his lifestyle meant that he couldn't be depended on. Obviously, she wasn't his main concern.

She'd continued with the care he'd initiated, washing her hands and cleansing the wound thoroughly, applying antibiotic cream, and wrapping the wound in a clean bandage. There'd been no signs of infection, and within a week the dead, burned skin had peeled off and new red skin had healed to a light pink.

When she'd inquired about Gabe's work, he'd dismissed the action film as a 'typical racing car flick.' When she'd pressed for details, knowing the film would most likely become another box office hit, he'd described action shots involving his jump from a twenty-foot cliff, or throwing his race car into a skid, or flipping the race car over while he drove.

She'd hold her breath, sometimes wishing she hadn't asked, telling him she felt sure that her hair was turning prematurely gray and she was developing a new wrinkle with every death-defying feat he'd described.

He'd laughed softly. "Airbags help," he'd finished.

Her piano practice had lessened as a result of their lengthy conversations, although she'd been able to squeeze in three hours every evening.

Gabe cared about her, he obviously desired her. And although she had little faith in deciphering her own emotions, she wouldn't deny her growing feelings for him, despite her fears of becoming vulnerable. That focused, powerful stuntman left no doubt that he wanted to be with her.

Fortunately, her aunt's piano had been fixed by the competent piano technician from Fisher's Crossing. The technician had replaced the damper pedal rod, fastened the pins on the upper and lower levers of the piano, and tuned the piano.

Although Gabe wasn't expected to return to Snowing Rock until Thanksgiving morning, Noelle occasionally caught herself looking up from the cash register when a customer walked in, half-expecting him to stride in and place another order for vanilla-scented beeswax candles. She could just hear him saying, 'To repay my kindness in adding to your sales, all I want is a sugar cookie in return.'

* * *

THE FOLLOWING AFTERNOON, Noelle went to the rehab center to enjoy Thanksgiving dinner with Aunt Joy. After saying grace, she and her aunt were seated at a long, rectangular table along with several other senior citizens convalescing from a range of injuries.

Long after Noelle had eaten more than her share of thyme-filled turkey, fluffy sweet potatoes topped with marshmallows, and a mountain of mashed potatoes drowning in boiled gravy, she sat back, hoping she'd still be able to fit into her black recital gown.

As the meal came to a close, Noelle lightly rapped her fingers along the tablecloth, practicing the first measure of Chopin.

Her aunt giggled affection beneath a wide-brimmed straw hat and evened out her long, lime-green skirt so that it stretched to her ankles.

"I'm so happy you came to Snowing Rock," she said.

Noelle smiled in agreement. "After holidays alone in Saint Augustine, it's good to celebrate with family."

"Holidays are about spending time with the people who matter most in your life, dear." Aunt Joy patted Noelle's arm, then dove into a creamy slice of pumpkin pie topped with whipped cream. "Your hand healed with little scarring," she observed.

"And I've practiced all week with two hands!" Noelle yanked the sleeves up on her black cashmere sweater and waved both hands in the air. "Gabe was right!"

"And where is your Gabe?" Aunt Joy prompted.

"He's not my Gabe," Noelle said.

Her aunt managed a wan smile. "Aren't things between you going well?"

"I'm seeing him tonight, after he's taken Lucia Crandall to dinner at the country club."

Aunt Joy's fork froze in mid-bite. "He was welcome to dine with us at the rehab center."

Noelle rubbed the back of her neck. "He couldn't. He'd promised Lucia."

Although Noelle attempted to exude calmness, she felt her muscles tighten. Gabe's friendship with Lucia and his

Thanksgiving promise were reasons enough why Noelle needed to return to Saint Augustine and succeed.

Noelle didn't respond to her aunt's upraised, penciled-in brow. Instead, she glanced at her cell phone. There'd been no messages from him since they'd spoken last evening. Still, if his flight had been delayed, he'd have contacted her.

"You always steer the conversation to me, Aunt Joy," Noelle said. "I'm glad you'll be back at the candle shop before I leave on December thirteenth. Although Caroline is knowledgeable, I want to learn the candle business from you, the woman who started it all."

"I'd love to see your performance in Saint Augustine. However, between running the shop and recovering from my hip injury—"

"And I'd love for you to attend," Noelle parroted, checking her aunt's explanation in mid-sentence. "Nonetheless, I completely understand. And, Colin emailed me last night. Ticket sales are brisk and the concert's slated to be broadcast on an FM classical radio station, so I'll give you the station's info and you can listen to the performance live."

Silently, Noelle cringed at the thought that her performance would be recorded. If she had a memory slip, would her audience judge her again?

She leaned back in her chair and took an easy breath. She could do this. She was skilled, and Gabe's nightly encouragements had deepened her resolve.

Her cell phone pinged, and she viewed Gabe's text message: 'Arrived safely. Rushed home for a shower, now at the country club for the quickest Thanksgiving dinner Lucia will ever eat. See you at 5. Ready for a sleigh ride?' He'd inserted a heart emoji.

'Yes,' she texted back. She'd make good on her promise to go to the O'Donnell farm with him.

A few minutes later, she bid her aunt farewell with a fierce hug.

The sun was setting as Noelle headed toward the cottage. While she drove, she admired snow-capped pine trees, the branches shimmering in the last wanes of sunlight. A fat snowman with a carrot nose stood on a street corner, most likely made by happy, squealing children.

She steered into the driveway, surprised to see Gabe's familiar black Land Rover pull in behind her. Simultaneously, they both shut off their engines. He vaulted from his vehicle and drew her into his arms before she'd taken two steps.

She stiffened.

"I missed you." He dropped his hands, stepped back, and examined her right hand. "Only a slight scar left from the burn."

"And my Chopin is much better. I've refined my phrasing and articulation."

"I'm proud of you, Noelle," he said.

"You can enjoy my concert along with the entire listening audience on the FM radio station." She shook the curls from her face and asked the question that had nagged at her all afternoon. "How was Thanksgiving dinner with Lucia?"

Gabe scowled, then shrugged dismissively. "Quick. How was Thanksgiving dinner with your aunt?"

"Very enjoyable. I admire Aunt Joy's business sense more each day. My mother used to complain that Aunt Joy was a non-conformist, although I've come to realize that's a good trait."

"She sounds remarkable, like her niece." Gabe slipped his arm around her shoulders and guided her to his SUV, opening the passenger door for her. "Are you ready for the sleigh ride?"

She nodded. That morning, she'd dressed ahead for the

arctic-like night air, wearing a cashmere sweater and woolen hat, leggings, thick coat, and leather boots.

When they'd settled into Gabe's Land Rover, she asked, "How did filming go in Wilmington?"

"The rain was nonstop and made the stunts more difficult." Gabe enhanced his statement with a theatrical groan. "Fortunately, they called a wrap, unless there's a moment in the film the director believes needs to be improved with a reshoot. Consequently, I can attend your piano performance in Saint Augustine, so I won't need to listen to it on the radio."

"You might be bored ... you're a stunt race car driver ... don't you prefer action?"

"I promise I won't embarrass you and fall asleep during the performance. I'll be the person in the audience clapping the loudest."

Cautiously, she ventured, "Colin said he'd give me a complimentary ticket."

"How generous of him." Gabe scoffed, then softened his tone. "Tell him I want a front row center seat."

Her old fears emerged. Could she trust Gabe to keep his promise and attend her concert? Could she take him at his word?

What if she had a memory lapse? Would he see her as a failure? Anything could go wrong during a live performance. Just thinking about it made her feel nauseated and sick to her stomach.

No, she told herself adamantly. She'd conquered her silent terror. Besides, this performance wasn't about her. She was giving something back to her audience, her gift of music.

As they drove in silence, passing a crisp, winter-white landscape, she asked, "Do you know the route to the O'Donnell farm?"

He smiled. "Like the back of my hand."

As they approached the left turn onto a private drive, Noelle leaned forward. "Why is there a high security fence around the entire property?"

"To keep out the paparazzi," Gabe explained vaguely.

She crossed her arms and focused on the high iron fence. "Do celebrities come to the O'Donnell farm to take sleigh rides and buy Christmas trees?"

He didn't answer. Instead, he idled the SUV and pressed a code at the entrance. The front gate swung to the side, and they followed a long driveway past acres of fir trees, the branches heavy with snow. They didn't stop, as she'd expected, at a wood-framed caretaker's cottage, aglow with flickering lights within, nor at an imposing red barn farther down the road. The distance widened and a magnificent, tri-level mansion loomed ahead.

Gabe drove his Land Rover to the entrance. He turned off the engine, got out and came around to open the passenger door for her.

She stepped out. Large flakes were beginning to fall and the air seemed quiet, her footsteps muffled.

"Why are we stopping here?" She tilted her head, surveying the main level wood deck wrapping around the impressive home. "Who lives—?"

"I do, Noelle. Do you approve of my cabin in the woods?"

CHAPTER 13

*N*oelle gasped and became still for a moment. "How big is this ... cabin ... er ... mansion?" she asked in a loud voice.

Gabe grinned as she stared in wide-eyed bewilderment at him. "About ten thousand square feet," he said.

"Are you the O'Donnell's caretaker?"

He laughed and shook his head. "I'm the owner. I bought the home and surrounding acreage a few years ago and fixed everything up. Actually, my cousin, Holly, oversaw the remodel and interior design. Want to see the inside?"

"Yes, of course."

He tucked her hand in the crook of his arm and led her to the covered front porch. They admired stunning mountain views before entering the spacious foyer.

"The house is on three levels," Gabe nodded toward the opulent central staircase and elevator and flicked on a low, overhead light. "On the left is the formal living room. I haven't found the proper furniture, so it's empty except for a couch and chair."

She removed her coat and red wool hat, shaking her

blonde curls free. He took their outerwear and hung their coats in the entry closet.

They walked to the living room and she glided toward the floor to ceiling windows. Gazing outside, she said, "A piano would go perfectly between these windows and the stone fireplace. And I can see the entire town of Snowing Rock." She whirled to face him. "You can arrange Christmas candles on the fireplace mantel. The shop just got in a new fragrance —chutney and cranberry."

Moonlight glinted through the glass, enhancing her soft skin to a rose-colored hue, giving her an ethereal appearance.

He paused, admiring her. "I don't need candles. You're so lovely, you light up the entire room."

She began walking toward him with that graceful elegance he'd always marveled at. "Your home is splendid, Gabe," she finished softly.

"Not as splendid as you." He closed the distance and slid his arm around her. "And something else of great importance is lacking in my home besides a piano."

"What's that?" she asked.

Noelle Wentworth, he thought to himself.

Aloud, he replied, "A sprig of mistletoe hanging in the doorway."

She leaned against the wall. "Gabe, it's not Christmas yet."

He braced his hands on the wall above her shoulders. "Do you remember Snowing Rock High's Christmas dance fifteen years ago?"

"Yes, my aunt and I discussed that dance recently."

"You wore a red sequined dress. You looked irresistible."

"I couldn't wait to leave," she said.

"And I also remember a mistletoe in the doorway." Briefly, his lips descended on hers. "I wanted to claim you for a dance and kiss you under the mistletoe. I turned to get some tortilla chips and you were gone."

Her cheeks pinkened. "I remember running through that doorway as fast as I could."

"Next time there's mistletoe, I won't turn around. And if you run, I'll catch you."

He bent his head to kiss her again, then checked himself. She seemed distant.

He sighed. Although he felt a sense of pride to show her his home, the home he'd worked so hard and so long for, he also felt the need to take things slowly.

"There's a wood-paneled library with a fireplace beyond, a guest bedroom, and sitting areas on this level," he said. "I'll show you the upper level first, all right?"

When they reached the top of the staircase, he guided her to the chef's kitchen containing a large breakfast nook, a family room anchored by a large fireplace, and the master suite with another fireplace adding romance to the decor. He led her out to the private balcony that held a hot tub, and they stared at the expansive snow-capped peaks, the moonlit shadows dancing in the cobblestone courtyard below.

He stood behind her with his chin resting on her hair. Ever so slightly, she leaned back against him. He stirred at the intense feeling of her body pressed to his, and his hand fell to her waist and pulled her closer.

For a moment, he debated about asking her to marry him right where they stood. They could plan a Christmas wedding within the next few weeks, send invitations, spend their honeymoon anywhere in the world. He'd explain his diabetes, a topic he'd avoided, hoping she wouldn't view him as a weakling and lose respect for him. He wanted her to see him as strong and dependable.

His mind explored wedding arrangements before he reluctantly forced the idea aside.

Noelle needed to concentrate on her upcoming performance. Despite her fearlessness, he assumed she still harbored insecurities and stage fright. Afterward, she'd be able to concentrate on rebuilding her self-esteem and he, in turn, would offer safety and security.

Since he couldn't ask her to marry him yet, he murmured into her fragrant hair the only other thought that was important to him.

"Noelle Wentworth, I love you. I've always loved you."

He felt the poignant effect of his words because she stiffened. With a graceful twirl in his arms, she lifted her gorgeous face to his.

"I'm slowly learning to trust again," she said quietly. "Give me time."

He wrapped his arms around her and bent his head, his lips moving over hers. She stood on her toes, hesitantly kissing him back. When he lifted his lips, he murmured, "I'm a patient man and I'll wait for you. Always remember you can trust me." Reluctantly, he released his grip and gazed into her jade-green eyes.

"I trust you more than I've trusted anyone in a long time," she said.

Her response made his throat tighten.

He held her hand as they rode to the lower level in his private elevator. The level boasted a work-out room with state of the art exercise equipment, a family room with fireplace, and a large projection theater room.

"Isn't tonight the opening for your film, 'Force of Thunder Two'?" she asked.

"I'm not comfortable watching my films," he replied. "I tried once, with Devin, and ended up leaving the room after ten minutes because I scrutinized every mistake."

They rode the elevator to the upper level and strolled to the kitchen.

"I bought you a gift while I was in Wilmington." He indicated a small box wrapped with red foil paper and tied with a gold bow lying on the table. "It was special ordered."

She arched her delicate brows questioningly at the small package. "I'm assuming this isn't a bouquet of flowers," she said. Carefully, she unwrapped the gift and spread the printed words on the table.

"I bought you a tattoo," he said. "You mentioned you'd always wanted one. Unlike mine, yours isn't permanent and should last only a week or two." He read the words aloud, "'Running away from your problems is a race you'll never win.'" A snowy mountain against a blue-gray sky loomed in the background.

An incredulous beam broke across her face. "This tattoo is the same as yours."

"Yes, we'll match." He studied her, his thoughts drifting to the day when he could ask her to be his wife. Her sweetness warmed his heart.

He cleared his throat. "You could've run far away from the concert stage, you could've hidden—"

"I did," she said.

"You mustered up the courage to face your problem head-on. Not many people have that kind of determination."

She raked her fingers through her hair. "In case you haven't noticed, I'm not the sort of person who wears tattoos, despite what I might've said in a moment of weakness."

"Yours is a temporary henna tattoo." He rolled up the shirtsleeves of his navy blue sweater, exposing his right forearm with the same words tattooed in permanent ink.

She took a quick breath and bit her bottom lip. "My tattoo will come off before my concert, right? My gown is sleeveless and Colin would be furious."

"And Colin can answer to me from now on. Here, take a seat." Gabe pulled out a kitchen stool and shifted his gaze to her pasted-on half-smile. "Noelle Wentworth, you're not nervous, are you?"

"Not a bit," she said, eyeing the doorway before settling on the stool.

He rolled up the right sleeve of her black cashmere sweater. She closed her eyes and breathed in.

"No needles, I promise, and this will take less than a minute." He wet a sponge from the sink and brought back a pair of scissors to the table. He felt Noelle's entire right side clench as he wet and applied the tattoo with firm and gentle pressure, then peeled off the backing.

"You're done?" she asked.

"In less than a minute."

She examined her tattooed forearm. "'Running away from your problems is a race you'll never win.'" She grinned. "Somehow, having a tattoo makes me feel giddy and reckless!" She rolled down her sleeve and sighed. "I hope I can show it off."

"Saint Augustine doesn't have Snowing Rock's winter weather," Gabe replied. "On the other hand, every time you look at your tattoo, think of me. I'll do the same."

"You're good to me, Gabe." Her eyes welled with tears. He snuggled her against his chest, her words muffling against his heart.

He offered her a white handkerchief from his pocket. "If you cry whenever I give you a gift, be prepared to have dozens of handkerchiefs with you at all times, because I intend to shower you with endless presents."

She drew back and dabbed at her eyes. Her lips twitched. "You mean showering me with endless tattoos?"

"As many as you want."

The night sky was dotted with stars by the time Gabe guided her to the front foyer and retrieved their coats. "Tomorrow's an early morning for you at the candle shop. I'll

248

text Stan, my caretaker, to harness the draft horses for our sleigh ride."

"Don't tell me you have a caretaker?"

"I can't manage this entire property by myself. We passed his cottage on the way in. He lives there with his wife, Elise, who cleans my house and sometimes leaves a meal for me. She's an excellent cook, and although I've reserved Snowing Rock Country Club to cater Holly's wedding, Elise will be there to supervise. I'll also show you the renovated barn for the reception. I could use some guidance because I can't begin to comprehend—"

"Gabe, sounds like every detail has been planned to perfection, including the candles."

"There's always details that I miss."

And the main detail that was missing was his beautiful Noelle standing by his side. How could his house ever feel like a home without her?

CHAPTER 14

*A*unt Joy had been right about Black Friday sales, Noelle reflected, looking back on how busy the shop had been on the Friday after Thanksgiving. Her aunt had also predicted how hectic the following days would become, stuffed with customers and roaring with activity. It didn't matter. Noelle felt comfortable in her surroundings, and happy working at the shop.

Two weeks had spun by in a marvelous blur. Noelle had purchased her dress for Holly's wedding ahead of time in one of the upscale boutiques in town. The red sequined tea-length gown featured sheer sleeves and a pleated, taffeta skirt. The fitted, deep v-neckline bodice was delicately enhanced with gold embellishments. She'd described the dress to Gabe, and he'd kissed her, tenderly and deeply. With a tigerish gleam, he'd remarked that he looked forward to Holly's wedding so that he could see Noelle dressed like an exquisite goddess, and he planned to kiss her under the mistletoe he'd purposely hang in the doorway of his home.

Noelle smiled. The future looked bright, almost too good to be true.

She spent her daylight hours at the candle shop while Gabe donated endless amounts of energy to his outreach center. Evenings, she and Gabe were inseparable. They alternated between bringing dinner and dining with either Aunt Joy or the Fernandez family on weeknights, and enjoying a sumptuous meal at the country club on weekends. Afterward, Noelle would practice piano at her aunt's cottage, taking a few moments between pieces to get up and stretch. Gabe sat in the kitchen, humming quietly and out of tune, while learning new stunt skills and networking with other stuntmen online.

Noelle had recommended fun, upbeat recorded music for his outreach center's upcoming Christmas musical. When they visited the center, she watched him admiringly while he interacted with the teens, especially those teens who were disadvantaged and at high-risk. Gabe encouraged their self-confidence, advising them to choose their friends wisely while clarifying his personal values. They were his fans, and thus, listened to him. In turn, he was always generous, attentive, and supportive.

He was also the most attractive man Noelle had ever met. More and more, she felt appreciated and cared for, protected and loved.

The day before Noelle departed for Saint Augustine, Aunt Joy returned to the candle shop. Just before the shop closed, Noelle knelt in the front window and arranged a lighted holiday display.

Gabe strode in, turned automatically to the front window, and bent to plant a kiss on Noelle's lips. "You and I are booked roundtrip from Fisher's Crossing to Saint Augustine tomorrow," he said, straightening.

Noelle continued to arrange white pillar candles in a glass container, wrapping greenery around the base. "I bought a round-trip bus ticket, remember?" she absently corrected him.

He held out a pair of airline tickets. "You're performing the most important performance of your career, and you don't need the extra worry of motion sickness. The plane ride will shorten your travel to Saint Augustine and I'll be with you."

She came to her feet and examined the tickets.

"Our return tickets are open-ended with a flexible date." He grinned broadly. "Although I may return earlier, whereas you may need a few extra days in Saint Augustine to sign autographs and book concerts and arrange your permanent move to Snowing Rock."

"Did I say I was moving here permanently?" she laughed.

He pressed his lips on hers for a leisurely kiss. "If you require extra persuading ..."

"Your beeswax candles have arrived, Mr. Waters! Now we're just waiting for the Candleglow and Mistletoe candles," Caroline and Aunt Joy shouted at the same time as they emerged from the back storage room. Caroline's arms were laden with boxes while Aunt Joy stopped to price a soy candle.

Caroline placed the boxes on the counter near the cash register, then joined Gabe and Noelle in the front display window. Slowly, Caroline flicked a skinny blue braid from her face and tapped Gabe's arm. "Mr. Waters, after supplying you with enough candles to light the entire town of Snowing Rock, we all expect invitations to your cousin's wedding."

"Holly said she mailed out the invitations and you're all invited," Gabe answered.

Apparently not one to be pacified so quickly, Caroline turned another tack. "Alan and I have never visited Hawaii. Did you purchase any extra airline tickets to warm, tropical places?"

Gabe's shoulders shook with noiseless laughter as he

retrieved Noelle's coat and slipped it around her. "Sorry. I'm only offering Saint Augustine tickets today, and they're both claimed and booked."

And this, Noelle thought with a beam, was why she loved Snowing Rock. Because of the supportive friends and family and splendid man she could rely on. Completely contented, she leaned against Gabe's arm as he opened the door for her, took her hand in his, and escorted her out of the shop. Scenic Snowing Rock reminded her of a Swiss mountain village, laced with aromas from hot chocolate and homemade gingerbread stands, a layer of pure white snow on the sidewalks. Miles of sparkling Christmas lights decorated timbered roofs and stone fences. Christmas was definitely in the fresh mountain air.

As she and Gabe strolled slowly hand in hand, her feet dragged. She really wasn't excited about the prospect of leaving this special town where she now felt very much at home.

The following day passed quickly as Noelle packed her luggage and carry-on for her trip.

Despite his assurances, the henna tattoo Gabe had applied on Thanksgiving Day hadn't disappeared, despite endless scrubbing and applying oil on the tattoo.

She shrugged. No matter. Colin could fume all he wanted. Gabe would be with her, supporting and cheering, beginning with their plane ride to Saint Augustine.

* * *

EXCEPT THAT GABE wasn't able to accompany her on the plane.

Three hours before their scheduled departure, he'd phoned and explained that the director hadn't approved one of the film's action scenes, pouring rain was predicted in

Wilmington, and Gabe had been requested to return for one last stunt before the shoot was considered a wrap and ready to go into post-production.

Noelle lowered her head and covered her face with her hands. "Can't your agent just call the director and tell him you have other plans?"

"I could never renege on this gag. The entire film would be delayed. They need me."

Noelle's stomach had clenched as he continued to expound on the details.

'What about me? I need you, too,' she'd wanted to say, although she said nothing, silently berating herself for wanting him near and relying on him, while knowing millions of dollars were at stake when producing a box-office hit.

"The scene will take less than a half day to film. I'll fly from Wilmington directly to Saint Augustine, all right?" Gabe was saying. He gave her his agent, Chris Swidering's, cell phone number in case she needed to reach Gabe while he was working.

A heavy sigh accompanied her words. "I'll arrange for the box office to hold your ticket."

"I'll be there. When you step onto the stage, look for me in the center of the first row. I'll be the guy who can't keep his eyes off you."

"And the guy who'll clap the loudest," she added with false cheer.

Because he was a man of his word. Wasn't he?

CHAPTER 15

$\mathcal{I}$n her dressing room at the Forum Theater, Noelle subjected herself to a full-length mirror scrutiny while she zipped up her black gown and adjusted a thin, rhinestone belt at her waist. Despite her concern that she'd gained weight, the gown still fit, clinging to her slender curves. She scrutinized the henna tattoo, boldly emblazoned on her right forearm.

'Every time you look at your tattoo, think of me. I'll do the same,' Gabe had said.

His words filled her with confidence, and she straightened her posture. Besides, there was no point in worrying about any shocked reactions because of an innocent henna tattoo.

Sitting at her dressing table, she drew her blonde curls severely up and back, threading a red velvet ribbon through her hair to contrast with the color of her black gown. Gabe had said he liked her hair that way because the style accentuated her high cheekbones.

She applied stage make-up with an exaggerated hand, knowing that otherwise her complexion would appear washed out under harsh onstage lights. Cream-colored foundation was followed by black mascara, muted red lipstick, and a fine dusting of light powder on her face.

Her dressing room was filled with the light, sweet scent of dozens of baby-pink rose bouquets, along with a handwritten card, all from Gabe. A bottle of rosé sparkling pink champagne sat chilling in a tall silver urn.

'We'll celebrate your success together after your performance, so look for me in the front row, all right?' the card read.

Then where was he? She'd checked her cell phone nonstop for the past hour, and had even phoned his agent and left a message.

She sank stiffly into a chair and briefly closed her eyes, reflecting on the previous afternoon's events. Colin had demanded a methodical run-through of their entire performance during dress rehearsal. Two seven foot grand pianos had been tuned and retuned, and acoustics checked. Several difficult sections had required practice at slower tempos with a metronome ticking steadily in the background.

After three hours of rehearsing, Colin had finally taken his hands off the piano keys and stretched his arms out wide. He'd swaggered over to Noelle's piano and surveyed her with a satisfied expression. "That went well."

"Your father will be pleased," she said.

Colin had slowly shaken his head. "My father passed last year, soon after you and I were divorced."

"I'm sorry, I didn't know," Noelle said. "I'm sure you miss him."

"I think of him every time I play piano." Colin had replied.

Noelle had wiped the sweat from her hairline and raised her face to a welcome blast of air-conditioning. Saint Augustine's sub-tropical climate at Christmas was typical beach weather, and she'd chuckled at the garland-wrapped palm trees outside the terminal entrance when she'd landed at the airport.

"As soon as our gig is completed, I'm returning to Snowing Rock," she'd said to Colin.

Gig, not gag, she'd smiled to herself, thinking of Gabe.

"How can you put up with those mountain hillbillies sitting in their rocking chairs, spending their days watching the snow fall?" Colin had smirked.

"You couldn't be more wrong," she'd said.

Colin had shrugged, his gaze brightening. "Our ticket sales have been phenomenal. After the concert, you'll be paid a flat fee of five thousand dollars per our agreement. I knew my advertising would pay off—the estranged husband and wife duo teaming up for a Christmas reunion."

"You didn't pay for advertising, the Forum Theater did," she'd contradicted. "And the revenue from a full house will be well over sixty thousand dollars."

"You're calculating gross ticket sales," Colin had said. "You've never had my shrewd business sense. I have promoters to pay, the venue ..." he'd sighed dramatically.

"You were paid a flat rate of forty thousand dollars," she'd said. "I checked. And I deserve half. Twenty thousand dollars."

"You agreed to five thousand and—"

"I changed my mind. Our agreement was verbal. We didn't shake hands, nor was there a witness."

Colin had cracked his knuckles. She'd forgotten how much she'd disliked that.

"Be grateful I've given you a second chance to redeem your career," he'd said.

"And be grateful I'm one half of your success. Enjoy this concert, because it'll be the last time we'll be performing together."

Her thoughts snapped to the present by an insistent rap

on her dressing room door, followed by an usher reminding Noelle that curtain time was in five minutes.

She stood and placed Gabe's card on her dressing table.

Now was the moment she'd been anticipating for months, the night of her successful return to the concert stage. She checked her appearance in the mirror, smoothing her gown with clammy hands. Sure, she was nervous and struggled with stage fright, and she'd learned to channel her nervous adrenaline into a dynamic performance. This performance would be no exception. She paused and whispered a silent prayer, thanking God for her natural abilities and talent.

Before she left the dressing room, she checked her cell phone once more, hoping Gabe had sent a text message. Perhaps he'd lost cell phone service because he was on a plane. Perhaps he'd gone directly to the Forum Theater as soon as he'd landed and hadn't had time to call.

The air-conditioning made her shiver. Perhaps he'd gotten hurt during the stunt?

No, she decided wretchedly. His agent would've contacted her.

She took a determined breath, reminding herself that she was a professional and expected on stage, no matter her personal life. With her head held high, she marched into the hallway and turned a glittering, artificial smile on Colin. Despite the fact that Colin employed a professional tailor, the sleeves and pants of his white tuxedo were too short.

Colin's gaze fastened on her right forearm. He loosened his collar. His face reddened. "What … is … that?"

"It's a—"

He jerked his arm out dismissively to silence her. "I know what it is." He snapped his fingers and an usher appeared. "Does anyone have a sweater to put over this woman's shoulders?"

Noelle stood tall. "I won't cover myself. If you don't like the tattoo, then perform this two-piano concert by yourself."

"Thirty seconds," the usher advised.

Colin scowled.

"And we never finished our conversation from last evening. I want my fair share. Twenty thousand dollars," Noelle said.

"I've already spent the money on a new—" His voice rose to a falsetto.

"If you don't agree, then go on stage and explain to the audience."

The usher wrung her hands. "Ten seconds."

"Shut up!" Colin snapped to the usher.

"Agreed?" Noelle held out her hand for Colin to shake. She glanced at the usher. "You're our witness if he reneges."

"Yes, I agree!" Colin roughly grabbed Noelle's hand and shook it. They walked onstage to resounding opening applause, dropped hands, and bowed deeply to the audience.

Noelle's gaze milled the crowd, searching for a handsome, tall man sitting in the front center seat. The gleam in his gaze when they made eye contact would convey his affection and support.

Except his seat was conspicuously empty.

Terrifyingly close to tears, she tried to convince herself this aching letdown was because she'd finally summoned up the courage to trust someone again. However, the desolate ache in her gut sprang from more than that. She wanted him to share in her important night.

As she walked to the grand piano and gazed at the black and white keys, a memory flooded her thoughts.

'Mr. Gabe, do you know what note this is?' Anjali had asked Gabe when he'd joined them at the Fernandez's piano.

His hard chest had pressed against Noelle's back as he'd joked, 'I'm tone-deaf.'

How, with them being so different, could she ever think they could make a life together, that she could trust and depend on him?

Silently, Noelle shook her head. She couldn't think about him now. She was a seasoned performer who was expected to remain focused.

With precise movements, she seated herself on the cushioned artist's bench and placed the music stand down, indicating her music was memorized. She poised her hands above the keys and made eye contact with Colin on the other side of the stage.

'Ready?' He mouthed.

She nodded curtly. Determined to enjoy this performance, she broke into the fast, opening bars of the Chopin etude, using the damper pedal sparingly. The acoustics in the concert hall absorbed the piano sound, and she relied on hand memory to take over the keys.

* * *

AN HOUR AND A HALF LATER, THE CONCERT WAS OVER.

Noelle had panicked for a split second during the Brahms, when her hand had slipped off the black keys when she'd played rapid octaves. The slip hadn't gone unnoticed by Colin, who'd glowered at her from his piano. Briefly paralyzed by fear of a memory lapse, she'd quickly extricated herself from her tight spot by relaxing and breathing in, then centering her attention on the music.

After she and Colin had performed the final notes of the Rachmaninoff finale, they both waited in silence until the music died away. Only then did they lift their fingers from the keys.

Noelle placed her hands in her lap and exhaled. Sweat poured down her back at the physical and emotional exertion involved in performing a vast amount of difficult repertoire.

Judging from the audience's shouts of 'bravo!', the concert had been a success, and she felt an emotional connection to her receptive and enthusiastic listeners. Her audience had forgiven her. In fact, they were embracing her.

Clapping grew faster and faster. She stood and turned, scanning the crowd for Gabe.

His seat was unfilled, and she swallowed hard. She'd performed the most brilliant concert of her career, and he hadn't been there. After countless hours humming the opening bars of Chopin while she'd practiced, he'd chosen his stunt job over her.

With one hand at her side, the other placed on the piano, she bowed to a standing ovation. Colin did likewise. They joined hands in the center of the stage and bowed deeply. As they'd rehearsed innumerable times, they straightened, smiled at the audience, and walked off the stage.

After another entrance and exit to great, gratifying applause, Noelle raced to her dressing room, shut the door, and snatched up her cell phone. Surely Gabe had called or texted. Her hands shook as she scanned the messages, consisting of only a missed phone call from Aunt Joy, as well as two congratulatory text messages, one from Mrs. Fernandez, the other from Caroline.

In desperation, she dialed his agent's cell phone again.

Christopher Swidering answered on the first ring. He stated rather vaguely that, yes, Gabe had finished the film shoot later than planned and been detained for several hours afterward before boarding a plane for New York City. Christopher, suddenly pleading busyness, had apologized for not returning her earlier call and hastily broke the connection.

Noelle sank into her dressing room chair. Gabe hadn't flown to Saint Augustine, he'd flown to New York City.

An usher knocked, delivering the news that several fans waited in the hallway for autographs. Also, the usher continued, Mr. Rudovich wanted a word with Noelle.

Pleading exhaustion, Noelle instructed the usher to apologize to her fans, close her dressing room door, and tell Mr. Rudovich to mail her check.

Noelle lowered her chin to her chest, anger and disappointment tramping dizzily through her mind. Somehow, she needed to stand, collect herself, and walk out of the Forum Theater.

She couldn't, her mind screamed. She needed to be alone.

She stepped to the full-length mirror and studied the tattoo.

'Running away from your problems is a race you'll never win.'

'Words to live by,' Gabe had said.

Perhaps she should call him. Anxiously, she wiped her palms along the folds of her black gown and picked up her cell phone. But what would she say if he answered?

Noelle trooped out of the Forum Theater, leaving Gabe's numerous rose bouquets, his card declaring that they'd celebrate together, and his bottle of pink champagne behind. She seated herself in the back of the taxi she'd called earlier, giving the driver her high-rise apartment address. Thankfully, the theater had cleared quickly and the sidewalks were empty. Colin was most likely celebrating in a fancy nightclub with his critic friends.

The taxi sped through muggy Saint Augustine streets, past a Santa Claus electronic display brilliantly flashing red 'ho, ho, ho' across a giant screen. Animated Christmas displays and wax myrtle trees were illuminated with white lights.

She sagged against the worn taxi seat and closed her eyes, her heart thudding dully in her chest. She'd imagined a fun-filled, snowy Christmas with Gabe. Now she'd be celebrating alone in Saint Augustine. A big city, just like New York City.

Her eyes snapped open and she jolted upright, recalling Lucia's conversation with Caroline on Noelle's first day at the candle shop.

'Did I mention I'm opening a second shop in New York City?' Lucia had asked.

New York City. Gabe was flying to New York City.

No, it couldn't be. Lucia and Gabe were just old friends.

Nonetheless, tears filled Noelle's eyes and she blinked them away. Her chest felt heavy. Loneliness and disbelief hurtled through her mind. Once again, she'd been a gullible, insecure fool.

She retrieved her cell phone from her purse to return Aunt Joy's phone message. Despite the late hour, concert offers were flooding Noelle's email inbox and optimism burst like a silvery ray of hope in the midst of a thunderstorm.

Her chin lifted. The heaviness in her chest lightened.

She'd sought esteem and recognition for all her hard work and she'd achieved her goal. She'd succeeded in reaching her dreams, hadn't she?

Then why was she crying?

CHAPTER 16

*O*ver the next few days, Noelle immersed herself in responding to concert venues across the country. With brave determination, she purposely kept herself too busy to think about Gabe. She'd answered text messages from both Mrs. Fernandez and Caroline with the same untruthful response. 'Thanks for your support. Lovin' Saint Augustine.'

Occasionally, she gazed out her apartment window at the clear, sunny sky, preceded on and off by a torrential downpour, before turning back to her computer.

Christmas was less than a week away. Perhaps she should purchase an artificial Christmas tree and hang a burlap stocking on a storage shelf hook in the kitchen.

However, she told herself, she was preoccupied with bookings, so Christmas would need to be put on hold for another year. She entertained the idea of spending Christmas Day walking alone on a beach, possibly dining at one of the resort hotels afterward, before deciding on a take-out from a local cafe.

Gabe had phoned soon after Noelle returned to her

apartment after the concert. At first, his messages were short, upbeat, and congratulatory, becoming longer as the days progressed, sometimes incensed, sometimes pleading with her to return his calls, always followed by an apology for missing her performance.

He'd explained he'd been detained in Wilmington, skimming over the details. And he'd never mentioned his trip to New York City, only that he'd returned to Snowing Rock and was waiting for Noelle while attending to last minute wedding preparations for his cousin, Holly. The preparations included obtaining Holly's marriage license and the resultant wait period before her vows were said.

Each time Noelle replayed his messages and heard his deep, male voice, a part of her died inside. When she'd first arrived in Snowing Rock, she'd been uninterested in a relationship with a man. She'd feared placing her trust in anyone again.

And then she had. She'd taken Gabe at his word. She'd relied on him. She'd started to let down her guard, and he'd left her for his stuntman job.

Perhaps Colin had been right all along and she truly didn't deserve happiness.

Colin's check for twenty thousand dollars arrived the morning after the concert, which she'd deposited in her bank account. The money gave her safety and security. Now, she didn't need to rely on anyone for her finances.

And, the same day her check arrived, Noelle snagged a booking agent.

However, that was the end of her good luck.

The following evening, on her walk to an artsy Cuban restaurant, she paused to stare at a billboard advertising the new blockbuster film, 'Force of Thunder Two', featuring a tough-looking, handsome man, seemingly flying through the air in a race car. Noelle knew, without glancing at the billboard twice, that the man was Gabe. Blindly, she raced back to her apartment, valiantly holding back tears until the door was safely closed behind her.

One day later, while sitting in her desk chair perusing forwarded mail, a Snowing Rock address leapt out at her. She read and reread Holly's wedding invitation, recognizing Gabe's return address on the foil-stamped response card. Remembrances of his magnificent home on Thanksgiving night flashed, and a painful tightness constricted Noelle's throat.

She'd leaned against him, with his hands wrapped around her waist, and he'd whispered, 'Noelle Wentworth, I love you. I've always loved you.'

Love. Dependability. Trust. She closed her eyes as tears streaked down her face.

Sternly, she told herself to open her eyes, marvel at the details of the embossed wedding invitation objectively, and stop crying.

She picked up a pen. On the smaller response card, she checked 'will not attend' and wrote in her name. She placed the response card in the stamped envelope, pre-addressed to Gabe. In the morning, she'd drop the card in the mailbox.

That was easy, Noelle decided, only to find herself in a crumpled heap a few minutes later, dabbing at her eyes, in that very same desk chair.

The following afternoon, Caroline called.

"Hey, Miss Saint Augustine, don't panic, but your Aunt Joy is in the hospital. We had another snowstorm and the power's been out. Anyway, your aunt took a spill inside her cottage and bruised her arm. She'll be convalescing for a few days in Snowing Rock Hospital and is in room 22, on the second floor. She can't work, and it's a few days before Christmas. I need help because I'm swamped here at the candle shop!"

"I'll phone the hospital now," Noelle hedged.

"Don't you have a round-trip plane ticket that Mr. Waters had purchased? Take the next flight from Saint Augustine to Fisher's Crossing."

Noelle stared apprehensively at her cell phone. "I don't know."

"Yup, that's a great answer," Caroline burst out, clearly annoyed. "And when you get here, you can give me an explanation as to why you're not returning his calls. He's visited the shop every day."

"Please. I don't want to discuss him again. He promised to attend my concert. I reserved a front row seat for him, I relied on him—"

"Why can't you be more understanding?" Caroline interrupted.

"I spoke with Gabe's agent."

Noelle could almost visualize Caroline throwing her head in her hands and muttering.

"Well, that explains everything," Caroline said. "Now get on the plane tomorrow and text me when you land. Alan will pick you up at Fisher's Crossing airport. Your concert is over and there are no excuses."

* * *

THE NEXT DAY, Noelle arrived in Snowing Rock. After she'd set her luggage in Aunt Joy's cottage, Noelle walked two blocks to Snowing Rock Hospital. The weather was unusually sunny, although a cold snap was predicted.

She stood outside the hospital, staring at the brightly-lit ambulance entrance sign. A woman in patterned blue scrubs walked by briskly.

"Coming inside?" the woman asked, holding the hospital's sliding glass door open.

Noelle hesitated, inhaling hospital smells of antiseptic and bleach along with her get-well arrangement of red and white spray roses that she'd purchased at the airport's gift shop.

The woman in scrubs waited expectantly and glanced at her watch.

Noelle reframed her hesitation. Yes, she was apprehensive, because entering the hospital would dredge up sad memories of her parents' deaths. On the other hand, how was she supposed to visit Aunt Joy if she didn't step inside?

Her thoughts went back to the first time she'd visited her aunt at the rehab center.

'Confront your supposed failure, view it as a learning experience, and keep moving forward,' Aunt Joy had said.

Her aunt was right. A hospital setting was an obstacle she could conquer, just as she'd rebounded from an embarrassing public concert by overcoming her fears and succeeding.

Thanking the woman in scrubs for holding the door open, Noelle walked through the entrance. She rode the elevator up to the second floor with two nurses writing notes in clipboards and conversing in low voices. Noelle quickly found room 22, and, with a deep breath, she entered her aunt's hospital room.

Aunt Joy lay sleeping in the hospital bed, looking frail and peaceful. Her favorite blue slippers were tucked beneath the bed, and a tiny Christmas tree sat on her bedside table. A TV played softly, tuned to a romantic, black and white Christmas movie starring Cary Grant.

Noelle set her bouquet on the window sill beside Gabe's exquisite copper tin get-well arrangement, filled with berry and evergreen aromatherapy scented oils, topped with a candy-cane foil bow. He'd signed the card, 'Warm Wishes For A Speedy Recovery. Best, Gabe.'

With a sigh, Noelle sat on a chair sandwiched between the bed and the window.

Aunt Joy opened her eyes and her thin face broke into a delighted smile. "My beautiful niece! Thank you for coming!"

Noelle drew her chair closer to the bed. "I came as soon as I could after Caroline called me."

"I meant, thanks for coming to the hospital," her aunt said.

"Slowly but surely, I'm learning to confront my fears." Noelle's fingers brushed against the cold stainless steel bed rail as she reached out and squeezed her aunt's hand. "More importantly, how are you?"

"Fortunately, I caught my fall, although I bruised my arm." Aunt Joy drew back the sheets and rolled up the sleeve of her hospital gown, exposing a significant bruise.

Noelle bit her bottom lip. "Oh, Aunt Joy, I'm so sorry."

"The doctor wanted to take precautions because of my age and stick me in this hospital, but I'm fine." Her aunt leaned back on the bed pillows and dismissed Noelle's concern with a sniff. "Your concert was wonderful, dear! I listened to the entire program on the radio."

"I proved to Colin I could step onto that stage and perform again."

"You didn't need to prove anything to anyone except yourself." Aunt Joy settled herself upright on the bed, then promptly asked, "Have you heard from Mr. Waters?"

Noelle stared down at her empty hands. "Yes."

"Then you know he's back in Snowing Rock." Her aunt's expression changed, and she studied Noelle in an extremely odd way. "How is he?"

"I assume he's well." Noelle pressed her lips together, determined not to ask for details, wanting to forget all about him.

"You should talk with him."

"There's nothing to say," Noelle said vaguely.

"I won't pry, although I believe he's a good man." Aunt Joy sighed, then said, "I'm getting out of the hospital in the morning."

"I'll work at the candle shop, and you can rest at the cottage all day."

"Rest?" her aunt countered. "I'm attending Holly Waters's wedding, and Caroline is picking me up early to fix my hair. Did you know Anjali's the flower girl? The flower basket is lined with organza and pearls, and Mr. Waters special-ordered it from Hollywood. Everyone in Snowing Rock is attending the wedding."

Her aunt's words hung in the silence.

Everyone in Snowing Rock was attending the wedding except her, Noelle thought with an unexplainable surge of sadness.

CHAPTER 17

*E*arly the next afternoon, Noelle added finishing touches to the candle shop's display window, featuring elegant white pillar candles in large hurricane vases, surrounded by loose, shiny red ornaments.

Caroline had left before lunch to pick up Aunt Joy and suggested Noelle close by one o'clock. Although Noelle had objected at first, she'd finally agreed. She planned to return to her aunt's cottage and tackle the sugar cookie recipe, this time waiting for the oven to pre-heat.

After a quick take-out lunch from Hal's Subs, Noelle tallied up the morning's receipts at the cash register. Although she'd placed a sign on the door stating that the shop was closed, she looked up as a customer walked in. Noelle regarded the lovely young woman and adorable little boy at her side. The woman's wavy chestnut hair was styled in a long pony-tail tied with a bright yellow hair bow. The style accentuated the woman's double pierced ears.

"Welcome to 'Scents of Joy'," Noelle said. "Sorry, we're closing early."

With a studious smile on her lips, the woman adjusted the

large tote slung on her shoulder. "I'm here to pick up a half dozen candles on back order. Candleglow and Mistletoe."

Noelle's head jerked up. Her stomach clenched. She openly stared at the young woman with the hazel eyes highlighted with gold specks. "And ... and your name?" Noelle asked, although she already knew. Heavens above, she already knew.

"Holly Waters. And this is my son, Devin. We arrived a few days ago, along with my fiancé, John, and John's older sister, Sarah. Gabe and Sarah are the witnesses for my wedding."

Noelle nodded, then smiled at the little boy before turning to Holly. "The candles arrived last evening, although I assumed you'd received them already. I'll check."

As Noelle walked to the back storage room, she silently cursed the ever-efficient Caroline who'd promised to call Gabe and arrange pick-up when Noelle wasn't at the shop.

Noelle found the candles, took them to the counter, and placed them in a shopping bag. Holly accepted the bag with a 'thank you' and settled Devin on the floor near the register. She dropped to her knees and handed him a coloring book and crayons from her tote bag. When she stood, she studied Noelle for a moment.

"What do you know about my cousin, Gabe?" she asked.

Well, Noelle thought, he was charming and certainly hard-working, and up until the concert, dependable, although Noelle didn't share her thoughts aloud. She merely met Holly's persistent stare with silence.

Holly plunked her hands on her slim hips. "How strange. I've heard you're a woman who's bent on succeeding, yet you accept defeat without putting up the smallest struggle."

Noelle shifted, glancing at the time. "Don't you have a wedding to prepare for?"

Holly shrugged. "Gabe's arranging all the details. He's a

planner." She shook her head. "He won't be happy I came here."

Noelle stared blankly at the display window. "If this is about him not attending my concert, I don't want to talk about it."

Holly sighed and took Noelle's hands in hers. "What happened in Wilmington is tearing Gabe apart. And from the haunted look on your face, you're not doing any better."

"He's so dedicated to his job, I know it will always come first." Noelle pulled from Holly's grip. "Besides, it doesn't matter."

"Listen, it does matter." Holly's tone rose. "And both of you aren't going to ruin my wedding by being miserable!"

"I'm not attending your wedding and—"

"Noelle." Holly's face grew speculative. "I thought you and Gabe were growing close, but you really don't know ... do you?"

"Know what?"

Holly put her hands on Noelle's arms. "After Gabe finished the film shoot, he was rushed to Wilmington Hospital because of a diabetes complication. His blood sugar dropped too low because he didn't plan his meals correctly. The filming ran late and he was in a hurry to see you so he didn't bother to eat." Holly released her grip. "Obviously, he missed his flight to Saint Augustine."

Noelle touched a hand to her mouth. Her mind registered shock. "Diabetes? Gabe? He never mentioned—"

Holly gave a bemused smile. "He wants everyone to think he's this strapping, tough guy. Truth is, he was very sick when he was young. His parents were negligent and he wasn't diagnosed with Type I diabetes until he was eleven years old. Since then, he's always been trying to prove himself."

"Why didn't he tell me?"

"Maybe he was waiting to explain in person. I've lived with him the last few days and he wants to see you, although he's not about to approach you again. He's too proud and stubborn."

Noelle's voice caught. She swallowed. "There's so much I want to say to him."

"That's why you're coming with me so you can attend my wedding."

"I ... I sent in my response card stating I couldn't—"

"And I'm the bride and overruling your response card. My car is parked outside the candle shop."

"I can't go to a wedding looking like this." Noelle rubbed her hands across her gray wool sweater and navy slacks. "I need to change. I'd bought a new dress, but it's at my aunt's cottage."

Holly bent to pick up Devin's crayons and coloring book and grabbed his hand. "Then what're we waiting for? I can't be late for my own wedding!"

* * *

NOELLE REGARDED her reflection in the cottage's bedroom mirror, buttoning a faux-fur jacket over her red sequined dress. She'd grinned at the henna tattoo peeking through the sheer sleeve of her dress. Although the tattoo had faded, the words were still prominent.

'Running away from your problems is a race you'll never win.'

With that thought, the knot in her stomach began to dissolve, and a few minutes later she pronounced herself ready. Black tights kept her legs warm, and she'd added red pom-poms to her black leather ankle boots for a wintry, festive air. She'd pulled her hair back from her forehead, the way Gabe liked, secured at the crown with a sparkly hair clip. Soft blonde curls framed her heart-shaped face, and pearl stud earrings completed her outfit.

She'd changed quickly while Holly and Devin waited inside Aunt Joy's cottage.

Now, an hour later, Noelle walked to the entrance of Gabe's barn where the wedding was being held. Holly had dropped Noelle off before driving on to Gabe's house to get ready. Holly had kept the bag of Candleglow and Mistletoe candles, saying she wanted them for her new home.

Darkness had fallen, and Noelle regarded the large, rustic barn doors lit by a twinkling string of bistro lights. She hesitated, trying to calm herself. What would Gabe say when he saw her? Would he demand she leave? Or worse, would he simply ignore her, his handsome face disinterested, yet cordial?

And what if Lucia were his date?

With resolve, Noelle pulled her mind away from defeating thoughts. He'd once told her he loved her, that he was a patient man, and would wait for her.

Her muscles tightened in readiness. She'd come this far and, if he gave her a moment, she'd apologize for misjudging him. All she would ask was a few minutes of his time.

Noelle stepped inside the barn and gasped at the gorgeous interior decorated in a wintry design theme. Blue ambient lighting transformed the large space into an icy hue, calling to mind a romantic winter fairyland. Crystal strands of garland dripped from a glittering chandelier hanging in the center. Silver tablecloths were draped over six long tables, shimmering beneath the warm glow of Candleglow and Mistletoe candles. Fresh rosemary, wrapped in burlap, was used as place cards for each table setting, and clear glass chargers framed gleaming white china.

Noelle wandered to the cake table on a rollable stand displaying a five-tiered pink wedding cake. Pink and white fondant roses cascaded down the front of the cake, and pink rose petals were sprinkled on the scalloped frosting. Mrs. Fernandez was certainly a gifted cake decorator, and white sheer curtains and a silver candelabrum added an elegant backdrop.

In addition, ten vanilla scented beeswax votive candles encircled the cake. Noelle grinned. Gabe had planned the occasion perfectly.

She glanced at her watch, knowing she was early. A violinist and keyboard player setting up their instruments, along with uniformed caterers from Snowing Rock Country Club, nodded to her. The clergyman stood at the front by the altar. He looked out an arched picture window to acres of wintry pastureland lit by moonlight.

Sprigs of fir branches hung from the backs of chairs that were set, ceremony style, facing the altar. White orchids in tall silver stands flanked the aisle.

Noelle hung her coat on a coat rack near the entrance and took an aisle seat in the back row. Soon afterward, the wedding guests filed in. Caroline, Alan, and Aunt Joy installed themselves in the vacant seats in Noelle's row, along with Mr. and Mrs. Fernandez.

Aunt Joy's gray hair was coiled in a low bun. True to her non-conformist style, she'd added a crown of shiny green leaves, which didn't match her bohemian style purple gown.

Aunt Joy's face was wreathed in a wide smile. "I'm thrilled you decided to attend, dear. You made a wise decision."

"I had a change of heart, along with some encouragement from the bride," Noelle replied.

With two opening blasts of organ chords from the keyboard player, the clergyman and John, the groom, took their places at the altar. Sarah, the only bridesmaid, walked down the aisle alone, followed by Anjali and Devin. Anjali's dark face gleamed with joy, her red plaid dress and black patent leather shoes fitting to perfection. She proudly held up her organza flower basket, skipping down the aisle while tugging on Devin's hand.

When the wedding march began playing, all the guests stood to watch Holly walk slowly down the aisle escorted by Gabe. She wore a short, embroidered, white lace gown with bell sleeves, her hair in the same pony-tail style she'd worn earlier at the candle shop. Gabe looked unbearably handsome, resplendent in an elegant black tuxedo hugging his tall, powerful frame.

Noelle stood a mere foot away from him as he passed, her hands tightly bracing the seat in front of her. She wanted to rely on his undeniably strong presence. Trusting him. Loving him.

* * *

GABE STOOD SILENTLY at the altar during the service. Holly and John's marriage vows held a keen sense of regret for him, because he'd debated asking Noelle to marry him only a few weeks earlier on Thanksgiving night.

A hollowness filled his chest. So much had changed in just a few short weeks.

Scarcely turning his head, he viewed the crowded rows, moving past Caroline and Alan. He greeted Mr. and Mrs. Fernandez with an appreciative nod, and grinned as his gaze went by Aunt Joy wearing an outrageous shiny green crown on her head, then to a beautiful blonde woman in a red sequined dress sitting at the end of the row.

His heart leapt, pounding wildly as a pair of gorgeous jade-green eyes locked with his.

He tore his gaze away. Noelle was in Snowing Rock! Despite her response card stating 'no', she'd come to the wedding after all.

Briefly, he closed his eyes. Why was she here?

She hadn't answered his numerous calls. She hadn't been interested. What had she meant when she'd told both Mrs. Fernandez and Caroline that she loved Saint Augustine?

His pride demanded he meet her stare with bland indifference, showing he was through pleading with her.

His heart, however, didn't agree with his pride.

'I'm slowly learning to trust again,' she'd said quietly. 'Give me time.'

He opened his eyes and found her gaze. Her lips parted and she smiled, her expression beseeching. Silently, she was asking him for a second chance.

He hardly stirred, could scarcely take a breath. Long ago, he'd been mesmerized by a brave young woman who'd been immersed in a posh musical world that a guy like him, from the other side of town, had never known existed. And now, fifteen years later, he longed to hear Noelle say what he read in her expressive green eyes.

'I love you.'

And he loved her, with an affection that had only increased over the years.

Briefly, he contemplated striding down the aisle and escorting her to the altar, requesting that the clergyman marry them alongside his cousin and new husband.

No, Gabe quickly decided. That wasn't fair to Noelle. His courageous, talented woman deserved her own exquisite wedding.

The fanfare recessional music struck a majestic cadence and, with a start, Gabe realized the ceremony was over. He waited for the bride and groom, followed by Anjali and Devin, before he walked down the aisle beside Sarah.

Looking through the celebratory, milling crowd, he spotted Noelle nodding and smiling with Caroline. A caterer, behind a cart, poured glasses of pink champagne, while Caroline scooped up several coconut breaded shrimp.

When Gabe reached them, he flashed a polite, dismissive greeting to Caroline.

She grabbed her champagne glass. "Good to see you, too, Mr. Waters," Caroline laughed and walked away.

He dragged air into his lungs and turned to face Noelle, pausing to feast his gaze on her. She looked like the exquisite goddess in a red sequined dress that he'd dreamed about, and she was heartbreakingly stunning.

He cleared his throat. "Champagne?" he asked.

"I'll wait."

"May we speak for a moment?"

"Yes, of course," she said.

He kept her close to his side, leading her to the barn door entrance. He lowered his head and whispered against her soft, blonde hair. "I've missed you very, very much."

Her taffeta skirt rustled gracefully as she turned to face him. "I've missed you, too."

"I'm sorry I wasn't there for your performance."

"I know," she said softly.

"You played brilliantly. I listened to the entire concert on the radio the day afterward on a delayed broadcast. Does that count?"

She laughed, despite the tears misting her eyes. "Please, don't apologize."

He drew her nearer. Gently, he brushed a shining curl from her cheek, then glanced around. "There are too many people here," he said. "My cousin won't mind if we leave the reception early."

"She might. She's the one who brought me here."

He scowled. "Holly?"

"Yes, she stopped at the candle shop this afternoon. She told me about what happened to you in Wilmington."

The back of his throat ached. Mentally, he debated about thanking Holly or being outraged that she'd interfered in his personal affairs.

"What did she say?" He tried to keep his tone casual.

"Everything." Noelle breathed after a long pause. "And I'm so relieved you're well."

He nodded a curt acceptance and took her hand.

"Where are we going?" Noelle asked. "I'd love a piece of Mrs. Fernandez's pink champagne wedding cake."

"We'll be back in time for champagne and wedding cake," he assured.

Noelle retrieved her coat from the coat rack near the doorway.

He slipped her coat around her shoulders and offered a slow grin. "There's something at my house I'd like to show you. An early Christmas gift."

CHAPTER 18

*T*he ride from the barn to Gabe's house took less than five minutes. They sat outside in the Land Rover while the engine idled and the heat blasted.

He sat silent, studying her.

She looked down at her hands. "I don't know how to begin. I only know I want a fresh start."

"Let's begin with truthfulness. You told me once you were slowly learning to trust again. Do you trust me now?"

She nodded.

"Then why didn't you answer my calls after the concert?"

She gave a little sigh. "I ... couldn't. I was so disappointed you weren't in the audience. Between my parents' deaths and my bad marriage, I assumed you'd let me down, just like everyone else."

"I'd never intentionally let you down, all right?" His hazel eyes held hers as he continued. "And then there's the matter of Thanksgiving evening when we were standing on my balcony together. Do you remember what I said?"

She looked up at him. "Yes."

"Then shall we try again?" He tilted up her chin. "I've been waiting for a more fitting reply."

She nodded, her voice too choked with tears to speak.

He cradled her face in his hands. "Noelle Wentworth, I love you."

She lay her trembling hand against his cheek. "I love you, too."

He grinned. "Much better."

She attempted to grin in return, which was thwarted by tears of elation streaking down her cheeks.

He wiped her tears with his fingers and his lips captured hers.

Intent on showing him how much she loved him, Noelle returned his kisses with all the happiness in her heart. By the time the kiss ended, the SUV's windows were fogged. He kept his arms around her while they both waited for their breathing to slow.

He kissed her forehead. "Shall we go into the house?"

Unwilling to end their discussion yet, she bit her lip and hesitated. "I have a question, too."

His dark brows drew together. "Go ahead."

"Why didn't you tell me about your diabetes? If I'd known—"

"I felt ashamed," he said. "You saw me fifteen years ago as a skinny, defenseless kid who needed protecting. I didn't want to appear even weaker in your eyes."

"Diabetes doesn't make you weak. You're brave, overcoming great obstacles and succeeding. Holly said you've managed your diabetes since you were a child."

He nodded soberly. "Yes, and if I take care of myself, there's no problem. However, because of my hectic schedule, I've made a decision." He transferred his gaze to his home, then Noelle. "I'm slowing down my stunt work and devoting more time to my teen outreach center."

He hadn't mentioned devoting more time to her, Noelle reflected. And there was something else she wanted to ask him. He'd flown to New York City and must've seen Lucia.

Noelle waved an airy hand in her mind, refusing to abandon all her dignity.

They'd reconciled. Everything was settled. They both wanted a fresh start.

A few moments later, they stepped inside the large foyer of his home. Gabe took her coat, as well as his own, hanging both in the entry closet.

Noelle looked up and smiled. A mistletoe was strategically placed in the doorway leading to the living room.

"Did you plan this?" She exaggerated an accusing look at him.

He chuckled. "I hung the mistletoe when I returned from Wilmington, because I was hopeful you'd be joining me here. However, when I received your response card that you wouldn't be attending Holly's wedding, I planned to take the mistletoe down. Then, between the eleventh-hour wedding preparations and the company, I forgot." He offered a guilty shrug. "Sometimes it's better not to be a planner."

She laughed.

He glanced up at the mistletoe. "Shall we?" He gathered her in his arms for a passionate kiss, leaving her trembling and straining to be nearer him.

He lifted his lips and threaded his fingers through her hair. "Did you miss me?"

"More than you can imagine."

His thumbs caressed her cheekbones. "Are you ready to see your gift?" He escorted her into the living room and flicked on the low, overhead light. "Sorry, it was too large to wrap."

Noelle stood stock-still. She blinked, staring at the black, glossy, baby grand piano and matching bench arranged at an angle, between the floor to ceiling windows and the fireplace.

"This piano looks just like mine," she murmured.

"That's because it is," he responded with a hint of amusement in his voice. He walked to the fireplace mantel and lit a half dozen candles.

Noelle shook her head. "My piano is in storage in New York City ..." Even as she spoke, she began walking toward the piano, slowly at first, then faster.

With Gabe striding behind her, she sat at the bench and checked the fallboard. Beneath were her engraved initials, N.W.

She whirled. "When? How?"

"After I missed your concert and was discharged from Wilmington Hospital, I flew directly to New York City. I'd arranged to get your piano out of storage and ship it to Snowing Rock and wanted to double-check that it was yours. A couple of weeks ago, I'd asked your Aunt Joy, and she assisted me in locating the storage facility."

"Aunt Joy never mentioned anything, although she encouraged me to talk to you."

"We both agree your aunt is a remarkable woman." He lowered his head and his mouth parted Noelle's for a deep, long kiss. When he lifted his lips, he whispered, "I want my own private piano concert, all right?"

The husky tone of his request sent a jolt up Noelle's spine.

He sat on the bench beside her with one arm around her shoulders. "With all the free time I'll have, will you teach me how to play the piano?"

"I thought you were tone-deaf."

"I know where middle C is." He struck the white key with his free hand.

She glanced up at his smiling, indignant expression. "I've

thought about teaching piano when I'm not helping my aunt in the candle shop," she said.

He traced her engraved initials on the shiny fallboard with his fingertips. "It's a good thing your last initial is the same as mine. Otherwise, I'd have to buy you a new piano."

His tone was light, although Noelle heard the roughness in his voice.

"What do you mean?"

"Besides piano lessons and volunteering at my outreach center, I'll want to devote my time to my beautiful wife." He looked meaningfully at her. "Noelle Wentworth, will you marry me? I can't begin to comprehend my life without you."

"Yes." She snuggled closer and locked her hands around his powerful shoulders. "Gabe Waters, my answer is yes."

"We can be married on Christmas Day," he said.

"You can't be serious." Noelle sighed. "We'll need time to plan and prepare."

"All right, I'm a patient man," he nodded with a grin. "We'll wait until New Year's Day. We'll book everyone tonight when we return to my cousin's reception. The cake decorator, the clergyman, the musicians, and the caterers are all there. Will the barn be all right for the ceremony and reception? You know I'm usually a planner."

Tears of happiness welled in her eyes. "Yes, perfect."

He stood, extended his hand, and nodded toward the piano bench. "I wonder if there's any Christmas music in there."

Surprised by his suddenly somber tone, she eyed him quizzically before she stood and lifted the lid of the bench. "I'd stored old sheet music, but doubt there's any Christmas music."

"Keep digging," he prodded.

A small, blue Tiffany box stopped her short.

She glanced at him and he nodded for her to continue.

She lifted out the box. When she unsnapped the lid, a magnificent diamond ring glittered in the glow of the candles.

In a soft voice, he said, "I hope you like the ring. It's not as beautiful as you, but—"

She stared at the ring in awe, admiring the shiny, flawless sparkle. Poignant tears filled her eyes.

"Merry Christmas, Noelle." He slipped the ring onto her finger.

She wanted to tell him that he was generous and thoughtful, that his exquisite ring was gorgeous, and that she trusted him completely. All she could manage to say through her tears was, "Merry Christmas, Gabe."

He crushed her to his chest. Assaulted by his intense kisses, her senses whirled.

Because for this man she adored, her love was as sweet and warm as a holiday candle.

THE END

A NOTE FROM JOSIE

Dear Reader,

As you can imagine, I learned a lot about making candles while researching *Candleglow and Mistletoe*.

I am a professional pianist and enjoyed writing Noelle's character. And Gabe made the perfect hero.

If you love this sweet romance as much as I loved writing it, please help other people find this book and write a review.

Candleglow and Mistletoe is available in Audiobook, ebook, paperback, Hardcover, and Large Print paperback.

My Spotify Play List for Candleglow and Mistletoe is here.

BUTTER BALL COOKIE RECIPE

Yields 3-4 dozen cookies

A small number of simple ingredients result in a flavorful, delicious cookie!

1 cup butter (2 sticks). Leave butter on counter at least 2 hours beforehand

(Do not use margarine or light butter.)

1 teaspoon vanilla

½ cup powdered confectioner's sugar

2 ½ cups flour

1 cup chopped nuts (optional)

Cream butter and sugar until well blended. Add vanilla, flour, and nuts if desired.

Mix thoroughly. Shape into small balls. Place on an ungreased cookie sheet.

Bake in a 400 degree oven for 15 minutes. Watch closely as they will burn if left in too long. Oven times and temperatures may vary.

Note: Dough is very crumbly, but the warmth of your hands will make them easier to shape.

While still warm, roll in a small amount of additional confectioner's sugar.

Enjoy!

JOSIE RIVIERA

USA TODAY BESTSELLING AUTHOR

A Portuguese Christmas

A HOLIDAY ROMANCE

CHAPTER 1

*I*t was simply the way it was in Portugal, another morning dawning so brilliantly. Dappled sunbeams reflected off the Atlantic Ocean; the surf pounded along a long, sweeping beach.

So this was a Portuguese December, Krystal Walters thought. It was so different from the cold weather battering her hometown of Newport, Rhode Island.

Here in Portugal, the sun never stopped shining.

She shaded her eyes, admiring the shimmering turquoise water. Feet snug in booties and reef socks, she wiggled her toes in the golden sand.

Hurray! Her anticipation grew with each breath of brisk, salty air. After a grueling year-long championship tour, the World Surf League ranked her as one of the top seventeen women surfers in the world. She actually stood on Medão Grande Beach's shoreline in Peniche, Portugal.

She tucked her waxed surfboard under her arm, hoisted her belongings, and headed for the competitor's area to check out the scheduled surf heats. Earlier that morning, she'd showered at the Oasis, an inexpensive hotel, and surfed for a short while. She'd encountered a sizeable wave and had spent a few seconds underwater. An hour had passed, and she still felt winded.

Shake it off.

Nothing would stop her, certainly not a little time underwater.

She gripped her water bottle, drained the contents, and refilled.

Slinging her lucky striped beach towel over her shoulder, she regarded the panoramic view of sky, tidal channels and mountains.

I wish you were here to see all this, Ernie.

A scream of sorrow slammed into her chest. Her carefree marriage to Ernie had lasted four months. And then, a week prior to their first Christmas together, he'd drowned while surfing.

"A huge wave will pack a big punch," the emergency medical responder had remarked. "Rip currents are drowning machines."

Ernie's death had left her disheartened. To escape a despair that never went away, she turned inward. Never again would she rely on anyone for emotional support. She couldn't bear the pain of loss, of abandonment, of defeat.

Sam Larson, an American surfer competing in the men's event, came to stand beside her. Playfully, he snatched her towel and dangled it in front of her. "Nervous?"

She seized her towel from him. "Absolutely."

"Ready to win?"

"I'm always out to achieve my personal best."

Sam nodded toward the voluptuous, sun-kissed brunette woman effortlessly riding a twelve-foot wave. "I gather from Wilhelmina's gutsy performance, she's aiming to win the preliminary competition too."

Krystal thoughtfully sipped from her water bottle. "She's an epic surfer."

"You're more proficient. Glad you're able to compete again. How long were you off the circuit?"

"Three years."

Sam's green-eyed gaze caught hers. The proverbial surfer dude, all bronzed skin and long, bleached-blond hair. "We missed you."

"Thanks." She swallowed the tightness in her throat and stowed the water bottle in her board bag. Affectionately, she patted her surfboard. "Angel and I are glad to be back."

"Angel?"

"My surfboard's name is Angel. You?"

"Umm, no. Although one of my buddies named his surfboard Rhino."

Krystal laughed. "I've always had a love affair with the ocean. I hope to generate a sponsorship from one of the swimsuit companies."

"Don't we all?" Sam smirked.

"Actually, lately, I've enjoyed sketching and designing swimsuits."

"Submit your designs. All the women's swimwear companies are represented here."

"Someday. For now, I'm here to surf."

Sam's smile was quick. "Conditions, swell models and the weather forecast are all textbook."

"Textbook is reassuring. I want to get out of Portugal as soon as possible."

"So you'll use all your feminine blonde, blue-eyed energy to accept your first-place winnings and leave this impressive climate behind?"

Krystal pulled sunblock from her purse and rubbed it on her nose and cheeks. "After the finals on December nineteenth, I'll return to Rhode Island."

"The purse is $15,000," Sam said.

"And if I win, I'm building an in-law apartment onto my bungalow so that my dad can live with me. We plan to celebrate Christmas together."

She was done with grief and heartache, and finally ready to celebrate the holidays again.

She scanned the spectators mobbing the shoreline, pleased to see her cousin Veronica, along with Veronica's husband, Clemente, and their twin six-year-old boys waving like mad cuckoo clocks in Krystal's direction. Veronica wore a wide-brimmed straw hat that covered her crimped auburn hair, a long rainbow-colored skirt, and pink floral scarf. Draped around her neck hung a camera and binoculars.

Krystal assumed her merriest smile and waved back. To cheer her on, they'd driven two hours from their olive farm in Évora. There was no reason for them to know her unease, or how much was at risk if she lost.

A tall man with thick, wavy black hair stood near Veronica. He crossed his tanned, muscular arms over his creased white shirt, and his worn denim jeans emphasized his fit physique. His expression was one of utter indifference to the entire competition—the crowd's lively applause, the announcer's incessant bullhorn, and the loud riffs of a guitarist strumming and singing that he wished all Portugal girls could be California girls.

Krystal studied the man's handsome features. No doubt he was Clemente's younger brother, Adolfo Silva. Although the men resembled each other, Clemente's softer, paler qualities suited his office environment, whereas Adolfo was tall and broad-shouldered, projecting an aloof strength.

Veronica had high praise for Adolfo. He worked the olive groves and consistently strove to build a more profitable farm.

How had Veronica persuaded her workaholic brother-in-

CHAPTER 2

*K*rystal clung to the edges of her surfboard and gathered a strong, brave breath.

Look up.

I can't.

You're a world-class surfer. You can. You must.

A wave with a fourteen-foot face bore down on her, its force the same as if her body were being hit by a sledgehammer.

A quick surge of dread tightened the muscles in her legs.

Paddle. Hard. Get through the lip of the wave.

She thrust her board to the side and dove under the water.

Breakers flung her toward a reef and protruding rocks.

She gulped, tried to break the collision. Her right wrist twisted.

She was little more than a rag doll being tossed about while her surfboard was sucked under. *No, please*, she prayed. Her ankle was attached to the board by the leash.

Too late. The wave released her board, which flew back at

her like a loose rubber band. A sickening crack sounded when the board connected with her head.

Hold your breath. She floundered, pushed her way to the surface, choking on a mouthful of ocean water.

Paddle. Breathe. Paddle. Breathe.

Don't be frightened. You'll use up all your oxygen.

Her lungs demanded air. She couldn't pull enough in.

Distant shouts resounded. She blinked, orienting herself toward the large group of people crowded together on the shore. Salt water burned her nostrils. Her eyes watered.

Lifeguards and surfers sprinted to the water's edge and yanked her out of the water, dragging her onto the beach. She attempted to get to her feet and stumbled. Her wrist hurt, her head pounded.

The twins were screaming as Clemente and Veronica tried to calm them. Sam hovered nearby.

Adolfo knelt beside Krystal, his fingers moving over her scalp. He grappled for a towel from one of the surfers and positioned it beneath her.

"Most likely, the surfboard slammed into her head," Sam was saying.

Adolfo ran his hands over Krystal's right wrist. "Some swelling already." His voice was composed, his manner soothing. She didn't recognize his next words. He must be speaking Portuguese.

Veronica angled above Krystal, her slim red brows drawing together. "We're taking you to the ER immediately."

Krystal groaned through the pain. She couldn't afford a hospital visit, seeing that every cent was necessary for her father's in-law apartment.

No words came. *Please, please no.*

CHAPTER 3

*K*rystal jolted awake when her body swerved forward.

Her eyes flew open. She sat in the passenger seat of a dusty red pickup truck bouncing along a dirt road, while Adolfo negotiated a hairpin curve. He drove dangerously fast considering the twists and bends in the road.

Disoriented, she peered down. A makeshift splint kept her wrist immobile. She wore a pair of royal-blue joggers and her black-and-yellow competition swim jersey. Her seatbelt was fastened, a downy fatigue-green jacket draped over her shoulders.

"Welcome back to Portugal," he said.

"Was I …" Her tongue. Oh, it was so thick she scarcely managed words. "Was I unconscious long?"

"A few minutes. Veronica helped you change your clothes at the car park. Do you remember?"

"No." The memory of the terrifying wipeout came back in a rush. She gasped. "I must return to—"

"We're heading to the hospital."

She stole a peek at Adolfo's sharp, angled profile. "I said I must—"

"And I said we're heading to the hospital, which is in the opposite direction of the beach." He glanced at her, his liquid-brown eyes filled with concern. "You've been through a lot and need to be examined."

Her brain—surely it was rattling inside her head.

"Don't think, just breathe, and I'll breathe with you."

In and out, in and out, she matched his rhythm.

The truck whizzed past orange trees heavy with ripe fruit. Acres and acres. And poinsettia trees in full bloom, the flaming red bracts set against the backdrop of an uninterrupted blue sky.

She licked her dry lips. "Where are we exactly?"

"I'm taking a quicker route to the Peniche Medical Center to save time. Veronica, Clemente, and their twins are in the car behind us."

"No hospital." Krystal tapped her trembling fingers together.

"I assure you our Portuguese doctors are as good as your American doctors."

"I can't afford …" The cost of a hospital exam in a foreign country was prohibitive without medical insurance.

"I'll cover any expenses."

"I don't take handouts."

"I'm driving, and it's a long hike back to the beach."

She was too weak to smile, to argue. In defiance of the blistering sun streaming through the car windows, she shivered and clutched the downy jacket more securely around her shoulders.

"All I brought with me," Adolfo explained.

She snuggled deeper, filling her nostrils with a pleasing, woodsy scent. "Your jacket reminds me of—"

"Olives." He kept his stare on the road. "I wear it on cold nights when I'm inspecting trees for pests and disease."

"How ...?" At least her hands had stopped quivering. So many questions, none having to do with trees. She couldn't get a full sentence out.

"You'll be all right." Along with a reassuring smile, something flickered in his hazel eyes—hazel, flecked with gold. And the gold radiated compassion.

* * *

AFTER EXHAUSTIVE TESTS AND X-RAYS, Krystal waited for the results in a wood-paneled office in Peniche Medical Center. Veronica and Adolfo sat diagonally from her. Veronica's husband waited in the car with the twins.

"Bento and Bernardo might disrupt the entire hospital with their antics," Veronica explained.

"*Might* disrupt?" Adolfo asked. At Veronica's raised eyebrows, he added smoothly, "In all fairness, your twins are well-behaved when they're sleeping." He caught Krystal's gaze and mouthed, "When awake, they're terrors."

The humor vanished as soon as the examining physician, Dr. Dantas, marched into the office, his white coat flapping behind him. A distinguished man, he appeared to be in his mid-thirties, despite the stark-white streak down the middle of his black hair.

He greeted them with a brisk, "*Boa tarde,*"—Good afternoon—while he shook hands with each of them.

He sank into the chair behind his polished desk and reviewed a summary of Krystal's test findings. Peering over wire-rimmed reading glasses, he asked, "*Senhorita* Walters, do you play football?"

His English was stilted, the hint of a Portuguese accent

accentuating his distinctive rolled *r*'s and singsongy intonation.

"Never, I ..."

"My cousin doesn't play football, doctor," Veronica supplied.

Adolfo tapped his fingers on his thighs. "Instead of football, Krystal has chosen one of the most dangerous, frivolous sports in the world. She surfs for a living."

Other than a quick blink, Dr. Dantas kept his countenance blank. "*Senhorita,* these test results indicate your brain has experienced concussion on top of concussion."

Krystal didn't answer, holding the silence.

The doctor's dark gaze assumed knowing consideration. "You've hit your head several times throughout the years. Are you aware this happened?"

"It's to be expected. The sea is unpredictable and wipeouts are normal."

"Some of your injuries may be micro-concussions."

"Micro means small, right?" Krystal wobbled to her feet. The room swayed and she gripped her fingers around the arms of the wooden chair to steady herself. "So when can I resume surfing?"

The doctor rubbed his black beard. "Not anytime soon."

"Don't concussions heal on their own?" She sat back too quickly and squinted against the mind-numbing thud in her head.

"*Sim.* Yes." Dr. Dantas angled to face her directly. "My question is, why risk additional brain trauma?"

"Surfing is my livelihood, and ..." Her benumbed brain refused to operate normally, begging for darkness in lieu of fluorescent overhead lights.

The doctor pushed back his heavy wooden chair and stood. "Give your body time to heal."

"For how long?"

"A few weeks, preferably forever."

She shook her head. "Out of the question."

"*Dotour* Dantas is not speaking Portuguese." Adolfo's voice vibrated with exasperation. "Are you listening to his excellent English? Your brain cannot tolerate any more jostling."

"Please Krystal, take it slow," Veronica broke in.

Dr. Dantas rubbed the middle of his forehead and briefly closed his eyes. "Do you suffer from migraines, *senhorita* Walters?"

"Thankfully, no."

He pulled out a pad and pen from the desk drawer and scribbled. "Just in case, I'll write you a prescription. Call my office if your headache symptoms become unbearable." He studied her wrist. "In spite of a bad sprain, we've ruled out a fracture and removed the splint. Ice your wrist every three to four hours for a couple days and keep it elevated and take an anti-inflammatory painkiller to reduce the soreness and swelling. Remember, rest is paramount."

"Thank you, although I can't rest.'" Her breath hitched. "The surfing finals are in a couple of weeks."

Veronica's hand shot to her throat. Her round, freckled face held alarm. "You won't be ready to surf again by then."

Krystal kept her manner steadfast and spoke directly to Dr. Dantas. "Once the finals are over, I'm headed back to America."

He ripped the prescription from the pad, retrieved a pamphlet from the drawer, and handed both to her. "With a concussion as severe as yours, plane travel isn't advised for at least six weeks. And no surfing, either. A second blow to your head could be fatal. I also suggest someone staying with you the next few nights, or until you are well."

The prescription and pamphlet slid from Krystal's grasp.

"My departure cannot be delayed. My father and I are celebrating Christmas together. I won't disappoint him."

"Your father can spend Christmas with your brother Julio in Newport," Veronica said, "and we'd love you to celebrate the holidays with us." She clasped her hands together. "On *consoada*, our Christmas Eve dinner, we'll boil *bacalhau*—salted cod—and attend midnight church service. My boys will be so excited."

"I can't."

"Of course you can. Clemente will send for your luggage at the Oasis Hotel. We own a small guest cottage on our olive farm. Aunt Edite stays there when she visits Évora at Christmastime, but she won't be arriving for a while yet. She's a freelance artist, extraordinarily successful, and manages our retail store."

Krystal lowered her head in her hands while reality invaded the doctor's office. A vow was a vow. Her father would never be alone. For the past three years, she'd been emotionally absent from him, from life. All this lost time, all those lost Christmases.

"What's wrong with staying in Portugal for Christmas?" Adolfo was asking.

Krystal shoved past him. "You don't understand. None of you understand."

Her father and her career were all that mattered, and Adolfo was concerned about her opinion of his eternally sunny country?

The office tilted. Her gait faltered.

Veronica came to Krystal's side, although Adolfo was faster.

Firmly, he held Krystal's arm. "In light of the fact that you can't walk farther than two feet without collapsing, it appears you'll be spending Christmas in Portugal whether you like it or not."

CHAPTER 4

*T*wo hours later, rows and rows of olive trees perfectly spaced at twelve metres apart were illuminated by Adolfo's truck's headlights. He neared the cobbled driveway of his home, slowed, and almost wheeled in by habit. Set back from the road and sitting at the edge of the Silvas' olive farm, he could just see his tiled roof and marble porch.

His house dated back a century, and it was a former wine press. Ironic, considering his last argument with his father had been about grape vines and wine.

As he continued to the guest cottage, he pondered, once again, how Veronica had managed to talk him into attending a surfing competition. She'd assured he'd only be gone a few hours.

"A break after an exhausting harvest is necessary to recharge," she'd said.

Well, she'd certainly been wrong. Saving a woman he hardly knew from near disaster was definitely the opposite of recharging. He bit back an exasperated sigh at Krystal's single-minded insistence to surf again. Her slight form and delicate features contradicted her stubborn nature.

He parked his pickup in front of the white-washed guest cottage and eyed his passenger. "Wake up, Krystal. We're home."

She opened her eyes, fire in her gaze, a pout to her full lips. Belatedly, he realized that he'd used the wrong term. Portugal was his home, not hers.

He blew out a breath. She was certainly one plucky American.

The entire drive she'd slept off and on. That is, until she'd hoarsely requested he stop his truck on the side of the road. In the dry grassland, he'd held her silky hair back from her face, consoling her through long shudders as she vomited. Her gaze stayed downcast while he'd offered small drinks from the water bottle in her bag, and he'd gently wiped her chin with his handkerchief.

He'd never minded taking care of sick people. After his father was diagnosed with prostate cancer, he'd moved into his father's home to take care of him. They'd gotten along relatively well considering their many disagreements over the years—until the terrible argument that had severed their relationship.

A familiar knot formed in Adolfo's gut. He knew it well. Even after six months, losing his father was much more difficult than he'd anticipated.

He ran his gaze over his traveling companion, the blonde beauty who was once again sleeping. Somewhere, he'd read that a person suffering from a concussion should be kept awake for twenty minutes of each hour, or they'd risked falling into a coma. So, he'd roused her twice during their drive, discussing surfing, America, any subject he thought might interest her. In reply, she'd offered long-suffering side glances and hadn't spoken. A one-sided conversation wasn't his forte, so he'd switched on the radio, changing channels before choosing an upbeat Portuguese station.

He pulled his keys from the ignition. Twilight had faded to pitch-dark, the sky bathed in the light of a bright winter moon. Shadows lengthened, and the canopies of olive trees swayed slightly in the breeze.

A lamplight glowed within the guest cottage, the curtains tugged closed. He counted on Veronica stocking the kitchen with bread and crackers, food Krystal might be able to keep down.

He glanced at his cell phone. Veronica had texted that she'd unlocked the cottage and was at the main house preparing dinner. She'd stay overnight with Krystal after the twins went to sleep, and he relayed the information to Krystal.

He came around the truck, appreciatively sniffing the pervasive scent of olives. Why wouldn't Krystal want to spend Christmas in his idyllically scenic country? Portugal was the most spectacular country in the world.

He opened the passenger door and extended his hand. "We've arrived, *senhorita.*"

Krystal's long, dark lashes fluttered, and she surveyed him with drowsy eyes. She ignored his outstretched hand and stepped gingerly from the truck. "I can walk by myself."

He stayed beside her. "You're too worn out to venture more than a centimeter."

For speaking so abruptly, he chided himself. To say her entire day had been traumatic was an understatement. Compensating for his sharpness, he moderated his tone and slowed his pace. "Please allow me to assist you up the porch steps."

"Nope, I'm fine." She started forward and wavered.

Sim, sure she was. Automatically, he took hold of her arm. "Just in case, I've got you."

Once inside the tidy cottage, she used the bathroom. Afterward, he settled her in the living room on an L-shaped slipcovered sofa, positioned thick pillows behind her, and covered her with a cotton throw. Portuguese nights were cool in December, and he built a fire in the stone hearth.

He came to stand behind her. "Olive wood burns well without having to dry out first. You should enjoy a warm night."

She didn't answer. She hadn't heard, or wasn't listening.

"Care for something to eat?"

She sank back. "I should call my father."

Lightly, he patted her elbow. She jerked back.

Loud and clear message received.

He moved away. "Veronica contacted your father and brother. They're aware of what happened and will ring you come morning. So for tonight, eat and rest."

Krystal opened her mouth, a protest surely planted on her lips. Rather than waiting for her rebuttal, he took off for the kitchen. A countertop and stools separated the efficient, up-to-date galley from the living room. A one-light pendant hung above a white-tiled kitchen table and chairs.

He rummaged through well-stocked cabinets and found blue-flowered china plates and matching teacups. He hadn't stepped inside the cottage in years, and made a mental note to praise Veronica. She'd accomplished an amazing feat in updating the abandoned stone ruins into a modern, inviting home, complete with a wall-mounted television in the living room.

He hunted for food, pleased to find slices of just-roasted *pernil,* pork shoulder, in the refrigerator.

He set the teakettle on the stove to boil and prepared a toasted Portuguese roll with butter and jam for Krystal. For himself, he readied a crispy roll wrapped around the pork and a glass of red wine.

When he reentered the living room, Krystal was dozing. Firelight illuminated her wavy blonde hair, her flawless complexion, and small, turned-up nose dotted with freckles. Compared to his harsh outdoor life, she resembled a fresh-faced teenager.

Nearing the sofa, he fixed the tray on an antique wooden steamer trunk that doubled as a coffee table. "Your tea and toasted roll are ready."

"Thanks," she mumbled. She opened her eyes and gripped her hands together. "Staying awake is a battle, and my head is exploding."

"Very understandable." Rather than a clipped rejoinder about her dangerous profession, he took the polite approach. "Do you take sugar in your tea?"

"Yes. Sugar is my weakness."

"Good. I mixed in three teaspoons."

She accepted the steaming cup and proffered a listless smile. "Thanks."

He planted himself in a slipcovered chair across from her and swirled his glass of wine. As usual, his thoughts roamed to the farm and the daunting prospect of covering thirteen hectares of land.

"You don't seem to be enjoying yourself," Krystal said.

He glanced up. How long had she watched him?

"I get sidetracked thinking about the farm. Pruning is the next step after the harvest. It must be done hard and will kick-start the trees to produce."

"And I'm keeping you from your work."

He raised the glass of wine to his lips. "Come morning, I'll rise extra early to make up for today. Really, you're no bother."

"You're lying."

He shrugged slightly. *Sim.*

She smiled, a measured smile, much like the one she'd

given him at the beach. He hadn't meant to stare at her then, but her wetsuit had accentuated each enticing inch of her slim curves. She was an alluring woman, although she obviously hadn't appreciated his admiring gaze. He'd noted the proud lift of her chin, her natural grace when she'd swiveled and walked away.

He regarded her brewed tea and roll. "Eat. Take a bite at least."

"I'm not hungry." She propped her elbows on her knees. "Can I ask you something?"

No. "That depends on the subject."

"How can you tell Veronica's twins apart?"

He attempted to keep his expression straight. He hadn't expected that question. Goaded by the good humor in her voice, he said, "Bento is right-handed and Bernardo is left-handed."

A genuine smile burst across her face. "Suppose the boys aren't eating?"

"They're two growing boys with boundless energy. They're always eating."

Her laughter was infectious and he grinned. "In truth, I can't tell them apart since Veronica and Clemente carried the twins down the steps of the hospital six years ago." He took a bite of his sandwich. "More important than a set of unruly twins, how are you feeling?"

She eyeballed her swollen wrist and grimaced. "I'll be completely recovered in a couple days."

Her eyes were a strikingly crystal-blue. He wondered if anyone had ever told her that her eyes matched her name. Krystal.

He swallowed and got to his feet. "Let's take care of your wrist." He strode to the kitchen, nabbed ice from the freezer and wrapped it in a soft towel. Circling back to the living room, he asked, "Do you want to take anything for the soreness?"

"No, my tolerance for pain is high."

He elevated her wrist on a pillow. "I'm the opposite. A little discomfort and I gratefully take a painkiller."

"I can't stay in Portugal, you know."

"So you said." He relaxed on the armchair and stretched out his long legs. "Stay. Go. The decision is yours."

"Dad and I are celebrating Christmas together in Rhode Island."

"So you said."

"Dad raised me and my older brother, Julio. Did you know Julio was adopted from Portugal?"

"No, I didn't. Growing up, did you learn any Portuguese customs?" He didn't like the dark circles under her eyes, the paleness in her cheeks. If only she would drink some sugary tea, or chew on a corner of the roll.

"Dad was too busy working in a factory and raising us." Thankfully, she nibbled at her roll, singling out the crust. "He was a single father. My mother was never a part of our lives."

Adolfo wanted to ask why not, but Krystal wouldn't meet his gaze. He tossed down his wine. "So now you'll repay the favor by taking care of your father?"

"He had a minor stroke a few years ago which makes it difficult for him to live alone, although rehab services come in every day. Julio is recommending that our father live in the Lakewood Senior Lifestyle facility. He believes Dad will benefit from socialization and the activities geared toward people of retirement age." A heavy tone strained her voice. "I don't agree. Dad will be uncomfortable in a strange environment where he won't know anyone."

"And which option does your father prefer?"

"He stubbornly said he wants to live alone." Wistfully, she sighed. "I'm planning a traditional snowy New England

Christmas." She set her teacup between the wooden slats of the trunk. "Dad and I have become incredibly close, and we talk all the time."

"Become?"

"Yes, become."

"Weren't you and your father close before?"

"Excellent tactic, Adolfo." She tugged at the hemline of her joggers and sat back. "Ask me about my family as a diversion to stop me from thinking about surfing, right? What about your family?"

Her reproof brought an unwilling half smile to his lips, along with unexpected sadness. He picked up his empty glass and stared into it. "My father died six months ago. We never said much of anything to each other unless we were discussing olives." Abruptly, he picked up the plates, preparing to head for the kitchen and fix another sandwich.

A stifled sob and suspicious sniffle made him swerve.

Krystal was crying. Sighing, he set down the plates and settled beside her. He never was good around crying women. "Should I get your painkillers?"

"No, no." She dabbed at her luminous damp eyes with the sleeve of her jersey. "Now do you understand why I must return to Rhode Island?"

He fumbled. "Because of an olive farm discussion?"

"Because every minute with our parents is precious, and I won't regret another Christmas."

With a slight head shake, he watched the crackling flames dancing in the hearth. Sudden memories of his father flooded his senses, undeterred by his attempts to banish them to a safe, locked compartment in his mind. Alone, he'd gone to his father's grave at the cemetery numerous times, preferring to mourn in solitude.

He scraped a hand over his bristled jaw. "I wish I'd spent more meaningful time with my *pai,* my father, when he was alive. We argued a lot. He elected to grow olives exclusively, and wanted to someday press olive oil. When I was younger, I begged him to plant grape vines as well."

"Did he?"

"No."

"All the same, you went along with his bidding?"

"Of course. He owned the farm and I respected him, although we never sold olive oil. I was vocal about that. The oil business is so risky."

"Don't olive oil and olives go well together?"

"*Sim.*"

He and his father had held tightly to their opposing views. A silent dispute. No oil. No grapes.

She offered a comforting smile. "I admire you for respecting your father, and I'm genuinely sorry for your loss."

Her smile softened the rawness of grief over his father's death. "Thanks."

"My dad loves glazed ham and cornbread stuffing and I plan to prepare a four-course meal for him on Christmas Day. For an appetizer, I'll stuff celery with peanut butter—" A fresh torrent of tears slid down her cheeks as she spoke.

He never talked about his relationship with his father. In quieter moments, he reviewed the many times they'd shouted at each over the years, what they did to hide their emotions.

And now Krystal was sobbing about ham and cornbread stuffing and stuffed celery.

He fumbled in his pocket for a clean handkerchief and passed it to her. She accepted and curled up on the sofa, bare feet peeking beneath the cotton coverlet. She was gorgeous, reminding him of a model. Her photo should be plastered on the cover of an All-American magazine. However, surfing was a nontraditional, nontypical, and an extremely perilous career.

They sat mere inches apart. His fingers hesitated before he reached out to smooth sun-streaked strands from her wet face. Her high cheekbones were tinted a slight rose, the result of a morning spent under Portugal's freckling sun.

She cast off his hand. Still the spitfire.

Massaging his temples, he pushed up from the sofa and gathered the plates and flatware.

She wiped her eyes with his handkerchief. "I plan to compete in the Peniche finals."

"Remember your doctor's advice."

"He's not my doctor. Besides, he knows nothing about surfing."

"And evidently you know nothing about concussions. As long as you're recuperating on this farm, I will not allow you to surf."

"You won't *allow* me?" Slowly and deliberately, she placed the ice and dish towel on the table, then she threw his handkerchief on the trunk and came to her feet. "You've known me for what ... eight hours?"

"And believe me, they've been a *long* eight hours."

"I'm sorry I'm such a burden." Her small hands balled into fists. "You can't comprehend how difficult these past three years—"

He set the plates and flatware back on the trunk. Again. "If you fancy being alive for the following three years and beyond, give up your freewheeling career and find something else to do."

She balked. Her eyes sparked. For a woman with a concussion, she came on full alert very quickly.

"And you won't be telling me what to do."

He gritted his teeth. Was nothing easy with this woman?

"When it comes to you risking your life, I most certainly will."

The entry door burst open.

"Here I am," Veronica called, her heeled footsteps tapping over the polished wood floors. "Bento and Bernardo were a little high-spirited tonight." She tottered into the kitchen carrying a sizeable wicker basket. "Bento helped me bake three dozen *biscoitos*. That is, biscotti cookies," she added for her cousin's benefit. "They're delicious dunked in a cup of hot tea." She plonked the basket on the countertop and laughed indulgently. "Bernardo preferred a game of tag, bolting around the kitchen table with his father in pursuit. Sometimes I think I'm raising three rambunctious boys rather than two."

Entering the living room, she stopped. Her gaze flew to Krystal's pronounced frown and the half-eaten roll. Then Veronica swiveled to meet Adolfo's scowl. "Am I interrupting something?"

"Not a thing," Adolfo replied.

"I told you to keep Krystal calm and quiet. Did you follow my instructions?"

"Every single word."

"Then why do you both look like you're contemplating murdering each other?"

CHAPTER 5

 anned by a temperate breeze, Krystal perched on a canary-yellow rocking chair on the guest cottage's front porch. Lightly, she pushed with her feet and rocked back and forth while waiting for Veronica's arrival. Green potted plants flourished in terra-cotta pots on the guest cottage's wooden steps.

Veronica planned a noon outing to see Évora's town square decorated for Christmas. She'd been so excited describing the festive city that Krystal had agreed to accompany her.

Black cotton slacks, a bell-sleeved navy blouse and comfortable leather loafers were the perfect choice, Krystal decided, smoothing her naturally wavy hair into a ponytail pulled tight at the crown.

She checked her wristwatch, squinting against the onslaught of another headache. "Not again," she whispered, willing the headache to go away. Falling back against the rocker, she pinched her lips together, seeking to come to grips with her frustration. Admittedly, her recuperation wasn't as quick as she'd anticipated. Her wrist still hurt, although the swelling was gone, the bruises faded. Her imagination? Possibly. Still, the burning sensation kept her awake at night.

Which was just as well. Her dreams were filled with flashbacks of her near-drowning, bringing her to a sweating, nauseating wakefulness.

Avoid activities which may injure you again, she'd read in the doctor's pamphlet before she'd shoved it into the bottom drawer of the bedroom bureau.

She shoved to her feet and took in the gnarled olive trees, the murmur of a creek nearby, the vivid purple carpet of lavender blooms, Portugal's national flower. Veronica's unceasing commentary about the numerous flowers native to Portugal—daffodils, sea daisies, and Portuguese squill—was a course in itself.

Brilliant sunlight sifted through the greenery of the old trees, the sky a cloudless denim-blue. Wilting in the heat, she shrugged off her red paisley tunic sweater.

It was all so picturesque, she debated slipping off her shoes and scampering barefoot in the grassland for the sheer, childlike enjoyment of it.

Since morning, she'd sketched ten new swimsuit designs. The creative process brought gratification, and the hours had sped by. And, she'd managed to blend ingredients for a round loaf of olive bread currently baking in the oven.

Olives, olives everywhere. The now-familiar scent oozed through the walls. Countless jars overran the kitchen cupboards, an outside container of glistening green olives was being brined for eating, and jammed olive barrels stood ready for the olives to be pressed for oil in the mill.

The previous evening, a World Surf League official had phoned, asking if she'd consider participating in the finals as a wildcard. The officials had taken into account the naive interference during her preliminary heat.

Her resultant injuries from the wipeout were being properly treated, she'd assured the official, and she fully intended to resume competing.

She wished that she could practice her surf maneuvers. A dozen times, she checked the global swell app on her phone for Peniche's latest surfing forecast.

The wipeout seemed as though it had occurred five weeks ago, not five days ago. Certain of her future, that her life was finally on track, she'd counted on a surf win.

Except that wasn't what had happened.

Instead, she was recuperating from a concussion and staying in a guest cottage in a Portuguese town she'd never heard of. And the town was located hours away from the Atlantic Ocean.

Twice, her father had phoned. He'd recommended basking in Portugal's sun, inasmuch as Newport's temperatures had sunk below freezing. Of course, she'd assured him of her arrival back in Rhode Island after the finals on December nineteenth. He hadn't replied, instead advising that she put all her efforts into getting better.

"Learn some Portuguese while you're there," he'd said, casually adding that he and Julio had scheduled a visit to the Lakewood Senior Lifestyle facility.

Surfing, always a prickly topic, especially after Ernie's death, wasn't broached beyond her mention of the finals. Her father hadn't asked further, and she hadn't wanted to worry him unnecessarily.

She wandered to the railing. Well past noon, and Veronica was late.

Veronica had married a Portuguese man and moved to his native land. With her inexhaustible good humor, the customs and language of a new culture had seemed an unproblematic adjustment for her. Most Portuguese spoke excellent English, the chief foreign language, she'd explained.

"All for the love of Clemente," Veronica joked, along with affection and commitment and a common bond of two adorable children. Veronica managed a household and the twin boys with ease, and she respected her husband. Chattering endlessly, she'd proven an enthusiastic caregiver, providing meals, tidying and tending to Krystal's injured wrist and occasional headaches.

Unlike Veronica's brother-in-law Adolfo.

Five days since Krystal's wipeout, and he hadn't bothered to stop by the cottage.

Veronica had mentioned the long hours involved in tree pruning, an insurmountable task for one person, even if that one person was Adolfo.

With a mischievous glint, Veronica had also elapsed into gushing detail on the number of times Adolfo had inquired about Krystal. Matchmaking was Veronica's specialty, so Krystal surmised that Veronica was spinning her own tales. Nonetheless, Krystal wasn't interested in dating, especially a man like Adolfo.

As the chat progressed, Veronica added that Adolfo didn't socialize as much as the eligible women in their area might like, and that he currently was seeing Isabel, who'd been a runner-up in a local beauty pageant years ago. Granted, Isabel seemed a current favorite with Adolfo, although many women, from Lisbon to Évora, competed for the possibility of being on his arm.

When Adolfo had stared at Krystal in her wetsuit, she'd assumed two things. First, he was a silver-tongued womanizer, followed by a close second—he had little else to do with his life than ogle women.

Right on the first part. He was a man who appreciated women, although she didn't know for certain if he was a womanizer.

Wrong on the second. The olive farm seemed to take precedence over everything else.

Something about his empathetic nature, the thoughtfulness that lay behind his strong features, disarmed her. Openly, she'd cried in front of him, something she'd never done in front of anyone. Granted, her emotions had been raw after the concussion, but she'd welcomed his soft tone and soothing gestures. Attentively and capably, he'd cared for her. Gently even.

Perhaps there was more to the man than his handsome, rugged exterior.

But while she'd been succumbing to her own emotions, that entire time they'd spent in the compressed confines of the cottage, Adolfo had seemed to suppress his own emotions behind a polite facade. Sure, he projected a quiet strength, an impressive appeal. Conversely, those attributes, combined with his intelligent hazel eyes, had little to do with his real attractiveness. He possessed an all-male way about him, combined with a silent barricade.

Perhaps that was why women found him so appealing. Adolfo Silva compelled women to find a way to penetrate his barricade, to temper him, to uncover what lay beneath his quiet, brooding exterior.

Krystal gave herself a firm mental shake. None of that barricade stuff mattered to her. One relationship in a lifetime was enough. All that mattered was winning the upcoming finals in order to afford her addition.

CHAPTER 6

A familiar pickup pulled into the dirt driveway. Adolfo emerged carrying a brilliant red poinsettia plant in one hand and a jug of pure, sparkling water in the other. Sunlight played across his good-looking face. His nose was crooked. Funny how she hadn't noticed that before.

He wore slim jeans and a charcoal-gray collared pullover with the tail out. His black hair was long and tousled, weeks past requiring a solid trim.

He smiled. *"Boa tarde, senhorita. Voca esta tao bonita."*

She lifted a brow. "I don't speak Portuguese."

"It means, you are beautiful." His smile, those words, caused an unexpected flurry in her chest.

"Do you use that line with all the women you know?"

His smile remained. "I've reserved it for foolish American surfers."

She ignored the barb. "Where's Veronica?"

"Chasing the disorderly duo around her garden. They got out of school at noon today." He bounded purposefully up the shallow stone steps. "How are you feeling? Your cheeks are still hollow and you're slightly pale."

"Thanks for the compliments."

"Sorry. I didn't mean—" He extended the poinsettia. "The trees grow throughout Portugal. Merry Christmas, or, as we say in Portuguese, *Boas Festas.*"

She didn't accept the plant. "What are you doing here?"

"I live a few miles up the road. By way of a bribe, I first brought the poinsettia to Veronica, hoping to coax her into feeding me a noon meal."

"So these flowers aren't technically for me? They're for Veronica?"

"Not anymore. Now they are for you." His grin beamed white against his tanned face. "She suggested I bring the flowers to you, and I took her advice." He edged open the door and sniffed. "Something smells good."

Krystal followed him inside and to the oven. The scent of homemade yeasty bread permeated the tidy cottage.

She tugged open the oven door, thankful the bread wasn't burnt. "I'm not a baker and scraped up two cups of flour when the recipe called for three. So for the third cup of dry ingredients, I substituted sugar. Being a master chef isn't at the top of my resume."

"Very enterprising. I'm impressed."

"At any rate, I prepared Veronica's recipe since the olives on the farm are rampant at reproducing."

"Welcome to a typical Portuguese olive farm." He stationed the jug of water and poinsettia plant on the kitchen counter. "Would you like a glass of spring water? I stopped at a stream." Without waiting for an answer, he brought two glasses from the cabinet and filled them.

"Water, sure. Flowers, no."

He twisted, the glasses in his hands. "Why not?"

She tested the bread for doneness and avoided his watchful gaze. "Flowers are too personal."

No man had ever given her flowers, not even Ernie.

Often, he'd tuck a gardenia in his own platinum blond hair, though.

"Well, the poinsettia wasn't for you. Does that make the plant more acceptable?" She glanced at Adolfo's persistent smile, uncertain how to refute the logic. He slid her a glass of water and dragged a stool to the counter. He drank quickly, set down the glass and wearily rubbed his fingers over the dark stubble covering his jaw. "My morning was difficult."

"I'm sorry."

"So accept the flowers."

"In view of your difficult morning?"

"In view of the fact I want you to have them." He successfully kept his expression bland, his voice insistent. Truly, the man was impossible.

"I can't. Flowers are too intimate."

He waved a dismissive hand. "Too intimate, too personal … Poinsettias will give your cottage the first taste of Christmas."

"This isn't my cottage, and I won't be here for—"

He touched his calloused fingers to her mouth, silencing her protest.

He was a man who worked the land.

She was a woman who swam in the sea.

Flinching, she drew back. He dropped his hand and poured another glass of water. "The Portuguese word for yes is *sim*."

"What is the Portuguese word for no?"

"I forget."

She couldn't help chuckling out loud. "Okay, I'll accept them." She arranged the plant in the center of the chrome kitchen table. She was being churlish, and the flowers were wonderful.

"*Obrigado.*"

"I'm sorry?"

"*Obrigado* means thank you in Portuguese."

"Yes, of course. *Obrigado.*"

"Excellent. These are your Portuguese words for the day." He took up her swimsuit sketchbook she'd left on the kitchen table. "What's this?"

"Design and fashion are my passions. Except for surfing, of course."

"May I open it?"

"Sure. Why not?"

He thumbed through her pencil drawings of one-piece swimsuits designed for women of all body types and sporting a flirty, feminine appeal. "These are good. Really good. Personally, I prefer two-piece swimsuits on women."

She laughed. "I'm sure you do. Much as I appreciate your compliment, my sketches aren't good enough because I'm no artist."

"I can help. I've had experience sketching building models in my spare time. Does that count?"

"A building and a swimsuit are very different. Plus, I'm a perfectionist."

His gaze held hers. "So am I."

She gestured vaguely. "Someday, I hope to submit sketches to the major companies that specialize in surfing. Now I just need to come up with the perfect name."

"You will."

"My dream is to inspire the companies to develop swim-suits for the average woman, not pencil-thin models."

"Like you."

She shook her head. "I'm hardly a model."

"Ah, you underestimate yourself." He ran his fingers over the lines of the sketches. "What about your intention to professionally surf?"

"Even *I* know I can't compete forever."

He considered each drawing. "You're talented, and your

surfing knowledge will be beneficial as you develop these ideas."

"A prayer won't hurt, either."

"I will pray." He nodded. "And now, one more request."

"I'm not taking orders yet."

"I don't need a swimsuit. I never learned how to swim."

Her gaze narrowed. "Why not?"

"I never had the opportunity. The farm is a distance from the beaches."

"Swimming is easy."

"For you, *senhorita.*" He grinned. "Now, if you will agree to accompany me, I'll show you my hometown of Évora. The city is quaint and also modern. Our town centre is partially enclosed by medieval walls."

Surprise, surprise. He had an agenda besides the poinsettia. "Aren't you busy pruning today?"

"I'm allowing myself a break. Besides, we'll only be gone a few hours."

She gestured toward the cooling bread. "What about my bread?"

"We will eat it another day."

We. She swore a male certainty showed in his grin.

"What about Veronica?"

He pressed back from the counter and carried his glass to the sink. "I reminded her that a restful outing is essential for your recovery, preferably without two wild boys let loose in the busy city streets."

Krystal took a long swallow of water. "Bento and Bernardo can't be as rambunctious as you claim. I love children and can't wait to meet them."

Adolfo made no attempt to stifle a laugh. "Be sure to wear your running shoes."

CHAPTER 7

*A*dolfo parked his truck near Évora's town centre, still surprised that Krystal had actually agreed to accompany him. Even though he felt more than a nudge of guilt for neglecting the farm work, he wasn't immune to the delight that came from appreciating the company of a lovely woman, the delightful afternoon underscored by a rich blue sky, and showing off his thriving city to his most intriguing companion.

He opened the passenger door for her. "The biggest and best Christmas decorations are in the town square." Noting the dark smudges under her eyes, he swallowed an unexpected lump in his throat, a protective urge he hadn't anticipated.

He hesitated. "Are you comfortable covering the short distance on foot?" He could carry her, he supposed. Delightful thought, actually.

She tied the arms of her paisley tunic around her waist. "I'm ready and able."

He surveyed her tall, athletic figure. Her shiny hair,

reaching down her back, was pulled tightly off her heart-shaped face. Her unblemished skin was devoid of makeup.

Very nonchalantly, he attempted to capture her hand. Very politely, she refused.

He wouldn't push. He respected a woman's boundaries. She was too pretty and polished for a man like him, anyway, a farmer struggling to make ends meet.

As they toured the city, he explained the history behind Évora's medieval walls and monuments. She listened intently to his narration when he pointed out a prominent cathedral.

"I love historic cities," she said. "I wish I could spend days and days here." She tapped her index finger to her lips. "If only I had more time ..."

She didn't, he knew. She couldn't wait to leave Portugal.

He lapsed into silence and studied a modern building, analyzing how the structure fit into the older architecture of the city. He'd wanted to study architecture at university. He'd never had the chance.

They strolled across a stone bridge and down cobblestone streets until they entered the old town. Raucous shouts from street-market vendors selling Christmas wares punctuated the celebratory atmosphere. Tinned fish and tawny Portuguese wine mingled with scents of dark, rich espresso and *filhoses* made of fried pumpkin and dough.

Near the curb, Adolfo halted. "Do you like chocolate?" He nodded toward one of the vendors.

Krystal rolled her eyes. "You obviously don't know women as well as you think. Of course I like chocolate."

He paused. "Who said I knew women well?"

"Veronica."

With a wry smile, he shook his head.

They stopped at a vendor's stall laden with chocolate Santas, bells, and pinecones neatly stacked in rows.

"How can I choose between so many shapes?" Krystal mused.

"If you're here in Portugal long enough, you'll consume more candy than you ever imagined. We use chocolate to decorate our Christmas trees."

She slanted him a smile and went back to contemplating the chocolate.

"Pick one," he prompted.

She pointed to a chocolate bell.

"The beautiful *senhorita* and I will share a bell." Adolfo paid and handed the chocolate to Krystal.

They stepped out from beneath the stand's awning and into the sunny street, lingering on the corner, relishing bite after chocolate bite. In between licking their lips and dividing the chocolate, half a dozen friends hailed Adolfo with a friendly *"Feliz Natal."*

As they spoke in rapid Portuguese, numerous women nodded toward Krystal, hiding their inquisitiveness behind good-natured smiles. Their consideration changed to blatant speculation when they learned she was an American surfer occupying Veronica's guest cottage.

After the women left, Krystal asked, *"'Feliz Natal'* means Merry Christmas, right?"

"Sim."

She wiped a chocolate smudge from her cheek. "And a couple of those women were your former girlfriends?"

"How did you know?"

"I could tell by the way they ogled you, and the way they pouted at me."

He didn't respond. Definitely, this beautiful woman was perceptive.

"The outdoor air will help your recovery." He considered smoothing a finger over the bloom of color appearing on her cheeks. Anticipating her response, he thought better of it and shoved his hands into his pockets. When it came to being touched, she was as jumpy as a newborn foal.

A towering Christmas tree greeted them when they entered the town square, and Krystal came to an abrupt halt. A slow, radiant smile worked its way across her face. The twelve-foot pine rose majestically, adorned in enormous clusters of silver, red, and green Christmas bulbs, illuminated by hundreds of tiny white lights.

"Are the Portuguese trying to outdo the Americans?" she teased. "These Christmas decorations are gorgeous."

He chuckled at her quip while he admired the relaxed elegance of her stance. Her black slacks and a navy blouse enhanced her lithe figure. Although sporting a casual pony-tail, she was a class act, carrying unassuming grace with ease.

He tried to decide what sort of Christmas outfit would complement her easy, natural style.

He shook his head. *What are you thinking? You'll never spend Christmas with her, escort her to Midnight Mass, Missa do Galo, or gather around the table for a traditional Christmas Eve dinner of codfish and boiled potatoes.*

He wouldn't be able to take her anywhere, for the holi-days or otherwise, ever.

Perhaps it was the way the rosy light of the afternoon sun enhanced her finely etched features or her easy-going smile. Regardless, the realization of her leave-taking left a surprising void in his chest.

He pushed the thought aside. He would accept the fact that she was here for a brief time, and not allow the thought of never seeing her again spoil an agreeable and memorable afternoon. And he would certainly never ask her to stay. Women required too much maintenance, and his life was here in Portugal, cultivating the farm. Hers was in America.

"Whoever drew that picture is very talented and creative." Krystal indicated a colorful crayon drawing.

"It is one of our many Portuguese traditions. School-children bring their artwork, and all decorations are welcome." He gestured to a particularly whimsical drawing. "We call the wise men from the Bible *Reis Magos*, so I taught you two more Portuguese words today."

Pinecones and homemade stars, and no fewer than twenty depictions of cows and donkeys, nestled amid an array of chocolate shapes and sparkling Christmas tree lights.

"Beautiful," she said. A few strands had loosened from her ponytail and framed her face. He resisted the urge to hook the strands behind her ears so he could better see the excitement shining from her captivating blue eyes.

"*Sim,*" he softly agreed.

She blushed and stepped away, navigating through the swarm of people, leaving him no choice but to follow her. Evidently, she didn't accept compliments well.

"Why is the city so busy on a weekday?" she asked when he caught up.

"As usual, there is a festival going on." He subtly navigated her to the perimeter of the crowd.

"A festival for what?"

"It doesn't matter. We use any excuse to celebrate an occasion. Today happens to be a local saint's feast."

A kaleidoscope of colorful dresses whirled past. The women wore eye-catching checked bouffant skirts and red scarves tied around their hair. Krystal watched the parade, but then she apparently caught the aroma of sizzling, crisp seafood floating through the air from an outdoor café. As her steps slowed, he guided her toward a wrought iron table and chairs situated on the sidewalk.

"Are you hungry?"

"A little. You forced me to share my chocolate bell, remember?"

He chuckled, drew out a seat for her, and accepted menus from a black-suited waiter. He sat opposite her and perused the menu. "Do you like fish?"

"I can eat almost anything. Surfing is a tough sport and uses up a lot of calories."

"Excellent. The Portuguese take long, leisurely lunches. Do you like grilled sardines?"

"I'm still recovering from queasiness, so I'll stick with coffee and dessert." She scanned the menu. "What do you suggest?"

He drew her attention to an image of a custard tart and grinned as she attempted to pronounce it: "*Pastel de nata.*"

He provided a thumbs-up and ordered two espresso coffees and three custard tarts, sprinkled with cinnamon and powdered sugar. He relaxed, entertained by the dance troops, the fancily decorated props, and the obligatory Portuguese celebrity holding up a sign advertising a bull fight.

The waiter set down their coffees and desserts.

Krystal eyed the prominent bullfight sign. "I've never seen a bullfight."

"It can be a fierce sport. Nonetheless, bullfighting is a well-established tradition." He scooped up a mouthful of pastry, smoothly changing the subject to something less violent. "In less than a week, a nativity will be set up, along with an ice skating rink and another marketplace. And then, we will have another festival."

She chuckled and polished off her pastry. "Is the third *pastel de nata* for me or for you?"

"We can share."

She opened her mouth, presumably to tell him he didn't share fairly. He'd eaten 90 percent of the chocolate Christmas bell.

"Adolfo, my good friend!"

Adolfo swung around at the booming, recognizable voice.

A full-bearded man wearing a black rumpled linen suit and smoking an ever-present cigar wended toward them.

"Francisco?" Slowly, Adolfo came to his feet. "What are you doing in Évora?"

"Early parole, old friend." The men exchanged Portuguese salutations and shook hands.

Francisco's mirrored aviator sunglasses kept his eyes hidden. *Convenient*, Adolfo thought. *He always had something to hide, especially as he grew into adulthood.*

Francisco plucked his sunglasses off and leveled a blatant gray-eyed stare at Krystal. "Who is this divine woman? An acquaintance of our mutual friend Isabel?"

Adolfo ignored Francisco's deliberate implication. They'd known Isabel since their teens, and news in a small city of less than 60,000 people certainly traveled fast. Unquestionably, Isabel was a striking woman. Be that as it may, he had tired of her seductive, throaty laugh, eager availability and avid interest in beauty pageants, which she helped to organize. She certainly didn't have a mind to talk business, which was why he'd called on her.

She didn't spar with him or challenge him, nor would she ever dream of leaving her house without makeup. She lacked something. A sparkle, a determination no matter the odds. She wasn't a splendid, willowy beauty. She wasn't … Krystal.

In the way of an introduction, Adolfo said, "Francisco, please meet Krystal, an American surfer."

"*Belissimo.* I am delighted, *senhorita.*" Francisco leaned in and kissed Krystal's hand.

She snatched her hand away.

"My country has miles of beaches," Francisco went on, "and I've always wanted to learn how to surf. Will you teach me?"

"I don't—"

He cut off her refusal. Francisco was always quick to try out all the angles. "How long are you in town, *senhorita*?"

"Only a few—"

"When were you released from prison, Francisco?" Adolfo interrupted.

"A week ago." Francisco tucked his sunglasses into a pocket of his emerald-green jacket. "My behavior was exemplary, because I know how to manipulate the system. Now I'm counting on finding employment somewhere. Is the olive harvest finished for the season?"

Adolfo inclined his head. "*Sim.* You've lived in Portugal long enough to know this."

"Will you ring me if you hear of any work?"

"Why? So now you are willing to toil in the fields?"

"Solely for a short while until I get on my feet financially. You know I'm experienced. How can I ever forget waking at dawn and sneaking port while I harvested olives on your farm? The wine helped steady my olive comb because your father was a hard taskmaster, constantly scolding everyone. Except Clemente—who was always studying for one test or another."

"No one wielded the pruning saw as well as my *pai*," Adolfo said softly.

Francisco's wolfish gaze landed on Krystal again.

Adolfo drummed his hands on his thighs. He might consider helping Francisco find work if Francisco could ever take his eyes off Krystal.

"At the end of a harvesting day," Francisco said, "I never knew on which terrace I left my olive rake." He slicked back a fringe of bleached hair. "Remember joyriding these streets in your souped-up truck? We attracted everyone's attention, especially one particular lady."

"*Sim.*"

"And the bonfires? We'd invite our friends from miles

around and secretly haul away empty kegs of beer before your parents woke. I can reveal many outrageous memories, my friend."

"I'm sure you can." Adolfo swore under his breath. "Keep them to yourself."

Often, Adolfo had wondered whether he and Francisco really were in agreement about anything, considering they weren't alike. Francisco was too irresponsible, too impetuous. Still, they'd boasted many a carefree day together in their youth.

"Let's reminisce over a bottle of port and a cigar," Francisco said.

A familiar flash of anger made Adolfo pause. "As you well know, I don't smoke."

"Of course you don't smoke," Francisco countered. "You're too taken with laboring over olive trees. Will you at least agree to sharing port with me?"

Never at a loss for words, this guy, and wouldn't know how to respond to the word no if someone shouted it in his ear.

Adolfo glanced at his wristwatch. "Certainly."

Stiffly, the men shook hands. Francisco blew a kiss over his shoulder at Krystal, then swaggered into the crowd.

"Who *was* that man—all dapper and charming?" Krystal asked.

Adolfo lowered himself back into his chair. "Try another question."

"Why?"

He pushed his espresso aside. "Because it's late and we should leave."

"What happened to our long and leisurely Portuguese lunch?"

"I changed my mind."

"Well, I haven't. Why won't you tell me more about Francisco?"

"I never knew you were so interested in ex-cons."

"He called you an old friend."

"As children, *sim*. We became rivals in our teens because of a woman."

"Is she the particular lady Francisco mentioned?"

"*Sim*. He pursued her relentlessly, and she wasn't interested." Adolfo tempered his tone. Francisco always knew what buttons to push to cause Adolfo's temper to flare. "As kids, we often dared each other to jump off the highest cliff or swim in the deepest streams."

She propped her elbows on the table. "Who won?"

"Whoever was the most reckless and fearless." He scrubbed a hand over his face, an attempt to wash away his and Francisco's foolhardy escapades. Where had those light-hearted days gone?

"Did you realize he was blatantly flirting with me?" she asked.

"Was he?"

"You know the answer. Is that why you don't want to talk about him? Are you jealous?"

He punted a stray stone near his shoe. "Absolutely not."

Her eyes sparkled, and she grinned, appearing a little too pleased by his denial. Her eyes reminded him of the Mediterranean Sea and the ocean she loved so much. A light, animated blue, darkening to navy when she grew angry. Her current shade, a blend of soft blue and softer turquoise, shone large and luminous.

In a tone of thinly veiled exasperation, he continued. "As we grew older, Francisco chose a different path from mine. His included rash decision-making. In contrast, the olive farm overrode everything in my life, including higher education. He earned an accounting degree at university. I staked and shaped trees, irrigated and fertilized." He fell silent, examining the espresso in his tiny cup.

337

"So, were you the most reckless and fearless?"

"Whatever the challenge, I won."

His *pai's* love had been conditional, based on Adolfo's achievements. His entire life he'd waited for parental praise, a positive *"muito bom"*—very good, very beautiful. Never, not once, was his father satisfied. Even Adolfo's mother couldn't please her husband, despite her attempts. Eventually, their marriage had become a polite, empty shell.

Krystal gazed at him over the rim of her cup and smiled.

Her whimsical smile warmed his insides. "Once I want something, I never give up."

She shifted her gaze, avoiding his stare. "If you're referring to me, to ... us, I don't date."

"Thanks for the information."

Her statement didn't deter him. She was much too fascinating, much too appealing.

She sipped her espresso. "So why did Francisco go to prison?"

Was persistence her middle name?

"He did some creative accounting at his job and got caught. He had developed an expensive drug dependency along the way."

The biting, bitter aftertaste of the espresso prompted a grimace. She pushed away her still-full cup. "He seems charming."

"He is, especially with the ladies. I assume he's now clean and free from drugs."

"I hope he finds work." She toyed with the crumbs on her plate. "When he was in his midthirties, my brother's job was outsourced, and he was ultimately blamed for something he didn't do. For over a year he couldn't find employment. He and his wife were pointed toward divorce."

"What happened?"

"Long story with a happy ending. A private company

hired him." Distracted by a costumed bull with a giant head marching by, she abruptly asked, "What *is* that?"

"Judging by his popularity, he might be the same celebrity we saw earlier." Adolfo drained his espresso and eyed Krystal's cup.

She nodded. He downed hers in one swallow.

Krystal cleaned the crumbs on her plate with her fork. "My brother's current employer said that everyone deserves a second chance and that's why he hired Julio. Do you agree that everyone deserves a second chance?"

Adolfo folded his hands on the table. "No. Not when they are unreliable."

There. Cool, quick and definite. Despite what he was feeling, he'd honed the art of acting indifferent. But she didn't have to know that.

CHAPTER 8

*U*nder sultry skies, another two days passed, and Krystal worked on swimsuit sketches. She'd asked both Veronica and Adolfo if they would drive her to Peniche so that she could practice surfing for the upcoming competition.

Veronica pleaded busyness, and Adolfo simply refused, stating that the predicted heavy rains and a string of storms that might make the beach roads impassable. Although, from what Krystal had experienced thus far, it never rained in Portugal.

Perhaps it was for the best, though, because the thought of surfing incited her wrist to burn and ache, a phantom pain that was no longer caused by her injury.

The previous afternoon, she'd finally met Bento and Bernardo. The boys' constant activity had been a welcome distraction, and she learned the words to a Portuguese Christmas carol entitled, "Pinheiros do Natal," which meant Christmas Pine Trees. While translating, Veronica chopped garlic, onions and tomatoes in the kitchen for dinner, frying the mixture in fragrant olive oil while howling with glee at the twins' antics. Clemente had to work late, she'd added, and wouldn't be able to join them for dinner.

Later, the quartet assembled around the dining room table and snuck extra pieces of *coscorões*, fried dough described as angel wings. A snowman cookie jar sat in the center of the table.

Scrawled Christmas wish lists were displayed on the refrigerator, calling forth Krystal's childhood memories of bundling up in furry snow boots and thick woolen scarves, tramping through the snow. She and Julio would help their father cut down the most beautiful pine tree in Newport.

Once. Long ago. When she was a child.

Brightly colored wrapped packages were assembled under the tree on Christmas morning, the tags reading, "Your Christmas Angel loves you very much."

They were supposedly from her mother, but Krystal recognized her father's handwriting. Although her mother had died and loneliness had pervaded the household, Krystal's father tried to make every holiday magical. As the memories swelled in her, Krystal had had to dig for a tissue in her purse to dry her eyes. She owed him so much.

After she had devoured more *coscorões* than she could count, she'd been shown the Silva family's retail store located at the far end of the property. Soon, with the anticipated arrival of Aunt Edite, olives, tinned fish, and local holiday crafts would be sold there. The small store even had an old-fashioned, working cash register. Krystal could only surmise that a time-travel machine had seamlessly transported her back to the 1950's.

A day later, she still felt melancholy over her Christmas memories. She pushed aside her sketchbook and grabbed her cell phone. Since it was the weekend, she caught her brother at home. Their conversation went as well as their previous ones.

"Julio, please listen. You can't continue with your plans for Dad at the same time I'm held up here."

As she spoke, a violent gust of wind sucked in the white lace kitchen curtains. Captured by the wind, a loose shutter flapped against the wooden sideboards.

She peered outside. The early darkness was unusual, and a storm undoubtedly brewed. How had she not noticed this earlier? Little by little, a recognizable panic quickened in her veins. Ridiculous, this senseless fear of thunderstorms. She was a grown woman, closing in on thirty years old, no longer a youngster huddling in a closet with a flashlight. She refused to cower like a child anymore. She was a strong and capable adult.

Through her cell phone, her brother's transatlantic tirade made her blink.

"Please, Julio, don't make any decisions about the Senior Lifestyle facility until the surfing finals are over. I know Dad will be happier living with me." She grimaced at the thick band of clouds forming in the sky, and wiped her palms over her jeans. "Yes, I'm better and plan to surf in the finals."

Lightning flickered. She quickened her steps to the window and slammed it shut. "Of course you should visit Portugal someday. I wish we could trade places too, and I *am* appreciative I'm here. Yes, I know you work a full-time job, besides helping your wife care for three demanding kids—"

Her cell phone quit.

She stared at the blank screen and then pitched the phone onto the kitchen counter. No cell phone service? Now, the next thing to go wrong was a power loss.

She raced through the cottage in search of a flashlight, rifling through drawers and cabinets.

Thunder shook the walls like a cannon blast, and she was pitched into utter darkness a moment later.

Seeking refuge in a room with no windows, she scurried

to the bathroom and curled her fingers around the sink. She blamed her sudden dizziness on a rapid pulse, not the concussion. While rain lashed the cottage's exterior, she critically appraised her reflection in the mirror. A sheen of sweat coated her pale forehead and cheeks, in stark contradiction to her scarlet chiffon blouse.

The sound of a vehicle motivated her to sprint to the living room. Bracing her fingers on the windowsill, she scanned the vast acreage of the farm. Jagged streaks of silver lightning lit the sky. A gale wind howled, mercilessly bending tree branches as though they were twigs. Already, the dirt driveway was awash in mud.

Through the driving rain, a familiar red pickup truck parked near the front porch. An instant later, rapid, heavy footsteps echoed in her ears, followed by a firm knock on the door.

She opened the door, so thankful to see Adolfo she covered her mouth with her hands.

He carried an armful of large logs. "A menacing thunderstorm is underway," he joked.

Fat raindrops spattered against the roof, and she tipped an exaggerated peer heavenward. "You noticed?"

Resting one shoulder on the doorjamb, he smiled at her. His black hair, wet with rain, was plastered to his forehead. They were so close, she almost considered wiping away the beads of rain streaming down his rugged face.

"This is the part where you're supposed to invite me inside," he prompted.

Her heart did a surprising leap, which she attributed to relief at seeing him. "Yes, of course." She shook back the hair whipping across her cheeks. "Please come in."

He carried the logs to the fireplace and pulled off his jacket. She accepted the saturated jacket and hung it on a brass hook near the entry.

She inhaled. The same forest-like scent of olives, the same promise of his competent, reassuring presence. Gratitude pervaded her jumbled thoughts. She clearly remembered how, after leaving the hospital that first day, he'd treated her with compassion and patience when she'd become embarrassingly sick in the tall grass.

Across the width of the living room, he yanked off his muddy boots and set them near the hearth. When he got to his feet, his broad shoulders blocked her view of the fireplace, and all she could see was him. In worn denim jeans and a charcoal sweater, Adolfo Silva was the handsomest man she'd ever seen.

Fate had thrown them together, the circumstances out of their control. And despite her resolution to side-step romance, the R word, she was drawn to him.

He reached for the matches on the fieldstone mantel. "I stopped pruning when the storm neared and texted Veronica. She said you were alone, so I volunteered to stop by the cottage."

His baritone voice held the same captivating quality as when he'd cared for her on Medão Beach.

She fiddled with the cuffs of her blouse. "I'm grateful you came. The lights went out and I … I … couldn't find a flashlight."

"Out here, surrounded by pastures and farmland, we lose power often."

"Great. Just great."

His brows furrowed.

"What I mean is, I'm glad you're here," she said.

"I wouldn't expect a beautiful woman to sit in the dark by herself in the middle of a thunderstorm."

Beautiful was the only word that stuck. She was so pleased by his compliment that she didn't know how to respond. She dropped onto the sofa and rested her head on the pillows, her limbs limp after the thunderstorm scare. "Did you bring more olive wood?"

"Oak." He knelt by the hearth and lit the fire. The faint, soothing tang of wood smoke floated through the cottage.

"The other day, you mentioned olive wood burns well and would keep the cottage warm."

"And here I thought you hadn't been listening to me." He quirked a smile. "I brought oak logs to complement the poinsettia for the Christmas season."

She rubbed the base of her neck. "I'm sorry, I don't understand."

"On the days leading up to Christmas and throughout Christmas Day, Portuguese tradition dictates a piece of oak wood must be kept burning in every hearth. We refer to our Christmas log as *cepo de Natal*."

"I told you, I won't be here for—"

"In exchange for teaching you another Portuguese word and bringing you the Christmas log, can you get me a glass of port wine?"

Why couldn't he understand she wouldn't be in Portugal for Christmas?

"Can't you get your own wine?" she asked. "You know where the kitchen is."

"Of course. I thought you might—"

"Or at least ask and not demand?"

"My apologies, *senhorita*." He added a grim smile. "I didn't realize I asked so much."

His quiet, velvety tone had a disturbing effect on her pulse. She busied herself with tugging at the fringes of the pillows on the sofa.

"Krystal, look at me."

She hesitated. Reluctantly, she met his gaze.

"Thank you for coming to Portugal. Spending time with you brings me great joy."

Mesmerized by the huskiness in his voice, she felt her heartbeat quicken. "Thank *you* for coming to my rescue, not once, but twice."

"Much as I appreciate the credit, I, along with several others, took care of you on Medão Beach."

"You saw the storm and you're the one person who came today."

He suppressed a chuckle. "My exquisite *senhorita,* I will keep you safe from any storm."

"As long as I am here in Portugal?"

He strode to her, his gaze caressing her face, mouth, figure. He took her small hands into his large ones. "As long as you are anywhere."

She read his meaningful gaze, the silent invitation, and retreated. If she cared for someone again, loved again, she would get hurt, and she couldn't go through the heartbreak that came from losing someone. Her mother, her husband—all her close relationships ended badly.

She pulled from his grasp. "I'll go."

"*Abrigado.*" He lit a row of fat, stubby candles on the mantel, reducing the room to a soft, mellow glow. "We can wait out the storm and sit by the fireplace together, where we'll be warm and comfortable."

Warm and comfortable, together, by the fireplace.

Her mouth went too dry to respond.

Strategically, she routed around him and stepped into the kitchen. She poured his wine into a slender stemmed wineglass, along with a glass of spring water for herself, stalling for time to gather her emotions.

Enthusiastically, he accepted the glass of port when she reappeared and set the bottle on the trunk.

"A toast." He lifted his glass and inclined her to do the same.

Spine erect, she seated herself on the sofa and held up her glass. "What are we celebrating?"

"The upcoming Christmas feasts, the fact you're here, and the fact it's raining, for the parched land desperately needs rain." He installed himself beside her, inches away. She snapped her head up, intending to launch into a discourse regarding his boldness to sit so near.

That is, until forked lightning sliced the sky in half, followed by a crack of thunder.

She set down her glass, settled back into the cushions, and pressed her elbows to her sides. He watched her with such intensity, she feigned absorption in the black metal corners of the trunk to avoid meeting his gaze.

"Are you all right?" he asked.

"I'm afraid of thunderstorms. Or rather, I used to be afraid of thunderstorms."

He lifted a dark brow. "You? Afraid? After watching you surf those huge waves like a pro, I assumed you were fearless."

She sat straighter. "You noticed?"

"Along with everyone else on Medão Grande Beach." His admiring grin reached all the way to his hazel gaze—brown or green depending on his moods. Currently, his eyes were an easy, hot-fudge brown.

She decided on a new direction. "I can tell them apart."

"Who?"

"Bento and Bernardo. Yesterday, I had a very lively day at Veronica's house."

"*Lively* is a good description."

"Have you noticed that Bento's hair is straight and a shade lighter than his brother's? Bernardo's hair sticks up in unmanageable swirls at the crown, and he's the inquisitive one."

"Never noticed. They're like two little clones of Clemente,

and both children are such chatterboxes, I can hardly think whenever they're around. Did you notice a minuscule mole on Bernardo's left cheek?"

She beamed. "Yes, indeed. You?"

He stared into his glass, muttering, "Never spotted anything remotely resembling a mole, although Veronica has tried to point it out to me many times."

Krystal smiled, but then she drank more water, allowing it to clear her throat in order to approach her next topic, one sure to turn Adolfo's affable gaze to a glowering, this-side-of furious green.

"Are you aware I'm completely recovered from my injuries?" she began brightly, holding out her arm. "My wrist doesn't hurt anymore."

Only in her imaginings, she told her intrusive conscience.

"Better," Adolfo answered with equal brightness. "Though slightly bruised, there isn't any more swelling."

"So ... can you take me to the ocean this weekend? I must begin surfing again."

He tightened his fingers around his glass. "You know my opinion on this matter."

A charged silence glutted the room, interrupted by a deluge of rain pounding against the windows.

"The twins can come. They can build sand castles."

He seemed to be attempting to keep his temper in check. "I don't have time for sand castles."

"Veronica can use a break, and it gives you—us—a few hours away from the olive farm."

"No."

"Adolfo, please. I need the money, assuming I win. And I *will* win," she corrected. She never wanted to appear weak in his eyes. She'd done that once already.

He said nothing.

"My dad is planning to come live with me."

"We've been through this. You mean that *you* are planning for him to live with you."

"The completed addition will boast five-hundred square feet of living space for Dad."

"I know."

She shot him a murderous glare. "So why don't you understand my dilemma?"

"Does your father support your surfing ambitions?"

"For many years, I've supported myself."

"I don't mean financial. I mean emotional."

She rubbed her forehead. "In all honesty, no. In fact, he vehemently disapproves. He spouts statistics on why surfing's too dangerous. In spite of his opinions, though, he wants me happy, and surfing makes me happy."

"In our conversations, you've never mentioned your mother."

"My mom died shortly after I was born. I never knew her. I was the natural child and, as I told you, Julio was adopted from Portugal." She bent her head to hide the rush of sorrow filling her heart. "Perhaps—perhaps she died because of complications resulting from my birth."

"What on earth makes you say that?"

She kept her head down. "I've overheard whispers regarding my mother's hard labor. My birth might have been the reason she died."

Oh, please. She'd said the words out loud. That made it real. She didn't want it to be real.

"Has your father spoken to you about this?"

"Never. He's so nurturing. Perhaps he feared that telling was more than he thought I could endure."

She whispered tearfully, her words quiet fragments of pain, *I love you, Mom. Another lonesome Christmas without you. Even after all these years, I'm having such a hard time. I know Dad is too.*

Adolfo couldn't hear her, could he? She glanced up at him, worried. Those empathetic eyes. So intense, so attentive.

The room grew eerily still. No lightning. No thunder, the solitary tap-tap-tap of a persistent rain.

"I'm sorry," Adolfo said softly. "I don't know your father, although from what you've told me, he isn't the type of man who'd withhold information, no matter how distressing. I don't believe your birth had anything to do with your mother's passing."

"You weren't there. You don't know."

"Neither do you."

"I believe that my mother is watching over me—like an angel."

She had never admitted that to anyone. She couldn't take the words back, and if she could, where would the words go?

He waited, as if she might have more to say.

She sniffed and waved an airy hand. "My dad is wonderfully supportive, and I'm certain your parents urged you to pursue your dreams."

"Don't be so certain." He took a big swallow of port. "My parents were never satisfied with my work in the olive groves, especially my father. So the answer is no, they didn't. And no, he didn't. Happiness wasn't part of the Silva equation."

"Did you resent your father because of it?"

His jaw visibly tightened. "My *pai* lived on this farm for seventy years, and olive growing is the only life he knew. I am trying my best to honor his legacy."

"From what Veronica says, you take your work very seriously, to the point of excess."

"*Sim*, and with no apologies, I will continue to do so."

"Sometimes you need a break from all your demands."

"Not often."

She bristled. "Will you please, please, please take me to Medão Grande Beach? The trip would mean so much to me."

Hard-bitten inflexibility settled over Adolfo's face. His spiky black lashes lowered. He splashed more wine into his glass and didn't answer.

CHAPTER 9

*A*dolfo stared out at the droplets of rain pattering against the double-hung windows of the guest cottage. Dark clouds rolled against a late afternoon sky. A half day of tree pruning lost, and he might lose another if the rain continued. Meanwhile, the bills steadily mounted.

"How do you celebrate Christmas in America?" he asked, forcing their conversation away from Krystal's request. "Any favorite memories?"

Her gaze narrowed. "Suppose you tell me why you want to know?"

"I'm interested."

She tore her glare from his and centered her attention on a water spot dampening the vaulted ceiling. "Why?"

"I don't know."

"What do you mean you don't know? You're the one who asked."

He raked a hand through his hair. "I haven't been certain of anything since the day I watched you on your surfboard. You were so calm, so well-balanced, so ... stunning. And my uncertainty grows stronger each time I'm around you."

"Should I be happy about that?"

"I'm certainly not."

She took her time and studied him. "And yet you continue to see me."

"Because I can't stay away." His gaze moved meaningfully to her full lips. It took all his restraint not to take her in his arms and kiss her.

Her cheeks pinkened. His admission hung in the ensuing silence.

He fidgeted and clasped his hands together. "I can't help worrying that the next time you're facing disaster; I won't be able to rescue you in time."

Memories surged. Memories of being helpless on Medão Beach while she'd nearly drowned. Senseless, that was what surfing was. No one could battle battering waves. His heartbeat had thrashed in his ears when he'd sped to the shore to help carry her to safety.

A hint of humor flickered in the corners of her eyes. "I'm flattered you're concerned. May I remind you that I can take care of myself?"

"Can you?"

His response was curt. He blamed the curtness on the previous month's labor-intensive harvest, combined with his angst and regret since his father's death. He'd been angry and irritable with everything. All these factors created chaos with his mood, reasoning and sentiments, especially when he sat a scarce few inches away from this captivating woman, her fragrance reminding him of freshness and the sea. Around her, his senses came alive.

"Will you at least consider taking me and the twins to the beach?" she asked.

"We can resume this discussion later in the week, after we learn the weather forecast. Sorry, it's the best I can offer."

She huffed an assent, apparently mollified. *At least for now.*

He braced his elbows on his knees. "Any more olive bread in your pantry?"

"Of course. I can't eat an entire loaf by myself."

"Do you want me to get a few slices for us?" He stood. "The bread has been on my mind."

As well as the exquisite woman who'd baked it.

"I'll go." She hurried to the kitchen, reappearing with a plateful of olive bread covered with creamy butter. "The bread is two days old," she reminded him, setting cloth napkins on the trunk.

He congratulated himself on successfully diverting her thoughts from surfing and helped himself to a slice of bread. "Tasty and a tad hard, the way I like it," he lied around a mouthful. He'd be chewing for hours.

"Thanks. I'm so glad." She arranged herself on the far end of the sofa. "I think I told you that I didn't have enough flour, so I substituted sugar."

"Ah, I can taste the extra sweetness." He planted a most charming smile on his face. *"Delicioso!"*

He was probably overdoing it.

"Are you lying?"

"I don't lie." Well, maybe now and then, when he didn't want to hurt someone. A white lie, a harmless untruth.

She arranged a napkin on her lap and picked up a corner piece of bread. "Will you share something about yourself?"

Was that a question? Yes, unfortunately. The conversation was supposed to be about her, not him.

He swallowed the bread, sat next to her on the sofa, and downed the port. "What would you like to know?"

Daintily, she chewed. "Anything, as long as you're honest."

"How about *dishonest?*"

She offered a curious look. "Sure. Go ahead."

He threw one arm carelessly across the back of the sofa.

"Earlier, I texted Veronica and she said you were alone in the cottage."

"You told me that."

"*Sim.* What I didn't say was that I bribed her. She was on her way here when I insisted I would check on you instead. We were both concerned."

"Another bribe like the poinsettia? What did you use this time?"

He withheld a laugh. "I volunteered to mind the twins. Believe me, a bigger sacrifice can't be found anywhere in all Europe."

"Should I be flattered? I suppose I should be. Does this mean you were worried about me?"

"Always."

She drew a shaky breath, her expression speculative.

"Now you," he prompted. "Favorite Christmas memories?"

"You didn't tell me any of yours."

He shrugged. "Someday, I will."

Actually, he'd prefer they make their own Christmas memories together, right here in Portugal.

She set her napkin on the trunk. "One Christmas, when I was five years old, my dad wanted my brother and me to send out Christmas cards. Dad asked me to lick the stamps and my brother sealed the envelopes. I treasured the thought that we were a real family, just like all the other families I knew from school."

The flickering candlelight accentuated her shimmering eyes. "I can still picture the front of that card—a big green wreath with a gigantic red bow. Inside the card was a glossy Christmas photo of my Dad, Julio, and me, all dressed up for Christmas. I wore a jade-green dress with a gold spangled headband, Julio wore a black vest, pants, and a red striped tie, and Dad wore a navy suit. On each card, Dad hand wrote, 'Merry Christmas from the Walters.'" She linked her fingers on her lap and gazed down at her hands. "So, that's my memory."

He imagined her, a motherless blonde and blue-eyed girl. Tenderness stirred in his chest. He wasn't a crier, but he still had to turn his head slightly so she wouldn't see him wipe the corner of his eye. Clearly, she missed having a mother.

"I love your story, I really do." Turning back to her, he slid his forefinger across her soft cheek.

She shrugged him off.

He pushed out a frustrated breath. "You did it again."

"Did what?"

He held up his hand and counted off three fingers. "You draw back every time I touch you."

"I haven't noticed."

"Sure you have. Care to tell me why?"

Her chin came up a notch. She was one stubborn American.

"If you explain, I'll take you to Peniche, as long as the weather cooperates."

"You're offering me a bargain?"

"*Sim.*"

"Unfair."

"On the contrary, my offer is beyond fair, considering my opinion on the subject of you and the beach."

She accorded him an uneasy smile. "Finally, I can surf?"

"I didn't say anything about surfing. I'll honor my bribe to Veronica." He skimmed Krystal's silky hair, pleased she didn't pull back. "Agreed?"

Her face reddened. "Do I have a choice?"

"The decision is up to you."

She pinched her bottom lip and studied the V neck of his sweater. "At least I'll get to play with the children and enjoy the ocean." When she finally connected with his gaze, she was like a magnet, all enticing charisma. Pulling him in, slowly, inexorably, her eyes a fathomless pool of wariness and want. Everything about her lightened his mood. She revived his flagging spirits—he'd been in such despair after his father's death. And he liked the feelings of revival, of lightness.

Women had accused him of being detached and aloof. Perhaps it was his nature, perhaps his upbringing. With Krystal, the urge to protect her from her foolish pursuits was so overpowering, he wanted to wrap his arms around her and never let go.

Unhurriedly, his fingers outlined the shape of her mouth, admiring the exquisite cupid's bow. He kept everything feathery—his caresses, his voice, his motions. Dressed in form-fitting jeans and a red blouse draped attractively around her enticing body, she was incredibly desirable.

His lips came within a fraction of hers. "What are you afraid of, Krystal?"

"Afraid is a strong word." In the course of shaking her head, she smiled, cancelling out both reactions. "Maybe you should explain why you feel so unbalanced around me, and why—"

"Why, why, why," he murmured. Her fragrance reminded him of crisp soap and clean water, a veil of sparkling simplicity. *Take it slow. Don't startle her.*

She was every inch the enchantress. She could be furious with him, and then disarm him the next moment with her charismatic smile.

Surely, she felt what he felt, this fate weaving a spell around them both.

She laid a finger on his jaw and drew a wobbly sigh. "Adolfo, I …I haven't been kissed in a long time."

He captured her sigh with a kiss. Their breaths mingled.

357

He claimed her quivering lips exhaustively, insistently, hungrily. Tentatively at first, her mouth answered his, surprising him with her eagerness.

His kiss deepened. His hands explored every inch of her flawless face, and he brought her tighter against him. Her exquisite body was made to fit against his.

When the kiss ended, she rested her head on his chest, her fingers flat against his shoulders.

He waited until their breathing slowed. Tenderly, he tilted her chin. "Please explain."

Her glorious eyes gleamed with disoriented tears. "Explain what?"

"Why you are so skittish."

"I don't know where to begin."

He pressed a kiss to her temple, content she allowed him to still hold her. "Start off wherever you're comfortable."

His answer seemed to amuse her.

She licked her lips, still lush and swollen from their kiss. "Do you know how old I am?"

Such an odd question. He chuckled against her fragrant hair, scents of leafy greens and musky soap. "According to Veronica, you'll soon be thirty years old."

"You're thirty-five. I asked Veronica about you too."

"And it cannot be disputed that Veronica is a wealth of information."

He was five years older than Krystal, and a million times more experienced. Work in the fields was grueling and back-breaking, while she was all softness.

She flicked him a glance. "Have you ever been married?"

"No. The perfect woman has eluded me."

Until now. The thought came unbidden, although he was already making plans for them—beginning with their excursion to Peniche, then intimate holiday dinners, a trip to

Lisbon to view the massive Christmas market, afterward taking in a classical concert at one of the local churches.

"Were you ever involved in a serious relationship?" he asked.

"Yes."

His heart rate increased, sending a flush through his body. He hadn't expected her response, at least not *that* response. He should have, though. It would be unusual for a thirty-year-old woman not to have had a serious relationship. But he doubted she was in one now. If she were dating someone, that man would have traveled to Portugal to support her at the surfing competition.

Still, he treaded carefully, picking up on her somber tone. "If you would rather not tell me …"

When had she grown so distant? She visibly was withdrawing into herself, like a turtle retreating into its shell. She folded and unfolded the napkins, her movements slow and uncertain. "No. I need to talk about my past."

Her conflicted features said otherwise, reflecting his fears. One part of him wanted to know every detail of her life. The other part didn't want to hear what she obviously had avoided telling him up till now.

He couldn't summon the energy to stand, so he sat where he was, his arm around her shoulders.

"I should've told you," she began. "I thought Veronica might have said something." She rubbed the heel of her hand against her chest. "My husband, Ernie, died in a surfing accident three years ago. You see, I'm a widow."

Adolfo loosened his grip. He tried to ignore the shockwave of her statement, the impact her gorgeous, tear-streaked face had on his gut.

"I'm sorry for your loss." He attempted to keep his voice emotionless, knew he failed. "What was your husband like?"

"Ernie was popular with our peers, for one. I waitressed

359

while he devoted his days to chasing waves. Nothing worried him, and I soon learned his priorities were much different from mine. We were married only four months and I kept my maiden name, Walters." She refused to meet Adolfo's stare. "In retrospect, we were so young. Too young."

CHAPTER 10

*L*ater that evening, Adolfo stomped up the marble porch stairs of his home and into the front room. He jerked off his jacket and flung it on a chair, followed by his boots skidding across the smooth pine floor. He flicked the light switch. No, in his mood, better to keep the lights off.

Krystal had been married to another man. His Krystal. His. Krystal.

She was a delightful blend of cool musk and satin skin and soft sobs.

He'd touched her as gently as his calloused hands allowed, kissed her so as not to frighten her. So many women welcomed his advances. With her, he waited for permission before a first caress, a tender kiss.

Never, never, never in his wildest imaginings had he supposed she was a widow.

He sank into his favorite armchair, gazing out the floor-to-ceiling windows at the moonlit mountain range beyond. The rich glow of an antique rosewood cabinet settled against an exposed brick masonry wall. His home blended the past with the present.

On the drive, his shock had faded. She was yielding to him and beginning to trust him. She'd allowed him to kiss her, touch her. Her mouth had answered his avidly. She was delightful, a combination of wholesome exuberance and fortitude, spirit and resolve.

He linked his hands behind his head and stared at the sweeping spiral staircase leading to his second-story bedroom.

He took joy in each minute of their time together. She forced him to work hard for her favor, and every smile was a triumph. When he considered their upcoming excursion to the beach, his pulse kicked up a notch.

Had she loved her husband? He assumed so, even if Krystal acknowledged that she and Ernie were too young when they married. Perhaps it was her girlish dream to marry the trendy guy in their tight-knit surfing community.

Love.

Love had no place in Adolfo's life. He welcomed bachelorhood, where life was regimented and made perfect sense. Finally, he was in control of the farm. Nevertheless, he had no control over his feelings for Krystal.

He leaned back against the leather armchair, recalling her twinkling gaze whenever she sparred with him. He shook his head. No use denying what was clear in his heart. He was already half in love with her.

Every movement she made, each time her cheeks flared with color when she laughed at one of his teasing remarks, his heart struck one unsteady beat after another.

To prevent being hurt again, she'd erected a tidy wall to keep men out of her life.

Understandable.

Nonetheless, he intended to breach those walls.

"Are the Portuguese trying to outdo the Americans?" she'd teased.

He'd prefer a tie. An American woman and a Portuguese man as equal partners.

Soon, he anticipated showing Krystal his home. Once it had been a deteriorating structure that no one wanted. He'd done much of the reconstruction himself, doing a full-scale mock-up beforehand, and was pleased with the results. He looked forward to Krystal's reaction.

With that final contemplation, he climbed the spiral staircase to his bedroom.

CHAPTER 11

*K*rystal awoke to bright sunshine streaming through her bedroom window. It was the morning of their beach outing.

A few evenings earlier, it had been a relief to talk to Adolfo about Ernie, and she'd appreciated Adolfo's reserved sympathy. He didn't interrupt, he'd just listened. As a result, her sadness over Ernie's death had lessened.

She threw back the bedcovers and opened the window, inhaling the thick, fruity aroma of—what else—olives.

The distinctive quality of rich coffee and corn bread smeared with strawberry preserves made her lips smack. Adapting to the Portuguese continental breakfast certainly came easy.

She luxuriated in a long bath, washing herself with gardenia and vanilla-scented soap in the soaking tub, then arranged her hair in a ponytail. For want of a better style, she tucked her stubborn waves beneath a royal-blue baseball cap so that the ponytail stuck out the back of the cap. A black scalloped bikini, topped with a turquoise T-shirt, cut-off jeans shorts, and casual leather sandals completed her beach outfit.

With a sliver of optimism, she placed her wetsuit and surf gear in her bag. *Just in case.*

Adolfo had mentioned a visit to Peniche's city center for dinner, so she also packed a change of clothes. And, he said he'd planned a surprise for her.

As he pulled up to the cottage, the twins in the backseat of his truck, she glanced at the clock. He'd assured her that he'd arrive by eleven, and, once again, he proved a man of his word.

For the picnic, Krystal crowded a wicker basket with bottled water and *chourico*—a Portuguese smoked sausage. She included artisan cheese for the twins, and Adolfo had brought a loaf of Veronica's sweet bread.

"Did you bring pails and shovels?" she asked.

"*Sim.*"

"I'll get a spatula. It's for a sand sculpture," she explained at his questioning look.

He was about to close the lid of his trunk when Krystal reappeared on the porch holding her surfboard and gear.

He stared at her, the surfboard, then back at her. "No."

She tightened her fingers around the board. "I can't go to the beach without Angel."

He blinked. "Your surfboard's name is Angel?"

"Lots of surfers name their boards, and I believe in angels."

He studied his knuckles before meeting her jutting chin. "Today is for having a good time at the beach and a picnic lunch. Agreed?"

She opened her mouth and then closed it again as her arguments warred with reason. Granted, he was right. This day was earmarked for the children, not surfing. She set the surfboard in the cottage and descended the porch stairs to his truck.

After assisting her into the passenger seat, he asked if she'd experienced any dizziness lately.

"Headaches, mostly. Dizziness, once."

He slid into the driver's seat and turned the key in the ignition. "More justification why I can't allow you to surf. I'm too concerned about your safety."

"Overly concerned." Despite her disappointment, she managed to keep her tone reasonable.

"I'm practical. There's a difference."

Any room in her mind for retorts was quickly forgotten. The twins chattered incessantly, interspersing their periodic backseat squalls with giggles when Krystal attempted to sing "We Wish You a Merry Christmas" in Portuguese.

Adolfo squeezed her hand while he drove, his low-toned laugh ever present. "Your voice is lovely. Please keep singing."

"Uncle Adolfo, is Krystal your *namorada?*" Bernardo bellowed from the backseat.

"Only if she wants. She may still be angry at me."

"Why?"

"Because today she wanted to bring her surfboard named Angel, and I said no. And I'll tell you boys a secret. She doesn't need a surfboard. Krystal is already an angel, my angel from America."

His voice, so quiet, so affectionate, brought unbidden moisture to her eyes. She blinked and glanced at him. "Will agreeing to be your girlfriend earn me another Christmas log and more compliments?"

A smile spread across his face. "I have something better planned."

* * *

"UNCLE ADOLFO, did you pack our pails and shovels?" the ever-inquisitive Bernardo asked when they arrived at the beach. "Mom said Krystal knows how to make sand castles since she spent so many years at the shore."

"And," Krystal said, "I know how to build award-winning sand snowmen."

"Award-winning?"

"Well, not exactly, although the locals applauded the second I was finished. They were easy."

"The applauding locals were easy, or your sculptures?" Adolfo asked.

"Both. Sand snowmen don't take a lot of skill."

He tugged at her ponytail. "I like your hair pulled back, by the way. The style shows off your high cheekbones."

"Thanks." She felt her face heat from the sincerity in his gaze.

Laden with beach gear and the picnic lunch, they crested the dunes and found a grassy spot bordered by dense forest a few minutes later. Adolfo had avoided Medão Beach, Krystal noted, substituting it with an unspoiled strand several miles away.

Frothy whitecaps glistened in the afternoon sunshine. Krystal checked the surfing forecast app on her phone, confirming her observations that the swells were nonexistent. She glanced at the ocean and then quickly looked away. A vivid memory of nearly drowning flew through her mind.

She yanked off her baseball cap and threw it on the sand. Today wasn't a good day to surf, anyway.

Despite the twins' protests, she applied sunscreen to their slender, wiggling bodies, while Adolfo set towels and blankets adjacent to a large shade tree.

"My striped towel is lucky," she pointed out. "At least, it used to be."

"*Boa sorte*, good luck, is the order of the day." Adolfo patted the boys' tousled hair. "The water's too chilly for swimming. You can run along the shore."

"*Viva!*" The twins frolicked in the shallow waves, splashing each other, while Krystal and Adolfo watched, occasionally waving. They emerged from the water with chattering teeth and lips blue from the cold. Krystal toweled them off and then bundled them in thermal sweat suits.

She and Adolfo sailed a Frisbee through the air with the twins. When the boys tired of Frisbee throwing and opted to scramble like crabs, she sat beneath a tree. Adolfo came to sit beside her. He dusted his sandy hands on his khaki shorts and drained a bottle of water without taking a breath. Giving her a wicked smile, he reached into his pocket and produced a tree-shaped chocolate.

She drew nearer. "For me?"

He raised a forefinger to his lips. "For us. I don't want to ruin the boys' lunches."

An eye roll was in order. "How considerate of you."

With a furtive glance toward the twins, he unwrapped the chocolate. "We can split a piece each."

"Split? As in fifty-fifty, or ninety-ten?"

"Whatever is fair."

"Fifty-fifty."

He laughed, snapped the chocolate in half, and granted her a piece. "See how well we get along?"

She sampled the chocolate and then she stretched, cat-like, her smile expanding.

After lunch, the boys wrestled for a few minutes on the soft sand. Giggling rascally, they scampered farther away with each of Krystal's fruitless attempts to pull them apart.

"I told you to wear your running shoes," Adolfo reminded her.

"Watch this. They will come to me." She slipped off her shorts and shirt, donning a sheer black cover-up over her bikini. She nabbed two pails, shovels, and the kitchen spatula. Walking along the shore, she occasionally paused and dug down, then finally dropped the pails and knelt.

"I found a good spot," she announced. "Good quality sand makes all the difference."

"What are you building, Krystal? Let me see!" Bernardo shouldered his brother in his race to reach her first.

"Each of you gets a pail of water and three buckets of firm sand. Be sure the sand sticks together like this. And bear in mind, no rocks. The finer the sand, the better." She packed a handful of sand into a ball and rotated the ball in her hand. "Our snowman consists of three round balls of different heights arranged on top of each other."

The boys and Krystal occupied the next hour creating various-sized snowmen, shaping and smoothing, while Adolfo snapped photos of the trio with his cell phone.

"Uncle Adolfo, will you help us?" Bento asked.

Adolfo stretched out his legs. "I'm relaxing my sore muscles because pruning took a lot of effort this week. Besides, you don't need me. You're learning from an award-winning sand sculpture expert."

Krystal laughed. "Is there such a person?"

"Her name is Krystal." Beaming a white smile, he placed his hands behind his head and leaned against the bark of the tall shady pine.

Afterward, when the twins settled on their linen beach blankets for a nap, Krystal sat next to Adolfo.

He was outrageously attractive, his navy polo clinging to his wide shoulders, the top buttons casually undone. As the day progressed, the lines on his forehead had relaxed. His entire bearing seemed younger, as though time had rewound him to his youth. Laughing often as he'd tossed the Frisbee, he'd displayed a laidback side she hadn't seen before.

He pulled her close. A raw teasing of salt and sea air stung her lips, and a cool breeze glided over her skin. Nearby, orange trees popped with fruit, sunlight filtered through the shrubbery, the woods halcyon and serene. Sun versus shadows. In the approaching dusk, everything appeared calmer.

Adolfo partially closed his eyes.

With an outbreath of satisfaction, Krystal leaned nearer him, savoring the view of the dramatic Atlantic coastline. "I love this spot," she said.

Of course, she'd never see this strand of beach again. She'd been so determined to quit Portugal ... but how could she leave this fairy-tale country—and this gentle man holding her as if she were a piece of precious china?

As the sun set over the hills, she pressed her cheek against his chest and sighed. "We should go before it gets any later."

"Not until you eat this last morsel of chocolate." He fished in his pocket and displayed the tiniest piece of chocolate she'd ever seen. "I saved this for you."

"I wouldn't dream of denying you of your favorite pastime—eating every bit of chocolate in sight."

He laughed and popped the chocolate into her mouth. She savored the sweetness on her tongue.

His amusement was replaced by a lingering stare. "There is another pastime I like even better than eating chocolate."

Intensity in his eyes grew and her pulse tripled. She gloried in the excitement of his hard chest pressed against her, his lips moving lightly, then more urgently on hers. Straining to be nearer him, she kissed him back, winding her arms around his neck.

"Let's stay like this," he whispered. "Just like this."

Eyes closed, she listened to the rhythmic sound of the surf, the cawing of seabirds, the palm trees lightly swaying in the early evening breeze. The sheer splendor of it brought a quiet, wonderful peace.

"If only I weren't leaving," she murmured.

"You don't have to leave." His arms tightened around her. She opened her eyes to see his half smile, although the previous light-heartedness had faded from his expression.

CHAPTER 12

*a*dolfo stopped smiling as Krystal withdrew from his grasp.

"You know my father needs me in Rhode Island."

"Do I?"

Her mutinous glare leveled on him. "If you've been listening to me these past two weeks, then you most certainly do."

She wouldn't like his next remark. He took a leap, anyway. "Your father is a grown man. Allow him to make his own decisions. Something tells me he would be happier in the senior facility where he could meet new friends."

"I know him. You don't."

"Fair enough." He rubbed his hands over his face. "We will agree to disagree, *sim*? No need to spoil a good day by quarreling."

She busied herself with shaking out towels, pulling on her cut-offs, T-shirt, and a pink terry-cloth jacket. No matter what she wore, she was gorgeous. It was difficult, but he turned away.

Their discomfort ended when Bento opened his eyes

from his nap. "I'm hungry!" His loud proclamation quickly awoke his sleeping brother.

"We'll stop for pizza," Adolfo said.

Thirty minutes later, they were window-shopping at the little seaside shops situated on Peniche's boardwalk. Afterward, sitting astride a stone wall overlooking the sea, they waited for their pepperoni pizza to cool and ate outside. A pastry shop located next door to the pizzeria sold *bolo rei*, king cake, an agreeably sweet Christmas cake, along with beautifully-crafted marzipan.

Krystal declared she'd eat dessert first, casting a wary eye on Adolfo and refusing to go halves with him.

He grinned. "In the past, king cake contained a broad bean, which hid a good luck charm. Granted, the tradition is no longer observed due to safety precautions. But the person who got the slice with the bean provided the cake the following year."

"So, no bean is inside, and therefore, no luck?" She plucked the crystallised fruit off the top and handed it to him.

He happily accepted. "On the contrary, you're in Portugal during the Christmas season. How lucky can you get?"

Dusk swiftly cooled the coastal air. Krystal tugged thick hooded sweatshirts over Bento and Bernardo before they dashed off to troll for seashells and colored glass.

Adolfo grasped her hand. "In your bungalow, did you invest in a real or artificial Christmas tree?"

"Artificial. Certainly, I prefer a real tree." She drew an unsteady breath. "For the past three years, there hasn't been a Christmas tree in my house."

"For the sake of honoring your late husband?"

"Yes. The memories were too difficult." Sadness shadowed her eyes. "We married on a whim, and I soon understood I'd wedded a lifestyle choice."

"Whose lifestyle choice?"

"In all fairness, both of ours. We were happy-go-lucky surfers—despite the fact I earned the actual income. Still, we struggled to meet our monthly rent payments." She shook her head. "Fortunately, I surfed in a lot of events and banked some winnings, which was how I afforded my bungalow."

And during that time, she'd evidently dismissed the countless concussions.

Adolfo considered her in thoughtful silence. Even if he disagreed with every aspect of her perilous sport, he was humbled by her dauntless resolve to succeed.

"The minute I traveled to Portugal for the competition, I vowed I'd never live in the past again." She squared her shoulders. "I'm ready to embrace life."

"You are one plucky woman," he said, his lips a hairsbreadth from hers. With his hands, he framed her face and entangled her spirited affirmation with a lengthy kiss.

The high color of her face, her magnificent eyes a bottomless indigo, dragged him deeper. Each time she allowed him to hold her, his blood raced like fire through his veins.

CHAPTER 13

*A*couple hours later, Adolfo swung into the U-shaped driveway of Veronica and Clemente's traditional country house. He had insisted on dropping the twins off before going on to Krystal's cottage, and she waited in his truck.

The boys tracked sand through the foyer as Adolfo propelled them into the kitchen. They struggled to one up each other, talking louder, one over the other, so that their parents were bombarded with two editions of the same beach adventure.

Offering a quick wave to Clemente and a quicker explanation to Veronica, Adolfo assured them that the boys would sleep well that night. "Besides tearing about all day, they sang constantly during the ride home."

Veronica beamed. "They sing like cherubs. They always remind me of the Vienna Boys choir."

Not quite, Adolfo thought, although he nodded.

"Did they sleep in the car?" Clemente asked.

"Never. They switched from one Christmas carol to

another, singing again and again and again." *And again. How many verses of "Jingle Bells" were there?*

Veronica finger-combed the boys' tangled hair. "Thanks for allowing them to join you for such a fun day."

"My pleasure." And, Adolfo realized with a start, that he meant it.

A few minutes later, he and Krystal reached the cottage. He cut the engine and placed a kiss on her cheek. "Ready for your surprise?"

She grinned. "I love surprises."

A slight gust flapped the hem of her pink jacket as he assisted her from his truck. The evening's fog slowed their footsteps.

"What's this?" Her eyes widened at the sight of a large pine tree on the porch.

"Your surprise. I arranged for it to be delivered while we were at the beach. No Portuguese home is complete without a Christmas tree."

They ran up the steps, the vivid evergreen scent permeating the night air.

"Do you like it?" He glanced at her, unsure of her reaction.

Tears welled in her eyes. "I love it. Thank you!"

He bowed his head and uttered a thankful prayer. Apprehension had chattered in his brain all the way to the cottage. He'd envisioned himself hauling the tree back to his truck under Krystal's furious stare.

He let out a huge breath and dragged the tree into the cottage.

After he'd deposited the tree in a corner, he wrapped his arms around her. "I'll buy bells and pinecone chocolates tomorrow. We can string and hang them on the tree tomorrow night."

"Adolfo, I can't wait!" Her laughter lit the room. "When I

was a little girl, I loved fat colored lights and silver tinsel on our tree."

He bit his lower lip to keep from smiling. "We'll trim your Portuguese tree with lights and tinsel and chocolate."

"And I'll prepare dinner."

"Really? You cook?"

She cocked her head, feigning offense. "I like cooking. I'm not a gourmet chef by any means. I'm better at baking."

He decided not to touch that comment and made a vague compliment about her exceptionally sweet and succulent olive bread.

They exchanged grins overflowing with contentment. And something else. Companionship. Kindred spirits, both searching for acceptance and love.

Krystal wedged herself into a corner of the sofa. A cool breeze kicked through the open living room window, blowing blonde strands around her face. She tucked a strand behind her ear and smiled at him.

He smiled back. There was an ethereal quality about her that captivated him, a slow burn rather than a sudden hit. But it was there. *Sim*, it was there. Their relationship had developed quicker than he'd ever imagined, and he was powerless to stop the attraction.

He drew a lungful of air and slowly let it out. The contented expression on her face mirrored his feelings. He pressed a kiss on her temple, then built a fire in the hearth.

"How do you harvest olives?" she asked.

He sat beside her. "Do you like to climb trees?"

"What does climbing trees have to do with harvesting olives?" She playfully shoved at his chest. "Julio and I once built a tree house in our backyard and climbed that tree a dozen times a day. Does that count?"

Adolfo sighed dramatically. "Where were you last month?

I needed you desperately when olive harvest season rolled around and we were short extra hands."

He needed her desperately now, although he didn't add that part.

He chucked her chin. "Harvesting is beyond time-consuming, and it takes three people several hours to harvest two trees."

"How is it done?"

"You can either climb a ladder, or climb the tree. I prefer to use an olive rake and smack the stick on the tree."

"Sounds exhausting."

"*Sim,* though when I'm outside on a wintry day, the sun on my face, appreciating the views of the hillside and every color of the rainbow … Well, these moments make a hard task incredibly rewarding."

"So rewarding you'll be adding grape vines to your workload?"

"Olives and grapes share similar processing, because each is pressed and put up. When wine-press work ends, olive pressing begins." He paused. "Do you think a winery is feasible?"

He didn't usually ask for other people's opinions, except for Clemente. However, here beside him sat his splendid, exquisite Krystal, and he valued her insight.

Pensive silence stilled the space for several seconds.

"Yes, it's an excellent idea," she said. "If I stayed, I'd help you plant the vines and start your winery."

She could. Stay. He left the thought alone, pulling in a sigh thick with the utter loneliness he'd feel in her absence. "Clemente approves, and he's the guy who writes the checks. Remember, the winery business is fierce and our family could end up losing money."

He spoke as if she were already part of the Silva family. Had she noticed?

For a moment, her body went rigid.

She'd noticed.

"Knowing you and your work ethic," she said, "your wine will taste better than any competitor." Her encouraging smile made his heart race. He wanted to hold her, to feel her small hand brushing against his chest. He wanted her to be attracted to him, an olive farmer with no formal education.

Sometimes, his sadness at his father's death, his frustration to produce a profitable farm, was like a needle jabbing at his skin. Sometimes, he thought about walking away from it all. He knew that would never happen, his obligation to his heritage long entrenched. And he felt safe there, amidst the vast acreage.

"I appreciate your confidence." He spread his knees and studied the hardwood floor between his sandals. "As I told you, years ago I suggested planting grapes to my father. I supposed he'd pat me on the back and congratulate me. On the contrary, he shot my idea down and insisted we stick with the old ways, the old traditions."

"Perhaps your father was a tad stubborn. Perhaps you resemble him more than you realize."

There was substance in her remark. "Perhaps." Besides, his agreement brought a perfect excuse to gather her in his arms and kiss her. She was a woman who needed to be kissed, he decided, thoroughly and often.

Once the kiss ended, they remained in companionable silence and stared at the fire kindling in the grate.

He brushed his lips against her temple. "What are you thinking?"

"When I first came to Portugal, I didn't want to like this country. And I definitely didn't want to like you."

He laughed. "I felt the same about you."

She drew back and studied him. "And now?"

"Now things are different. Do you agree?"

"Yes, very different." Her cornflower-blue eyes softened with affection. She brushed a hand back and forth across his cheek. "You don't need to take care of me anymore. You've had enough of that."

"I didn't mind."

"And I'm sorry you've lost so much work time because of me."

"So am I."

Her fingers halted. "I said I'm sorry."

"You're forgiven." Nuzzling her neck, he chuckled. "I've hired someone to help me so I'll have more free time."

To spend with her.

She tilted her head. "Who?"

"Francisco. He starts tomorrow."

He could almost see the questions pushing into her busy brain. "You said you wouldn't hire him because he's unreliable."

Adolfo's smile had no penitence. "I changed my mind. I thought about your brother's story, and you're right. Everyone, even Francisco, deserves a second chance."

Indisputably, prison had changed Francisco. For better or for worse, time would tell.

CHAPTER 14

*T*hree more days gone. Krystal used the time to develop a business plan for her still-unnamed swimwear company, perusing specialized artists' and manufacturers' websites. If only her sketches were more expert. She could envision the swimsuits, but hadn't managed to convey the ideas to paper.

Despite that frustration, she was anticipating another amazing evening with Adolfo. The hours with him brought a contentment she could scarcely explain.

After work, he stopped by his home to shower and then was knocking on her cottage door an hour later, laden with unique Christmas trimmings—a festive wreath, a tiled keepsake ornament, a campfire-plaid tablecloth. Always, he presented her with a jewel-toned bouquet complemented by greenery from the ever-abundant gardens surrounding the countryside.

She'd thank him and bury her nose in the sweet fragrance. And then he'd kiss her.

He brought ingredients for dinner, seafood being the norm. He proved to be an excellent cook, attesting to his years of living alone; and he taught her how to season cod with olive oil and vinegar, to prepare a simple clam stew, and to grill mouth-watering sardines. His homemade *piri piri*, a spicy hot sauce, usually accompanied the meals, as did a field-greens salad tossed in an oil and vinegar dressing.

She marveled at how a strong-shouldered, formidable man like him could move so capably around the kitchen. His tanned, muscled arms revealed by the short sleeves of his white cotton T-shirt, he attended to last-minute dinner preparations—setting the table, placing a single purple bud in a vase, summoning her to the table with another exquisite, lengthy kiss.

"Your cooking is so good," she told him after she'd tried a grilled sardine. Did she dare to dip it in the hot *piri piri* sauce?

He'd quirked a thick, dark eyebrow. "I also can iron and sweep a floor and wash windows fairly well when asked nicely."

He was generous, reliable, and a romantic. Whenever her glance lingered on his handsome face, he'd flash a teasing smile, and her pulse skipped a beat.

When dawn broke the following day, Krystal rushed to the kitchen. The surf finals were imminent, and she needed to practice. Her phone app stated the swells were ideal. Today was the day.

She called her cousin, setting her cell phone on speaker as she peeked out the window at another steamy December day.

"Can you please take me to Peniche, Veronica?" she asked. "If I want to improve, I have to get back in the water. You're pushing me against the wall."

On cue, Krystal's wrist burned. *That pain—it wasn't real. Her wrist had healed.*

While she spoke with Veronica, Krystal peered at the recipe for rice pudding—that Veronica had given her. Adolfo had offhandedly mentioned that rice pudding was a traditional Portuguese Christmas dessert and one of his favorites. Krystal glanced at the kitchen wall clock and calculated the hours to Peniche and back. He had already accepted her invitation for a formal dinner, and she planned to surprise him.

Veronica expounded on the dozen and one reasons why she wouldn't be available for Krystal, while Krystal measured rice and water and brought the pudding ingredients to a boil on the stove. Had she added enough brown sugar? She flooded the mixture with sugar, then gave the mixture a stir.

With a thin 'good-bye' to Veronica, Krystal disconnected the call. She began to suspect Veronica and Adolfo were in silent agreement, both deciding surfing was too risky a sport for Krystal to pursue.

Her stomach hardened as she replayed the conversation with Veronica.

Why don't they listen to me? I told them I'm fine.

A trace of pine scent, bringing childhood remembrances of Sunday morning waffles drenched in maple syrup, wafted through the cottage. Krystal drained the rice in a colander, ladled out a bowlful, and stepped into the living room. Pausing between spoonfuls, she delighted in the tree, decked with numerous chocolate Yuletide shapes. Pieces of oak burned in the hearth, the scent toasty and Christmassy. She hummed the first two measures of "We Wish You a Merry Christmas" and closed her eyes.

The previous night, she and Adolfo had trimmed the tree and set up a crèche to represent the Nativity. On Christmas Eve, many Portuguese families gathered around their crèches before attending church at midnight.

After his explanation, he'd traced her cheekbones with his thumbs, and gazed at her with unbearable gentleness.

"Please stay in Portugal for Christmas. I promise our time together will be magical. In January, we can travel to the

States and, hand in hand, we will make it up to your father. He'll understand why you postponed your return."

Gaze downcast, she stared at her hands.

"Will you at least consider my suggestion?"

His question held a guarded hope, and tears sprang to her eyes.

The subject of surfing was never mentioned. Apparently, he considered it no longer an issue.

But she did.

So she'd forced her lips together and lifted her gaze, studying his attentive face, resisting the temptation to fling herself into his capable arms and agree with his request. *Yes, yes, yes.*

Somehow, she'd managed not to respond at all.

Krystal shook away the thoughts, seated herself on the living room sofa and set down the bowl. Worn-out—by unfinished dreams, indecision, her inability to be a worthy daughter, her feelings for Adolfo—she splayed her fingers over her eyes and sobbed. Didn't Adolfo realize all those years she'd practiced to become one of the top seventeen women surfers in the world, and that all that work and sacrifice could culminate in winning the finals? Didn't he realize she couldn't disappoint her father?

Her mind spun. She couldn't let her scary wipeout damage her image of herself. The definition of Krystal Walters was strong, not weak.

Admit defeat? Never. She was an accomplished woman pursuing an up-and-coming career.

Numbly, she wandered to the bedroom and glided her fingers along the flat, familiar surface of her surfboard. "I'm trying, Angel. Adolfo told me that whatever challenge he faced, he intended to win. Well, he's met his match, because I mean to succeed too."

She carried the board into the living room, intending to

wax it.

A knock on the cottage door made her pause. Perhaps Adolfo had finished early.

Despite their last discussion, she was always happy to see him. Summoning a smile, she swung open the door.

Francisco lounged against the door frame, aviator glasses clipped to his button-down linen shirt. "*Bom dia*, my lovely *senhorita*." He kissed her hand.

Her smile faded, and she jerked her hand back. "What are you doing here?"

"Were you expecting someone else?" His thin lips twitched with laughter. "Don't tell the boss I'm taking a respite from the hot sun. For over an hour, I've pruned his precious olive trees, while he hightailed it off to price grape vines."

"How did you know where I lived?"

Francisco jerked a shrug. "Common knowledge in a town like Évora. You're a fine-looking American woman who's also a world-renowned surfer." With a hawkish peer, he assessed the interior of the cottage. "Will you invite me inside for a drink?"

Coolly, she nodded and allowed him entry. He didn't give her much choice. Besides, he was Adolfo's friend.

Francisco made a show of complimenting the Christmas decorations. "Very cozy," he remarked in a sarcastic tone, sprawling in the armchair Adolfo frequented.

Krystal disappeared into the kitchen. "Is water all right?"

"For what?"

"You said you wanted a drink. I supposed you were thirsty."

"Anything stronger than water?"

For an overlong moment, she stared at the empty glasses in the cupboard. "Adolfo drinks port wine in the evening."

"I drink whiskey in the morning."

"Well, port is all I have."

He smirked. "Port it is."

Doubling back, she handed him the glass of wine.

"Do you always keep your surfboard in the living room?" he asked.

His gray-eyed appraisal unnerved her.

"I planned to wax my board. I anticipated practicing my surf maneuvers before the finals."

"What day are the finals?"

"Friday, and I haven't surfed since my wipeout. Today, I wanted to get to Medão Grande Beach. As usual, no one can take me."

Francisco took a liberal slug of port. "I can."

"Aren't you working?"

"I arrange my own hours. I'll ring Veronica once we're there and she can tell Adolfo. He'll understand. The shore beckons for a *belissimo senhorita*."

Krystal ran a hand through her hair. "Adolfo's one hundred and ten percent against me surfing. I had a concussion during the preliminary competition. Several concussions through the years, actually."

Francisco stood and closed the gap separating them. "Is that why you've been crying?"

Most people required at least three feet of personal space, and Francisco obviously hadn't gotten that memo. She took a step back.

"I miss being in the water. Surfing is my job, although it's more the thrill of nailing the ideal wave ..." She shook her head. "Don't misunderstand, I appreciate why Adolfo feels the need to protect me."

"Hours tick by while you sit isolated in this cottage, waiting for him to decide if he should or shouldn't take you to Peniche. He wants total control over every situation, and never liked to share his women."

"I'm not his woman."

"Aren't you?"

"He's concerned about my health."

Francisco choked back a laugh. "You're defending him?"

"Yes, I suppose I am."

"Typical Adolfo. He charms the ladies and keeps the best for himself. He has dangled around you ever since you arrived." Francisco used the right amount of scorn, tempered by flattery.

She rocked on her heels and stared at the floor. "In fairness, I don't understand myself anymore. I want to surf, and then I don't."

"Therefore, I will decide for you. Let's go to the beach."

"I should finish the pudding preparations first. Adolfo said he loves—"

"Adolfo has a lot of loves, and the olive farm will always be his first. Meanwhile, Medão awaits your triumphant return."

She deliberated, shivering from an imaginary blast of Adolfo's icy gaze if he found out. *When* he found out. "You mean now?"

"Not everyone abides by rigid rules, unless you fancy a boring life. You're a surfer girl—you like being exposed to danger. Or are you afraid to ride your surfboard again after the wipeout?"

She wasn't afraid of surfing. She just wasn't certain she could muster the courage to face Adolfo's disappointment.

Her gaze darted to the kitchen. "We might be gone too long, and I promised—"

"Adolfo will be late getting back tonight."

"Did you know that this year we'll sell olives in the retail store? And in a few years, with the purchase of grape vines …" She tried to piece disjointed ideas together. Had she said *we*?

Francisco subjected her to a long appraisal. His expression was so blasé, her self-control slipped a notch. "Are you aware his plans in Évora include meeting a woman for lunch? Since you're here by yourself, I assume he's seeing the stunning Isabel."

Her astonishment of Adolfo's betrayal stalled Krystal's breath, cut through her thoughts.

Sure, she didn't feel duty-bound to honor his request not to surf, though he hadn't asked, simply stated *no* in that flat, dismissive way of his.

"Isabel is the woman who won the beauty pageant several years ago?"

"*Sim.*"

Intending to gorge on carbohydrates and uncertainty, she sank onto the sofa and retrieved her half-eaten bowl of rice. "Adolfo didn't say a word about meeting anyone."

Francisco's smile never wavered. "It appears I'm the sole person around here who wants to help you."

She ran through her objectives.

Win. *Must* win.

Her wrist burned, and an unexpected headache struck with a vengeance.

Live your life boldly and with temerity, her father had encouraged.

"I'll be ready in five minutes." Like the determined athlete she was, she trooped to the bedroom and changed into her swimsuit, then snatched her wetsuit and surf equipment.

She peered into the kitchen. So much for finishing the rice pudding preparations.

Francisco clinked her bowl into the sink, singing "Jingle Bells."

In English.

He would be a nice rest from the intense Adolfo.

CHAPTER 15

*A*fter learning about Adolfo's luncheon date, Krystal felt more like a deflated balloon than a world-class surfer. In the cottage's bathroom, she splashed cold water on her face and stared in the mirror. Her cheeks and lips were so thin. Was that a gray root peeking out from her blonde hair?

She stepped into the kitchen. Francisco had raided the cupboards and packed a jar of olives, a loaf of corn bread, bottled water, and the unfinished bottle of port for the drive to the beach.

When they left the cottage fifteen minutes later, her mood had lightened. Francisco's car, a sleek convertible, washed a bright red in the sunlight. Just as they buckled their seat belts, he disclosed, rather vaguely, that he'd borrowed the convertible from a friend.

Oh no, I hope I'm not making the biggest mistake of my life.

She slid into the passenger seat. Regardless of Francisco's easy-going manner, she wasn't certain his remark about Adolfo and Isabel rang true. The disbelief niggled, a reminder that despite whatever Adolfo might be doing in Évora, he had spent every evening with Krystal.

Perhaps the acres and acres of scarlet and bright yellow fields heard her reflections, because the trees rustled and sighed. She imagined the murmurings of secrets and dreams, ancient as the country of Portugal itself.

Francisco bore down on the accelerator. The car responded, careening along the narrow roadways. "Adolfo and I used to play in these streets, shoot at cans with rocks, drink foamy cups of cold beer on hot summer nights." He focused on her while he swerved around corners scarcely wide enough for one car and a skinny pedestrian.

"Typical males," she responded.

"What did Adolfo tell you about me?"

"You work in finance," she answered evasively.

"*Sim*. I rose to vice president of a manufacturing company before I was caught embezzling funds. My penchant is money, so finance proved a natural choice for my university studies."

And stealing, although she didn't add that.

"Adolfo didn't attend university," she said. Yet, a sharp intellect shone in his eyes.

"When we attended primary school, Adolfo never mentioned becoming a farmer. He planned to apply to a prestigious university in America," Francisco said. "Architecture interested him, and he was brilliant in math, analyzing and solving problems in half the time it took the rest of the class. But even though he graduated at the top of our class, he never quite fit in."

"Why didn't he go to college?"

"Probably because he was too busy thinking about olives." Francisco laughed. "His father needed him, and Adolfo's motto is obligation above all else."

Francisco kept reminiscing, and to avoid his endless prattle, Krystal feigned sleep. When he finally got the message and the conversation quieted, her thoughts shifted to Adolfo.

He was a handsome enigma, valuing his privacy and his ability not to rely on anyone.

She'd grown up without a mother, the odd person out, her solitary path. In an attempt to prove herself, she'd filled the void with surfing. Ernie came along, all sea-salty pizzazz, a guy who embodied the surf culture of perpetual youth, popularity and year-round summers.

Skinny, always shirtless, happy-go-lucky Ernie. The man she'd loved.

Right?

She frowned, repeating the question to herself.

Her mind raced, searching for answers.

Well, so she'd thought. Except when a swell brewed, Ernie could disappear for hours. Responsibility was a fleeting consideration on the fringe of his mind, and that was why he couldn't hold a job. Ernie was the exact opposite of Adolfo.

Adolfo's name brought a quiver to her chest. He paid attention to her, his hazel gaze unflinching. With him, she felt protected and secure. He was self-sacrificing and self-sufficient. Plus, his sense of humor was wonderful.

And those were merely some of the reasons why she was falling in love with him.

Her eyes flew open. What? No, no, no. She hadn't known him long enough to love him.

Or had she? She recognized that emotion flooding her heart. Without knowing it, he'd broken through her boundaries.

"I'll shield you from Adolfo's fury," Francisco was saying. "His temper can be fierce."

"I've never seen his temper. And please don't say anything bad about him."

She was in love with Adolfo, a Portuguese farmer. A loner. A kind and generous man. A brilliant man. A man she innately knew would guard her with his life.

She loved him with a solicitousness that made her fiercely protective of him, and a desperation that left her vulnerable and breakable.

He had a clear mind for business, foreseeably why his *pai* had chosen him, not Clemente, to assume the farm tasks. A sense of honor propelled him to accept his responsibilities. To please his father, he'd set aside his personal aspirations.

Francisco gestured to a patch of strawberry runners tangled over wooden fences, pasture dotted with sheep. "Not for me, this hard, thankless labor. I want people to look up to me."

Adolfo had taken up his father's olive rake rather than studying at his dream university. Meanwhile, Francisco had landed in prison. Thus the difference between honor and dishonor. People worked the edges. Some minded the guardrails, others didn't care. Adolfo was a man of integrity.

Francisco angled to face her. "Once he reached his teens, Adolfo wasn't permitted to have a good time. I never heard laughter coming from his house, probably why he snuck out with me and my friends." He waited a beat. "Did he ever tell you about his shouting matches with his father?"

"Their relationship was rocky."

"There's an understatement." Francisco's smile was quick. "More like two stubborn people who never gave in—father and son."

With a nod, she closed her eyes again and courted sleep. For the first time since getting into Francisco's car, she agreed with him.

CHAPTER 16

*H*ours later, Krystal awoke when Francisco's convertible came to a stop and the bitter scent of raw ocean reached her nostrils. She hauled her surf gear out of the car and traipsed over broken driftwood and sandbanks to Medão Grande Beach. Francisco trailed beside her.

"Since all the locals think the water is too cold in December," he said, "the strand is yours. I prefer this cooler weather. In the summer, the temperature can exceed one hundred degrees Fahrenheit." Francisco peeled off his shirt, exposing a full-sleeve tattoo of an attractive woman with a spill of long black hair.

"A woman I love," he provided, at Krystal's quizzical stare. "Adolfo and I both got tattoos the day we graduated from secondary school."

"Is she the particular lady you mentioned when Adolfo and I met you in Évora?"

"*Sim.* When we attended secondary school, she didn't hide the fact that she preferred Adolfo, although he wasn't interested. Still, I continued to pursue her. She at least was my friend, but once I was arrested, she wanted nothing more to do with me."

"What is her name?"

"Isabel."

Krystal stiffened. "As in Isabel, the beauty queen?"

"*Sim.*"

"So Adolfo's tattoo is of Isabel, also?" Krystal turned away, intending to shake out her towel and place her surf gear on top. Her arms and legs refused to move, though.

"No, *senhorita.* His tattoo is inked on his back and is one unique word. *Saudade.*"

"What does *saudade* mean?"

"It is difficult to translate. Think of an occasion or person you keep forever in your heart and would miss if they were gone." Francisco positioned his emerald-green jacket on the sand and sat on it. "After secondary school graduation, he was undecided about his future. While the majority of our class planned to go on to university, he knew his formal schooling had ended. His father was slowing down and Clemente had been hired to work at a law office in town." Francisco popped open the olive jar and mopped up the juice with a slice of bread. With the bottle of port beside him, he sloshed himself a glass. "*Saudade* is joy and sorrow mixed together."

She waxed her surfboard in silence. *Joy and sorrow. Two different spectrums. Perhaps life could be found somewhere in the middle. Compromises. A new mindset.*

Atlantic breakers roared against a backdrop of sandstone cliffs. More and more, the same thought resonated in Krystal's mind: she'd miss Portugal, the fervor of the jubilant festivals, the jaw-dropping scenery that rendered her speechless.

And Adolfo. Adolfo most of all.

A dull ache settled in her chest when she pondered never seeing him again. How could she carry on if they were separated?

Francisco donned his aviators. "Aren't you jumping in the water?"

She glanced at the ocean, then away. The strong desire to surf whenever she was within walking distance of the sea eluded her. Did she *want* to surf anymore? She could scarcely look at the ocean without remembering how the enormous waves had tumbled her, tossed her, nearly drowned her.

"First, I'll take a walk to warm up." She hung a right, carving sandy footprints along the shore, avoiding tangled seaweed as she splashed through rocky pools, shallow and overrun with seawater.

She had gone behind Adolfo's back, and he would be furious. She knew him well enough to know that. Guilt overwhelmed her, because he credited her with being as honorable as him, and she'd betrayed his trust. Nonetheless, in his high-handed way, he limited her. And he was arrogant and exacting.

She shrugged the thoughts aside because he was also thoughtful and considerate. In her mind, she heard his roguish chuckle when he'd offered her the tree-shaped chocolate at the beach.

I saved this for you.

They shared so much more than chocolate—laughter, memories of their fathers, Christmas tree-trimming, and a stroll through his charming, historic town. There was no point in denying how much she cared for him just to keep her surfing goals alive. Even now, she longed for his lazy smile, approving glance, and the sound of his deep voice.

Sighing, she scuffed at a glossy-pink seashell with the toe of her sandal.

She'd appease Adolfo's anger by telling him what he wanted to hear, for she'd decided to remain in Portugal and spend Christmas with him.

When had she made that decision? That morning, last night, last week? Somehow, she'd known since she'd confessed to him that she hadn't wanted to like him. But she did. With a smile, he'd admitted the same.

She'd tell him tonight at the cottage. She envisioned his affable grin, the quiet hope in his eyes changing to gladness. A good man like him would never abandon her, knowing she'd given up so much to be with him. Assuredly, her caring father would understand.

Satisfied with her choice, she paced back and forth along the shore and planned their upcoming evening. First, she'd pin her hair in a casual upsweep away from her face, the way Adolfo liked it, and dress specially to please him. She'd brought a stunning satin sheath dress to Portugal in case of a formal occasion. It was embellished with lace sleeves, classic and elegant.

In her enticing outfit, Krystal would serve him her homemade rice pudding, and then, in that bold, sensual way of his, he'd compliment her on a tempting meal, take her in his arms, and kiss her.

Long, hard, and lingering.

Her heart galloped just at the thought of the kiss.

Yes, her life was finally in balance, and she was in love with a noble, unselfish man.

She walked back to Francisco.

"Ready to show me how well you navigate those waves?" he asked, slightly slurring his words.

She frowned. He wanted a performance? She'd give him one.

She pulled on her wetsuit and adjusted her reef socks and booties.

Fat, gray clouds had assembled in the sky, underscoring her need for haste. The swells were ideal, although conditions could suddenly change, dependent on the weather.

She secured the leash to her surfboard and paddled out, soon catching and riding a wave. *She could do this. The sudden stinging pain in her wrist? Only her imagination.*

The cool water refreshed, and the familiar rush of gliding up and down the waves invigorated. Her first maneuver, the frontside turn, required placing her weight on her back foot and bending her back knee. With ease, she leaned in the direction of the swell and reverted to the center.

She could see Francisco hold up his glass and toast her. Surely he hadn't been drinking all the while.

She pointed her attention to her next maneuver. Her backside turn was a little more complicated. To see the wave, she needed to peer over her shoulder, and she transferred her weight as she reached the top of the swell.

Stay aligned and balanced.

She tugged at the sleeves of her wetsuit, willing her muscles to relax. Normally, this maneuver came easily. Not today. Today, she felt lightheaded. Her body was overheating in the wetsuit. Her breath came short and fast.

Ignore the wrist pain. It isn't real. You're very different from the child who huddled in a closet with a flashlight.

She knew the moment she'd successfully accomplished the maneuver. Thrusting a fist toward the clouds, she let out an elated "Hurray!" Her gaze skirted the shore for Francisco's upraised glass.

Now where had he wandered off? Apparently, he couldn't sit still.

She kept scanning—

Her breath came to a halt.

Francisco stood at the water's edge with another man. A

tall, handsome man. The man's arms made sweeping gestures at Francisco before he swerved jerkily toward her.

Adolfo. Before she could avoid eye contact, his hard, flinty stare cemented on hers.

CHAPTER 17

*I*t couldn't be Adolfo. He was buying grape vines in Évora, eating lunch and sipping espresso with the beauty queen.

The air became thin, sparking of disaster. Krystal couldn't breathe.

With a tumble off her surfboard, she wiped out into the frigid Atlantic waters.

"Krystal!"

She heard Adolfo's unnerved shout, saw his frenetic dash toward her. Hadn't he said he couldn't swim?

She regained her strength and paddled to shore. The brisk breeze cooled her heated face as she surfaced and unleashed her foot from the surfboard.

Slowly, she inhaled, intending to pick up her pace and hurry past him.

Adolfo seized her forearm. "What were you trying to prove out there?"

She noted the betraying hoarseness in his tone, the fear in his hazel eyes.

Her arms fell limply to her sides. She couldn't bear to see him upset.

"Don't worry. Please don't worry. I'm a pro in the water."

He held her firm. "Were you planning to walk right past me with no explanation?"

She yanked from his grasp and attempted to get by him. "Let go of me! Who do you think you are?"

His one-step twist blocked her path. "By your own admission, I'm the man who came to your rescue not once, but twice. Were you trying for a third time?"

She pressed back her hair, knowing it was a soaked, tangled mess. "You broke my concentration!"

"Suppose you got dizzy on those heavy waves? Then what? Dr. Dantas advised giving your brain time to heal."

"I'm so tired of you parroting the doctor's advice." She knew her face telegraphed her guilt. Who was she to pretend to know more than the doctor?

"No one fights the ocean and wins. Admit your limitations." Adolfo's voice grew softer. "Please, Krystal."

Through a blur of tears, she spun toward the parking area. He was in no state to listen to reason. "You're the one trying to limit me! You ruined my practice and I was doing well. I can't surf with you standing on shore glaring at me."

"I'm standing ready to save you."

"How? You can't swim." She shivered. The sun felt stiff and bleak against her wet skin. "I'm going back to the cottage. Francisco will take me."

Adolfo looked tired. And livid, his hazel eyes glittering a dangerous green. "You're coming with me."

"You're joking, right?"

Adolfo frowned at Francisco. "He's too drunk to steer a car. Knowing him, he probably misplaced the keys."

"Both of you are talking about me as though I'm not here." Francisco whipped off his aviators, exposing bloodshot eyes. He shrugged into his shirt, taking his time, fumbling with each button. "She's an expert and knows what she's doing." He swayed, and Krystal eyeballed the empty wine bottle. He'd consumed an epic amount of liquor.

All six feet two inches of Adolfo's wrath landed on Francisco. "Why did you risk Krystal's life by bringing her to Medão Beach?"

"Why are *you* seeing Isabel when you know how important she is to me?"

"This isn't about Isabel. It's about Krystal."

Francisco's expression radiated cockiness, although he stood six inches shorter than Adolfo. "Is it? Or is it about how you think you can get any woman you choose? When Isabel finds out I was at the beach with a world-famous surfer and your latest love interest, she'll come back to me."

Before Krystal had time to react to the news that Francisco had used her to provoke the woman he claimed to love, Francisco said, "By the way, you're fitting the role perfectly, Adolfo."

"What role?"

"The role of a tyrant like your father."

Adolfo's muscles bunched beneath his gray T-shirt. "What did you say?"

Francisco pointed a thick index finger straight toward Adolfo's face. Too close. Krystal knew Adolfo wouldn't like it, but Francisco's conception of personal space was conveniently nonexistent.

"You're marking a never-ending report card. No one can reach your lofty standards," Francisco said.

"Leave. Now." Right before Krystal's eyes, the soft-spoken Adolfo she'd known since that first day at the cottage had been replaced by a seething, furious Adolfo.

Neither man had ever acted like a raging bear before, compelling Krystal to either dash for cover or physically separate them. Fortified by her exasperation at the universe in general, she used her board as a barrier between them. "Stop. Stop. Both of you."

"Whatever you wish, *senhorita.*" Francisco retreated quickly, stomping and stumbling, carting himself off as if he had something to prove.

Adolfo caught her by the shoulders. "Give up this absurd path you're bent on. Do it for me."

She dropped her surfboard into the sand. The ocean air she loved so much was fragmented by his statement.

Adolfo, please understand. How can I choose? I love you and want to please you. I also need to prove to myself that I'm a winner. I've held onto this dream for so long.

The briny depths of the ocean churned; seagulls skipped along the chaotic waves. The wind blew persistently, those fat gray clouds amassing into the beginnings of a thunderstorm.

"All I've ever known is surfing," she said quietly.

"I'm warning you for the last time. Do not surf. It's too dangerous."

She balked at his commanding tone. "Must you overthink every situation? Can't you be spontaneous like Francisco?"

"I swear, if you ever say his name again—"

"You'll what? Prevent me from becoming a winner? If so, let me congratulate you for accomplishing your goal so admirably."

He stared down at her. Nope, no warm chocolate-fudge gaze there, still a sizzling green. "Someone must protect you from yourself."

A couple smudges of dirt were on his cheeks, a dark stubble on his strong jaw. He was the man who worked the land.

She almost reached out to stroke the dirt from his cheeks, to calm the worry in his gaze, but she didn't deserve to touch him, to comfort him, anymore. She'd betrayed his belief in her that she'd be sensible and do the right thing. Had she ever been worthy of a man like him?

"You're successful," she said. "Let me be successful like you." Her voice cracked.

"I'm a far cry from success."

"Your father may have led you to believe otherwise, but you are brilliant and will succeed." She blew out an frustrated breath. "He must have praised you once in a while."

Judging from Adolfo's impassive expression, that had never happened.

He planted his feet wide. "This is the end of any conversation about my father."

"Can't you deal with the world when it doesn't spin your way?" She whipped her towel up from the sand. "My American driver's license is valid in Portugal and I'll drive Francisco's car back to the cottage."

"Your decision to leave without talking this out is unwise, Krystal. I suggest you reconsider very carefully."

"Is this your idea of asking me to stay? I'm sorry you don't like my observations regarding your father."

His shrug proclaimed aloofness. "What about you, fussing over *your* father like he's a child?"

"He's always been there for me and I'm going to be there for him. One of the nurses from rehab said he's becoming forgetful. He can't live alone any longer."

"He won't be alone at the senior facility. He'll be surrounded by friends. And he's happy."

He's happy. Present tense.

She moved backward. Tiny grains of sand blew around her face, and her skin prickled. "How do you know he's happy?"

"Julio and your father rang me this morning."

"Rang *you?* Why didn't they call me?"

403

"They wanted to speak to me and Veronica gave them my number."

Her cheeks warmed to crimson. "How dare you go behind my back?"

"I didn't. Your father moved into the senior facility last week. They were concerned you'd be disappointed and wanted my input."

"You withheld this information from me? While I begged to surf again and again?"

"I found out this morning. Now you won't need the money from any winnings."

"Suppose I want to surf because I want to show *myself* that I can win?"

"You're here. I'm here. Your father is happy. That's all that matters."

"That's not all that matters to *me*." She removed her wetsuit and dragged on her jersey and sweatpants. "I'm surfing in the finals on Friday."

"I won't support you. Meet me on my terms."

"Or what?"

He shrugged.

Roughly, she seized her surf bag and zipped it closed. "So now our relationship is conditional? I either abide by your wishes, or else?"

Veronica appeared over the dunes, shouting and waving. She raced to Krystal, a polka-dotted kerchief tied askew around her hair, her tiered, ruffled skirt reaching her ankles. Her cheeks were smeared with off-kilter red blush. "Thank goodness you're all right. Adolfo finished early in Évora and stopped by my house on his way to your cottage. He flew out so fast after I told him Francisco had called, I jumped into my car to follow him and left the boys with Clemente." She glanced briefly at Adolfo, then at the surfboard and bag Krystal had picked up. "Are you leaving?"

"Yes, with Francisco. I expect he's sleeping off the liquor in his car." Although Krystal was furious with Francisco, he was her ride back to the cottage.

"If you came with him in that flashy red convertible, he isn't there. He probably wandered to one of the local pubs, so I'll bring you to the cottage. Settled?"

Forced into agreement, Krystal said yes. "Although on Friday, I'm competing," she added. "I'm a wildcard, and this chance to surf in the finals comes once in a lifetime."

Veronica reared back. "Is a serious brain injury worth a few thousand dollars?"

Purposely slow, Krystal hoisted her surf gear. "It's no longer about the money."

"It's about a free-for-all nonsense sport that might get you killed." Adolfo's quelling frown seemed to silenced the air. Barely a leaf stirred, the wind buttoned up. "This is my last word of warning. No surfing. Call it a recommendation, if you will."

Recommendation? His voice brooked no argument.

Krystal pushed back her shoulders. "I never excelled at obeying a dictator's orders."

"Forget surfing. Leave it in your past where it belongs."

Her throat constricted and she forced back tears. There was only one thing she was going to forget. Him. Because after Friday, she was saying goodbye to Portugal and Adolfo forever.

For a split second, she thought he might pull her back as she shoved by, imagined his plea. *Don't leave, Krystal. Carry on. I'm here for you, in sickness and in health …*

He didn't say a word. Not one word. Nothing.

And neither did she, for anything she said would be wrong.

She wanted to tell him that her whole being lightened whenever he gazed at her. She wanted to tell him that her heart was finally, irrevocably broken with the choice he'd forced her to make.

She thought of Rhode Island and her typical snowy Christmases.

She thought of lush, steamy Portugal, and the delights of a holiday in a country still unknown to her.

It's too much. Don't look back, don't come apart in front of him. You've lost everything important in your life. Winning is all that's left.

CHAPTER 18

"You weren't talkative during the drive," Veronica said when they arrived at Krystal's cottage. Veronica shut off the car's ignition, although she made no move to get out.

Krystal shrugged. "There's nothing to say."

Daylight waned through the canopy of olive trees. Silvery-green leaves turned in the balmy breeze, and there was no sign of the earlier impending storm.

"Hmm. I think you have a lot to say." Veronica tapped her pink manicured fingers on the steering wheel. "Although I'll admit Adolfo has a bit of temper when his buttons are pushed."

"You mean when things don't go his way."

"He's worried about you, and understandably so."

"His concerns aren't necessary. I don't need him to take care of me." *My self-image has suffered enough.*

"Forgive my prying, but what is your relationship with him?"

Krystal hesitated and pulled her terry cloth jacket tighter

around her. "Our relationship is developing. *Was* developing."

"He cares a great deal about you, more than he cares to admit, even to himself."

"Wrong topic, Veronica." Determined to remain aloof, Krystal let her gaze wander aimlessly, taking in the faded orange bougainvillea dripping over the front porch trellis. "As long as I obey his wishes, he'll continue to see me. Meanwhile, he met another woman for lunch today, the famed 'Miss Portugal.'"

"I don't believe it. And if he did, it's because her parents own a winery near Lisbon. Adolfo mentioned he might purchase supplies from them, which is why he's met with her before. So there, you're wrong. Besides, I see the way he looks at you."

Krystal glanced at her cell phone, which had pinged repeatedly during the drive. Adolfo's number blinked on the screen.

She shoved her phone in her purse and covered her face with her hands. She refused to listen to his messages, wouldn't read his texts. Because if she did, she'd cry. And if she cried, she wouldn't be able to stop.

Veronica squeezed her shoulder. "Are you okay?"

Krystal shook off Veronica's hand and managed a half-hearted smile. "Please don't. I know you mean well."

Veronica blew the air out of her cheeks. "Well, anyway, I wanted to tell you before now … But, you had a lot to process between hearing about your father's move to the senior facility and your argument with Adolfo."

"Tell me what?" In the stingy light of dusk, Krystal corralled her gear and exited the car as Veronica started for the cottage. A television set hummed from inside.

Krystal blinked. She hadn't left the television on. In fact, she hadn't watched any TV since arriving in Portugal.

An elegantly coiffed woman wearing fuchsia-colored lipstick opened the door. Her shiny black hair was shot with gray tips. Her dimples winked with her welcoming smile. She came to the porch's steps and extended her hand. "I'm Edite Silva. You must be Krystal. I've heard so much about you."

"As I was about to say," Veronica filled in rapidly, with a glance in Krystal's direction. "Aunt Edite stays at the cottage in December and runs the cash register in our family store during the Christmas season. She's the talented artist I told you about, remember?"

Krystal set down her gear and shook the older woman's hand. "Oh, it's a pleasure to meet you, Ms. …?"

"Silva. I never married. My brother, who recently passed, was Clemente and Adolfo's father."

Aunt Edite smelled of paints and canvas, her manner saturating the air with color and kindness.

"I'm sorry for your loss." Krystal glanced at Veronica. "For both your losses."

"My brother and I weren't close," Aunt Edite said, "although I always spent Christmas with him and his family. This holiday will be our first without him. We'll set an extra plate at the table for *alminhas a penar.*" At Krystal's inquiring glance, she clarified, "'The souls of the dead.' We offer a food gift to ensure they will do well in the future." She linked arms with Krystal and guided her inside the cottage. "In any event, the loss of a loved one is difficult, especially during the holidays. Men don't show their emotions the way women do, although I'm certain both Clemente and Adolfo are struggling with their grief."

Veronica picked up Krystal's surfing gear and deposited it inside the cottage. "Clemente has immersed himself in his office work since his father's death. I've hardly seen him."

"Typical male response," Aunt Edite said with a heartening smile. "Continue to be there for your husband. Everyone mourns in their own way."

Krystal took a silent, pained breath. Besides his endless work demands, Adolfo was swamped with sorrow. This was a difficult season in his life, and she'd made their relationship all about her and her selfish demands.

"We'll be roommates, and I moved my luggage into the upstairs loft," Aunt Edite was saying.

"Please, I don't want to put you to any trouble," Krystal said.

"Aside from the fact that I'm forty years older than you, I'm still spry." Aunt Edite's dark-lashed almond-shaped eyes scrutinized Krystal. "I can see why you're a surfer. You're so tall and thin."

"What I meant is, I won't be in Portugal after Friday. I'm booking my airline ticket back to Rhode Island."

"Well, that's my cue to leave." Veronica rubbed her palms over her skirt and then glanced at her wristwatch. "I have to check on the twins to be sure my house is still intact, so I'll leave you two to get acquainted and ring you tomorrow."

Aunt Edite nodded. "I stopped at the market in Évora on my way here. *Caldo verde*, kale soup, is simmering on the stove. Krystal and I are two capable women and are all set for the night."

"No surprise there. You always have everything under control." Veronica waved a cheerful good-bye followed by a hasty exit.

Aunt Edite nabbed Krystal's elbow and led her to the kitchen. "Let's be blessed with a delicious dinner and have a heart-to-heart talk."

Krystal glanced downward. "I may not be up to a heart-to-heart anything."

"Then I'll talk. It's my favorite pastime. By the way,

cooked rice and a pudding recipe were left on the kitchen countertop."

"Right. I intended to—"

"From what I understand, you were preoccupied today at the beach. No worries. I prepared the pudding."

Krystal sniffed the mouth-watering scent of smoked sausage and kale. Normally, she didn't eat kale, preferring a thick hamburger and French fries. Today, she found the strong cabbage aroma comforting.

While Krystal set the table, Aunt Edite slid onto a stool and snapped up a pencil and paper napkin.

Noting the quick strokes, Krystal peered over Aunt Edite's shoulder. "May I ask what you're drawing?"

"I'm drawing you. If I added color, your eyes would be a flash of blue. And your hair is magnificent. You must have a mile of it."

"No one's ever drawn me before. I'm sketching, or rather, trying to sketch, swim designs for my yet-to-be-named swimsuit company."

Aunt Edite focused on Krystal's face, then went back to her pencil and napkin. "May I see your sketches sometime? I'll offer a helping hand, if you'd like."

"Certainly. Yes, thank you, and I'd be eternally grateful. I'll show you the sketches tomorrow."

With a nod, Aunt Edite pushed back her stool. Taking the thick creamy soup off the heat, she ladled potatoes, sausage, and kale into speckled-blue pottery bowls and placed a basket of crusty bread on the kitchen table. She settled into the seat across from Krystal and prayed a simple grace.

Lively conversation accompanied their meal, and Krystal scarcely believed an hour had passed by the time she'd cleared the soup bowls and brewed a pot of herbal tea.

Aunt Edite set the rice pudding on the table, then sat and

perched her chin on her slim folded hands. "So, you won't be joining us for Christmas?"

Krystal sank into the white-tiled chair across from Aunt Edite. "No."

"What a shame. I could use help in the retail store, and Christmas Day is such fun with Bento and Bernardo. Portuguese tradition accords that the Three Wise Men, not Santa Claus, bring the gifts on Christmas Eve."

Unable to get comfortable, Krystal crossed and uncrossed her legs. "All your holiday traditions are fascinating."

"Indeed. And Christmas is one of the most magical. I've celebrated Christmas with the Silva family since Clemente and Adolfo were boys."

"What was Adolfo like when he was a boy?"

Aunt Edite smiled. "One Christmas in particular is fixed in my mind, when Adolfo was a toddler. He played for hours with a toy train set, designing and redesigning the tracks round and round the Christmas tree. He was very creative, and solved the smallest of problems in unique ways. He wanted to be an architect."

Krystal nodded, imagining a dark-haired boy, his nose a tad crooked, most likely tall for his age, his wide hazel eyes brimming with complexity beyond his years.

She dragged herself from her musings. "Any boyhood transgressions?"

Aunt Edite sipped her tea. "There was the time when he was ten years old and didn't come home for Christmas lunch. I still remember whiffs of the stuffed turkey baking in the oven before the family realized he'd been gone too long. We all went outside and combed the farm looking for him."

"Where was he?"

"Much to his parents' dismay, he'd snuck out early in the morning to design and build an elaborate fort. He was positively covered in dirt by the time we all came running up.

With a pile of twigs in one hand and plans for the fort he'd drawn up in the other, he gaped at us, probably wondering what all the fuss was about."

"Should I laugh or cry?"

"His mother wept with relief at finding him. His father, however, delivered a deafening rant regarding Adolfo's rash and reckless behavior. Even though it was Christmas, Adolfo was sent to his room."

Krystal plucked up a napkin and dabbed at her eyes. The thought of Adolfo as an exuberant child with high expectations, and then the hard-working man he'd become, the man who'd shouldered his duties without hesitation, brought a dull throb to her chest.

Aunt Edite reached out and touched her hand. "Christmas carolers came to the door later that evening, and Adolfo was allowed out of his room. He immediately went to his father and hugged him. That boy always had a heart of compassion."

"He cares for everyone around him."

Astuteness shone from the elderly woman's eyes. "And he's smitten with you."

"You couldn't be more wrong."

"I'm never mistaken about my nephew. He and I lunched in Évora today. He laughed out loud and seemed content and happy for the first time in a long while. I'd feared he'd never come to grips with his father's death. His father was so tough on him, and, as Adolfo matured, he began to argue back, and rightfully so."

Krystal's napkin dropped to the floor. "*You* were his luncheon date?"

"Didn't he tell you?" Aunt Edite helped herself to a heaping tablespoon of rice pudding directly from the pot and grimaced.

"No, he didn't." Krystal twisted her wristwatch. "We had a

terrible row at the beach and I split." She'd left first, before he had the opportunity to leave her.

"In Évora, I helped him purchase a Christmas gift for you, and an ornament for the top of your Christmas tree."

Vigorously, Krystal shook her head. "It's not my tree, Ms. Silva."

"Please, call me Aunt Edite. From what I gathered, you'll soon be part of the family."

Krystal studied her cup of tepid chamomile tea. "He can't seem to understand my need to prove myself."

"One of my favorite pastors once said, 'The most important story is the one you tell yourself.'"

Krystal linked her fingers together. "Do you want to hear my story? I'm a champion surfer."

Aunt Edite wagged her spoon. "There's more to life than that."

"My father is waiting for me in Rhode Island."

Setting down her spoon, Aunt Edite place her hand over Krystal's linked fingers. "Adolfo mentioned your devotion to your father. Although admirable, perhaps you've limited yourself. There is a man here in Portugal who needs you. Don't exclude him from your life."

* * *

IN HER BEDROOM later that evening, Krystal set her surfing gear by her nightstand, and smoothed her fingers over her surfboard. She loved the smells of the ocean, the wet wood and salty fish, the sense that the world was just waiting for her to achieve her goals.

"Angel, I must surf in the finals. You're the only one that understands how far we've come to reach this goal."

The scent of the ever-burning oak log, blending with

fragrances of pine, seeped through her closed bedroom door. The scents of Christmas in Portugal.

Setting Angel aside, she padded to the window, opened it, and rested her hip on the sill. Fresh, cool breezes flooded the room, entering her as the inspiration for a new life. For a moment, she closed her eyes and absorbed the night sounds of Portugal—the peal of church bells, the chirping of noisy crickets, a dog barking somewhere in the distance.

She glanced at the woven wool rug covering her bedroom floor. Her first night at the cottage, she'd hunched over that rug with the lights off and suffered the worst headache of her life.

She retraced her first days in Portugal—her wipeout and resultant concussion, Adolfo's reassuring, subdued voice while he spoke to her in Portuguese. Always, her thoughts veered to him, his sizzling hazel gaze when he kissed her, the scruff of his dark beard against her cheek, his thick black hair, casual and careless after a day's work.

Despite her craving for all things Adolfo, why would she change her goals, her lifestyle, to suit him? All those years perfecting her techniques. All those sacrifices.

If she participated in the finals, he'd made it clear he wouldn't want to see her again. Her ambitions meant little to him. And if she didn't participate? Well, then, inch by inch, she'd lose her foothold on everything she'd once deemed important.

Her heart thudded hard in her chest. Her conflicting thoughts threatened to break the dam holding back her tears.

She crossed to her nightstand, retrieved her cell phone, and pressed *play* to hear Adolfo's voicemail messages.

His baritone voice resonated into the silence.

Krystal, please answer the phone.

Krystal, answer the phone.

And she read and reread his text messages:

Next time I call, pick up your worthless cell phone.

Followed by: *I'll text you tomorrow. Please, we need to talk.*

"I make my own path and live by it," she whispered. Yet, her loneliness was bottomless without him.

She stared at the phone. She wanted to call him. Of course, she didn't. Instead, she set the phone on her night-stand and ran her fingers along her leather-embossed sketch pad.

Aunt Edite was a talented artist and successful entrepreneur. Could she bring Krystal's visions, her swimsuit designs, to reality? Could Krystal leave her dusty story behind and find a new life, a happier Christmas, in Portugal? Could the despair from her repeated abandonments be assuaged by Adolfo's love?

She shook off the inertia accompanying her conflicting emotions. The soft woolen blanket on her bed had been turned down, probably by the thoughtful Aunt Edite. With a weighty sigh, Krystal slid beneath the blanket and shut her eyes. Sleep would enable her to consider her future in a clearer light.

Daylight wasn't near when she woke. A full winter moon rode high in a charcoal sky smeared with gray. She rolled onto her stomach, chasing the truce of slumber before she lost it to an endless night of tossing and turning, and the anguishing dilemmas plaguing her.

CHAPTER 19

$\mathcal{A}$t precisely eleven o'clock in the morning on Friday, December nineteenth, Krystal let her gaze roam over Medão Beach. The Atlantic Ocean sparkled, crashing against the shore. Beachgoers in bathing suits sat cross-legged on the blistering sand. A mild sea breeze carrying scents of coconut suntan lotion and salt water brushed through her hair.

She lifted her face to the comforting warmth of the sun. People called Portugal the edge of Europe. To her, this incomparable country was the center of her heart.

Spectators, each rooting for their favorite contestants, mingled along the sloping rise. This modest fishing town was splendid, resembling a picture book of laughter and sunbeams.

And she felt so alone. The special event held no sign of a tall, ruggedly handsome man with compassionate hazel eyes.

Surely Veronica had told Adolfo of Krystal's decision.

And Krystal had hoped, a small, quiet hope, that he would show up to support her. But he hadn't. He hadn't bothered to call nor text.

It took every bit of her self-control to turn away from the spectators, to rest her hands silently on her surfboard.

As she waited for her heat to be called, Sam Larson came to stand beside her.

"Thanks again for bringing me to the surfing finals," she said. "I'm sorry for phoning you last minute. I was undecided about today."

Below bleached-blond brows, Sam's green-eyed gaze zeroed in on her. "More than glad to help out a champ. We were all wondering where you disappeared to, and then I find you've been staying on an olive farm of all places. Are you ready to win this heat by a landslide?"

She glanced at the ocean, and her mouth went dry. If only time would speed up and the heat was over.

"I managed to surf once since my concussion, and it didn't go well," she said.

He crossed his arms. "Then should you surf today? Concussions and surfing don't mix."

"The World Surf League deemed me worthy enough to be granted another opportunity. Otherwise, I didn't qualify." Krystal gestured to the curvaceous Wilhelmina, who'd already completed a successful surf. "She's in the lead for the women's events."

Sam whistled through his teeth. "Yes she is."

"And you're in the lead for the men."

"A double hurrah for me."

"Double?"

A dazzling white smile wreathed his face. "Wilhelmina and I are together."

"As in dating?'

With a decisive clunk, Sam planted the nose of his surfboard into the sand, and then leaned against it. "Ever since I congratulated her on her win at the Peniche preliminaries, we've dated. We're flying back to the States on Sunday."

She grinned. "The media will love a jaw-dropping, glamorous surfing couple. You'll get plenty of sponsorships."

"We're counting on it. When are you traveling back to Rhode Island?"

Krystal's assigned heat blasted through the announcer's bullhorn and she didn't have time to answer Sam. Wearing a pasted-on smile, she attached her surf leash, swept up her surfboard and sprinted to the ocean's edge.

Surfers emerging from the water warned of a rip current, and how even the strongest swimmer could be swept out to sea.

She paused in midstep.

Rip currents are drowning machines.

Please, please, anything but that. She'd warned Ernie not to surf that fateful day, pleaded with him. Intent on pursuing his own interests and disregarding everyone else's opinion, including hers, he'd opted for his surfboard. Nevertheless, she should have insisted. Why hadn't she insisted?

Ignoring the phantom pain in her wrist, she flexed and unflexed her fingers. All of a sudden, conditions seemed windier, the sea churned rougher, the water murky and foamy.

Her heartbeat went erratic. Dizzy, she leaned over and put her head between her knees. Conceivably, the spectators would think she was limbering up. The blood raced to her head, emboldening her.

Lightly, she patted Angel. *Don't be scared. You need to see this through. If conditions were dangerous, the officials would have canceled the competition.*

She threw down an invisible gauntlet, determined to overcome her fears, ignoring the butterflies taking up permanent residence in her stomach. With a long-held breath, she mounted her surfboard and paddled into the icy waters of the Atlantic Ocean.

* * *

STEPS away from a rocky enclave at the far end of Medão Beach's shoreline, Adolfo stood stiffly with Veronica. Bento and Bernardo were sandwiched between them. Why he'd agreed to Veronica's suggestion that she follow him to the beach in her own car, her ever-talkative twins in tow, was beyond him.

"Krystal's an expert surfer." Veronica's smile came easy as she kissed one son's hair, then the other's. "She'll be so happy when she realizes you're here."

"I sincerely doubt it."

A gleam appeared in Veronica's eyes. "Believe me, Krystal will be delighted."

Krystal. The only woman he'd ever loved didn't love him. She had come to Portugal with a surfboard and rigid aspirations, and, less than a week ago, she had been softer, brighter, when he'd held her. He'd never anticipated finding a woman like her. She was brave, too brave for her own good, with bewitching blue eyes. A woman who loved chocolate, and Christmas, and believed in angels.

He watched as she stood near the shore, holding her surfboard. Firmly, he gripped the twins' shoulders as they giggled and wrapped their arms around Veronica's legs.

He rolled his shoulders in a vain attempt to shrug off his tension. "Nonetheless, I'm here to support Krystal, and to pull her out of the water if anything goes wrong."

Veronica pivoted as the boys ducked beneath Adolfo and streaked toward a nearby hot dog stand. "I brought some towels and a pail, and I'll settle the boys underneath a beach umbrella. Hot dogs will keep them occupied, at least for a while." She laughed affectionately at the twins, already halfway to the hot dog stand. "After Krystal's surf event, we'll leave. I assume you're sticking around?"

"*Sim.*" Adolfo eyed the rough Atlantic. Suppose Krystal floundered in that churning water? Suppose she went under, and the waves sucked up every bit of her precious oxygen? He rubbed a hand over his heart, his stance restless. "I can't watch. I'm not suited to standing idle."

"You can't pull her out of the water if you're not watching," Veronica called over her shoulder.

He snatched up the twins' pail. "Believe me, I'll be listening to the announcer's every word."

Farther down the beach, he filled the pail with water. Hauling the pail a few feet up the beach, he knelt, immersed his arms elbow-deep in sand, and started digging. He should build Krystal something impressive, something special and exquisite, while he waited for her.

Once, when he heard her name being called by the announcer, he viewed her. Only once. Although she effortlessly glided through the water on her surfboard, his breath hung in his throat.

He went back to the sand.

On this very same beach, he'd demanded that she choose between him and her sport. Barring the fact that he disagreed with her views on surfing, who was he to stop her? She was a widow and had fended for herself for several years. She'd lost her mother and had endured tremendous sadness at a young age.

What if he had told her that she could surf, but that he'd trusted she wouldn't because he was too afraid of the outcome—of losing her. Would she have responded to his relentless phone calls and texts then, before he'd decided to ease off and give her a couple days to think about their disagreement? What if he'd *asked* her to reconsider competing, instead of issuing an ultimatum?

All week, he hadn't been able to switch off the "what ifs," although he'd tried, burying himself in his farm work, seeking any distraction. His father's maxim had flown through his mind.

Work, work, work.

So Adolfo had pruned, and planted, all the while thinking exclusively of her.

That infernal bullhorn again, announcing the next heat. He peered up. He didn't know anything about surfing, although by the ebb and flow of the crowd and their reaction, she hadn't surfed well.

"Adolfo?"

His heart stopped beating at the sound of Krystal's voice. How many minutes had gone by? He lost the capacity to breathe as his gaze fixed on her.

"Adolfo, you came to the beach to watch me surf? Veronica was at the water's edge and just told me." Krystal's face was flushed, her eyes huge and blue.

"You sound like you can't catch your breath," he said.

"I've been running—trying to find you."

His gaze stayed on her, only on her. The sight of her, her striped towel thrown over her shoulder, still wearing her form-fitting wetsuit, jolted his insides with an electric current. Never had she looked so gorgeous, or so peaceful. She was a glimmer of sunshine moving toward him, glistening wet with droplets of ocean water streaming down her face.

He didn't stand.

Was she delighted to see him? Was she disappointed?

Keeping his fingers occupied, he continued sifting double handfuls of cool sand, applying a fair amount of water to help the sand stick together. Hadn't she said something about good quality sand containing no rocks? This sand was loaded with tiny pebbles.

She leaned her hands on her knees. "What are you building?"

He wanted her to grin, to see her infectious smile when he was finished. He wanted her to think of this moment, of him, always.

"It's a surprise." He wanted to say more. His words were enmeshed in the blue sky, in the relentless surf, in her nearness.

* * *

"SURPRISES SEEM TO BE YOUR SPECIALITY." Krystal knelt beside Adolfo and drizzled a small amount of water into the sand.

Adolfo drew a labored breath, gave a curt nod. All potent vitality and attractive masculinity.

At first, she'd wondered if he'd heard her when she approached, although he'd stared at her before turning back to his sand sculpture. When she'd finally found him on this far end of the beach, she'd felt a stab of desire so great that her knees had weakened. He was so grand, so impressive in his fitted gray T-shirt and jeans. If he'd only look at her again, tease her with a genial smile rather than being so absorbed, she'd wrap her arms around his hard, muscular shoulders and plead with him.

Plead with him for what exactly? Forgiveness? Understanding? Patience?

Sand spilled through her fingers. "You found some decent quality sand. It should be a little finer, though."

"All I could find."

He was certainly occupied with whatever he was making.

She added more water to pack the sand firmer. "You need to smooth out the edges of your sculpture once it gets higher. Where's the kitchen spatula?"

"Forgot it."

She snuck a peek at him. His dark stubble was thicker than usual. His gaze was lowered beneath his dark lashes.

The noonday sun emphasized his dark tan and the minute creases on his forehead and near his lips. Creases of hard work, of levity, of worry. His Mediterranean nature was innate—tempers deeply experienced and strongly contained.

She pulled in some air. "I didn't surf well. I lost the heat."

"I know." His hands stopped, then started again. "Despite your loss, I'm proud of all you've accomplished. You surfed extremely well."

"How do you know? You've been building castles in the sand."

He smiled, but not at her. His gaze remained fixed on his task. "It's not a castle."

"When I heard talk from the other surfers about rip currents, I—I was afraid." She flashed a peek at the ocean. "I faced my fears."

He looked up. His hazel gaze had changed from anguish-shadowed green to something richer. A deliciously warm hot fudge. "Since we've met, I've regarded you as the most coura-geous person I've ever known."

Blood hummed through her veins. He was finally acknowledging her, not seeming hundreds of miles away.

"And I learned something else—something important about myself this morning," she couldn't resist continuing. "The in-law apartment I wanted to build for my dad was more to assuage my guilt for not being there for him these past three years, rather than for him. I believed that I'd neglected him after Ernie's death to nurse my own wounds. And I did. Dad and I spoke on the phone last evening and he's forgiven me—although he assured me there was nothing to forgive. So, I confronted my faults and failures, and I forgave myself. Nobody's perfect."

"*You* are."

She shook her head. "I'm far from perfect."

"When will you be traveling back to America?"

424

"I'm not. My dad is the happiest he's been in a long time, and the Senior Lifestyle Facility is planning a big Christmas celebration. He's on the decorating committee, and has made lots of new friends."

Adolfo's hands paused in the sand as he looked up, his expression stunned. "You're spending Christmas in Portugal?"

"Aunt Edite asked me to help her in the Silva family store. In turn, she's sketching my swimsuit designs. The woman is a gifted artist. We're roommates."

"Not for long." Their gazes came together, hers and Adolfo's, private and swift. Her pulse flittered. He was so close, the scent of soil and earth clinging to his clothes, even here at the beach.

"What do you mean?" she asked, daring him to continue.

He brushed the sand off his hands and cupped her face, his breath whispering against her temple. "You're coming home with me."

"I don't understand."

"Try this." He embraced her, his arms warm and strong through her wetsuit. "Krystal Walters, will you marry me?"

"You mean right here in the middle of the beach?"

"I'll give you a couple of weeks to plan the wedding. Do you want me to ask you to marry me on my knees?"

"You already are." She grinned. She'd missed him so much, the feel of his calloused hands, his breathtaking smile.

"Well?"

She snuggled nearer, her arms winding around his shoulders. She wanted everything about him. "Adolfo Silva, the answer is *sim*, I will marry you. *Sim, sim, sim.*"

Aunt Edite was right. There was more to life than surfing, and that included Adolfo.

He brushed his lips over her hair. She tilted her head to

gaze at him and her heart kicked. Oh, how she loved this powerful, charismatic man.

He crushed her against his chest. His lips on hers were moist and earnest. When he finally tore his mouth away, he settled his forehead against hers. The moisture from his sweat melded with the dampness of her wet hair.

"That's settled then." He stood and assisted her to her feet, brushed the sand from her wetsuit. His fingers lingered on her hands. "Krystal?"

She faced him, cautious of his reproach because she'd ignored the doctor's advice and had surfed. Adolfo hadn't mentioned it. Surely, he would. The subject needed to be broached.

"I won't prevent you from surfing again, if that's what you want to do." His voice was quiet, his eyes downcast. "Is that what you want?"

She turned and gazed at the ocean. One last look. Scores of seabirds squawked and swooped through the heavens before plunging into the water for fish. Clouds covered the normally blue sky. The beach breeze had turned chilly on her skin. A light, foamy mist sprayed her face, a gentle farewell.

"Not all dreams are meant for a lifetime," she said. "New dreams take their place. Better dreams."

"Either way, I will support whatever you choose."

Arching a brow, she grinned. "Really?"

"As long as I don't have to watch." His solid arms closed around her. "Krystal Walters, I love you so much."

She attempted to repay his smile with one of her own. Instead, she blinked back tears. "I love you, too."

He cradled her face, stroked the tears from her cheeks. "Then why are you crying?"

"Because when I decided to surf in the finals, I assumed I'd never hear you say those words."

He hugged her. "I loved you this morning, last night, last week. And I love you now more than ever."

Everyone deserved a second chance at love, especially at Christmas.

She grasped her striped towel. "I'm officially retiring my lucky towel, although it wasn't so lucky after all."

"I disagree. That towel made me the luckiest man in the world, because it brought you to Portugal."

She smiled and straightened her shoulders. She could still smell the salt from the ocean as he guided her away from the beach. The spectators had disbanded. The finals had ended. The shore had emptied.

"Let's get your surfing gear and go back to the olive farm."

She paused and swung around. "You never told me about your sand sculpture. What were you building?"

And then she understood. She could see the heart-shaped face, the doe-like eyes, the wings.

An angel.

CHAPTER 20

*K*rystal layered boiled, sliced potatoes onto the boiled and shredded salted cod. In another baking dish, she added sautéed onions, black olives and hard-boiled eggs. "My first Christmas Eve supper in Portugal," she declared.

Veronica smiled. "Your first of many *Consoadas.*" She wiped her hands on her frilly green apron adorned with mistletoe and then tended to flash-boiling an array of shellfish, including crab, clams, and pink shrimp. She arranged the seafood on a white ceramic platter to serve warm in their shells. "How's this?"

"Looks delicious," Krystal said. "Truly, I've never seen so much food."

The women paraded into Veronica's expansive dining room. The shiny mahogany table fairly groaned beneath an assortment of hazelnuts, olives and garden-fresh collard greens drizzled in olive oil.

Krystal peeked at her reflection in the hallway mirror as she passed. She'd fussed with her appearance, wearing her hair in a side-swept chignon and donning a candy-apple-red crepe shift she'd purchased in Peniche, along with black kitten heels.

Aunt Edite placed a silver candelabrum, lit with a half dozen red and green candles, in the center of the table. "*Consoada* literally translated means 'to comfort.' Traditionally, we abstain from meat dishes on Christmas Eve because Advent is our 'little lent' and we fast and repent the days before Christmas."

"Until Christmas Day," Adolfo added, "when pork and roasted lamb are served."

He had stood as the women marched into the room. He was so strikingly handsome, Krystal thought, so unbearably splendid, wearing a linen shirt and gray dress pants. His thick, wavy black hair framed his face.

He strode to her and claimed her with a kiss. "*Boas Festas,* beautiful." Arm in arm, he led her to her place at the table. As he seated her, he whispered in her ear. "After we attend Midnight Mass, *Missa do Galo,* I have a surprise for you."

"Surprises are your speciality."

"*Sim.*" He grinned sheepishly. "Gift giving is an important part of a Portuguese Christmas."

"I don't have a gift for you, Adolfo. I'm sorry. I'll buy you something when we fly to America to see my family."

"You're here in Portugal. That is my gift."

His oddly rough voice gave Krystal pause. The clean-air scent of him fused with the aromas of olive oil and pine trees and olives. Her spirits flooded with happiness, marveling at the sincere goodwill reflected on the faces of the Portuguese family she loved. *Her* family.

And her family in America who were also experiencing a wonderful holiday. She'd spoken to her brother and father earlier that evening. Her father was spending Christmas Eve with Julio's family, and Christmas Day would be enjoyed at the senior facility, where he'd perform in a Christmas carol concert, along with other residents. He'd discovered a love for singing.

She scanned the Silva family table, savoring the scene, tucking it away to reflect on for years to come. Clemente was seated at the head, Aunt Edite on his right and Veronica on his left. Krystal was next to Aunt Edite, and Adolfo took a seat across from Krystal. Bento and Bernardo sat on either side of Adolfo. At the other end of the table was an empty place set for Adolfo and Clemente's father, *alminhas a penar.*

After they bowed their heads and said grace, Clemente poured red wine into the adults' glasses and sparkling water for the children.

"Uncle Adolfo said that Bento and I should behave and be extra good tonight," Bernardo said, "so that Father Christmas will put presents in our *sapatinhos.* Those are shoes," he translated for Krystal. Despite Veronica's obvious attempts to slick down his wavy brown hair, it whirled upward in undisciplined wisps at the crown. "Is he right, Krystal ... I mean, Aunt Krystal? Uncle Adolfo said we should start calling you that."

She laughed. "Absolutely."

"Aunt Krystal, do you know that Christmas Eve is my favorite night of the year?" Bento asked. He reached for his water glass and knocked it over, spilling water onto the floor and Adolfo's shoes. He glanced up at Adolfo. "Sorry, Uncle Adolfo."

Adolfo ran his fingers through his hair, then set the glass upright. "No worries. I'll wear my work boots to church tonight. I always keep a spare here. You're a good boy and all is forgiven." He patted Bento's unruly brown hair, which grew in short spikes around his face.

Bento glanced at Veronica. "Sorry, Mom."

Clemente grimaced and Veronica smiled as she grabbed some napkins to wipe up the mess. "It's only water, dear."

Krystal gazed across the table at Adolfo. "Christmas Eve is my favorite too."

"And mine. And the Portuguese make Christmas Eve the longest night of the year."

Veronica dashed salt and a pinch of black pepper on the vegetables. "I never tell the boys when to go to bed on Christmas Eve."

"They play until they drop." Adolfo leaned back in his chair and regarded both boys. "Thus, the longest night of the year."

Along with a crack of laughter, Aunt Edite raised her glass of port. "*Bom apetite e Feliz Natal*. Good appetite and Merry Christmas!"

Conversation crisscrossed the table, along with the clinks of silverware and the clanks of chili-red glazed dinnerware. By the end of the meal, Adolfo had the boys giggling as he pretended to pull pennies out of their ears.

After they were finished, Clemente put down his fork and knife and addressed the table at large. "We'll leave for Midnight Mass within the hour."

After a last sip of coffee, Krystal assisted the family in clearing the dishes and setting the table for dessert. Veronica waltzed into the kitchen with her arms around the loves of her life—Clemente, Bento and Bernardo.

* * *

AFTER MIDNIGHT MASS, the family returned to Veronica and Clemente's home. In the formal living room, Clemente switched on the television set for a singalong with the *Coro de Santo,* the holy choir.

Bento and Bernardo hastened to their *sapatinhos* by the

fireplace, squealing with excitement as they opened their gifts.

Krystal abandoned her heels, hung her light cotton jacket in the foyer closet, and stifled a yawn with her hand.

"Tired?" Adolfo asked in a laughter-tinged voice. His gaze shifted to the wall-mounted clock chiming one a.m. "The night is young." He took her hand and led her to Clemente's study down the hall. Beside a bow window stood a miniature Christmas tree wrapped in twinkling white lights. An elaborate crèche displaying the three main figures of the nativity, Infant Jesus, Mary, and Joseph, sat beneath the tree.

"As you can see, we celebrate Christmas everywhere." Adolfo closed the door behind them. "Clemente, Veronica, and Aunt Edite will be awake for hours, unwrapping and setting up all the toys the twins received."

"Don't you want to join in the festivities?"

He grinned. "Later."

He sat beside her on a leather loveseat tucked into one corner of the wood-paneled room. A wool rug stretched across the tiled floor. He stared at Krystal, still scarcely believing that she was in Portugal.

She was here, after her courageous surf, when she'd been determined to win a contest she hadn't won. She was here, after fighting with him so fiercely.

How close he'd come to losing her because of his stubbornness, his inability to listen to anyone's side other than his own.

She had run through the crowd on Medão Grande Beach, intent on finding him after the surfing finals. And then she had stared at the ocean after he'd told her that he wouldn't stop her from surfing if that's what she wanted to do. After a long minute, she'd turned away from the sea, her chin lifted high. Then she'd taken his hand, apparently comfortable in the decision to leave her surfing life behind. Her huge blue eyes had shimmered with love and resolution.

Now she sat quietly, staring at the tree. The soft wash of Christmas lights illuminated her beautiful face.

He hooked an arm around her shoulders. "What are you thinking about?"

"You." She brushed back a wavy blonde strand of hair from her cheek.

He regarded the warmth in her gaze and grinned, both touched and pleased. A wave of tenderness for her gladdened him to the core. He'd come to her with a full heart and total commitment. He wanted to be sure she felt the same.

"Care to elaborate?" he asked.

A flicker of a smile touched her lips. "You know what impressed me most about you?"

"My work ethic?"

"Your crooked nose."

He laughed out loud. He couldn't help his reaction. He captured her in his arms, burying his face in the gardenia and vanilla scent of her hair.

She snuggled closer to his chest. "And I have a confession."

"This better be good. We just attended *Missa do Galo*."

"And everything about the Mass was beautiful—the crib, walking up to the altar to kiss Baby Jesus, and the hymns we sang. The Portuguese appreciate the true meaning of Christmas."

"The season is meant to bring joy, and having you here to share it with me ..." His mouth descended on hers.

"Adolfo—"

"I love when you say my name," he murmured, his lips still on hers.

"Remember my confession?"

Reluctantly, he lifted his head. "Of course. Please continue."

She drew an unsteady breath. A reddish tint, the color of a poinsettia, crept up her cheeks. "From the first day I saw you, I kept thinking, this is my love, my husband-to-be. He's here in Portugal. And then I'd think, no, that's impossible. He's high-handed and arrogant."

He chuckled. "Maybe sometimes."

"Many of the times I was railing at you because of your demands, I was distracted because I was thinking about you … kissing me."

"You mean like this?" He drew her nearer, his mouth moving with intensity over hers. It took all his effort to break the kiss, to compel his hands to stop caressing her exquisite figure. He shifted and rested his chin on her head. "Always, you were on my mind. And I have a confession, also."

She tipped up her chin. "I'm almost afraid to ask."

"The day I took you to the beach with the twins, you were dressed in a bikini with that black cover-up."

"I recall every detail of that day."

His lips traveled down her temples, lingering near her ears. "I kept hoping for a strong wind so I could catch more than a glimpse of your shapely legs beneath that cover-up. The weather didn't cooperate. If you remember, it was a clear, sunny day."

She grinned. "As usual."

He nuzzled her neck, muffling a laugh. "May I remind you that I have a gift for you."

"A chocolate bell to share?"

"Better." He reached into his shirt pocket and produced a small black velvet box. "I've carried this around with me since Aunt Edite and I shopped in Évora. Look inside."

Carefully, she opened the box. An exquisite diamond ring flashed, caught by the radiant lights of the Christmas tree.

"Adolfo." Her eyes welled with tears. "I've never seen a ring so beautiful. How?" She swallowed. "I remember Aunt Edite had mentioned you went shopping together."

Taking her left hand, he slid the ring onto her finger. "You and I will be married on January sixth."

"Less than two weeks from now?" She shook her head. "Impossible."

"It's perfect. Epiphany Eve is January fifth, so we'll marry the day after. We can get married at the beach you like—the one we took the twins to. I've already invited your family to the wedding and Veronica is arranging the flights. They arrive January first. After the wedding, we'll all fly to America so you can collect your belongings and return to Portugal to live in my home."

"They never said a word to me."

He smiled. "Surprise."

"I love being here in Portugal, although I'm sorry I wasn't able to spend Christmas with my father."

"In a way, you will." Adolfo threaded his fingers through the soft curls that had slipped from her upswept hair. "Epiphany Eve is another Christmas tradition. Bento and Bernardo will fill their shoes with carrots and straw and place them on the windowsill, because this will lure the Three Wise Men, who leave candied fruit and sweet bread. So your family can continue to celebrate the holiday along with us."

"Thank you for including my father in all your plans."

"I know how much he means to you."

"And I know how much your father meant to you," she said quietly.

"He carried an aura of control about him. Despite being feared for being such a hard taskmaster, he was respected."

"And you were the most considerate son a father could want. Despite disagreeing, you abided by your father's wishes. You're a hero because you always do the right thing."

"Please don't call me that. I'm just an overburdened man with a father who needed him." His denial had come out sharper than he'd intended. He softened his tone. "In hindsight, my father knew more about olive farming than I ever gave him credit for. Although ..." His voice trailed off.

"Go on." Her blue eyes were compassionate. She was too attuned to his emotions.

He sighed. "Despite the work, I learned that life doesn't need to be so serious. I've put down my olive rake in order to truly enjoy Christmas and to love life again. You taught me about communication, about forgiveness. My shame I carried, arguing with my father before he died, couldn't find healing in an olive grove, nor in grape vines, nor in my attempts to close off the world and live alone. In the end, I couldn't succeed. Not without you." He covered her lips in an undemanding kiss.

"I'll help you establish your winery. That is, once I get my swimsuit company up and running."

"Aunt Edite is sketching your ideas?"

A faint crimson flush crept up her high cheekbones, the flush he loved, one of excitement and enthusiasm. "Yes. And I've finally decided on the perfect name."

He gazed down into her impossibly gorgeous face. Truly, this was a most perfect Christmas. "What is it?"

"When I realized how much I would miss you if I ever left Portugal, I decided on my company name. Aunt Edite agreed. So, you want to hear what it is?"

"*Sim.*" He closed his eyes, but he already knew.

"*Saudade,* because I love you so much."

It was a noun, not a verb, and unique to Portugal. A longing for, a yearning.

In aching tenderness, he snuggled her closer. "And I love you."

And he added another word connected to *saudade*. She didn't know the word yet, but he did.

Fado. Their destiny. It was simply the way it was.

THE END

A NOTE FROM JOSIE

Dear Friends,

Thank you for reading *A Portuguese Christmas.*

I wanted to write a sweet holiday romance in a unique place, and set *A Portuguese Christmas* near the town of Peniche, Portugal, because the heroine, Krystal Walters, is a world-class surfer. As a non-swimmer, I was fascinated by the skill it takes to surf.

The hero, Adolfo Silva, is an olive farmer. In my research, I learned so much about olive farming and have a great respect for the expertise, patience and perseverance that goes along with a successful olive harvest.

Set against the lushness of beautiful Portugal, it is my hope that you learned some new traditions and celebrated the wonderfully festive Portuguese holiday along with me and the characters.

If you loved this sweet romance as much as I loved writing it, please help other people find *A Portuguese Christmas* by posting your review.

A Portuguese Christmas is available in ebook, paperback, Large Print paperback, Hardcover, and audiobook.

Happy Holidays and *Feliz Natal*!

Spotify Play List Here.

A TRADITIONAL PORTUGUESE CHRISTMAS RECIPE

Bacalhau A Braz (Dried Cod Dish)

5 Large potatoes

3 pieces of boneless, skinless dried cod (previously soaked for 24 hours)

4-5 jumbo eggs

3 large onions

4 large garlic cloves

1/3 cup half and half or whole milk

oil to fry potatoes

salt, pepper, paprika to taste

½ cup olive oil

The salted dry cod needs to be presoaked inside a pan with water, in refrigerator, for 24-36 hours. If cod has been pre-soaked and is frozen, boil for 5 minutes to defrost it.

Cut the potatoes into fine sticks (as close to shoestring as possible) and sprinkle with salt. Fry potatoes in hot oil and put aside.

In a large pot, place the olive oil and sliced onions. Cook onions until transparent. Add cod broken into small pieces (about the size of your fingers) and chopped garlic. Cook for about 10 minutes, stirring occasionally. Add the eggs (that have previously been beaten with half and half) alternating with the fried potatoes and mix well. Add salt, pepper and paprika to taste.

To serve, place in a platter and garnish with fresh parsley and olives. Serves 6.

Enjoy!

ACKNOWLEDGMENTS

An appreciative thank you to my patient husband, Dave, and our three wonderful children.

ABOUT THE AUTHOR

Josie Riviera is a *USA TODAY* bestselling author of contemporary, inspirational, and historical sweet romances that read like Hallmark movies. She lives in the Charlotte, NC, area with her wonderfully supportive husband. They share their home with an adorable shih tzu, who constantly needs grooming, and live in an old house forever needing renovations.

To receive my Newsletter and your free sweet romance novella ebook as a thank you gift, sign up HERE.

Become a member of my
Read and Review VIP Facebook
group for exclusive giveaways and FREE ARC's.

josieriviera.com/
josieriviera@aol.com

ALSO BY JOSIE RIVIERA

Seeking Patience

Seeking Catherine (always Free!)

Seeking Fortune

Seeking Charity

Seeking Rachel

The Seeking Series

Oh Danny Boy

I Love You More

A Snowy White Christmas

A Portuguese Christmas

Holiday Hearts Book Bundle Volume One

Holiday Hearts Book Bundle Volume Two

Holiday Hearts Book Bundle Volume Three

Holiday Hearts Book Bundle Volume Four

Candleglow and Mistletoe

Maeve (Perfect Match)

A Love Song To Cherish

A Christmas To Cherish

A Valentine To Cherish

A Christmas Puppy To Cherish

A Homecoming To Cherish

A Summer To Cherish

Romance Stories To Cherish

Romance Stories To Cherish Volume Two

Cherished Hearts Six Book Volume

Aloha To Love

Sweet Peppermint Kisses

Valentine Hearts Boxed Set

1-800-CUPID

1-800-CHRISTMAS

1-800-IRELAND

1-800-SUMMER

1-800-NEW YEAR

The 1-800-Series Sweet Contemporary Romance Bundle

Irish Hearts Sweet Romance Bundle

Holly's Gift

A Chocolate-Box Christmas

A Chocolate-Box New Years

A Chocolate-Box Valentine

A Chocolate-Box Summer Breeze

A Chocolate-Box Christmas Wish

A Chocolate-Box Irish Wedding

Chocolate-Box Hearts

Chocolate-Box Hearts Volume Two

Chocolate-Box Double Hearts

Recipes From The Heart

Leading Hearts

New Year Hearts

SENIOR HEARTS

Summer Hearts

Christmas in the Air (1-800-Book)

A Very Christian Christmas

Most books are available in ebook, audiobook, paperback, Large Print paperback and Hardcover.

Many are FREE on Kindle Unlimited!